"Ninth Street Designs"

HOLLYWONDRA

JOE LA FOUNTAINE

ISBN 979-8-88832-980-1 (paperback)
ISBN 979-8-88832-981-8 (digital)

Copyright © 2023 by Joe La Fountaine

All rights reserved. No part of this publication may be reproduced, distributed, or transmitted in any form or by any means, including photocopying, recording, or other electronic or mechanical methods without the prior written permission of the publisher. For permission requests, solicit the publisher via the address below.

Christian Faith Publishing
832 Park Avenue
Meadville, PA 16335
www.christianfaithpublishing.com

Printed in the United States of America

Contents

1 The Race to the Tree...1
2 Able and Harley...4
3 Montana Teen Life 12
4 A New Land 17
5 Harley Reports 20
6 Meeting Perdition...24
7 Rile Recon 31
8 Captain at the Valley...39
9 Titus the Tracker..43
10 No Dice..48
11 Jarius Returns 54
12 Hamman Turns 63
13 Jarius Reveals Himself..70
14 Wisp Away 78
15 Jarius Discovers Amanda's Necklace and Roots 82
16 Trespass 88
17 New Allegiance...96
18 Sir Allendale 106
19 Amanda's Rite..111
20 Hollywondra 116
21 The Return..126
22 Growing Alliance..135
23 Arrival 141
24 Elvan Recon 151
25 Biander's Bluff..156
26 King's Road 162
27 Great Greys 172

28	Ezen Kroach	178
29	Fair Warning	190
30	Bierland's Ferry	197
31	Warning Hollywondra	204
32	Kayuni Trail	211
33	Kobold Assault	225
34	The Kellene	233
35	Kobold Arrive	239
36	Lake Kellene	245
37	The Sepien	256
38	Falling Hollywondra	262
39	Gormund's Escape	271
40	Hollywondra	282
41	Zel Camber	295

The rain that rested on the leaves jumped off the branches and into his face as he ran through the brush. He could hear the dogs drawing closer. He pushed himself to run as fast as he could through the cold dark woods. Jarius rushed deeper into this forest that he knew so well. He knew he would not be able to outrun the hounds. He knew the swords of their handlers would not be far behind. It was only a matter of time. He could not allow himself to falter.

Jarius was considered one of the swiftest and strongest of his clan. Running through this forest was something he had done his entire life. This night, his speed and knowledge of this forest would determine the length of his life. These hunters had two goals: kill him and recover the key he was carrying. It had been given to him in faith. He could not afford to be caught.

The baying hounds were drawing nearer. He could hear them crashing through the underbrush. Jarius rushed through the woods in the dark of night. The moon would have been full, but it was not providing any light through the densely forested canopy. If he had a torch, it would have only told the trackers his location, plus he knew these woods in the same way a person would know the house in which they had lived their whole life.

Jarius was not worried about beating his hunters to the Tree Gate. He knew it was not far. His concern was making this key work before they caught up to him. Throughout his childhood, the stories had been told of this mystical old fir tree and how it was a gate to another land. Elvin legends spoke of Tree Keys that allowed travelers to walk through the tree to another distant land. What Jarius had recently come to learn was that one key took you one direction and a different key brought you back.

As Jarius ran through the forest, he carried what he believed was just such a magical key. Periodically, he raised the stick in his hand to knock away tree boughs as he fled. Once he realized the risk of using this ancient piece of wood in this fashion, he determined to try some evasive maneuvers rather than flee in a straight line. He knew places along this deer trail where he could leap from the path. He hoped these small breaks in the scent of his trail might slow the dogs a bit.

He altered his route to a small creek. After running a few dozen yards down the shallow creek, he came up on the other side near a well-known badger burrow. Deftly kicking dirt into the badger's hole, Jarius continued up the trail. Rounding the corner of the deer trail, Jarius knew the tree was nearby. He also knew he could probably hear the splash of creek water to alert him of the hunters drawing near.

Jarius arrived at the base of the ancient fir tree that grew atop a gentle slope. Coming to a stop at the base an ancient fir, Jarius began to run his hands over its knotty burls. His fingers sought an odd indentation in the surface of the bark. After feeling the rough surface for only a few moments, he found a place in the bark that was similar to the shape of the key. The key itself was nothing more than an odd-shaped stick. When he examined this stick more carefully, he could tell it was not a product of nature but of some magical creation. Just like the burls at the base of this tree, the natural surface of this tree had been corrupted by the powers of magic. The Tree Key had four very flat sides to it. One end was cut flat, while the other end was cut into a point. Still, that did not make placing it in the tree any easier.

Jarius could hear the dogs splashing in the nearby creek, just as his fingertips were tracing the indentation in the tree's bark. Finally, he was able to find the straight edges from the shape of the key. Taking the key, he tried to place it into the wooden pocket he had found in the curvy surface of the tree's trunk. The darkness made the work clumsy. He spun the key in his hand, trying every viable way to make it fit into the bark of the tree. Just as one of the dogs began snarling at what he guessed was the badgers, his fingers found a flat surface that came to a point.

Frantically, he tried to make the key fit. He knew his hunters were only twenty yards away. For a moment, his mind wondered if this had all been a set up and his life was about to be taken in vain. Then the wooden key suddenly clicked into place. As it locked into place, a bright luminescent green glow surrounded the seam of the key and then his hand. Quickly the glow surrounded him in a bright flash of green light.

In his last frantic moments of trying to place the Tree Key, Jarius failed to hear the call of his hunters. They had spotted him at the base of the tree. He could not hear the twang of their bows releasing their arrows. Nor did he see one of the arrows glance off the tree right in front of his face. He was not even aware that one of the arrows nicked his arm, as he stood motionless and glowing of green. At the same moment that Jarius was wounded, his entire body became engulfed in a green magical glow. Then in a bright flash of green, he was gone.

Moments later, Jarius's hunters arrived at the base of the great tree. Scouring the area, they could find no sign of the elf they hunted. Their dogs wandered around them, looking for the scent they had been following for miles. Confused, the bay of the hounds began to echo throughout the woods.

Harley, Able, and their dogs searched the area for a couple of hours. They could never find the trail of the elf. Returning to the trunk of the great fir, Harley wiped the sweat from his brow with the left sleeve of his smoke saturated tunic. Turning to look directly at Able, he spoke the words that neither of them wanted to hear. "I can't figure out where he went."

"I'm telling ya, his tracks end right here!" Abel emphasized by pointing at a specific place on the ground. "It just doesn't make a lick of sense." Certainly, their torch light helped them to see the tracks that had been left, but Harley just knew they had to be missing something. The two had been searching the area for hours looking for any sign or trail that the elf might have left.

"Did ya see that green glow? I'm telling' ya, he went into this tree!" Able stated with conviction as he carefully examined the bark of the tree under his torchlight.

"Oh, come now. We can't be takin' that kinda story back to Zel Camber. Do you have any idea what he'd do to us?" Harley reminded him.

"I don't know what to do," said Abel. "We can't go back and tell them that we lost him. We can't follow him. I can't find even a hint of him." Abel lifted his torch up high to look up into the limbs of the tree.

"If he were in that tree, the dogs would have yelped themselves hoarse," reminded Harley. "You know he's not up there."

Abel had exhausted all his ideas. "We can't go back to Zel Camber." Then pausing, as if considering all his options, he announced, "That's why I'm headed north."

HOLLYWONDRA

"North?" Harley repeated with surprise. "You mean to tell me that you're making a run for it? You know he'll hunt you down and have you killed, just like we were supposed to do to this tree flea."

"Oh, I know," Able said as he walked his dog to the creek for a drink, mindfully walking around that badger borough. "I just don't see Zel Camber very pleased to hear our report. I think I'd rather extend my miserable life a few more nights than to take this news straight to the general."

Harley followed him to the creek with his dogs, concerned for the choices Abel was about to make. "Well, if you up and run off into the hills, how do ya think that's gonna make me look?" Harley suggested.

"Well, come with me," Able quickly replied before considering Harley's circumstance.

"I can't just take off into the woods. I've got Myrna and the kids to worry about. That sick bastard might just take his rage out on them," Harley reminded Able.

"Yeah, you're right, I s'pose." Changing his tone to one of certainty, Able restated his plan, "That doesn't mean I have to go!"

Harley bent over to cup water into his pitch filthy hand for a drink. Then he suggested that he would "just make up a story about how you had not come back from our search of the area. That maybe the elf got you and your dog."

"Damn, Harley! That would be great of you." Able thanked him. "If it's all the same to you, I'm gonna set out tonight. I don't see any reason to stretch my luck by staying put."

"I understand," Harley said as he stood. Extending his hand to his old friend, he wished him well, and the two began to head back to where they had left their horses. As they walked, the two quietly listened to the gentle crunch of leaf mulch under their boots. The dogs loped along beside them at a casual pace.

As they started to near their horses, Able asked, "Well, what are you gonna tell him about the elf?"

"What is there to tell?" Harley replied without consideration. "The little tree flea gave us the slip in the forest?"

Able grabbed his old friend by the sleeve and spun to speak to him directly, "Good grief, man! He'll run you through as you stand there." Digging into his imagination, Able began to create a story worthy of their defeat.

"I'd tell him that we got to the edge of the forest and ran into a pack of those tree fleas. They outnumbered us." The men had arrived back to where they had left their horses. As Able tied the dog leashes to the horn of his saddle, he continued his story. "No less than a dozen of them began to fire on us. No wait, let's not be ridiculous, a half dozen." Able checked his saddle to make sure it and his pack were secure. He took the leashes off his dogs so they could run along beside him. Then he stated plainly, "We had to back away or be killed. By the time we were able to skirt their fire, we had lost the scent of his trail."

Able paused to see what Harley thought of his story. Harley was upset. He was looking at the ground gently shaking his head from side to side. "I don't think he'll buy it," Harley said.

As Able placed his left boot into his stirrup and threw his leg over his horse and landed atop, he suggested, "You can work out the details however you see fit, my friend. I won't ever be back this way to tell the story any different." At that suggestion, Able nodded and reined his horse to turn.

Between the first kick into the ribs of his steed and the second, Harley whipped his bow from his shoulder, nocked an arrow, and fired it squarely into Able's back.

Able let go the reins with his right hand to feel for the arrow that was buried deep into the middle of his back. He gave his horse a second kick, but then he fell. Pulling his long dagger from his boot, Harley walked to where Able had fallen into the grass. Standing over Able, Harley could barely make out Able's feeble attempt to ask him why he was killing him.

"Oh, come on, Able. You know the truth. If I go back there and lie to Nictovius, he will surely kill me in the most horrid of ways. If I let you desert his force, then I would be killed for that too. My only

hope is that he will show me mercy for my loyalty in these deeds."
Then Harley ended Able's suffering.

*****

Barrick and Burk were safely concealed high in the trees. The brothers had climbed high into the trees to watch things unfold at the base of Tree Gate. They had been assigned to ensure Jarius got safely away and to recover the Tree Key. From their posts, they were able to witness the bright green flash that signaled the departure of Sir Raphael. With their bows drawn and ready, they saw no reason to kill the dogs or the inept humans, who had been chasing Jarius.

They watched as the two human trackers circled the great tree. The only thing their dogs seemed interested in was the trail left by Jarius. The dogs would run up to the tree then turn around and start backtracking the scent. One hunter had his bow drawn and arrow ready while his partner used the torch to illuminate the tracks and the branches of the tree. The two men looked for any clue of the elf they had been chasing. The brothers knew exactly what had happened. So, beyond the glow of the torches, they tucked themselves safely behind the trunks of their trees. From the safety of their cover, they listened to the two human trackers begin to panic.

As the hunters realized that it was only them and their dogs at the base of the tree, their frustration turned to anger. The hunters lit new torches and searched every inch of the area several times. They went over the tracks and scent trail left by Jarius but reached the same conclusion each time. He was gone. He had vanished before their very eyes. He walked right up to this tree and then disappeared.

Barrick and Burk waited silently, amazed at the fact that humans could not see mystical emanations coming from the Tree Gate. The hunters passed back and forth right in front of the magical Tree Key and did not give it a second look. The brothers watched with satisfaction as the dejected hunters finally left the Tree Gate. Once they heard the hunters talking in the creek, the Elvan brothers quietly descended their perch.

As a precaution, Burk readied his bow and watched in the direction of the trackers. Carefully approaching the Tree Gate burl, Barrick reached his hand into the wooden pocket where the key was placed. He ran his fingers down the shaft of the key to find its pointed end. After pushing down on the pointed end of the key, it popped from its pocket in the gnarled bark. Plucking the Tree Key from the old tree, Barrick looked at it with reverence. Pulling a cloth from his pack, he carefully wrapped the key and secured it in his backpack.

Their journey back to the hallowed woods of Hollywondra was uneventful. Careful to not be seen or followed, the brothers made good time. Since it was just the two of them, they could travel smaller trails and take routes that would surely be untraveled. They knew they carried in their possession an artifact of Elvin history. They felt heroic since they had snatched it from under the eyes of their human enemies. The return to their Elvin capital would certainly be reason for celebration.

The Elvan city of Hollywondra was a masterful creation. Hundreds of gigantic old oak trees were formed into the homes and businesses. Destroying the tree itself was not an acceptable practice, so the structures had to be carefully carved out of the trunks in a way that preserved the tree yet created a living space. Many of these wondrous lodgings wove up the tree in systems of stairs and handholds that made travel very fluid for the elves who called this home. Every tree housed a family or a community service. It was not predicable as to where the business might be in the multitiered designs of these homes. It was not unusual for any of these homes to have as many as five or six rooms on four or five distinct levels of the tree.

The floor of Hollywondra was a vast carpet of sweet white alyssum. The flowers were only worn in those places where foot traffic restricted it from covering the entire forest floor. Three little brooks flowed across the city floor. They all converged into one large creek that eventually dove off a cliff into the Raven Rift, turning the stream into nothing but a mist.

Burk and Barrick wove their way through the trees of Hollywondra. Recognizing folks, they only slowed long enough to wave. They had only one destination: an audience with the Elvin high priest Barnabus Malactus. Next to King Elfanwisel, there was not a more revered elf.

The audience with the high priest was not what the brothers thought it would be. After being ushered into the antechamber of the high priest, the two were left standing and waiting. The High Priest Malactus stood across the room at a book stand, reading something, while the two waited for him. Elves were known to take their time, when compared to human terms of time passage, but this was a long awkward wait even in Elvan terms. As they stood waiting, they took in the full effect of their surroundings.

This room was an ancient Elvan work of art. The floors, walls, and ceiling were all highly polished wood grain. Both men knew the amount of time and care it took to polish oak. It was a technical process that took days to do the smallest piece of wood. A room this size would have taken a team of finishers years to have completed so beautifully. Certain parts of the room were intricately hand-carved to create tapestry hooks and even a place for a window.

While the two waited, they imagined the great wealth and honor they might receive for this service to the temple and community. Being asked to sit at the priest's gold leaf gilded table only reinforced their enthusiasm. The two mustered as much grace as they could as they came to the table. As is the custom, they waited for the aged Malactus to sit first, then the two sat down.

The High Priest Malactus seemed cold and distant as the brothers permitted him to speak. Hoping to lighten the spirit of the meeting, Barrick removed the Tree Key from his pack. As if to add to the impact of the moment, he carefully placed the wrapped key on the table and pulled back the cloth to reveal it. Nodding his head, the priest unceremoniously offered, "You have fulfilled a great service for your community."

Waiting for Malactus to suggest a great reward or feast in their honor, the two brothers nodded in agreement. When Malactus became aware of their gaze upon him, he said, "My apologies. Forgive my tenor." Looking squarely into the eyes of each man, he explained, "Your accomplishments will not be forgotten. My mind was on the journey of our brother Jarius. Pray that the grace of God travels with him in that foreign land. When you return home, be sure to pray for all Elvin kind. For should he fail to return, I do not know who else among us could be sent to find the Ray of Light."

The brothers looked at each other and then back at the high priest. Barnabus Malactus turned and looked at a nearby acolyte. Without words, the acolyte came to his side. The acolyte carried a large red silk pillow to the table. Malactus took the Tree Key from the cloth and placed it on the pillow. Then bowing his head, Malactus whispered a short prayer. The prayer was so short, the two brothers paused, uncertain if they should bow their heads as well. Before they could make up their minds, his prayer was over.

Turning back to the men, Malactus pulled two leather bags from under his table. "Inside these purses, you will find twenty-three gold pieces and twenty-three silvers. Each gold piece represents the family heads attributed to your family crest in Chronus's Book of Life. Each silver piece represents your future generations. It is my prayer that the same twenty-three generations that have brought you to this place will mirror your service in the future of Elvin kind. May twenty-three generations of your family lineage find honor and glory in the eyes of God and our Elvin nation."

At that, each brother took their bags of coins from the priest. Then Barrick said, "We would be honored to serve you for the next twenty-three generations."

Malactus paused to look at Barrick, his brother spun in his seat to look at him. A faint smile came over the face of Malactus, then he stood. His standing superseded anything that could be said. In honor of his presence, the two men quickly stood and bowed as Malactus turned away.

As Malactus stepped behind a large forest green tapestry and out of sight, Burk quickly backhanded his brother's arm. "What was that? You're gonna serve for the next twenty-three generations?" Shaking his head, Burk turned and headed for the door. As he made his way toward the door, he tied the leather thongs of his new purse to his belt.

HOLLYWONDRA

Catching up with his brother, Barrick whispered, "We're rich!" Burk stuck his arm out and across his brother's chest to slow him down. "I whispered it," Barrick offered in his defense.

"Just relax," Burk said. They exited the temple onto some high bows of the majestic tree in which the temple was carved. As they walked away, Burk could only shake his head.

Barrick was confused by his brother's attitude. They had done many things that were far more dangerous for far less than one piece of silver. This was truly a fortune. Walking the through Hollywondra, Barrick grew anxious to discover what disturbed his brother.

3

The brisk fall breeze that chases most indoors did not bother the teenagers assembled in the field. Jumping and cheering as they circled the two figures at the center. The clack, clack, clack of wood striking wood echoed in the nearby canyons as two figures circled each other with large sticks in their hands.

The boy was much larger than the girl he fought. Though he was only sixteen years old, his size was that of a large man. His scruffy, unkempt facial hair hid most of his concern in its shadow. Although she was probably half his size, his quick retreat from her lunge showed his respect for her skill with the stick.

"Now remember the deal. No headshots," he reminded her. The girl only smiled and nodded as she continued to circle and watch him carefully. She seemed to be studying him and his movement as she circled and prodded with her stick. His words brought a chuckle from the gallery of classmates. Periodically, she reached out with her stick and allowed him to block her strike. Like a small cat playing with one very large mouse, they continued to circle each other.

On the edge of the audience, two brothers argued. The smaller of the two, Titus, was telling his brother, "You know she's gonna take him down."

Webster, quick to defend his friend, stated the obvious. "If Brent can get her flat-sticked, she won't stand a chance," he stated without ever taking his eyes off the two fighters.

"Oh yeah, I'm sure that part of Amanda's plan is to get locked in a physical struggle with Brent," Titus remarked sarcastically. Titus took a moment to look at his brother to see if he was actually serious about his comment. All he saw was his older brother hoping his friend might be able to salvage his honor and not fall to the pastor's skinny blonde daughter again.

Just a week ago, the two had collided in what had since become local legend. A bunch of the kids from the high school were out gathering wood for the homecoming bonfire when Amanda and Brent began to have words. Brent suggested that if she were not a girl, he would "make her see things his way." Amanda suggested he forget that she was a girl and picked up a stick to defend herself. After Brent took a sharp rap off his shin, he quickly understood, he might need a stick to defend himself. What followed was a brief combat between the mismatched youth. Brief, because Amanda quickly gave Brent the end of her staff to his groin. Having doubled him over, she walked to him and pushed him over. Today's rematch was all about Brent reclaiming his dignity.

"You don't have to do this," Amanda suggested with a note of kindness and confidence in her tone. The comment made Brent's eyes quickly survey all his classmates.

"Oh, yes, I do," he whispered. Then he lunged at her with a foray of blows apparently intended to break her stick in half. Each blow causing a loud clack as Amanda's shaft blocked each of Brent's blows. Gently hopping backward to lighten the impact of each blow, she flowed with grace as her hair and necklace rose and fell with each hop. In her retreat, she found the strength and balance to make a counter blow. Her blow was not on the middle of Brent's stick. It was closer to his hand than any blow he had made.

The close nature of her strike made Brent hesitate and reconsider how he was holding his shaft. Then he came at her again charging, with the hopes of overpowering her. He needed to only put her in her place, but to do so decisively. Any wasted time would make him look weaker than he already did in the eyes of his classmates. His size and speed had made him a physically intimidating presence in his high school.

Amanda quickly bounced to the side as Brent charged past. Poking her stick between his ankles, she caused him to stumble. By no means was Brent a clumsy oaf. He caught himself before he fell. Spinning toward her, he swung his staff like a bat, unsure of her exact location behind him. The arc of his swing made the wall of onlookers jump back, as suddenly the combat was too close for their safety. Arching her back, Amanda was able to lean back far enough to avoid Brent's swing. His stick whistled past her face into the thin Montana air.

"Hey!" she yelled at him. "I thought we weren't going for any headshots." Amanda's brow was creased as her serious tone was met by Brent's respect for her agility.

Squaring himself for another attack, he sarcastically suggested, "Sorry! I was a little off balance. Someone tried to trip me!"

Immediately, he attacked her again. Continuing to swing his stick like a bat, he swung from his right, then left, then right again. Each time Amanda was able to block the blows. But the blows were beginning to get violent. She knew that if she didn't end this quick, she could get very hurt by one of his strikes. As Brent paused, Amanda could see a large cloud caused from his breath hitting the crisp Montana air. His breathing was far more labored than it had been. She knew he was beginning to tire. Any moment she should have her opportunity.

Brent stalled to regain his air as he began to circle her to his right. Watching carefully, Amanda timed his steps. She knew that if he kept a steady gait, that she could catch him off balance between steps. First one, then the other, and finally the window came. In his midstride, Amanda faked a jab to his head. Not fully certain that she would not strike him in the head, his instinct went to block her attack. Using the same end of her shaft, she came down squarely on top of Brent's left foot.

Though he was wearing cowboy boots, they still were not designed to take that type of force. The shaft hit solidly to the bones on the top of his foot. The pain was immediate. Not even realizing his reaction, Brent dropped his stick and bent over to see what damage was done to his foot. Dropping his stick, he was fully vulnerable. Realizing that too late, Brent quickly shot Amanda a glance to see what see was going to do with him. She simply smiled at him. Then she placed the butt of her stick on the ground and relaxed.

"You broke my foot!" Brent screamed as he hopped around, trying to massage his wound. Plopping himself down on the high grass, Brent quickly pulled off his left boot. Then he pulled off his thick wool sock. Looking at his foot, he began to gently rub the blackening knot that had already risen from the top of his foot.

The crowd began to disperse into two groups, those who wanted to give Amanda a pat on the back and those who wanted to see what damage had been done to Brent's foot.

As they began to walk toward Amanda, Titus bragged to his brother, "Hah! I told you!" Titus gave his brother a slap on the shoulder as he turned to check on his friend.

His brother stopped and turned. "You gotta be kidding me? That was a lucky shot. No way was she aiming at his foot."

Appalled with his brother's denial of the obvious, Titus replied sarcastically, "Yeah, lucky!" Then with a light chuckle, Titus walked over to congratulate Amanda. His brother shot him a quick glance of disapproval and turned to check on his friend.

"Look what you did, Amanda!" Brent yelled as he thrust his foot in her direction. His pain tugged at her attention, so she went to see how badly he was hurt. The late afternoon sunlight made it hard to see, but a black knot was clearly bubbling up on his foot. The students gathered around him collectively gasped at the sight of the knot.

"Damn! That's gotta hurt," Titus said with a smile. His comment brought laughs from those less sympathetic to Brent. Brent shot a quick glare in the direction of the laughter, but he could not place his anger on any one person, since the whole group seemed to find humor in his pain.

Fuming mad and embarrassed at losing to the girl, Brent began to put his sock back on his exposed foot. Stepping forward, Amanda asked, "Come on. Let me see it." Reaching for his foot, Brent's initial reaction was to withdraw the foot from the same person who had hurt it so badly. Then he paused and extended his meaty foot for her to examine. Looking at it carefully, she twisted it lightly, bringing a cringe to Brent's face.

"This will hurt for a second, but then the throbbing pain will subside," she explained to her enemy turned patient. Placing a hand on each side of the foot, she paused, closed her eyes, and whispered to herself. Then she pulled both sides of the foot down, and the bones made a crack. Brent, trying to be the toughest guy he could salvage from this fight, grimaced at the sound.

Amanda, acting as if she had just accomplished something, told Brent, "You'll be fine. If you just put some ice on it, the swelling will go down."

Before Brent could get his sock on, some of the group noticed the swelling had already begun to subside. The mark had a bluish hue, but much of the swelling had begun to disappear. "How did she do that?" one student asked Titus as he stood near Amanda. Titus simply shot the student a smile and remarked, "She's just amazing."

Now that the fight was over, the cool Montana breeze began to get the better of the crowd. With Brent still sitting on the ground, the group began to all head back toward town. Brent almost wished his foot had been broken. It would have made his losing far less painless, if he had been hobbled. At least that he could hold that against her. He could have had the sympathy of his classmates. That might have made this seem better somehow. Webster stood by his friend as Brent gently pulled his boot back on his injured foot.

4

As the bright flash subsided, Jarius quickly looked around. To his surprise, he found it was daylight. Whatever the Tree Gate had done, it had teleported him to another time and place. Then his surroundings began to sink in.

Though it was still cold, he was still standing in a forest and at the base of a large pine tree. It was not the same tree. This was not the Tree Gate burl he had known as a child. It was a different Tree Gate. At the base of the tree, Jarius recognized a flat surface much like the tree key he had just used. Touching the surface of the large pine reminded Jarius of his new reality and his need to find another Tree Key to go home.

Then he began to feel a burning sensation on his left bicep. Thinking that to be an odd symptom of this teleportation, it quickly became an all too familiar sensation. Looking at his arm, he could see his blood matting the light leather of his tunic by his arm. The burn he knew was the result of his skin being sliced by iron. Tearing a strip of fabric from the hem of his tunic, Jarius created a small bandage. Using some moisture from some familiar-looking tree moss, Jarius dressed his wound.

Through the underbrush, Jarius could see the forest give way to a large grassy plain that stretched out toward a village in the distance. He knew that at some point, he needed to make the trek into that village, but leaving this unfamiliar forest was not something he was in a hurry to do.

The forest and trees were truly where Jarius was most comfortable. His entire life was in the comfort of the trees, though this forest was truly foreign to him. The pine trees were familiar but much smaller versions of trees he had known in his youth. Many of the small forest creatures he had seen since coming to this forest were also familiar. This wood had a youthful vigor to it that left Jarius a little unsettled.

Jarius stood a few trees away from the edge of the grassy field, considering his next move. For whatever the reason, his journey was meant to bring him here to this place. He did not really understand why; he just knew that his success was critical to the success of his people.

He was certain his leather slacks and tunic would appear strange to the youth he watched leaving the grassy field in the distance. He also noticed none of them appeared to be armed. The quiver and bow he always carried might seem out of place. Yet somehow, he needed to make his way into the town to begin his search for the Ray of Light. If he could do so undetected, that would be best. Realistically, he realized that he may have to expose himself and try his best to fit in. Somewhat shy by nature, this was clearly his last option.

Taking a moment to examine the bandage on his left arm, Jarius noticed the initial bleeding had slowed. Removing the cloth he had tied over the wound, he could see that the arrow had indeed ripped through his leather tunic and made a neat slice in the flesh of his bicep. He looked carefully at the wound for signs of discoloration. He was pleased to see the wound was not deep. The wound was clean, but the blistering that commonly came from Elvin skin touching iron had begun on both sides of the small slice. The people of Jarius's clan had always avoided iron because of these poisonous properties. The blisters and the pain from contact with iron were things Jarius had learned to avoid. The blisters were not a good sign. He knew that they could grow and cause him serious health issues if he was not able to care properly for this wound.

He carefully changed the cloth bandage with a clean strip of linen. After securing the bandage under the sleeve of his tunic, Jarius tucked the dirty bandage into a pocket. He did not want to leave any trace of his presence. Then he returned his attention to the kids playing in the distance.

HOLLYWONDRA

Watching these children play at sticks only reminded Jarius how foreign he was to this place. The clacking of sticks and the laughter of the kids reminded him of his youth. That seemed ages ago. Yet the play of youth was not something he could afford himself. His responsibility was far too great. He had to remain focused to his mission of finding the Ray of Light.

While he knew he did not have the luxury of time, he also knew he had to calculate his moves. There would be no second chances. Having his first glance of this new world, he now needed to consider how best to proceed. His mission was urgent. His success would determine if his people would continue to exist in the land of Namron Rae.

Considering this, Jarius turned back into the woods and began walking away from the clearing. He walked the short trail back to the base of a great pine tree. This great tree, like the great fir from Namron Rae, had a burled base radiating the same mysticism Jarius equated with the old fir. Having the light of day, Jarius examined the trunk of this great tree. He did not want to find himself at the base of this tree trying to figure out how to use the Tree Key while under fire.

Sitting down on an exposed root, Jarius swung around his quiver and took account of its contents. He noted that he still had nineteen arrows. He wished he had the Tree Kay and an obvious way back to Namron Rae. His mission had just gotten tougher. Not only did he have to find the Ray of Light and get it safely home, he had to find a Tree Key too.

He noticed it was beginning to get very cold. He did not want to burn anything that was going to send a lot of smoke into the air. So he began to look around the camp area for the best fuel for a small fire.

That night, by the dim light of his fire, Jarius took stock of his supplies and clothing. He knew he had to be prepared and he could not make any mistakes. He had to be fully prepared for whatever destiny had to throw at him.

Harley reviewed his reasoning as he was awaiting his audience with Zel Camber. *Surely, returning with this specific information and this show of devotion will show Zel Camber that I am worthy to stay in his charge.* He had created about a dozen different stories he thought he might offer but decided to stick to the truth. He was afraid any lies could be deciphered. The bench he sat on was crude oak construction but solid in structure. It sat across the hall from the double doors that led to Zel Camber's headquarters. Two large guards in leather armor held their swords ready and pointing at the floor as they stood at attention on each side of the entry.

Trying to break the tension or to create some brotherhood with the guards, Harley asked, "So…what's it like being the guard for Zel Camber? Is he as ruthless as people say?"

One guard broke his stare to look down in Harley's direction and said, "If you come to this room with hope, you will not find any inside."

Before Harley could double check the guard's expression to see if he was serious, a bolt on the other side of the doors slid, and suddenly the doors were pulled open from inside. The doors were two solid oak planks framed with heavy iron and hinges. The craftsmanship, while crude, was very sound, and the heavy doors opened without a squeak or creak.

Standing behind each of the doors was another armed guard. One guard did not have his sword drawn. He held an oak plank that secured the doors from the inside. The room was deep and wide. About forty feet from the door was a large oak table. Two five-candle candelabrums lit the table surface. The rest of the room was dimly lit from torches that hung on the distant walls.

Standing behind the table was a large man with long wavy black hair that had thick streaks of gray. The gray could also be found in the thick mustache and goatee that hid his facial expressions. He wore a blackened plate armor that seemed weightless on his build. Harley knew this to be Zel Camber. Behind Zel Camber was another man. The other man was seated and wearing the robes of a magi. The magician was being hand-fed fruit by two female assistants. He seemed unconcerned with anything that was going on beyond the attention he was being given by the ladies in waiting.

On the table was a map and some scrolls. The scrolls' seals had been broken, and chunks of the broken wax were all over the table-top as well. A map was being held in place by an incense dish and a leather coin purse.

Leaning over his map, Zel Camber looked up to see who had entered his office. When he saw Harley, he began to examine the map he had on the table. With a commanding voice, Zel Camber asked, "Well! What have you?"

With that direction, Harley mustered as much courage as he could and stepped forward with confidence. "Well, sir…I'm afraid I have some bad news."

At that, Zel Camber raised his attention from the map and looked squarely into the eyes of Harley. "Just tell me you stopped him. I don't care if you failed to get the key, just tell me you stopped him from reaching that tree!"

Harley began to sweat. He could see that his loyalty was not nearly as important to Zel Camber as his mission to stop this elf. "Well, sir, we gave him chase to the wood. Then our dogs pursued him deeper into the woods. There was a light that lit up the night, and it gave me a chance to fire a shot at that tree flea. But at that very moment, we were attacked by badgers, and I did not get to see my shot land. Then the light disappeared. We searched the area three times. We found some fresh blood, but no elf."

Harley paused to see if there were any questions, Zel Camber just glared at him, and so Harley continued. "We searched the area for hours. If he were there, we'd have found some sign, but he disappeared like some kinda ghost."

Zel Camber turned to look at the priest being fed by the servants. The priest simply nodded. As Zel Camber turned back to face Harley, he could see that his face was beginning to redden. Harley was not sure if he had seen Zel Camber even take a breath since the moment he told him they had not stopped the elf. "Able wanted to run," Harley shared quickly. "He didn't want to come back to tell you that we hadn't killed him. So when he tried to desert your army, I killed him. I know there is no room for deserters, sir."

Zel Camber slowly walked around the edge of the table and approached Harley. Taking in the first deep breath that Harley was able to note, he said in a measured tone, "Let me see if I understand you fully. You let the elf get away. Some magic was done to allow him to escape. You killed your friend to show me that you can be trusted, because he was afraid to return to face me with his failure?"

In the pause, Harley took a moment to nod, never taking his eyes off the eyes of Zel Camber. He did not want him thinking that he was weak or unworthy.

Then a sly smile came over the face of Zel Camber. He leaned over to the Harley's left ear and whispered, "Maybe your friend had the right idea." Before Harley could process what Zel Camber had said, a loud *shing* sounded in his ear. A knife blade shot from the knuckles of the Zel Camber's gauntlet into the left side of Harley's neck.

Almost as quickly the blade had been shot through Harley's neck, Zel Camber withdrew it. As Harley fell to his knees and tried to stop the bleeding from his neck, Zel Camber used the shoulder of Harley's tunic to wipe the blood off his dagger. Then placing the tip of his dagger on the edge of the oak table, he reloaded the blade in his gauntlet. With a click, it was once again hidden among the chevrons that decorated the knuckles of his gauntlet.

Walking back around the table to examine the map, Zel Camber commented to the man in magicians clothing, "I cannot tolerate failure. This was important."

HOLLYWONDRA

"Then why send such buffoons to carry out such a critical task?" the robed man replied. Zel Camber was not accustomed to being spoken to in such tones, but this man was of immense value to him, and he could tolerate some things when he needed to.

"In truth, I'm glad to see that elf go. I don't know where he's gone to, but at least he won't be around here to deter our progress any longer. With him out of our way, we can proceed," Zel Camber shared.

Then pausing, Zel Camber shot the magi a glance and asked, "I am assuming this man was telling me the truth?"

"For the most part," he replied coyly. Holding up his right hand to signal the girls to stop feeding him, he went on. "They did fail to catch the elf. The elf did jump into some green glowing portal. The men did have doubts about coming back. He did kill his friend," the magician reported. Then he added, "Oh, and the guy did think that killing his friend might save his own life."

Harley made a thud as he fell into a pool of his own blood.

"It's dangerous business, Sythene, thinking that one can guess my nature." Zel Camber was looking directly at the magi now, and the magician stopped chewing. While Zel Camber was not making a specific threat to the magician, he did recognize that his behavior in the service of Zel Camber might have been more careful. Sythene nodded that he did understand. Then he opened his mouth as a request for another grape.

Jarius looked out onto the open grass land. While he watched the tall grass change color in the afternoon mountain shadows, he thought through the details of his mission. It was not even a moon ago he had been honored to become the newest knight of the Elvan realm. It really was the culmination of his work for the kingdom. It has been a goal of his from his youth. As far as he was concerned, there was no higher honor.

On the green of Hollywondra, Barnabus Malactus, the high priest of the Elvan nation, bestowed upon him the honors of knighthood by performing the Prayer of Empowerment. On his knees, he knelt before the entire city. At the time, Jarius was still trembling from the weakness of his wounds. Humbled by this honor, Jarius's mind wandered to this tattered tunic he wore for this life-altering event. The little strength he had remaining he used for focusing on keeping himself still for the ceremony.

Fear and awe rushed through Jarius as the high priest unsheathed the holy sword known only as Perdition. Perdition was rumored to be a holy artifact of power that only the truly sanctified could touch. There had been stories of men careless enough to have laid their hands on Perdition's ornate golden hilt. Their fate was to suffer a sudden and painful death. The idea that the high priest was about to knight him with that sword was both frightening and assuring to him. He knew that he and God had a connection. If they did not, he would never be allowed to be knighted by the power of Perdition.

Barnabus Malactus was a small elf. Perdition, though it was a short sword, was still half his height. His size truly had nothing to do with his power. To look into the eyes of the priest, you could see

HOLLYWONDRA

the wisdom of the ages. His pale wrinkled face was framed with long wispy white hair and beard. The sheen from his bright blue silk cap offset his pale complexion. The ceremonial robes he wore that day were rich and ornate. The long flowing wrap had fine needle point depicting stories of Elvan heroism. Written around the hem of this blue silk masterpiece was a well-known Elvan prayer. The gold thread was such a sharp contrast to the blue robe that it created a bright frame around the fabric.

In the center of Hollywondra was a large green. It reached across the floor of Hollywondra to the door of the temple. The green could be followed through the town, until it began to slope up to the royal residence of King Elfanwisel. Most everywhere else, the white alyssum grew. Malactus stood at the edge of an ivory-pillared balcony that had been built out from the Temple Tree. Overlooking the green, the balcony was about thirty feet up the side of the Temple Tree. Malactus was barely visible to the throng of elves assembled on the green below. Only his head and shoulders could be seen over the short railing of the ivory balustrade. Looking directly out over the crowd, Barnabus Malactus stood with his hands behind his back, waiting for the crown to quiet.

As the Elvan nation hushed, Perdition was ceremoniously delivered by two temple acolytes. They carried the sword on a blue sheet of silk that matched the blue of priest's robes. With each acolyte holding two corners of the fabric, the sword rested gently across the length of the fabric. As the acolytes arrived, they stepped back to pull all four corners tight. As the sheet pulled taut, it exposed the holy sword to the crowd. Jarius recalled how the crowd had made a sudden "Ahhh" then turned quiet. Almost as if they held their breath, they watched as Barnabus Malactus lifted the sword and sheath from the tapestry. With Perdition secure in his hands, the acolytes bowed and backed away.

Turning to the crowd, the high priest raised Perdition for all to see. Secure in his two hands, the crowd still dared not utter a sound. Then Malactus began his address. "Through the ages, Namron Rae and our Lord has sustained us safely in our sacred Hollywondra. Now everything we know, our very existence is being threatened by the evil of Zel Camber and his minions. Our Lord has bestowed upon us great beauty and trust. We have a responsibility to sustain the beauty of Namron Rae in the same way in which it was created. Like all duties, they do not come without challenge. Many of you have heard about setbacks we have had in defeating Zel Camber. I will not deceive you into thinking we are not in peril. Indeed, these are dark days for our Elvan kingdom. His armies approach Hollywondra with one goal in mind: the eradication of all Elves. Every man, woman, and child are at risk.

It is in these darkest days that we know to call upon our Lord with our faith: faith grown from centuries of events of His grace and support. Each time he reminds us of our duty to Namron Rae. Today, we celebrate the accomplishments of a new champion. A champion, who, if deemed worthy, will launch himself forward in the name of our God and the Elvin race.

Here in my hands, I hold the holy artifact known only as Perdition. Through the centuries of our existence, Perdition has been a constant arbiter of truth. As I unsheathe this holy sword, I unsheathe the eyes and will of our God. And through his power bestow the honor of knighthood upon Jarius Raphael.

Still holding the sword overhead, Malactus turned from the audience to the kneeling Jarius Raphael. Pulling the sheath off the sword with his left hand, Malactus held the sword in his right. Holding the sword high in his right hand allowed the sun to glisten from the blade as he bowed his head for a short silent prayer. Then extending the sword forward, Malactus laid it gently upon the right shoulder of Jarius Raphael.

As Perdition fell upon his shoulder, Jarius experienced a warm sensation that quickly surged through his body and soul confirming his holy appointment to the rank of knight. Then a flash suddenly shot through his conscious mind. It was like he had been given a full recounting of Perdition's life. This flash recounted all the knights who had been sanctified, as well as a lengthy history of fools and dead who touched Perdition willfully and otherwise. The entire sensation was energizing like a good night's rest. He noticed after being touched on his left shoulder that his strength had returned to him before the sword ever touched his right. No longer was he struggling to sustain his poise and strength. Instead, a wave of refreshment ran through him as he felt his posture straighten.

After the confirmation decree of the ceremony, Jarius rose. He could not remember the last time he felt so strong and refreshed. Still feeling the rush from the ceremony, the roar of the city seemed like only a fog to his memory. The rest of the ceremony was a blur. He did recall his right arm being lifted high by the priest and the words bringing another roar of approval from the city. Jarius felt badly that he could not recall the entire ceremony; his recollection kept returning to the powerful connection he had felt with his God.

The day after his appointment, Malactus called Jarius for an audience. "You, Sir Raphael, are indeed a blessed man. I pray the blessings of God may continue to shine on you in these difficult days ahead." Malactus greeted him. Concerned about the intention of his words, Jarius settled into a chair at a table with the high priest. Shortly after sitting, an acolyte brought a hot cup of herbal tea and saucer to match the one being held by Malactus. "I'm afraid there is no time to waist, so forgive me for being so direct. Jarius, you know our kingdom is struggling in this fight. While we are still able to control the key mountain passes and forest buffers that surround us, the sheer numbers of Zel Camber's legions will overwhelm us."

Pausing to sip from his cup, Malactus glanced at Jarius over the rim of his cup and said, "The time is upon us. From a distant land, we must bring forth the Ray of Light! You, my son, shall bring forth the ray."

The Ray of Light was an ancient Elvan myth as old as the Elvan race itself. How could Barnabus Malactus be considering him for such a deed was all Jarius could wonder. Many of the words that followed Jarius had to ask him to repeat, because the size of this mission overwhelmed Jarius from the beginning. Jarius felt he was too young to be considered for such an important task. Jarius knew there were plenty of capable warriors in the Elvan legion. Why him?

"Why me?" Jarius asked. "Sir Kluvarner is such a powerful warrior and has the respect of every elf. Why are you not considering him?" Jarius knew his comments were a bit brazen, but he really did not understand why he was being chosen.

"Ah, Sir Kluvarner is truly a great warrior," Malactus confirmed as he sipped his tea. "The truth is, Sir Kluvarner is needed by his men. To simply withdraw him from his current role in leading our forces could put his entire army at risk. They have come to believe in his leadership and wisdom in battle. Leadership in battle is not something you can simply assign to someone. A trust in that leader must be built, before men will follow you to their graves. You, Sir Rafael, will one day garner such devotion from your men. Today, the kingdom has a greater need for your skills." Malactus paused to accentuate the importance to the task. "Do not misunderstand the urgency of this mission." Malactus locked eyes with Jarius. "The fate of our nation depends on your success in this matter. I cannot imagine a more dire time in our history. This must be the time for the Light to come. You can be sure that elements of evil will unite to try to stop you. Stay true to your faith, and know that our God watches over you.

I have something I want you to carry with you on this journey. I know you will be going to places foreign to you, so I want you to have every possible advantage. Moving to his desk, Malactus pulled open the drawer. This was a gift to the temple. It was left at the gifting alter three moons ago. It's as if someone knew it would have an immediate purpose. Malactus pulled a bright-green silk cloth from the drawer. It was wrapped tightly around something. As Malactus pulled back the silk, he revealed a beautiful silver knife and sheath.

Grabbing the knife by the hilt, he handed it to Jarius. Jarius was a little surprised to see him handle the weapon so casually. He was surprised to see that the metal did not burn the priest. Not grabbing it right away from the priest, Malactus pushed it toward him a second time. "It's safe, son. Take a close look at the hilt."

Taking the knife from Malactus, Jarius found it surprisingly light in weight. He carefully examined the hilt of the dagger. The handle was made of silver, and the hilt was intricately engraved. It appeared to be two ropes starting at the end of each hilt wounding their way to the center of the hilt. There they crossed and formed a knot on each side of the knife. In the center of each knot was a ruby the size of his fingertip. The ropes then continued up the hilt to the end. A third knot was formed at the end of the hilt. Instead of a third ruby being located at that place, Jarius saw magical runes. Runes he recognized as those of his church, but not truly of his understanding.

The sheath was every bit as beautiful. It, too, was designed in the spun rope motif. The edges were the only part that had the rope lining the sheath. It had no rubies, but it did have the same markings as the hilt.

Jarius knew this was truly a one of a kind artifact. He looked up from his examination at Malactus and said, "This is far too fine." Then he tried to hand it back to Malactus.

The priest smiled and said, "Sir Raphael, you are in the service of your people. What we have, you will use to protect us. Take it. It is now your property. Anyone else to be found in possession of that knife will be known as a thief in this kingdom."

"Thank you for this fine gift," Jarius said as he stood and withdrew his belt on which he placed the sheath. He pondered the meaning of this. As legend has it, an imperiled Elvan world would be spared when the Ray of Light returned to Namron. The Elvan people would suffer, but with its return, new clarity would be provided to their defense, and the tide would be turned on the evil forces. The evil forces of Zel Camber have been trying to eradicate Elvan kind for the last several years. Zel Camber believes he is cleansing the land. His mission had not been taken very seriously until the growth of his army these last few years.

The legend was not merely one of Elvan hope. The legend of the Ray of Light was known in many of the cultures of Namron Rae. Some had slight variations that differed slightly from culture to culture. It was believed to be a weapon of awesome destruction that could level mountains and calm the seas. These legends were told of this unknown artifact without anyone having ever really seen it. One commonality was that it was a weapon of unmatched power.

The problem was, nobody really knew what the Ray of Light was, where it could be found, or how to retrieve it. What was clear was that there was no better time than the present. The human hordes under command of Zel Camber had united themselves for the purpose of ridding Namron Rae of the last remaining elves. They were making serious forays into the surrounding forests. The forests, until recently, had only been traveled by elves and wildlife. It was only a matter of time before they were in the streets of Hollywondra.

It was this sense of urgency that compelled Barnabus Malactus, the High Priest of Hollywondra, to commission this charge to Sir Raphael. Raphael had just returned from a campaign in which he and his men were able to infiltrate the battle lines and retrieve the Tree Key from Zel Camber's fortress at Biander's Bluff. It was a miracle that he was able to succeed. It wasn't a surprise that most of Jarius's men lost their lives in this task. To Malactus, it was a sign. A sign that this hero was a man of destiny. Malactus only needed to confirm his suspicions through the ceremony of knighthood. Yet Malactus knew he was taking a great risk in asking him to take on this new mission. Malactus knew Sir Raphael had become a hero in the eyes of an Elvan nation that was downtrodden. The lives they were losing were beginning to affect the entire city. Celebrating this victory meant a lot to the Elvan nation. To send him away and out of sight could place the whole Elvan nation at the risk of depression. Not to mention the chance that their new hero might also die in trying to accomplish the deed. Yet these were chances that Malactus felt he must take. He had prayed extensively. This is what he believed they must do. They had to do something quick if they were going to change the momentum of this war. Jarius and the Ray of Light was their only hope. The Elvan nation was never more at risk.

His initial instinct was to ask how to find the Ray of Light in this foreign land. Then the answer came to him. Faith. Just have faith that he will be guided to it. To utter such a question would only display a lack of faith in a God who had bestowed faith in him. He was a new man. He was incredibly young for knighthood, nonetheless a hero in the eyes of his nation.

Reviewing these responsibilities only confirmed Jarius's need to take his bow and arrows into this foreign village in this foreign land. He could not afford to be surprised or captured. He had to draw on every resource he had. Particularly, those resources he knew so well. Someway, somehow, he knew his Lord would show him a path to this Ray of Light.

7

A harden rock-tar surface stretched away from the village and into the distance. This hard surface was wider than two carts and created a very smooth surface for travel. White stripes were painted down the center of this path as it stretched into the distance. Tall posts illuminated the streets of the town with glowing fixtures Jarius did not recognize. The lights were far too high for someone to light nightly. Nor did they glow like the light of a candle. They were much brighter. Cables appeared to run from pole to pole and then from some poles to buildings.

In the village, a solitary street ran from one end to the other. Then it stretched off into the distance. Seven crossing streets created this small town. Jarius stayed at the edge of the town to observe the people and their way of life. While crouching down in the tall grass at the north end of town, he heard a sound in the distance behind him. Two beams of light seemed to rise in the distant road. The two lights moved quickly in the direction of the town. They came at a pace greater than any carriage he had ever witnessed. Jarius could only imagine what devastation he was about to witness.

As the lights drew nearer, Jarius could see that they were affixed to some form of wagon. This wagon was moving at incredible speed down the main street toward the village. Jarius began to feel relief when he could hear the wagon's roar lessen and the vehicle began to slow down as it approached the town. As it went by, Jarius could see that this vehicle had wheels on each corner and windows on the front and sides. The back of the vehicle was empty of cargo. It went past him so quickly that he couldn't tell much more about the vehicle itself, except it was blue. The vehicle slowed down, and suddenly the red lights on the back of the vehicle glowed brighter. It slowed down and turned into a building and stopped. Watching carefully, Jarius wanted to assess who held such power and speed. A door on one side of the vehicle popped open, and a tall human stepped out. The human wore blue trousers, a plaid woolen shirt, and a strange broad brimmed hat. Then throwing the door shut, he walked into the building. At this point, Jarius began to take notice that other vehicles with similar wheels dotted the streets in various locations. Some of them were at the same building. Others were parked in front of what appeared to be homes rather than businesses. Some of these vehicles were for carrying cargo, while others seemed to be merely transports.

The village was no wider than ten homes on any one cross street. Still, Jarius elected to skirt the town and observe from the cover of high grass. That night he was able to circle the town without little attention paid to his presence. The exception was hounds in a backyard kennel at the south end of town. They were a sudden reminder to Jarius that he had just left one reality for this one. The hounds were suddenly one very stark similarity. Evidently, the local folks were accustomed to hearing them bay, because nobody came to see why they had started to howl.

Jarius took his time circling the village. He made his way to the back of the building he had seen the visitor enter. The night air was crisp, but he had no choice in his clothing. He approached the back of the building to discover the building was two structures. The two buildings were separated by a large dirt breezeway with steps going up to the mercantile the visitor had entered. The breeze informed Jarius that the other building stabled horses. The stable had a large open door. As he looked inside, it seemed more like a barn than stable. Uncertain what other kinds of beasts might befriend a horse in this land, Jarius decided to not risk going inside. Instead, he went to the back of the mercantile to study the people inside the building.

On the backside of the building, Jarius discovered that someone had taken the time to cut down trees, cut the wood into small pieces that were all approximately the same size, and then stacked the wood in long neat rows against the back of this building. The roof of the

HOLLYWONDRA

building seemed to be extended a bit further than it had to be to create some cover for this wood. Jarius peaked over the edge of the wood pile to peer through the building window.

Inside he saw two men. One was at a counter and appeared to be writing something. The other sat in a rocking chair by a large iron pedestal stove. Inside the stove, Jarius could see flames but no smoke. A large black pipe running from the top of the pedestal removed the smoke. Jarius could certainly smell the burning fire. The man in the chair was drinking periodically from a small brown bottle with a label. The other man had a similar brown bottle on the counter near him.

Besides the similarities in what they drank, Jarius also noticed similarities in what they wore. The man sitting in the chair was wearing trousers very similar to the ones the visitor wore. He also wore a plaid shirt with long sleeves. The differences were the colors of the shirts and the fact that the one sitting by the stove had his shirt buttoned up. Both men appeared to be very comfortable in the company of the other.

Jarius listened carefully to see if he could pick out any words he might understand. The man standing had mentioned "oats" and "horses." He seemed to be joking with the other man, but he also seemed to call the other man more than one name. The man in the chair appeared to be the owner of the mercantile, and the other man was acquiring supplies from him. That was about all Jarius could figure out. Some of the words he understood, but the dialect was so rich that he could not be entirely certain. It was a human dialect. That he knew. It was just odder than the human language he knew from Namron. As he realized how cold he was becoming, he patted himself on the back for not just walking into the town and asking questions. With a little more study, he figured he could speak very close to the same way as these people.

He looked around the inside of the store and noticed that shelves had burlap bags of goods, jars with food contents, and clothing. Jarius knew that at some point, he would have to get his hands on some clothing that could be acceptable to these townsfolk. While the language difference might be something to overcome, nobody was wearing weaponry. He wasn't sure how he felt about entering this town unarmed. Fighting back the cold of night, Jarius took extra time to listen to the two men talk and to examine the contents of this mercantile.

Jarius determined to make his way back to his camp for the night, where he could create his own small campfire. He decided to skirt the west side of the town on his way back to the woods in the north. As he began making his way through the shadows, he was startled when someone yelled at him.

"Hey! What are you doin'?" The question came from an oak tree at the back side of a house. Jarius thought he was skirting wide enough around the town; he had not considered the possibility that someone might be in one of the trees. It wasn't like humans to be hanging out in trees.

He froze in place and did not move a muscle, hoping that he was not the one being addressed. Then the call came again. "I see you. You were just sneaking around the back of the Fletcher place." Looking carefully into the trees, Jarius could see the figure of a large boy climbing down the tree. The boy had been high in the tree, and that somewhat excused Jarius from not noticing him. Jarius knew the seriousness of this encounter. He was not prepared to engage locals. This could place his entire campaign at risk.

The boy was clearly coming down the tree to either confront him or to call alarm. Deciding he did not like either of those choices, Jarius turned and took off running to the west. Behind him, he heard the boy yell, "Hey! Come back!" but Jarius had already broken into the same stride he used to cover miles at a time. Few were able to keep up with him when he ran. He could not imagine a human crawling out of a tree would be able to keep pace.

Jarius took off running into one of the many tall grass fields that surrounded the town. He set off to the west so not to draw a straight line to his camp. He ran a long-arched route to the north and back in the direction from which he had originally started. The run began to make him warm again. The night was dark, and much of the brilliance of the moon was blocked by clouds. This was fortunate for Jarius, because as soon as he seemed sure he was out of reach, he heard the familiar sound of horse hooves.

Pausing for a moment to listen carefully, Jarius quickly noted that it was a single horse. So laying low in the grass and drew an arrow and nocked it to his bow. Watching just over the horizon of the tall grass, Jarius saw whom he imagined to be the boy from the tree. He had not run much further west before arching to the north, this boy would be about on top of his location. Fortunately, he was slightly north of the boy. The boy reined in his horse and spoke in a normal tone. "Are you there, stranger? I mean you no harm. What are you doing out here in the cold?" The boy paused to carefully listen. Jarius did not even breathe during the boy's pause. "I'm harmless," the boy tried to assure him.

Then it occurred to Jarius that he understood most of what the boy was saying. The boy spoke with different inflections, but it was basically the same language. Even with that realization, Jarius was still not ready to meet these people from this strange land. He could not afford to make any mistakes. The entire Elvan race counted on his success. If he was going to err, it was going to be on the side of caution. So Jarius waited him out, just like he had waited out so many other creatures in his life. He knew the constitution of humans was not that of elves, so it was only a matter of time. Though he was ready for him to leave at any time.

Even after the boy gave up and began slowly walking the horse back toward town, Jarius stayed still and watched him. He did not want this guy doubling back and surprising him again. His prior carelessness was unforgivable. This time he made certain he would be clear out of sight.

Once he was certain his tracker was indeed gone, he made his way east to his camp in the woods. Jarius took care to cover his tracks to the tree line. Then he walked several hundred yards into the woods before he circled back around to his campsite. There he finally warmed himself by a tiny fire. Digging through his small backpack, he found some of the bread and cheese he had packed for the journey. Settling in, he began to contemplate his newfound knowledge of this local settlement. This little trip into town had provided him good information. Besides, this town was just too close to the tree to not contain some clues to the whereabouts of the Ray of Light.

*****

"I'm tellin' ya, someone was out there last night!" Titus protested as Amanda and her friend Chloe continued walking beside him up the steps to the school. At the top of the landing, Titus grabbed Amanda by the elbow. That was huge. Titus may not have ever touched Amanda before, but he cared so much about what she thought that he had to know that she believed him. Spinning to face him, Amanda allowed him to ask again. Titus spoke calmly, "You *do* believe me...don't you?" Then he whispered, "Don't you?"

Amanda waited just a moment to see if he had more information to offer, then smiled and replied, "Of course, I do, Titus. I just don't know why you're making such a big deal out of it. It has to be someone we know from town. Nobody in their right mind would come all the way into town just to prowl around. It has to be somebody from around here." Changing her tone and lowering her voice, she leaned toward Titus and suggested, "Frankly...I don't think I'd mention it. The guys are probably playing some kind of trick on you." Amanda knew that Titus didn't exactly fit in and that he had been the butt of more than one teen prank.

Amanda's friend saw no need to even entertain his concern. Chloe added, "Get a grip, Titus," then she turned to walk away. Her spin away from the conversation was so quick that her shoulder-length hair spun around in an arc. Titus had to lean back to not be hit by her swinging hair.

Standing between Titus and her departing friend, Amanda looked to see where Chloe was walking. Then she returned her attention to Titus. It was clear to her that he was not done expressing himself. She could tell he was frustrated.

Having never seen Amanda treat anyone poorly, Titus paused to consider her thought. Then he responded, "But they didn't know I was there. I took him by surprise!"

Having lost track of what he was talking about, Amanda asked, "Huh?"

"I was in the tree," Titus stated before he realized how silly that might sound. Amanda's eyes narrowed as she was trying to reconnect with Titus and his story. A bit embarrassed that he might have to explain himself, he whispered, "The tree outside my bedroom!" Amanda's eyes lighted up as he then realized what tree he meant. Then a look of bewilderment came over her face. Rather than taking the next question, he knew she was going to ask, he moved forward.

"I was in the tree sitting quietly when I saw him prowling around the back of the Fletcher place. He was trying to not be seen. You see? It couldn't be a trick on me. He didn't want to be seen," Titus concluded.

"Hmmm?" she purred as the tardy bell rang. With a quick smile, for Titus, Amanda turned. Then she made a couple of quick steps to catch up with Chloe, who had stopped just inside the doors to stare at a couple of the guys getting books out of a locker. Titus stood and watched the girls walk away. Then he tried to assess their conversation. He wasn't sure if she believed him or if she left because school was starting. He began to ponder this as he slowly entered the school's front doors.

Adoring her, as he always had, he just watched her walk away. She and Chloe merged into the crowd of students rushing through the hallway of this small country school. Titus had never been able to tell her how he felt about her. Just touching her elbow to get her attention brought a rush to him that he did not expect. He wasn't sure if he needed her to believe him or if he was trying to believe himself.

Titus and his family moved to this remote part of Montana when his father purchased a cattle ranch a few years earlier. From that time on, Titus had grown close to Amanda. She did not present herself in the same way many of the others in the town behaved. She was kind and considerate. It seemed many of the people of the town required boys to be tough and muscular. Titus was always the opposite. He was quick witted and understood people's motives better than most. These two talents had managed to keep him out of trouble, though his mouth tended to be too quick at times. Nobody at the high school was close to matching Titus in his intellect. He extended his talents by studying physics and Latin online. He dreamed of studying Pre-med at the University of Washington and leaving this small town behind.

His older brother on the other hand settled very easily into the dust and leather of this small Montana hamlet. His quickness and athleticism helped him to quickly fit in with the middle school football team. It was there that Brent and Webster first became friends. Webster quickly became the quarterback and made his team a winner by constantly handing the ball off to Brent, the man-child.

Webster's six-foot-tall muscular frame combined with his quick tanning skin and sandy colored hair made him a popular guy with the local girls too. Everything that Webster was seemed to be absent in Titus's life. Sure, Titus was two years younger, but he was only 5'7" and seemed to sunburn every time he spent more than a half hour outside without sun block. As hard as he tried, he still could not seem to add any weight to his 145-pound frame.

While this tiny Montana town was so ordinary in so many ways, there was clearly something extraordinary about Rile, Montana. Very extraordinary.

8

The hooves of the huge black war horse scattered sod as Captain Nictovius reached the bluff. Allowing his steed to slow to a light trot, he and his horse walked up to the edge of a cliff. There the Valley of Shayna unveiled herself below. Lightly patting the shoulder of his old friend, Nictovius paused at this precipice to study the terrain below.

The Valley of Shayna was a spectacle to behold. The valley began at the base of the mammoth Crescent Crags Mountains. The Crescent Crags rose sharply from the valley floor, making it exceedingly difficult for travelers to enter the valley through those mountains. The Crescent Crags reached out for miles to the north and wrapped themselves around the entire region. Forming the eastern edge of the valley floor was the great Raven Rift. This enormous chasm made a natural boundary that stretched from the northern tip of the Crags to their southern end of the valley. At the northern end of the Valley of Shayna were Shayna's Tears, a majestic waterfall cascading down the rocky face of the crags. Shayna's Tears gathers into a small lake at the valley floor, before it trickled off the edge of the valley floor and into the Raven Rift. The drop into the Raven Rift is so high that the water from that stream disappears into a mist before it ever reaches the river below. Few could be truly certain, since the cliff is so high, and the waters below are so remote.

The floor of the valley is framed by the Crescent Crags to the west and the great Elvanwood to the east. A thin strip of the Elvanwood reached to northern and southern ends of the valley. The majority of its expanse lies to the east. There it stretches miles until it meets the edge of Raven Rift. The trees of the Elvanwood are ancient. From his perch, Nictovius could see how the trees seemed to get even more enormous the deeper into the woods he looked.

Lifting the visor of his helm, Nictovius looked again at the mystical woods. Some of these trees seemed so large, he could not imagine how they could be harvested for lumber. Somewhere inside that wooded maze was Nictovius's prize, the ancient Elvan city of Hollywondra.

Hollywondra was known to be the capital city of the elves. Rumored to be deep within the Elvanwood, few humans had ever set sight on its natural beauties. As Nictovius rested upon his horse, looking north into the Valley of Shayna, he could not begin to count his encampments that now dotted the lush green carpet of the valley floor. From the southern end of the valley and stretching halfway across the valley floor, Zel Camber's legions had come to this remote corner of Namron Rae for only one reason.

With the Raven Rift on one side and the Crags on the other, Nictovius grew pleased at his chances of finishing this job. The elves clearly had nowhere else to go. He knew better than to underestimate the crafty elves. He just knew that he had finally pushed them into this corner. He began to ponder how his feats would be scribed by Chronus's feather in the Annals of Time. His name would be on the lips of men for centuries. His name would be forever associated with bringing about the extinction of the Elvan race.

His daydreaming was dashed at the sound of his lieutenants arriving behind him. As they reined in their horses, they saw their captain resting high in his saddle and looking off into the distance. They walked their horses toward the edge of the bluff overlooking the valley. Streams of blacked smoke rose from the scores of campfires below. Dusk was coming to the Valley of Shayna. The camps below were buzzing with men preparing evening meals and posting guards for the night.

Captain Nictovius extended his right arm and pointed off into the distance. His musculature was covered with black iron plated armor. His black gauntlet pointed down into the valley. "See that place where the forest extends out into the field?" he asked his lieutenants. "We will begin there. Let's capture that edge so that we can use those trees for siege machines. That will also give us some idea how they will respond to our presence. Once we have taken enough timber to construct the trebuchets, then we can begin to lay waste to that forested fortress they call home."

The lieutenants all chuckled under their helms and nodded in agreement. With his back to his men, Nictovius continued to look off into the distance. The Elvanwood was a broad expanse that extended for miles. He knew that it ran to the very edge of the Raven Rift. He just wasn't sure how far that would be. He knew they would take less casualties if he used fire to lead their charge. Next to iron, fire was the most detestable thing to Elves. The burning of their sacred forest satisfied Nictovius in a dark way. Slowly a smile grew his face. His helmet hid this pleasure from the faces of his men.

The lieutenants were busy discussing who would take which part of the attack on the woods. Nictovius's dreams of greatness were broken by their argument over who would attack which part of the tree line. Listening to them bicker only reinforced his concern for the leadership of this army. He finally interrupted, "Have you never thought to wonder why I hold these meetings away from the men?" His tone brought the argument to an immediate end. All three lieutenants spun their horses to look directly at him.

Spinning his horse around to face them directly, he shook his head with disgust. "You fools could not agree on the light of day, if you were not told the sun was up! This is a simple three-pronged attack on a region that probably doesn't have four possums and a squirrel. You three talk like you're laying siege to the Elvan capital." Wrapping his reins to his saddle horn, Nictovius grabbed hold of his helm and pulled it off to make sure his men could see his eyes as he spoke.

Pulling off the helm had an effect greater than just showing his eyes to his men. It also revealed the horrible scar that ran from the corner of his left eye to the left corner of his squared chin. This scar, like many earned in battle, was not given the luxury of field poultice to heal cleanly. So the skin had discolored and settled unevenly on his face. The marking was so hideous, it was hard for someone speaking with him to not become lost in the sight of this unsightly flesh. His sweat ran off his forehead and onto his cheek. The natural direction of the sweat was interrupted as it fell into the scar that ran the length of his face. Quickly it joined other droplets and dripped out the end of the scar at the corner of his chin.

"Let me make myself perfectly clear. If this is your best work, then I am sure I can find three men with better minds," Nictovius challenged as he spit to the ground. "Every campaign, every battle fought for the last three years has been to confine the elves to this one corner of Namron. The real war is in front of us, and you three can't decide who's to fetch water. If your men were to see you behave in this fashion, I might promote the man who ran you through from their sheer disgust." All three began to hang their heads in shame.

Nictovius continued, "Now is not the time for such foolishness. We need to be organized as one, and our men need to see that we operate as one voice. Tallarand!" The man sitting in the middle of the three riders quickly raised his head and straighten himself in his saddle to look at the captain. "You will take the frontal assault on this wood. Your men will attack it from the point where it extends furthest onto the valley floor." The other two men looked up to receive their orders as well. "Silas Pei, you shall take the northern flank, and, Alec, you shall take the south. Do you have any questions?" Nictovius finished with a tone of sarcasm. Allowing for a pause, that he knew would be silent, Nictovius said, "Good! I would imagine I will never have to have speak of this with any of you again."

All three men began to reply to the captain in unorganized gentle replies of "No, my liege." Nictovius, still a bit disgusted, put his helm back on his head and leaned forward in his saddle. His heavy armored hand patted the horse's thick muscular neck, and it turned to look back at Nictovius. He knew the horse would never let him down the way all three of these men might at any given moment. The look he got from his horse was almost a confirmation of faith. Almost to say, "You can count on me, and yes, those three are idiots."

At that, Nictovius turned to look back at the valley filled with his army encampments. The first campfires of the evening stood out as the Crescent Crags' shadow crept across the valley floor. Realizing how far they had traveled, Nictovius thought it was just as well they eat and rest. Pulling gently on his reins, the horse spun away from the cliff and toward his lieutenants. The four riders descended the mountain trail back to camp.

9

Titus rarely found himself unable to focus on his studies, but his conversation with Amanda left him struggling to focus. He was not sure if he was struggling with the fact that she may not believe him or if he was struggling with the fact that someone was prowling the town in the dark of night. Both things disturbed him. He could not determine which was responsible for keeping his mind off his online physics course.

The school library was certainly quiet enough. He had a good connection to the website. Yet he found himself looking at the screen, as if it were the start of the lesson, only for him to struggle to catch up with what the instructor had been discussing. He knew this was not like him, and it caused him to consider why he was struggling to focus. Then after a few moments of consideration, he found himself trying to catch up with instruction again.

Finally, Titus realized that these other issues were too important, and he would not be able to focus on his studies. So that he did not attract the attention of the librarian, Titus kept his computer class running, took out some paper, and began to logically try to resolve his thoughts about these two issues. Making a T chart, he wrote "Amanda" on the left side, and on the right side, he wrote "Prowler." Then he began listing things about each of them to understand his thoughts more clearly.

The first thing he wrote under Amanda was the word "trust." Then he wrote her "believing in" him. Then her words took hold, and he listed her idea that the others might be playing a trick on him. As much as he was sure this could not have been the case, he respected her so much that he wrote down her idea. Pausing to examine his notes about Amanda, he turned his attention to the right side of the page.

Under the title of Prowler, he wrote "Who could this be?" "Where is this person from?" "What is he doing?" "Where did he go?" As he paused and looked at what he had written, he realized that he kept calling the person a "he." This forced him to stop and reexamine what he really knew. Was he certain this was a guy?

He was certain the person was truly prowling the edge of town. The prowler did not see him until he yelled out at him. For whatever reason, this prowler must have felt they could not be found out. The person would not stop to be confronted by someone of even his slight stature. The person was fast. The person was slight of stature. He began to try to consider who at school had this build and speed. When he realized none of his classmates really fit the description of the person, Titus realized this had to be a stranger. This prowler could be some transient passing through the area. There was a railroad spur not too far west of Rile.

While making his notes, Titus peeked over the monitor of his computer to make sure the librarian was not coming over to check on him. This was a reflection in his conscientious nature. The librarian never considered checking on Titus. He was without question the most responsible and accomplished student in school. The idea that he might be misbehaving, or off task, was something she never considered even possible.

As Titus looked back at his notes, he realized that he needed to find out who this person was or drop it all together. He knew he could not be making accusations without more evidence. He realized that he had no proof and that nobody important to him shared his concerns. He would have to find this person on his own.

Titus decided to revisit the trail he made chasing the person last night. He knew he had chased him through the hay field behind his house. There might still be a trace of the trail he could see in daylight. At the very least, he could find and follow the route he had taken with his horse. That might point him in the right direction.

Once school got out, Titus was anxious to see if he could find the path of the chase. After dropping his backpack on the sofa, he went right out the back door to see what he could find. He was excited to find that he could easily see the crushed grass path he and his horse had made the night before. He went straight to the barn to saddle his horse. After grabbing a quick bite to eat, Titus threw on his jacket and set off to see what else he might find.

At first, the tracking was pretty easy. Titus and his horse had made a large path through the tall dry grass. They were able to easily follow the path as it went west. When Titus came to the place where he stopped his chase, he found himself looking at the rolling fields of hay and the distant hills. He even found that the person had turned north before the path began to dissipate. The sea of hay blowing in the breeze looked like a blank canvas. There was no sign of any path. Sitting on the back of his horse and looking back at his house, he could see that his path was a fairly straight line from his house. Putting himself in the mind of the prowler, Titus tried to imagine what he would have done if he were being chased by a horsed rider. This led him to begin to slowly search the hay field between his path and his house.

The about halfway back to his house, he found what appeared to be a narrow path through the hay. It was so small, he almost talked himself out of following it. Then he realized the unusual nature of a path like this. He turned his horse to follow. The path did not turn directly east, it slowly arced off to the north. After following it for about a hundred yards, it turned directly east.

While this did not tell him a lot about where the prowler went, it did suggest that the prowler did not come from the railroad. The railroad was a good mile west of town. After running this far into the field, someone coming from the railroad would have turned off in that direction. Turning east baffled Titus. That suggested the person was either living in the hills or they had a horse waiting in the field a safe distance from town.

Knowing he had a little time before dinner, Titus decided to make his best guess and ride off to the east to see if he could find any signs of where he may have left a horse or car. It was a nice afternoon for a ride, so Titus zipped up his jacket a little snugger and decided to take his time.

For almost an hour, Titus had been watching the hypnotically waving grass looking for some clue of the prowler's path. His mind wandered to his horse and how little he had spent riding her as of late. Titus was startled to have found the path again. It was small. It was caused from someone on foot. Looking off in the direction of the path, the only thing he could see was the tree line ahead. There was a large gap between the grass field and the tree line, just enough to turn around the farm equipment. The tree line marked the edge of the forest. Titus knew that it was wooded for miles beyond that tree line.

Reining in his horse, Titus spun the horse to see how far from his house he had traveled. Off in the distance, he could make out some of the first buildings at the edge of town. He could not actually see his house. Turning back to look at the tree line, Titus considered the possibility that the prowler had come out of these hills and ventured into town. Then once he'd been caught ran all the way back into the hills. Looking back at the town, Titus realized that it would have been quite a run, but it was possible.

The path disappeared again, as he walked his horse to the edge of the hay field. There he stopped and looked up into the trees at the base of the hills. If there were someone hiding in the hills, he knew they could be watching him, and he would have no idea where they were. The whole idea made Titus a little uncomfortable, and his initial reaction was to spin his horse and head home.

Titus knew this feeling well. This is the same feeling he gets every time he is physically challenged by one of his classmates. The sheer difference in size and strength always leaves him at a disadvantage in any struggle. For years, his first reaction was to run. This only led to further embarrassments. He learned he couldn't run from his fears. He had to find another way to combat them.

Now from the back of his horse, he felt the same fear wash over him. This time, it wasn't from confronting high school classmates, but some unknown person. For years, Titus learned how to deny that initial emotion and work through the fear. This time he wasn't sure if that was a good idea. He knew it would be foolish to ride into the hills alone. Then he thought, *Maybe I'll just take a look along the edge of the hay field for any tracks.*

Pulling his horse to the left, Titus decided to ride north for a little way and then track back to the south and the old highway. That way he could just ride the highway shoulder home. Not really expecting to find anything specific, Titus galloped a couple hundred yards north before turning his horse around. Then walking back toward the highway, Titus watched the nicely furrowed loamy edge of the field for any signs of tracks.

A few dozen yards south of where his path had brought him to the edge of the hay field, he found what he had been looking for. There in the fluffy tilled loam at the edge of the field were footprints. As he walked his horse closer, he stopped and stared down at what he could not believe he found. These were indeed footprints. These were the tracks of a person who was running from the field. They were further apart than a walking stride apart. Titus considered getting down off his horse to check the tracks more closely.

Then he looked up into the nearby woods and considered how far and fast this person had run. They could be in the cover of the trees watching him right now. Then he thought he should be getting home. The woods were too close, and if he were off his horse, someone could come out of the woods faster than he could mount.

Besides, he convinced himself, now he had the evidence he needed to show Amanda. Looking back into the woods, Titus quickly mounted his horse and kicked her into a trot. As they headed south for the highway, Titus began considering his next message to Amanda.

10

The days had been busy. The prolonged ride of the campaign had not provided anyone with time for leisure. All Hamman Drew was able to think about was his need to sharpen the edges of his scimitars. Finally able to get some rest beside a warm fire, Hamman Drew found solace sharpening edge of his scimitars. As he slowly stroked the blade with his whetstone, he reflected on how well these blades had preserved his life. These were his tools of trade. He cared for them, and they cared for him. Leaving them unkempt made him very uneasy.

He paused to examine his progress. This blade had taken a direct block that left a chink in the edge of the blade. Hamman Drew had been working on it for several minutes. He knew if he didn't work it out that it could work against him the next time he really needed to use it. The crackle of the campfire and the grating sound of the whetstone on his blade gave him comfort.

Suddenly, something tugged at his senses, and he quickly looked around. The smell of burning meat caught his attention, and he looked toward the cook's fire. Above the fire hung a boar on a spit. The spit must not have been turned for some time because flames were shooting high enough to sear the boar's flesh. The fat from the boar dripped into the flames, only causing them to dance further up the sides of their dinner. Nearby, four men were enthralled in a game of dice. Clearly failing to mind the cooking of the food, Hamman Drew yelled at them, "Mind your pig!"

The last roll of the dice resulted in three of the men leaning back and groaning as the fourth man slapped his hands together and began to pick up the copper coins from the wooden deck of a

HOLLYWONDRA

wagon. At Hamman Drew's words, all four men turned to see who had addressed them in such a tone. One of the three losers replied to him with a snide, "Go home and mind your own pig, if she'll still have ya!" This caused the other three men to bust out laughing.

Far too busy for insults or nonsense, Hamman Drew paused to consider his next move. Obviously, these four guys did not care how their cooking was going to affect the rest of the men in their camp. Was that out of stupidity or lack of authority? After a moment, he couldn't imagine it was anything less than stupidity. Hamman Drew stopped honing his blade and put the stone in his pack.

As Hamman Drew paused, the man who had insulted him noticed him stop tending to his sword. "Oh, what have we here?" he asked of his friends as he saw Hamman return the stone to his pack. The man spun around to look at him more carefully, as Hamman Drew casually returned his scimitars to their sheathes.

Still reclined against the wheel of a wagon, Hamman Drew explained, "I was just trying to save your dinner from burning." Then Hamman Drew casually pointed at the boar that was sizzling over the fire. Crossing his arms, each of his hands disappeared behind the bulge of his biceps. Hamman Drew was both strong and lithe. His biceps extended below the edge of his leather armored tunic.

One of the other men who had just lost at dice challenged his friend who had already insulted Hamman Drew. "You gonna let him use that tone with you, Travor?"

Travor Pei turned to the man and said, "You go mind the pig. I'll take care of this one." Travor Pei spun around and stood up to address Hamman Drew. The man Travor Pei spoke to hurried to tend the burning boar. While he lowered the flames, he watched to see how Travor Pei would address this scout. Hamman Drew knew Travor Pei was not going to be able to let go of this. He had known other such foolish men.

Travor Pei's tone became challenging as he asked, "So what are you, the fire pit patrol?" This brought laughter from the other three men. "Isn't someone waiting for you to bring them firewood or something? You certainly must be a man of noble stature?" Each of his comments got his men laughing louder. Hamman Drew could tell this was going to get stupid if he didn't just walk away. Drew got up, turned, and began to leave the camp sight.

"Oh, no, you don't!" Travor Pei ordered. "How dare you come into our camp, insult me and my men, and then think you will be allowed to just walk away. I should thrash you for such impedance." Hamman Drew chose to ignore this man's words and continued walking away.

As he bent over to pick up his pack, he suggested, "We don't need to be fighting amongst ourselves." His logic was cut short from Travor Pei's boot clobbering the side of his face. Travor Pei's kick knocked Hamman Drew to the ground.

Enraged by the attack, Hamman Drew rolled to his feet and instinctively drew his scimitars. Realizing he had his scimitars in hand and that the man had taken a full step back, Hamman Drew pressed the back of his glove to his mouth to see if he was bleeding. Sure enough, this man had drawn first blood. Seeing the blood on his glove, he glanced up at Travor Pei and said, "It takes a pretty brave man to kick the face of a man who has his back to him. I'm gonna guess you're not brave enough to pull that long sword and deal with this like a real man." Hamman Drew had no reservations about fighting a man with a long sword. He knew he was a skilled fighter and that was some of the reason he had signed on as a mercenary. He was quite sure he could make some silver and live to talk about it.

"Sure, two swords to my one sounds fair," Travor Pei replied sarcastically.

Confident, Hamman Drew smiled and cleanly sheathed the scimitar he had been working on back into the sheath on his right hip. Hamman Drew never took his eye off Travor Pei.

Turning to address his gambling buddies, he suggested, "If he draws that other scimitar, I may need some help." Then without even turning to address Hamman Drew, Travor Pei quickly drew his sword and lunged. With a long sweeping overhead arc, Travor Pei appeared to want to split Hamman Drew in half. Hamman Drew's scimitar was overhead in plenty of time to deflect the blade to his right as he stepped to the left. The clang of metal on metal was a sound all the fighters knew too well. The sound of the fight quickly drew the attention of others nearby.

Hamman Drew allowed Travor Pei to exhaust himself. Hamman was fairly certain that Travor and his friends had been drinking. It was also clear that while Travor Pei was a much bigger man, he was not necessarily more muscular.

"You know, you don't have to die this way," Travor Pei offered as he continued to circle Hamman Drew. Travor Pei was clearly trying to catch his breath for another assault.

"It's either die here or die later," Drew replied with no concern in his tone.

Travor Pei had made four assaults on Hamman Drew, and each set of blows were blocked or deflected. Travor Pei began to catch onto Hamman Drew's strategy. So he thought he would use the one advantage he had: size. With that, he started a series a feigned blows all designed to bring his long sword overhead into a two-handed crushing blow. Everything went exactly as planned for Travor Pei. When the heavy blow came, Hamman Drew made the mistake of making a direct block on the blow. The force of the blow was so powerful that it snapped the blade of Hamman Drew's scimitar.

Fortunately, for Hamman Drew, he was able to lean back and dodge the blade that had crashed through his scimitar. The tip of Travor Pei's sword was close enough to etch a slash across the leather breastplate of his armor. Hamman Drew did not have time to contemplate what had just happened. Travor Pei moved in for the kill with a two-handed chop leveled at Hamman Drew's head. Drew was able to duck under the chop, draw his other scimitar, and strike the leg of Travor Pei all in one motion.

The blow brought a roar from the crowd that had now assembled around the campfire fight. Blood from the wound began streaking down Travor Pei's thigh. The wound had damaged his dignity more than injured his ability to fight. Wanting to play possum, Travor Pei embellished the size of the injury. "You've rendered my leg useless!" he claimed while continuing to close on Hamman Drew.

"You rendered my scimitar useless," Hamman Drew replied, holding up the broken blade he still carried in his right hand. While the comment brought laughter from some of the crowd, Hamman Drew was clearly not trying to be funny. If anything, this entire matter seemed to have become personal. What was he going to do with only one scimitar? His whole fighting style was based on having two swords.

Then Hamman Drew attacked with the broken blade in his right hand and scimitar in his left. He lunged into Travor Pei. With a left and right, followed by more left and right combinations, it was everything Travor Pei could do to stop the onslaught of blows. In a sudden change in his attack pattern, Hamman Drew slashed with his broken scimitar and then thrust with his left hand. Pei mistakenly tried to block the blow from the broken scimitar. This gave Hamman Drew the opening he needed. It took only a moment. His thrust went past the long sword of Travor Pei and deep into his ribs. As quickly as it had gone into him, Hamman Drew withdrew the scimitar.

Hamman Drew took just a moment to look into the eyes of the man would was about to die in front of him. Then showing him no more regard, he turned and walked back to where his scimitar blade that had fallen to the ground.

Travor Pei was shocked. First, the pain was awful. Secondly, why would this guy so foolishly turn his back to him. When Pei realized he was going to pick up his broken blade, it became more of an insult then he could manage. So he stepped forward to attack the back of this man who had just stabbed him. For some reason, his legs faltered, and then he fell facedown. Travor Pei was dead.

The semicircle that surrounded the fight was broken by the camp guard. Assigned the responsibility of keeping the camp safe from intruders, the guard also had the charge to make sure the men behaved themselves. This guard unit of seven men. Six of them carried bronze-tipped spears, leather armor, and wore the black scarf of Zel Camber. The seventh man was wearing leather armor as well but carried a bronze-plated shield with the crow of Zel Camber emblazoned upon it. He was clearly their corporal. He wore a long sword on his hip.

"Step aside! What's going on here?" demanded the corporal of the guard. The men moved back from the fight scene to create room

HOLLYWONDRA

for the guard. Some of the men stepping away went back to their business. Others stayed to see what was going to happen to this man who just killed one of their own.

As the corporal stepped into the ring of men, he saw a man bending over to pick up something from the ground. He saw another man coming at him from behind. He had his long sword held high and was going to strike this man who had his back turned. Then to the corporal's surprise, the man who was attacking fell to his knees and onto his face. Still with his long sword held high, the man laid still on the ground behind the man who was mourning the broken blade of a scimitar.

"What is all of this?" the corporal demanded of Hamman Drew.

Looking over at the corporal, Hamman Drew began to explain what had happened. Five words had not gotten out of his mouth when the man who had won the pot of coins playing dice chimed in, "He attacked us while we were playing at dice." Then he raised the dice to show the corporal as if they were evidence.

Almost as if that were a cue, several of the others around the circle began to give their versions of what they had seen. The raucous was more than the corporal could make sense of, so he shouted, "Silence!" Slowly the men quieted themselves.

Then the corporal turned to the guards and said, "Take him into custody." Waving his hand at the three friends playing dice, he said, "And get me the names of these men." Then stating it loud enough so that the others in the camp did not get any stupid ideas, he said, "Nictovius will not tolerate us fighting amongst ourselves. You can be sure that this matter will be dealt with harshly."

Hamman Drew knew he had not really done anything wrong, so he easily complied with the guard. He even took his scimitars and belt off for the guards so that they did not have to feel he was a threat. In truth, what could he do? He knew he had to rely on truth to preserve himself. As one of the guards waved his spear toward the middle of the camp, Hamman Drew nodded and began walking off in that direction. The smell of the boar reminded him that it had been a while since he had a hot meal. Why did the day have to go his way?

11

Jarius Raphael found peace in prayer. Holding his new knife and looking at the magical runes, he felt a little ashamed. He had allowed doubt to enter his mind, doubt that his God might not have a presence in this foreign world. He had always enjoyed a close relationship with God. He could truly feel the power of his Lord watching over him. It's just that this place was so different than anything he had ever seen. Coming out of prayer, he found himself with renewed focus. It was now clear to him what he needed to do to effectively get himself into this town.

Over the course of the next five nights, Jarius made forays into the town. His mission was to acquire clothing that would allow him to appear "normal" to these people while, at the same time, being careful nobody spotted him. He intentionally returned to the area where he had been first spotted. He wanted to see if there were some type of watchman at a post there or if this was an accidental discovery.

Jarius did not fear the person who had pursued him. While his pursuer was not the most physical specimen, Jarius could not afford to be discovered. His return to this area was to get a better sense for what happened and who his pursuer might have been. The time he spent at that location did not give him much information. For whatever reason, there was no sentry posted, and he concluded the incident must have been accidental.

One night he stole a shirt from the mercantile. He was surprised to find the store's front door was the only entrance that was locked. He was able to easily gain access through the window with the firewood under it. While inside, he was sickened by the amount of iron and iron alloys that were used in this community. He was able to find

HOLLYWONDRA

a variety of plaid wool shirts. Once he found one that fit his shoulders, he searched the rest of the store.

Up by the counter, Jarius found what he recognized to be dried meat strips. Uncertain as to what kind of dried meat it was, he thought he had better take some to try. He may find himself in a situation where he had to eat the food of these town folks. It would be good to know what it tasted like. Besides the shirt and the jerky, Jarius left the rest of the store undisturbed.

On one of his journeys into town, Jarius noticed clothing hanging from a line to dry. As he examined it from a distance, he noticed a pair of blue trousers like those the men had been wearing hung from the line. From a distance, it seemed they might be about his size, so he carefully approached the clothesline and quietly removed the pants. As he was being careful to not be seen, he failed to notice that the pants had metallic buttons.

Once he had the jeans in hand, he turned and ran for the high grass. The jeans flailed in his hand. When the metallic buttons from the fly of the jeans slapped the back of his hand, Jarius first thought he had been hit with something hard. As he crouched down in the tall grass, he took stock of his new merchandise. It was then that he realized these pants had metallic buttons. Looking at his right hand, he noticed an iron blister beginning to form.

This little blister on his hand only reminded him of the greater problem brewing on his shoulder. His repeated attempts to clean and poultice his wound had slowed but not stopped the growing infection. He knew he had the right herbs for his poultice. He feared that they may have somehow been affected in his travel to this land. Whatever the case, he knew that if he did not accelerate his mission, the fever and illness that can come from this type of injury could overtake him. His urgency had been amplified.

Upon returning to his camp, Jarius used his beautiful new knife and a pair of thin leather gloves to surgically remove metallic buttons from the trousers. That would mean he would have to wear a belt. The idea pleased him, as his belt and boots would be the only two things that were truly his to wear. Then he considered the idea of packing his knife in one of his boots. He really could not see himself leaving the knife in the woods after such a wonderful gift had been given to him. He felt like it had a clear purpose, and when the time came, he needed to have it with him.

Jarius's reconnaissance was nearing completion. There were just a few more things he felt he needed to understand before he would try to walk into town. He needed an entrance strategy. He needed to find a way that he could arrive in this town and not be considered suspicious. Jarius knew the nature of small communities and knew they were already tightly networked. He had to have a solid answer for how and why he had come to Rile, Montana. Maybe jumping on the back of one of the hay harvesting vehicles? They moved slow, even after they were loaded.

Jarius could smell the pending snow. That combined with the fact that he knew someone in town was already aware of him, and his shoulder was becoming more infected meant he could not delay much longer.

*****

Curiosity was making Titus restless. He knew something strange was going on, but he didn't know how to prove it. He had taken the time to ride out and examine the tracks again. The second time he noticed, they were about the same size as his own. This reduced his fears of being attacked but increased his curiosity. How could a any-one be running around in the wilds of Montana? Especially this late in the fall?

Then while returning to town, he found another set of prints. These footprints profoundly disturbed him. It was more a path than a set of prints. Back and forth through the soft soil were tracks going to and from the field. Looking carefully at the path, he could see the gait was tighter and the person walked this path. They had walked this way at least three or more times. Titus then realized this person was coming into town for a reason then returning to the woods when they were done.

As Titus rode home that afternoon, he began formulating a plan to catch this intruder. Not physically, but in some kind of a trap. The idea made Titus's mind race.

*****

Coyly Chloe asked Amanda, "So have you had a chance to see the new guy?" Honestly unaware of what Chloe was talking about, Amanda looked at her bewildered. "Oh, you cannot be serious? This guy just walked into town yesterday?"

Totally unaware of what she was saying, Amanda asked outright, "What are you talking about?"

Acting as if she were the only one to know the story, Chloe leaned in and began to unravel the tale with her usual drama. "So it's like this guy just fell from the sky. Right into Rile. He's kinda cute for a guy suffering from road rash. Yeah, I guess, he fell out of the back of a truck as it was traveling into town. I understand some folks found him and took him to Dr. Allenby's. I guess she's been patching him up."

"Well, he couldn't have been hurt too bad if they took him to Dr. Allenby." Chuckling, Amanda reminded her that Dr. Allenby was a veterinarian. The closest actual doctor was fifteen miles away in White Sulfur Springs.

"So? What do you think?" Chloe prodded Amanda's imagination with a smile.

"Think about what?" Amanda replied looking into the eyes of her friend.

"What do you think this guy is doing way out here…falling off the back of a truck?" Chloe reached across the table and lightly touched her friend's forearm. "Maybe he's that 'destiny' that you always talk about." Chloe shot Amanda a smile dripping with sarcasm.

Pausing to consider what Chloe had said, Amanda reflected on the fact that she had always felt larger than Rile. Her father had always told her she was destined for great things. She had come to believe she had some great destiny, but how could that ever come to her in such a small town. She knew she had talents and skills beyond many of her classmates, but she didn't have any true earthly desires for wealth. Even to her, her life and her future were unclear.

Amanda's father had been the pastor in this small town for as long as she could remember. Through his preaching and her faith, she knew the world held amazing things for her. She just couldn't imagine how it was all going to come together in this Rocky Mountain hamlet. She just had faith that it would.

"There you go again," Chloe broke the silence. Aware that she was still sitting at a cafeteria table with Chloe, Amanda dropped her hand and picked up a carrot stick. "Every time your mind wanders off, to wherever it is that it goes, you start to rub your cross." Looking down, Amanda was indeed caressing her cross. She quickly let go, and the necklace fell back onto her blouse.

Over the course of their friendship, Chloe had drawn Amanda's attention to the fact that each time she let her mind wander, she began to rub the cross on her necklace. The cross, to hear her dad tell it, was her mother's. Amanda understood that her mother had died at her birth. Her father had been left to raise her by himself.

The silver cross was fairly plain in appearance but very old. Amanda wore it every day. She never took it off. The surface had suffered from regular use. Lightly scratched by wear and worn smooth on the back Amanda had always wondered what the words were that had been lightly etched into the back surface. The wear had made the letters unreadable.

Realizing that she was holding a conversation with herself, Chloe began to think aloud, "I wonder if he will be going to school here? There are some lockers at our end of the hall…"

For the first time Amanda realized that this guy must be their age. "What? He's our age?" she asked with a newfound enthusiasm.

"Duh!" Chloe responded sarcastically. "Like I want some eighth grader moving into a locker next to me."

This was indeed a curious development in Amanda's life. Then returning to her daydream, she wondered what change this guy might bring to Rile. Chloe had piqued her curiosity.

*****

HOLLYWONDRA

Down the street, Jarius was leaving Dr. Allenby's home. As he walked out the door, Dr. Allenby reminded him to "be sure to come back in a day so I can change those dressings. I don't want this to get infected." Dr. Allenby, a middle-aged woman of small stature, then gently patted him on his back and shut the door behind him. Jarius, protecting his odd speech by simply nodding and smiling at the doctor, stepped off her porch.

Jarius made his way toward the gate of her picket fenced yard when he noticed a teenage boy standing under a tree across the street. The boy was watching him. As Jarius made the gate, he turned and began to walk toward the center of town. From across the street, the boy spoke loud enough that Jarius knew he was speaking to him.

"Where do you think you're going?" Titus asked. This was clearly one of the most courageous acts of Titus's life. He had no certainty that this guy was the night prowler he had chased. He simply noted his size as being similar to what the footprints suggested. He had no idea how aggressive this guy might be. When he saw the stranger stop and slowly turn his gaze upon him, Titus's heart began to race.

Knowing he could not ignore the verbal challenge, Jarius stopped and slowly turned to look over his left shoulder at the boy across the street. Pausing and deciding to try to walk away, Jarius tuned and began to walk away again.

Taking his willingness to walk away as a clue of his fear, Titus spoke again. "Where do you imagine you're going? Are you going to walk all the back to your camp in the woods!"

At that, Jarius knew the boy had to be the same one that had pursued him that night. Stopping, Jarius took a moment to weigh his options. When he realized there was no getting away from this confrontation, he decided to address this situation head-on. Turning around, he stared directly at Titus and began walking directly toward him. The intent in his stride was confident and caused Titus new levels of anxiety.

Titus knew he was in his own hometown, and in broad daylight, this stranger wouldn't try anything. Or would he? Then Titus felt the deep loneliness of rural living. There wasn't another person

59

he could see on the street. Where was everyone? *This guy could kill me, and there wouldn't be a witness.* It was too late. The stranger was nearing, and he could not turn and run. He knew this guy was fast. Assessing his situation, he determined his best chance was to stand confident and bluff this guy into believing he held all the cards.

Jarius came to within a sword's length from the young human and stood before him. Unspeaking, Jarius allowed the boy the chance to speak first.

As Titus mustered the strength to confront this stranger about his behavior and his camping in the nearby hills, he paused. He found himself looking into the blues eyes of a young athlete blonde teenager. The straight white hair was longer than most of the locals wore theirs. It wasn't too long to hide the fact that his earlobes came to an unusual point. This gave Titus even more pause.

Titus had always considered the pointed earlobes that Amanda and her father shared as a cute little birth defect. Certainly, there were things that could have been more distracting. The cute little tip had always been a target of Titus's affection for Amanda. Who was this guy to have similar lobes? This changed Titus's entire thinking to how he wished to address the stranger.

"It occurs to me that it's a long walk back to the hills. Certainly, you can't stay there through the winter. It won't be long before our first snow. My name is Titus. I am the guy who saw you sneak into town the other night. I was the guy who chased you on horseback. What brings you to our town?"

Jarius was prepared to draw his knife if he must. Then surprised by this boy's candor, Jarius paused and considered what the boy might be suggesting. Then struggling to articulate his speech, he carefully stated, "I am an explorer who has somewhat lost his way? What is the name of this village?"

The accent was thick, and the notion of this guy being an explorer was intriguing. "What do you mean you're an explorer? This is Rile, Montana. These parts have been settled for a hundred years," Titus responded.

Realizing that his guise as an explorer might have been a poor choice, he chose to focus on the town of Rile, Montana. "It's not that

HOLLYWONDRA

I am I trying to discover unknown lands. I am simply a nomad who roams the land searching for answers. My Lord has brought me to your village…Rile…Montana."

The reference to religion only heightened Titus's concern that he should tell Amanda about this guy. Then again, why should he risk losing Amanda to this guy? Even if he does have strange earlobes, that should not make a difference.

Titus had a hundred questions he wanted to ask. Not knowing where to start, he chose some simple ones to see if he could learn more about the stranger. "You know you're at least fifteen miles from the next closest town? Which way are you heading?"

Realizing that this human already knew he was camping nearby and that he had been there for days, the notion that he was on the move was not an honest question. Jarius decided to turn the table on the young man and stated, "You know I am camped nearby and not moving anywhere. What is it you want from me?"

Startled, Titus responded with honesty. "I wanna know what you're doing here and why you are sneaking around town at night!"

Admiring the honest question, Jarius quickly assessed his surroundings. Realizing that the boy was growing increasingly uncomfortable, he did not want to alarm him and send him running an alarm into the streets. "Calm yourself," Jarius whispered as he took a small step back. "I mean no one any harm. I am on a mission of tremendous importance. I cannot be delayed. You are the only person of this town who has any idea of my presence. My security cannot be compromised, so I need you to work with me for both our sakes."

Titus's initial instinct was to laugh. This guy thought Titus was the only one who knew of his presence. He had no idea how many eyes had already been on him. Titus listened carefully. His accent made him hard to understand. More importantly, what might he reveal about his purpose in Rile. How did this guy's mission impact Titus?

"My name is Jarius. My family lost an extremely valuable artifact somewhere in this region. I have been asked to find it and return it."

"Dude, I don't know what kind of artifact you could be looking for in Rile, but it's clear to me that you and your family have not lived here in the last century. I can barely understand a word you say," Titus replied.

Jarius could tell the conversation was awkward at best. He needed to be sure to contain the situation. "Is there somewhere else we could speak?" Jarius asked as he looked around.

Realizing that the guy had been living out in the wild, Titus took a chance and offered him to come to his home for some lunch. After a couple of hand gestures to his mouth and inviting him twice, the two of them headed across town.

12

The camp had been under constant attack since setting up in the lush green fields of the Valley of Shayna. Their efforts to construct war machines had been hampered by nightly attacks. Small groups of elves kept sneaking into the camp and cutting the rope work on their trebuchets. Sometimes the guards might catch them and chase them back into the woods. Sometimes the guards were just found dead the next morning. This nuisance strategy was wearing at Nictovius and the timeline he had imagined. Since all the other attacks had come at night, it was easy to understand why the camp was taken by surprise by a midday attack.

The day started out like so many of the others. As the watch guards changed shifts, they took time to check the war machinery for any obvious damage. It was at that time that a shrill whistle echoed through the valley. Suddenly, a small army of elves sprung from the high grass between the army and the woods. With their bows drawn and ready, it was clear they had their targets predetermined. Their first salvo let fly, and many of the watch guard were hit.

Klofgar were large humanoid creatures. Generally, they were despised by man and elf. Klofgar did not share the same cultural values of either man or elf. Frankly, Klofgar were not opposed to eating a man or an elf. For that matter, a dead neighbor might be cause for a Klofgar feast.

The Klofgar and elves were natural enemies. Klofgar found elves delectable, and the elves opposed the notion. The elves, by their speed and agility, could usually outrun or outmaneuver any Klofgar pursuing them. Klofgar were not the most intelligent of creatures, but they knew they could not catch an elf, so they resorted to throwing or swinging large objects at them.

Nictovius had formed an allegiance with a large group of Klofgar. He could see their size and brute strength as a resource in building and arming his large war machines. He also knew that coin did not motivate them, but the promise to ransack the Elvan nation was too much for this legion of Klofgar to resist. For that reason, they left their ancestral home in the Axel Major Mountains to join rank with Nictovius.

In the construction of the war machines, it had become apparent that the Klofgar played a very important role. Their strength was used for moving the heavy timber that was being used for framing these war machines. So it was no surprise that the elves made them the target of their attack.

Arrows flew from the grass in waves. Each wave seemed choreographed at specific targets. A flight of arrows rained down on the Klofgar camp, rousting several from where they lay in the grass. As they stood in surprise of their attack, the arrows hung from their torso like barbs from a briar. Klofgar plucked them from their tough hide and roared inaudible shouts of anger in the direction of the attack. A rare shot might hit one critically, but for the most part, it seemed like this assault on the Klofgar was designed to anger them more than kill them.

It wasn't until several arrows had found their way into the tents of the camp that the men had organized themselves and ran out to face their attackers. By the time the men organized a charge, they found themselves chasing the elves back into the forest.

Silas Pei was in charge of the legion that included Klofgar. He was busy organizing his men for pursuit of the elves when one of his sergeants reported that Silas "might need to speak to the Klofgar" himself. Turning to his sergeant to see what he meant, the sergeant explained that they were behaving strangely. "I think they may have broken into the mead wagons, sir."

"Great," was all Silas Pei could say. Then he ordered the sergeant to get the red regiment on horseback while he goes to speak with the Klofgar. Quickly agreeing to the easier of the two tasks, the sergeant hastened away. Silas Pei headed off to see what the problem was with the Klofgar.

The Klofgar did not fit in well with others, so their camp was a little more isolated from the rest of the camp. Not that they camped a long distance away. They just didn't seem to have any nearby neighbors. Most of the men found them to be foul-smelling beasts.

Silas Pei arrived just in time to see one large male Klofgar strike another Klofgar with a large wooden pole that was hewn for building a trebuchet. The pole struck the other Klofgar at the base of his neck and head, snapping the pole in two. The broken piece of the pole flew right at Silas Pei. He was forced to jump over the pole as it flew under him into the grass.

The Klofgar who had been hit wobbled and then fell with a great thud. His attacker then moved in on him to strike him with what he had left of the pole. Silas was mortified to see the Klofgar camp in total disarray. Some lay openly asleep on the ground, while others fought fist to fist directly above them. Still others were arm in arm gurgling something that must have been a Klofgar song. Nobody seemed to be in charge or cared to be.

Silas Pei searched for the Klofgar known only as Tromak. He had been the contact for Nictovius. Tromak seemed to have some sway with the other Klofgar. When he finally spotted Tromak among the Klofgar mayhem, he found him sitting upright and applauding the singing of two other Klofgar. The whole thing made no sense to Silas Pei.

As Tromak saw Silas Pei approaching, he smiled and waved him over. Silas had never seen a Klofgar smile before, so this made him even more uneasy. Klofgar patted the ground next to him, encouraging Silas to sit next to him.

Silas was careful to stay a little more than an arm's length away from Tromak. Then he addressed him. "Why are your men not coming to arms? We have been attacked." Silas had to speak a little louder than usual to be heard over the fighting and revelry.

Tromak looked at Silas with a smile and agreeably said, "Okay." As he began to stand, he teetered and fell to the ground laughing. Lying on his back, the Klofgar began staring at the cloudy sky. Then

Tromak pointed and said, "Look! That one looks like a horse." Silas started to look into the sky then realized the rant of a drunkard. Silas looked around for the evidence that the mead cart had been raided but only saw the camp to be littered with arrows.

"Sparrrrgum," someone behind him uttered. Silas turned to see a half dazed Klofgar plucking an arrow from his club. The giant looked at the arrowhead then handed it to him. At first Silas didn't know what the giant was talking about. Then as he looked more carefully, he understood. The arrowhead and much of the shaft had a sticky purple substance on it. Silas held the arrow to his nose to smell the liquid but did not recognize the scent.

"Is it poison?" He turned to ask the Klofgar who seemed to have most of his senses.

Shrugging his massive shoulders, the Klofgar said, "I dunno. It makes us funny." Then pausing to regain his focus, he continued, "I don't like it. It makes me head hurt."

Realizing that the Klofgar were of no value to him and his counterattack, Silas took the arrow and marched out of the Klofgar camp, careful to watch each one of them to make sure no more flying trees came his way.

The counterattack was not productive. Sure, they were able to slay a few retreating elves. But as the elves reached their Scurriers, all pursuit was lost. There was no way the humans, even on horseback, could keep up with the eight-legged Scurriers.

Scurriers had a hard exoskeleton. Their color varied from light to dark brown, so they blended in very well with the trees and underbrush of the forest. They were extremely quick. Even with elves mounted on their back, they could move very quickly across the forest floor or though the branches of the trees. Once mounted on their Scurriers, the elves quickly rushed into the forest. Many of the Scurriers leaped from the forest floor onto the underbrush and then into the trees. Just that quickly they were gone. This Elvan attack did not focus on the working of the siege machines. Their attack was successful by delaying the builders of the siege machines.

The inebriation of the Klofgar made them useless for a couple days. Some might say three days, when men who had to work with them discovered how poorly the Klofgar felt after their Spargum poisoning.

The alarm and the shouts of combat had become nightly rituals in the camp. It seemed like every night between last guard and the morning sun the elves would attack. Some nights it might be a single elf sneaking into camp. Other nights it was all-out war.

Peter and Soldac stood watch outside the tent of a prisoner. They didn't have much to do. They just had to make sure nobody came in and he didn't leave. It was coming to the end of their watch when shout of alarm came from other guards in the camp. The two guards looked at each other wondering if they should fall into a field muster or stay outside this tent. Then they heard the cry of someone on the other side of their tent. Soldac took off to rush around the tent. Peter took off after him. Soldac suddenly stopped, allowing six men with spears and shields to rush past him toward the fighting. As Soldac turned to follow the men, he quickly learned why they were running. Two arrows suddenly thudded deep into Soldac's chest. They came from the same direction the guards had come from. Peter turned to run in the other direction just in time to see a wall of elves rushing him.

*****

These late-night alarms troubled Hamman Drew. He felt like he was at the mercy of the elves. He didn't hate elves. He just needed to make a little silver to get him a ship ride home. In truth, he hadn't really had to use his talents, except against poor Travor Pei. He knew the real work was still in front of him. Even if he escaped this camp, he had miles of what could only be considered a war zone. No solid structure stood as far as the eye could see. Nictovius's troops had stolen every available resource en route to this valley. What they left behind was a smoldering wasteland. This valley was as nice as it got. Well, that is, except for the Elvan Woods.

He pondered his fate. He could be found guilty and made an example of by Captain Nictovius. The army might retreat to a place where his escape might be a good option. One thing he knew was he could not do was rush into the Elvan Woods. He'd be a pincushion of Elvan arrows. No human would be welcome in those woods.

While he was trying to imagine other methods of escape, he noticed the two guards at the entrance to his tent shout and attack someone at the front of his tent. Up to this point, Hamman Drew was a willing captive. He was confident he could escape at almost any moment. He just wasn't sure where he'd go, once he left the camp. This attack on his guards forced him to make a decision.

Recognizing the distraction as an opportunity, Hamman Drew went to work on the lock on his foot shackles. He knew this crude lock. As he considered the best approach, the tent door was pulled open. In stepped six Elven warriors. Two with arrows nocked and four with short swords draw. As soon as they saw Hamman Drew, the archers pulled back on their bows and aimed. Then a fighter at the front of the group held up his hand. The others froze in their approach. In Elvan, he told the rest of the war party. "He is in shackles. He is defenseless. Save your arrows!"

One of the other fighters slowly stated the obvious, "He is a human."

The elf who was clearly in charge said decisively, "Let him choose his own fate. Grab the keys from the guard."

One elf walked back to the dead bodies of his guards and returned with some keys. Quickly taking the keys, Hamman Drew surprised the elves when he suggested that he was no friend of these armies. He quickly explained that he was due to be executed in the morning. He asked if he could join their ranks. The Elvan guard didn't seem at all interested in his offer. As Hamman Drew reached for his pack and scimitar in the corner of the tent, the elves started out the tent door. Hamman Drew paused and tried to emphasize his point. "I am dead if I stay. If I run, they will find me. If I run into the woods, you kill me. My only hope is to run into the woods with you in hope that you will allow me to join your ranks."

Realizing that they had stayed too long in this tent, the platoon leader told him, "You'll have to keep up. Then you will have to find the graces of our captain. Do that at your own risk." Turning, the elves rushed from the tent. Following this small group, Hamman Drew helped them ransack more tents and fight the men of Nictovius's legion. As the elves ceased their attack and took flight for the forest, Hamman Drew followed.

Hamman Drew was fully aware that the elves did not care for humans. He also knew that any chance he had of surviving rested in the graces of some Elvan captain. Whoever that might be, Hamman Drew was willing to test his luck in a more neutral court. That was if he could keep up with these elves. They ran through the underbrush as a fluid part of the forest ecosystem. Hamman Drew knew he needed to not just keep up. He needed to appear in the ranks of their group. If he fell behind, he knew he could be mistaken for a human chasing the elves. Chasing elves into this forest would be certain death.

*****

The damage from this attack was as bad as it had ever been. As Nictovius heard the reports from his lieutenants, his anger grew. Over eighty men killed! Nictovius only relaxed slightly when Tallarand reminded him that they would get revenge. "The machines and men are ready." They were going to lay siege to the Elvanwood and reduce it to ashes. Nictovius paused his anger. He could feel the end was near. Soon all the elves would perish at his hand.

13

"Here," Titus said as he offered Jarius one of his brother's older shirts. Jarius's shirt had been ripped badly from his jump from the truck. Titus realized he couldn't continue wearing it around town. Scoffing at the notion, Titus shared, "He gave this to me and told me that I might grow into it."

Without haste, Jarius undressed to his bare chest and took the shirt offered by Titus. Looking up to thank him for this gesture, Jarius found Titus staring at his scarred chest. Proud of each battle scar, Jarius took his time putting on the new shirt.

Astonished at the scars, Titus asked, "Good Lord! What happened to you?" Remembering that the guy had just fallen off a truck, he wondered if he had some type of death wish.

Understanding that this world was not in the type of conflict he lived through in Namron Rae, Jarius simply replied, "God is good. He has seen me through many important struggles. These are just reminders of those struggles and that he has a larger plan for me."

The conversation they shared was mysterious, but Jarius left Titus with a sense of trust and confidence. Jarius spoke with a clarity and single-mindedness that Titus found entrancing. He could tell that some of what he said was true, yet it didn't make a lot of sense to him. Befriending him would be the only way Titus might come to understand more of what Jarius had seen. Jarius was obviously more worldly than his youthful exterior suggested. Titus also considered that Jarius could just be a lunatic.

Jarius spoke of another world and a mission he must complete. He wasn't ranting and raving about his goals. He was matter-of-fact and spoke with a determination that left Titus feeling that Jarius was not someone to cross. Jarius spoke of a mythical Light that he was supposed to find and then return to this foreign land from which he came.

All the complexities of this scenario were intriguing to Titus. He turned to ponder the numerous scars he had seen on Jarius. Clearly this young man had seen great conflict. The whole story only makes sense from Jarius's perspective. Titus knew that when Jarius spoke of magic, or a war to eradicate the elves, that he had to be speaking of another world. But those scars were real and plentiful. Either this guy is something amazing or he's delusional. The one thing Titus couldn't get out of his mind were the scars!

Titus considered his reality and this stranger's story. He knew he could stay close to this stranger and gather more information about his story. Maybe he could expose what said to be lies. If so, maybe he could get some public acclaim and appreciation. The only risk seemed to be that he could be pulled further into Jarius's conflict. What were the chances of that?

Despite the absurdity of this story, Titus got a genuine sense of peace and honesty from this stranger. His simple truths just made the rest of the miraculous story distantly possible. It was a puzzle that Titus had not yet been able to solve. Clearly, this was the most interesting thing to happen to Titus since moving to Montana.

Turning back toward Jarius, Titus asked, "So what's your plan?"

Looking up from the last of the shirt buttons, Jarius shot Titus an intense look. "A lesser man might come to a new world and leave behind his beliefs. Stumble through that world forgetting the path that brought them there. I believe my Lord will illuminate this Light for me. I believe he will make my path as long or as short as is necessary for me to succeed. My Lord will clear the paths of evil for me to succeed and save my people!"

As Jarius began to take a breath for what was going to be an even more serious detail of his faith, Titus held his hand up to silence him.

Trained in the field to become immediately silent, Jarius had no choice but to react to the hand sign for quiet. He was compelled by code of combat. Instantly, his senses heightened. Ashamed that he had let himself slip like this in the field. He should have heard the approaching boot steps. These were heavy boots. They were climbing stairs. Aware that Titus's room was on the second floor of this home, he knew the steps were coming toward the room. The gait was constant as it made its way toward them. Each thump was a blast of pride.

The sound stopped just outside the door. As Jarius looked more carefully at the door, he could see where the door jamb had been damaged from the door being previously kicked in. Glancing at the hand that Titus still held in his face, Jarius's eyes returned to the door in time to see the handle jiggle. Feeling the room was about to be broached, Jarius began reach for his boot knife.

Titus quickly rose and held out his hand, as if it would hold Jarius back. For the second time in as many moments, Jarius was surprised by this guy. He was so quick to assume leadership and assert those thoughts on him. Jarius looked at Titus and for the first time could see the fear in the eyes of his newfound friend. Having respect for both his leadership and his home, Jarius paused perfectly still.

"You in there, Titus?" came the husky whisper through the door.

As Titus quickly shot the door a look, he turned and held one finger to his lips. Jarius made not sound.

After several moments of silence, the boot steps continued down the hallway. After five thumps, they stopped. Another door opened and closed as Titus exhaled.

"Why do you cower in your own room?" whispered Jarius.

"It's my brother, Webster. He would not understand your situation. It's just best that we not involve him."

Jarius turned toward Titus and said, "I really do not want to cause anyone any harm. My failure is not an option. I will not let anyone stand in my way." He looked carefully at Titus to see if he embraced what he said. After watching Titus cower at the approach of his brother, Jarius needed to be clear about his aims. He could not afford to ally with someone he could not trust.

Glad to see his new friend was totally aware of his commitment, Jarius spoke in low tones. "I need to know more about this town, this kingdom, this place…I need to find the Ray of Light. I cannot just

HOLLYWONDRA

rush around the town in the dark. I need to be able to move freely about your town." Then turning to Titus, Jarius asked, "Will you assist me?"

He'd already made his calculations. There was no way Titus was going to miss out on anything his guy was going to be doing while in Rile. "It'd be an honor," Titus replied with a hint of sarcasm that was lost on this stranger.

They spent the rest of the afternoon talking about Rile. Sometimes they would pause quietly as his brother came and went. For a while they even went to the tree outside Titus's window. Titus had used paper and a "writing stick" to draw a map of the town. They used this to discuss the whereabouts of significant places in town. Once Titus showed Jarius their location on the map, Jarius was able to quickly identify Dr. Allenby's office.

Titus was impressed by his quick mind. He had also noticed that Jarius was trying to pick up colloquialisms. Titus took ten minutes trying to explain the meaning of *jerk*. They laughed for more than half of it. They laughed even more when Jarius was able to use *jerk* correctly.

As the sun hit the ridge, the cool evening shade came to this Montana valley. "Where are you staying?"

Smiling at his new friend, Jarius said, "You know where I'm staying."

"I knew it was you!" Titus quickly responded. "Man, you are really fast."

That day they made a pact. Jarius would come to town just before sunup. From the tree, the two would descend on the town and search the town for the Ray of Light. For Titus's help, Jarius agreed to tell him stories and facts about the land from which he claimed to have come. Titus knew this was only going to get more interesting.

*****

Jarius's interest in Rile was short-lived. As soon as Titus mentioned a girl in town who had ears like his, she became Jarius's focus. That afternoon, all of Jarius's questions were about Amanda. Titus did not like his sudden interest in Amanda and tried to steer him away from her as a subject of discussion. Each time it failed. Jarius came back with new questions about this girl with similar earlobes.

The next morning, Jarius never came. Somehow Titus knew Jarius bypassed him and was going to go straight to Amanda. Titus wasn't sure if the emotions he felt were jealousy or fear for her. He didn't really think Jarius would cause her any harm. He just didn't like it.

As Titus readied himself for the day, he wondered where he would find Jarius.

"I must speak with you," Jarius asked calmly.

Amanda was startled by the sound of a male voice coming from behind her. She quickly spun and took a step back to balance herself. There she saw this new guy standing beside a large rhododendron. She quickly surmised he had to have been hiding behind it, or she would have noticed him sooner. This was the same guy she had seen with Titus. He had seemed quiet when they first met, but to come to her house was very bold. She stood balanced and ready for anything. "Do you always sneak up on people?" she asked with a sharp tone.

He recognized the sarcasm in her tone and offered his own question. "Where did you get such a beautiful necklace?"

The change of subject caught Amanda off guard. She quickly grabbed the heirloom that hung from her neck. Now she was starting to feel like this could be a bad situation. Maybe this stranger valued the silver of the cross. Keeping her eyes on him for any sudden movement, she took a step back. While she carefully backed away, she asked, "What do you want?"

Seeing that she was becoming uncomfortable, Jarius asked her, "Be at ease. I would never harm you. It is just that that symbol on your necklace…it's the symbol of my God."

Still holding her cross necklace, she paused. Feeling a sudden sense of comfort, Amanda gave Jarius a gentle smile said, "It is the symbol of my God."

Jarius asked if he might walk with her to school. Amanda's home was just north of town on a hill that overlooked the north side of town. The church her father preached at was on top the same hill. The whole property was surrounded with a white picket fence, even the adjacent graveyard.

This sign from his God offered him the assurance he needed to ask questions of Amanda. As they strolled down the driveway and into town, Jarius began telling Amanda his story. Though it seemed preposterous, Amanda listened carefully to every word. She got no sense of danger from this stranger. If anything, his tone and confidence were assuring to her. The walk to school took no time at all. Soon Amanda found herself wishing she had more time to talk. They agreed to meet at the park after school.

*****

When Amanda found Jarius in the park, he looked like he had been waiting for some time. The first thing that came to her mind was how he was able to sustain himself. "Where are you staying? Have you eaten any lunch?" she asked.

"Lunch?" he asked.

Raising her hand to her mouth like sign language might help him understand, she asked, "Have you eaten?"

"This morning...prior to meeting you."

Realizing he had spent the majority of the day without food, she offered to buy him something to eat. "You want to get a burrito?" she asked.

The bewilderment that came over his face made her laugh at her question. If the guy didn't know what *lunch* was, he certainly wouldn't know what a *burrito* was. "Let me get you some food," she suggested. Then standing up, she waved for him to follow her.

As they approached the highway that ran through the middle of town, Jarius couldn't help but fixate on the vehicles that moved up and down the road without any visible horsepower. Waiting for a vehicle to pass, the two walked across the road to a business where vehicles fueled themselves. Walking past cars taking on fuel, Amanda led him into the mini mart.

Walking past a person at a counter by the door, the two walked to a glass-doored refrigeration unit. There Amanda selected two plastic-bagged burritos. Closing the door and turning toward the microwave, Amanda lost him. Amanda walked all the way to the microwave, before she turned to see Jarius back at the refrigerator.

Jarius had the door open and was admiring the cool air. Bending over, he looked deep inside the unit to see if he could understand how it operated.

Amanda let him examine the refrigerator while she heated his food. She knew she did not have time to explain everything to him. Whether he was truly from another world, or if it was part of a ruse, she just didn't want to take the time.

Jarius made it to Amanda just as she pulled the first burrito out of the microwave. Carefully holding the burrito by the corner of the plastic wrapper, Amanda warned Jarius that it was extremely hot.

Taking the burrito from her in the same fashion in which she held it, Jarius watched her microwave her burrito. He could not even begin to fathom how the microwave worked. Jarius opened the microwave three times to see if there was anything inside it to make the food hot. By the time he was done looking at the empty box, Amanda had paid for their food and called to him to leave.

As they stepped out the front door, they ran into Titus walking up the street. Not too surprised to find Jarius with Amanda, Titus began, "Don't you two look cozy."

Disappointed at the suggestion, Amanda replied, "Really, Titus. That's all you have to say. How long have you known Jarius? Has he told you his story?"

Titus was unsure what Amanda wanted from him. What he did know is that he would do anything for her. He had never used that tone with her, and he was instantly feeling badly. All he could offer was a quick and quiet, "I'm sorry."

"My lord has given me a sign," Jarius enthusiastically shared with Titus. "Amanda is going to help me find the Light."

Titus's heart sank. The thought of anyone being close to Amanda made him jealous.

HOLLYWONDRA

Amanda turned and looked at Titus to see how seriously he was considering this stranger's story. She saw that Titus seemed to both understand and believe what Jarius was suggesting. She whispered, "He thinks that it may be somewhere around the church." As if she had just opened a new present, Amanda smiled at the idea. All Titus's worries disappeared with her smile.

After pausing from his gaze at her smile, Titus quickly suggested the obvious. "Well, let's go check it out!"

The walk through the graveyard seemed a little morbid to Titus. Amanda seemed at ease, while Jarius keenly inspected every nook and tombstone. Amanda pondered the idea that this stranger and her destiny could somehow be linked. She felt an unusual devotion to him and his words, a feeling she only got when her dad talked about her mother. It was obvious this guy was a million miles from home.

After searching the church, the church grounds, and the graveyard, they looked around to consider what they may have overlooked. The only other place on the grounds they had not searched was her house.

Amanda realized the choices and quickly suggested, "No, we're not going to go traipsing through my house looking for something we can't even describe. I can hear me now... Yeah, Dad. He's not from here, but he goes to our church! Somehow I don't see this making a lot of sense to my dad."

The two boys considered carefully, then Titus suggested, "We could come back at a time when we know your dad won't be at home."

Amanda knew Jarius was driven and felt he needed to look around her house. It was the only home she had ever known. Having someone search through it was such an invasion of her privacy. How could she allow this to happen? How could she mange this?

77

14

They had been traveling for almost a week. Wisp was quiet and surely not much of a traveling companion. As they finally had reached the edge of the forest, they knew the search for the tree could still take hours. For entirely different reasons, both men were tired of their company. Gormund knew the path to the tree had to be fairly distinct, since it had been traveled so much as of late. Wisp agreed but was still unwilling to light a torch as the sun began to set. The two men searched well past sunset before finding the tree.

"Patience! Patience!" came the squeaky words from Gormund. The well-known magic user was a little bit out of his element. Fumbling through the dark woods was crazy enough. The fact this guy wouldn't let him use a torch made Gormund uncomfortable and defensive. Gormund had to just kept thinking about the prize. Once he was successfully able to transport Wisp, he would be awarded access to the magic Tome of Wythargle. All he had to do is make this teleportation device work.

Frankly, all he had to do was make this guy disappear. He didn't have to teleport him anywhere specific. He just had to be able to say with certainty that he did "send him." He knew he had taken a calculated risk because this guy was a professional assassin. If Gormund struggled with his spell, this guy might kill him before he could convince the assassin of any alternative plans.

Gormund had been studying ancient Elvan magic for years. He was trying to uncover the secrets that made Elvan magic so unique. In that process, he had made a discovery that he felt might set him apart from other young magicians. He thought he might have made a discovery on how to engage the ancient Elvan portals without the use of their keys. From what he read, he believed he could use herbs to make the Tree Gate engage. It was a calculated risk Gormund wanted to take. Some of his colleagues were being sent to Shayna's Tears for the final assault on the elves. The whole idea of being in combat was just too random and risky for Gormund.

He had decided that now was the time for him to make his move up the ranks of magi. He knew that several spells he had worked on had come from the spells of Wythargle. By having access to one of his spell books, he was sure he would be able to find the final details that would help him grow in his abilities. So he went to his arch-mage, Sythene, and presented his proposal. He knew that if he were wrong, he would have to dispatch the assassin or slip away. He would be on the Crow's list of "unwanted." He would never be able to show his face in certain regions of Namron Rae. He would be on the run the rest of his life. He felt confident in his research and skills. It was a risk he was willing to take.

Standing at the base of the Key Tree, Gormund fumbled with his pouches. Then mumbling to himself, he stated how much easier this would be with a little light on the matter.

"I've already told you, mage. No light. No noise. Just get this thing working so I can be on my way." Wisp was unfriendly at best. His speech was more a whisper that a voice. He kept his head hooded so that very little of his face could be seen. Sythene had made Gormund's orders clear. He was to take this man to the Tree Key and send him through the portal. If he could not, then he would have to answer to Wisp. Gormund did not have to be skilled in divining character to know that Wisp would willing kill him at the drop of a hat.

"You understand that you must recover a Tree Key on the other side, or you will be stranded in this foreign land," Gormund reminded Wisp.

"Obviously, that's a chance I am willing to take, so long as I am given the chance," he replied with sarcasm and a twinge of impatience in his voice.

"Just relax," Gormund offered as he continued to carefully check the contents of the pouches that hung from his hip. "Yes, I think I've found it." With a vial in one hand and a pouch in the other, Gormund knelt at the base of the tree. Feeling along the bark, Gormund found the indentation where he believed a Tree Key would be inserted. He noticed how the face of the indentation was flat and made a good surface for establishing physical contact.

Turning his face in the direction he knew Wisp to be standing, Gormund directed him to move closer. "Come down here."

The assassin pulled a dagger and said, "No tricks, mage. I'm pretty quick with this blade."

"No tricks," responded Gormund. "I need you down here to clearly understand where you need to touch." As Wisp took one knee, he extended his left hand while holding the dagger with his right. "You feel that unusually flat surface right there?" Feeling Wisps hand bumping his while he was still touching the surface, Gormund continued, "I will pour this oil over this part of the tree surface. As I sprinkle this powder on the oil, I will begin an incantation. As my words engage the mixture, the tree will begin to glow. It will not glow long or very brightly, but it will begin to glow. Once you see it glow, you must be touching that exact surface with your bare hand. That will engage the tree and transport you to the same location as the elf you seek."

Wisp suddenly stood up without answering the mage. This initially frightened Gormund. Gormund knew the assassin had no reason to attack him. Then the assassin slowly took one of his black leather gloves off and stuffed it into a pants pocket. He kept his knife out and continued to hold it ready in his gloved right hand. Kneeling back down next to the mage, Wisp felt for the flat surface next to Gormund's hand. Once he found it again, Wisp nodded at the mage.

Gormund did exactly as he said he would. He poured the magic potion on the tree burl where the Tree Key would have fitted. Through the faint moonlight, Gormund could see the oil make the bark darken. He sprinkled a mixture of herbs and powder where he thought the oil would puddle on the bark surface. Seeing that Wisp's fingers were directly covered, Gormund began to chant. After his third recitation, the tree burl began to glow. Suddenly, there was a bright-green flash, and the assassin was gone.

"Well, that could have happened a little sooner," Gormund mumbled to himself. His fear that that his spell might fail was quickly replaced by the awareness that someone owed him a big favor. As far as Gormund was concerned, that evil fellow could stay wherever this tree sent him. This magic act was going to gain him access to a tome of knowledge he had only dreamed about. His confidence was bolstered, thinking he might be the only person to have ever utilized an Elvan portal without a Tree Key.

15

Waving her hand in the direction of her dad's dresser, Amanda suggested, "You can go through that stuff, just put it back exactly as you found it. If my dad suspected I was going through his things…" Shaking her head, her words trailed off as she realized that she had never given her dad reason for concern. Her entire life, Amanda had always been a good girl and tried to make her father proud of her. She found herself wondering how she had allowed herself to get caught up in this crazy search.

"It's just not here," Titus offered as he pulled his head from the bedroom closet. "We've turned this place upside down. I not only don't see your Ray of Light, I haven't even found a flashlight."

That was an interesting thought. Amanda paused to consider the fact that they had never owned a flashlight. Or they never had a need for one. It never seemed that night was too dark that she ever really needed to use a flashlight. She has seen others with them. The glare they caused seemed to be more trouble than of use.

Then Amanda thought, "Wait! What if this light glows? You might only be able to find it at night. I mean…after all, it is the Ray of Light, right!?" Titus and Amanda looked at Jarius. They all stopped searching to consider the idea.

Almost embarrassed at the simplicity of the idea, Jarius paused and said a prayer. This prayer had always provided him the ability to see auras of power emanate from things that had magical powers. The Ray of Light must be an item of extreme magical power. That's why it had to be hidden in a realm beyond Namron Rae.

Opening his eyes from his prayer, Jarius surveyed the room. Everything appeared to be rather mundane. That was until he turned

HOLLYWONDRA

toward Amanda. The necklace she wore glowed in the magical brilliant opaque golden hue Jarius knew very well. Even in the daylight, the glow was unmistakable. Watching Jarius pray and then begin to survey the room left the other two wondering what he was doing. Then his eyes fell on Amanda.

Amanda suddenly became very uncomfortable. She wasn't sure if it was that they were searching her dad's room or the weight of Jarius's gaze. She just felt a sudden urge to flee. Jarius began to slowly approach Amanda. As she began to step away from him, Jarius raised his hands to show he was no threat. "Your necklace," Jarius mumbled. "May I examine it a little more closely?"

Feeling extremely uncomfortable, Amanda suggested, "Let's get out of here first." Then she turned and walked from the room. Jarius would have followed her anywhere. He needed to see that necklace. Surely it contained some clue for him.

"Let's go out on the porch," she suggested. "Can I bring you guys a lemonade?" She used this opportunity to regain her composure. She could tell Jarius had something he needed from her. Oddly, she knew she needed to help him with whatever he needed. Not because she thought he was a nice guy, she felt compelled. She had never felt more compelled in all her life.

Both guys casually accepted their lemonade from Amanda. Jarius was trying to be as calm as possible. He could hardly take his eyes off her necklace. At first glance, it looked worn and not very ornate. He knew the necklace had to mean something. He had never seen that magical glow on something that wasn't important. He knew this was a sign. While he was anxious to see the necklace, he also knew he had to be calm. This was a foreign land, and he needed to make sure he did not rush or accidently offend any of these new acquaintances. The three of them pulled chairs up to the patio table.

Unable to control himself any longer, Jarius sat his glass on the table and extended his left hand. "May I examine your necklace now?" Jarius tried to remain calm as the possibilities raced through his mind. Amanda lifted the cross from her chest and pulled it toward Jarius. Jarius leaned in close to get a good look at it. The silver cross was small. To carefully examine it, Jarius would have to place his face very close to hers. Jarius knew about the detection of magical items, that there would have to be runes. Those runes would glow even brighter than the aura. The problem was that on an item so small, the opaque nature of the glow hid the tiny runes. He would have to get closer to see them clearly. So he asked if she might take it off for him to examine.

Surprised by his suggestion, Amanda quickly replied, "I never take this off. I wouldn't even know how." Lightly pressing the cross to her chest, Amanda realized she could never remember not wearing the cross. She truly cherished this necklace. Her dad told her that it had been her mother's most cherished possession. Amanda's wearing it reminded him of her mother's beauty and her love for them. She had never considered ever taking it off.

The thought of her mother was a passing emotion. Amanda had no actual memory of her mother. The home was devoid of pictures, except those her father had taken of Amanda. Everything in the home was a celebration of his little girl and the glory to God.

"I can't take it off," explained Amanda. "It is too dear. I have never removed it."

Realizing that he would have to lean very close to her, Jarius asked, "May I look more carefully, then? I'd like to see if I can read what is written on the cross."

Amanda understood Jarius was asking permission to look even more closely than before. "Sure," offered Amanda. "I've got to warn you. I have looked rather carefully at this, and I can't make out what is written on the back." Then she turned pulled the cross toward Jarius and turned her face away, hoping that might allow him the room he needed to fully examine her necklace. As she turned away, Jarius leaned in to take a closer look. As Amanda held the cross out for him to see, she wondered if he still struggled to see it clearly. Not really sure why she offered, Amanda suggested, "You can move closer if you need to."

Getting up from his chair, Jarius circled the small table and came up to her right side. Amanda lifted her chin for Jarius. Taking the cross in his hand, he looked at both the front and back of the cross and saw nothing. Yet the magical glow was unmistakable. It

HOLLYWONDRA

was easily as strong as the power that came from the magic dagger Malactus had given him.

As he drew closer to examine the necklace, Amanda's discomfort was no longer about his attention to the cross. It was how close he leaned in toward her. She could feel his breath on her neck. It gave her a sense of excitement she had never known before. The tiny blonde hairs began to stand as she tried to remain still and unwavering.

For a moment, Jarius's thoughts wandered to his forest camp and the fact that he had to secretly secure all his property in his camp. It was obvious nobody else wore weapons in this town. To wear one might offend them. Like the mountain abbey at Kelora. No weapons were allowed inside those walls. Realizing that he had allowed his mind to wander, he refocused.

The brilliance of this cross was almost blinding to his ability to see the magic. The necklace chain was magical as well. But it was only a vehicle of the far more powerful cross. Then he saw it. The edges of the cross glowed brightest. As he continued to focus, he found that the runes began on the top of the cross and read counter-clockwise around the cross. Slowly twisting the cross, he uncovered the magical secrets of the Cross of Amanda.

Amanda sat still as this strange young man carefully examined her heirloom. She felt herself beginning to blush at his extended presence. Looking across the table at her friend Titus, she could see the concern on his face. Sensing the awkwardness of the moment, Amanda gave him and awkward smile and shrugged her shoulders. Her nervous smile revealed her true emotions to Titus.

Feeling as if she had waited long enough, Amanda broke the silence. "Well? What do you see?"

Jarius did not immediately respond. Her voice had broken his concentration. So he took that moment to respond, "Just a moment." He refocused his energies and continued to examine the cross. Slowly he moved the cross in a strange manner. Finally, he paused and released the cross. Stepping away, he returned his seat at the table. He was clearly processing his thoughts. Taking a moment to sip his drink, the others waited anxiously.

Suddenly, Jarius shook his head and shivered from the bitterness of Amanda's lemonade. Looking down at the glass, he carefully took another sip before addressing the others at the table.

Jarius paused as if to piece things together. Her cross is both amazing and powerful. He was baffled how a powerful religious relic could exist in this land of Rile? Was this the Ray of Light? Not only was it a magical artifact, but the runes of power also suggest Amanda is in extremely high favor with his God. His God? How could this be? All this confused him. This was clearly a sign, but what did it mean?

As Jarius pondered the details, questions from his friends broke his concentration.

"Well?" asked Amanda again. Grasping her cross, she stated, "Don't think for a second that you are going to take my necklace." Saying this aloud seemed to make the thought a possibility. Did he plan to take her necklace from her? Is her necklace the Ray of Light he seeks? Suddenly uneasy, Amanda leaned back to a perfectly erect 90 percent angle in her chair. She readied herself to flee or defend. Then she asked, "What is it about my cross that has you weirded out?"

Breaking his concentration, Jarius asked, "Weirded out?" The term confused him, so Jarius turned to look at Titus. Titus realized that he had become a sense maker for Jarius. Jarius should have more knowledge of the area than he possessed.

Continually, Titus was surprised to find what Jarius did not understand. Then he explained, "'Weirded out' means that you were behaving strangely."

Realizing the likelihood that he was distracted for a lengthy period of time, Jarius began to explain. "I just don't understand."

Titus began to elaborate with a deeper explanation of the idea of someone being "weirded out" when Jarius raised his hand to stop him.

"No, my friend. I understand that I was 'weirded out.' What I don't understand is my discoveries on her cross." As Jarius began to explain, Amanda unconsciously tightened her hand over her beloved cross.

HOLLYWONDRA

Staring into Amanda's eyes, Jarius began, "I've never been honored to see anything so powerful." Titus had to fight off his emotions of jealousy to listen. Jarius went on to explain that the cross was a holy Elvan relic of protection. He explained to Amanda that the necklace was magical as well. He noted that the necklace was made without a clasp, with which to take it off and on. The runes of protection protected Amanda from harm and protected her from detection by evil beings. While this necklace was an amazing artifact, it was not the Ray of Light. He had seen some similar creations to protect people in Namron, just nothing as powerful as hers.

What Jarius found odd was that something of such immense Elvan power could be found in this foreign land. Then he asked to take one more peek at it.

Amanda agreed then held it out. Jarius came around the table and leaned in. He extended one hand toward the cross. Then suddenly, his had shot past the cross and toward the nape of Amanda's neck. Then he quickly pushed her hair back to expose her ears. To his satisfaction and amazement, he found that she had the ears of an elf.

Self-conscious of her unusual ears, Amanda quickly batted his arm away then, in a single fluid motion, jumped up from her chair and spun to confront Jarius. "Hey! What the heck do you think you're doing?" Glaring at Jarius with an ire that Titus had rarely seen from her, he wondered if he should do something. It all happened so fast that Titus had missed what Jarius had seen.

"You need to go!" Amanda stated coldly. "Both of you! My dad'll be home any time."

16

As Jarius approached the perimeter of his camp, he stopped. Something wasn't right.

Quietly he pulled his short sword and began to survey his camp. This wasn't right at all. Jarius could tell that someone had walked through his camp. The cool fall Montana breeze was now knocking pine needles from the branches above. Though it was nearing nightfall, he did not need that much daylight to detect that someone had walked through his camp. He could see where the broad-leafed underbrush had no fallen needles. As he surveyed the passage of his intruder, he could tell the person passed through his camp but did not seem to look in the area where he had hidden his gear. After careful examination, Jarius could tell the tracks belonged to someone of his approximate height and weight. They had moved carefully to avoid detection, but their passage did not escape his expert tracking eye.

Jarius was able to trace the tracks back to the stump of the Tree Key. Realizing that the tracks started there, he paused in disbelief. How could this be that someone else had come through this passage? Had he somehow mistaken his own tracks for those of a stranger? As he reexamined the tracks, it was perfectly clear that these were not his own. These tracks moved slowly, and they meandered, as if searching for something. Pausing to survey his surroundings, Jarius realized that he was now being hunted again. Somehow, the Zel Camber had found a way to send someone through the gate to this world. If they were not here for the Ray of Light themselves, they were here for him. Either way, he needed to act fast.

*****

HOLLYWONDRA

Carefully raising his head to peek above the tall grass, Wisp surveyed the town from a distance. *These homes literally glowed*, thought Wisp. The lighting in this little town was so bright that it would make finding the elf very easy. Bright light creates dark shadows. It was there that Wisp felt most at home. This town would provide him more than enough shadows to easily stalk his prey.

Searching the horizon, Wisp considered how much time had passed since the sun had gone down. He figured that he had plenty of time to make it into the town and look around. A wry smile came over his face as he imagined the elf getting comfortable in this new setting. He could understand how his prey might think he was beyond the grasp of Zel Camber. This element of surprise was Wisp's greatest advantage. Killing someone before they even realized they were dying was one measure he used to gauge his performance. If the prey saw him coming, then he would consider that kill done poorly.

His mind wandered to how he would find his way home. He understood that he had to find some special artifact to reengage the Tree Key. There was always the chance that the elf might have done his work for him. He noted that he needed to search the elf's body carefully for a Tree Key. He wasn't entirely sure what it might look like, but there was a chance the elf might save him the work of finding one. Then again, maybe this world might hold better opportunities for a man of his talents. Surely, he would be well paid for the completion of this very important mission. But Wisp had a heavy heart. The idea of a fresh start elsewhere did have some attraction. Living in the shadows and the constant worry of being found had weighed heavily over the years.

Realizing that he had allowed himself to become distracted, Wisp quickly drew his attention back to his surroundings. He was in a hostile location, and he needed to remain alert at all times. Considering the large open field that lay between him and the town, Wisp drew a deep breath and pulled his dagger from its hilt. His razor-sharp blade was coated in a poison he had carefully poured into his hilt. Over the years, when he was not able to make solid contact with his prey, the small slices always served his need to kill them. Sure, it was a little sloppier, but in the dark of night, all that mattered was that he was able to kill those he wanted to kill. With his dagger in hand, Wisp slowly rose above the high grass and reached forward to pull the grass open so he could pass.

The tracking had led Jarius to the edge of the forest. This exit from the woods was a little closer to the highway than the route he had been taking. That gave Jarius some assurance that this stalker was not tracking him. If he had, he would have followed his tracks into the grass.

Night tracking was very slow. It didn't help that his stalker was not walking in a straight line. While the intruder searched for him, the trail took plenty of twists and turns. Fully aware that he was being stalked made the work even slower. He could not afford to miss something and then get himself caught off guard. As the path left the safe confines of the tree line, Jarius paused to recognize that the person was heading for Rile.

Jarius knew that whoever he was tracking was at least a few hours ahead of him.

He realized that the person was probably in town looking around. He weighed his options. He knew that Amanda was somehow connected to his mission. He was not sure how she fit into the puzzle. He just knew that she possessed a holy artifact and that had to be a sign for him to follow. He knew he could not let harm come to her. He also knew this to be a peaceful town that could easily fall prey to someone with violent tendencies. If Zel Camber was willing to send someone after him, they would clearly try to kill him at all costs. Nobody in Rile was safe.

Wisp circled the town in a fashion similar to how Jarius had done it a few days before. What were the odds that this night Titus would again be out in his tree? Titus was surprised to see a person creeping through the grass. He wondered why Jarius would continue this practice. Knowing that Jarius was aware of his perch, Titus pulled himself quietly behind the main trunk of the tree and continued to watch his friend in the grass. Titus was almost certain Jarius was going to bypass his place and head for Amanda's home.

Oddly, the figure moved very slowly for a person who had become familiar with Rile. Titus could only wonder what he was

HOLLYWONDRA

doing. As Titus watched, he noticed that these were different clothes for Jarius. His clothing was much darker than anything he had seen him wear. He wondered why Jarius didn't wear these darker clothes the night Titus had first spotted him.

Those wonderings were shattered when Titus noticed a second figure in the grass.

This one was coming up behind the first person. From his tree perch, Titus witnessed something he had only ever seen on TV or in a video game.

The second figure was closing quickly on the first. It seemed the first figure was distracted with selecting a careful path into town. The second figure was far enough away that he had not yet spotted the first person. A light crunch of the dry field straw alerted the first prowler. The first prowler immediately ducked below grass line. Titus could no longer see the first prowler, but he could only see the straw parting. The first prowler had changed his path. He was no longer heading toward town. He had turned north to get off his own path.

As the second person drew nearer, Titus could see that it was Jarius. He was carrying a knife and was crouched low as if he were ready to jump onto someone. Then it occurred to Titus the first person was circling around to get behind Jarius. He knew he did not know entirely what was going on, but he did know Jarius was in danger. Titus broke his silence and came out from behind the tree trunk and shouted, "Behind you, Jarius!"

In that same instance, the tall grass behind Jarius parted, and Wisp sprang for the kill.

Jarius knew his whereabouts and knew that it had to have been Titus who shouted the warning. Acting in confidence and instinct, Jarius spun with his dagger held high.

The two sharp-edged forces met in the pale moon light. A short thick click of metal on mithril sent a message to Titus that this was no schoolyard fight. Quickly he began climbing down his tree.

The warning had come just in time for Jarius to block the attack of Wisp. With daggers drawn, the two slowly circled each other in the tall grass.

"Who sent you?" Jarius asked as he watched his stalker preparing to lunge.

"You can't figure that one out yourself?" Wisp replied.

Titus had made it to the ground then wondered what he could possibly do to help his friend out of this situation, when he saw the pitchfork leaning against the wall of the barn. Not really sure what he'd do with the pitchfork, Titus grabbed it and rushed toward the fight.

"It's you or me, elf," Wisp said as he lunged at Jarius, taking swipe at his free hand. Jarius pulled his hand back and poked at the assassin with his magical dagger. Neither made contact, and they continued to circle each other.

As Wisp circled Jarius, he noticed Titus rushing through the grass with a pitchfork. Realizing he was about to be outnumbered, Wisp took a step back from Jarius and pulled a second dagger. This put Jarius into a new defensive posture.

When Jarius saw Wisp throw his dagger, he knew it could not have been meant for him. It flew too far afield. He took the opportunity to roll into the standing assassin to grapple with him. Jarius had determined that he was probably stronger, and if he could get in close, his chances would be better. What he didn't realize was the skill of his assassin.

Wisp anticipated the move in his follow through. He countered by diving over the top of the rolling elf and slashing at Jarius's shoulders as he flew over him. Wisp felt his blade make contact on the back of the elf. A grim satisfaction came over him. Within a moment, he had dispatched the farmer and his prey. As he tucked and rolled to his feet, he knew that his poison would take the life of his prey. He had to only keep the elf at bay.

Jarius knew he had been cut. He could feel the burning flesh that came from his skin touching iron. He knew he was in trouble. Quickly to his feet, he began to circle the assassin. The in the back of his mind, he realized that Titus was nowhere to be heard. Fear for his new friend came over him, and it nearly cost him his life, as Wisp spun into a round kick.

HOLLYWONDRA

The kick narrowly missed Jarius's face. Right behind the kick was the blade.

Jarius recognized this move. In instinct from his combat training, he quickly dropped and spun to sweep the legs out from under the assassin. Jarius's leg found its mark and sent Wisp falling to the ground.

Jarius beat Wisp to his feet, only to see that the assassin had his dagger by the blade in the same way he had thrown his earlier dagger. There was no time to move or dodge. Jarius was an open target for a fighter with the skill of Wisp.

A quick sneer came over his face, as Wisp's energy moved through his torso and into his arm. He had his target at point plank range. At this range and in this light, he knew he could hit a gold coin with his blade tip. This elf was his!

Suddenly something struck his wrist, and pain shot up his arm. Turning to examine what had happened, Wisp found that one of the tines from the pitchfork had suddenly pinned his wrist to the ground. Turning back at Jarius, the last thing he saw was Jarius lunging on him.

The blood from his shoulder wound had saturated the shirt Titus wore. The entire left side of the shirt was soaked and dripping. After killing Wisp, Jarius came to Titus's side. Looking at his friend, Jarius could not tell if Titus was in shock from witnessing the death of Wisp or if it was from the blood loss. What Jarius did know was he needed to get him help. He also knew that he was in trouble as well.

*****

The dream had taken as strange turn. It was a dream that Amanda had had several times before, but she had never shared it with anyone. It was just too strange. It was in a foreign land. The only thing that she enjoyed of the dream was that she believed that her mother was a part of the dream. She found that this dream gave her a sense of peace. It also seemed to come at a time when she needed it most. The encounter with her friends had left her upset and confused.

Each time the dream was a little bit different. It always had two consistencies.

There was a woman she felt was her mother. The other was that it took place in this ancient city of beauty and exotic mystery. This night she dreamed that she was asleep in a palace. High in a towered room she rested. Her slumber was disturbed by the tapping of pebbles striking the glass.

When her mind registered the incongruence of someone being able to toss small pebbles to such a high window, it made her wake. She realized that pebbles were not being thrown at her tower window. It was Jarius and Titus tapping at her bedroom window.

Still dazed by her broken slumber, Amanda moved to the window and lifted it to speak to them. Even after opening the window, she wasn't able to immediately make sense of what the two were telling her. The two stood arm in arm. They were speaking at the same time. Raising her hand, she asked, "Wait a minute! One at a time." Then she noticed the blood-soaked shirt on Titus.

Without hesitation, Amanda crawled through her window onto the lawn outside.

There she had Jarius lay Titus on his back. She could see that Titus was more ashen than usual. He was beginning to shiver and asked for a blanket.

"What happened?" she asked as she pulled his shirt down from his shoulder.

There she could see the hole Wisp's dagger had made. The skin around the wound had begun to discolor in shades of bright red and gray.

Jarius watched her carefully. He knew some field first aid practices, but Titus was insistent on Jarius bringing him to her.

Without hesitation, Amanda tore the cleaner side of Titus shirt from his body.

Shooting Jarius a glare, Amanda asked if he would "Like to take a picture?"

Jarius wasn't sure what she meant by that. He was pretty sure that this was sarcasm and that she actually wanted something else. "What would you like for me to do?" he asked.

"Get the blanket at the end of my bed and cover him," Amanda directed him.

Reluctant to leave the scene, Jarius jumped in the window and quickly found a blanket that had been folded and laid at the end of the bed. As he came back to the window, he paused to see Amanda. She had taken the torn piece of shirt and placed it over the wound. She was compressing it with both her hands as she stared into the night saying a prayer.

Jarius stared in awe at her power as her hands, or maybe it was the wound, began to glow. Suddenly, a rush of nausea came over Jarius. Grabbing the windowsill with both hands, he paused before climbing out of her room. The nausea turned into a dizzy rush. His legs became limp. They no longer supported his weight. Inside her bedroom window, Jarius fell backward to the floor. Barely conscious, he said a prayer of his own.

17

Hamman Drew ran for his life. The fighting around him was as intense and chaotic as any he had ever seen. Making his way toward the Elvanwood seemed like the best plan. His hope was that he could retreat with the elves. Outside of that, he didn't really have a plan. He had known enough elves in his time to know that they could be reasonable. Then again, this was their last bastion of defense, and it was a war against humans. Even in that scenario, he knew his best chance of survival was to escape this camp. He was most certainly going to be tried and executed for the death of another soldier. So he kept running toward the ancient oaks.

As he made it to the tree line, he witnessed something he had never seen before. Elves riding on the backs of large spiderlike creatures. The elves rode two to a beast. Each elf was able to shoot arrows with incredible accuracy as the Scurriers hopped from tree to tree or raced across the forest floor. Their movement was so quick, he could not tell how many there were. Klofgar were hurling large rocks at elves, while others swung small tree trunks. In some cases, Klofgar picked up injured elves and smashed them to the ground. The humans who raced after the retreating elves were fighting them hand to hand, up until they were killed by arrows arriving from the shadows of the Elvanwood.

Hamman Drew fought Nictovius's men on his way toward the woods. The flicker of fire shadows made things hard to see. He had made his choice. He found himself attacking humans who were fighting elves. Commonly, while the two were in combat and the human mistakenly didn't consider Hamman Drew a threat. And then it was too late. Each time the elf was surprised by Hamman Drew's attack-

HOLLYWONDRA

ing the human. After killing a soldier, Hamman Drew just kept running for the woods. He made no effort to engage the elves. He just kept pressing through the fight toward the ominous wall of ancient oaks that made a thick black veil against the starry sky.

Reaching the tree line, Hamman Drew took a new approach. He knew the elves were fast, so if he was ever going to keep up, he had to move quickly. Still with his scimitar in hand, he began to run past the fighting so he could move deeper into the woods. He really didn't want to kill any more humans. Then again, he could not afford to kill any elves either. He had determined his best plan would be to just get as far away from the fighting as possible.

Moving through the underbrush, Hamman was surprised to find how fast and how far he was able to move into the woods. He thought to himself that the mystery of these woods was truly undeserved. If anything, the towering trees made movement very easy. Growing winded, he pushed on.

Soon the underbrush changed. The brush gave way to a canopy of small oak trees.

Periodically, he would encounter the trunk of an exceptionally large oak tree. There was no longer brush in which to hide. For the first time he realized that he might be the only one retreating this far into the woods. He began to slow down and look around him. He could not see or hear anyone or anything. He knew if he kept moving forward, he was certain to encounter Elvan military. He knew all along that he would have to surrender to the Elvan authorities.

Suddenly three arrows thumped into the forest floor in front of him. Looking around, he realized he had been surrounded by a patrol of elves. He could only see about twenty of them. Many had their bows drawn and aimed at him. Those that carried swords had them at the ready. Hamman Drew immediately stopped, dropped his scimitar, and raised his hands to surrender.

Stepping through the row of archers, a stately looking elf addressed Hamman Drew, "What makes you think you can trespass on our sacred ground? What makes you think we would be willing to spare your life? Human!" the elf said with distain.

Hamman Drew wasn't sure how to answer the questions. What he did know was that elves believed humans were impetuous and impatient. So Hamman Drew kept his tongue and waited for the leader to speak again.

"Why do you believe you can abandon your ranks, only to find refuge in our woods?"

Hamman Drew knew he would die before he drew a second breath if he misspoke. So he carefully considered his words and said, "I will not lie to you. I joined those ranks as a mercenary. I intended to only make enough money to pay for a voyage home. I have yet to raise my sword on any elf. Truthfully, I became a prisoner of their army. I was considered a traitor for defending my own honor. Had your patrol not attacked so deeply into camp, I would still be their prisoner. I in no way meant to dishonor or disgrace your holy woods. I saw it as my only hope. Truly, if I were to die, I would prefer that it be at the hands of more honorable men then those I left.

"I understand why you must hold humans in such a high degree of disgust. I mean no harm, I simply wish…" Hamman Drew paused as he saw one elf step from the ranks and whisper in the ear of the leader he was addressing.

Once the Elvan solider was done, the leader returned his gaze to Hamman Drew and said, "You were saying?"

"I just recently hired on with this army. I did not understand their goals. Every elf I have had the honor to stand beside in battle has fought with courage and righteousness. Even some this very evening." Dropping reference to the fact that he was fighting for them this night couldn't hurt. It was a long shot, but he hoped one of these men might have been in the tent or at his side during the fighting.

"So I am told," replied the Elvan captain. "For that reason, I am to trust you and allow you safe passage through our sacred wood?" He continued with disgust.

Trying to find a point of compromise, Hamman Drew offered, "I am willing to skirt the edge of your forest until I find a path of safe passage. Surely that is a reasonable request from someone who fought at your site this night?"

This idea made a couple of the elves chuckle. There noise made him suddenly realize that these archers had held their bows drawn this entire time. That was an amazing display of stamina. It also made him a little nervous about how much longer they could hold them drawn.

Then the captain said, "Surrender your weapons. I will consider your fate." At that, four elves carrying short swords approached him slowly. He backed away from the scimitar he had dropped to the ground. Then he raised one hand at the four elves that approached him. Taking his left hand, he carefully lifted the broken bladed scimitar from his right hip scabbard. Being careful to not make any sudden movements, Hamman Drew openly displayed a willingness to disarm himself. He knew if they wanted to kill him, they could have. If these were going to be the terms, then he could manage these terms.

One elf in front of him pulled a felt blanket from his pack. He partially unfolded it and laid it at Hamman Drew's feet. Hamman Drew took his belt and scimitars and placed them in the blanket. Pausing for a moment, he also took the knife from his hip and the two from each of his boots. Then gently placed them on the blanket. The elf bent over and wrapped them in the blanket then picked up the blanket and walked away. Once again looking the captain in the face, Hamman Drew extended his arms to suggest he was defenseless. Then a sharp blow rendered him unconscious.

The pain was excruciating. Hamman Drew didn't even want to open his eyes. His head was woozy, and he was sure if he moved, he would get sick. Yet he felt an urgency. The roar of rushing water was so strong the earth shook. A heavy mist had gathered on his face and covered his clothes. Wiping the moisture from his cheek, Hamman Drew mustered the strength to slowly open one eye.

The last thing he remembered was surrendering to the elves. Now it was daylight. He had hoped to sneak a little peak with one eye. As he opened one eye, he found a young Elvan warrior sat cross-legged in front of him. As soon as he moved his eyelid, the elf said, "Good! Get up. Let's get going."

Realizing there was no use in playing opossum, Hamman Drew opened his eyes to examine his surroundings. As soon as his sight adjusted, he found that he and the elf were alone. He had rested on a fairly dry patch of ground that was part of a larger outcropping. This rock formation jutted out from the middle of some large waterfalls. The water rushed past in a powerful cascade and then disappeared over the ledge and into the mist. A few hundred feet below, Hamman Drew could see the forest lining the other side of the stream. The height of the sun was blocked by the mountainside on which they stood. He couldn't really tell how long he had been out. From the pain in his head, he might have guessed days.

The elf quickly stood and said, "I cannot afford to be away long. You need to gather your weapons and be on your way." Then he waved an arm out over the waterfall.

Still groggy, Hamman Drew tried to slow the elf down. "On my way?" he asked, looking side to side. "What am I supposed to do, dive off the side of this mountain?" The outcropping appeared to be situated right between two rushing walls of water. The two cascades struck rocks on both sides of them and then continued their decent into a deep ravine. In the distance, Hamman Drew could make out the tops of the Crescent Crags. He knew he was still somewhere east of the massive mountain range.

He wasn't sure how long he had been out. With the sun still low in the sky, it was probably midmorning. What didn't make any sense was his location. There was no way he could have covered that much ground that night. And how did they get him onto this landing in the middle of these waterfalls? He imagined that he was somewhere inside Shayla's Tears. Then he began wondering if he had been out for more than one night.

"It's a bit deceptive," the elf explained. "But if you'll just follow me, I can show you how we can walk right under." The elf turned toward one of the arcs of cascading water. Without waiting for Hamman Drew, the elf ducked his head. Before he could step under the rushing water, Hamman Drew yelled, "Hey, wait a moment." Seeing the elf pause, he added, "I need just a moment for my head to clear." Looking around, Hamman Drew noticed a green felt blanket laying by his feet. Flipping it open, he found his beloved scimitars and knives, such as they were. It was his scimitars he could not part with. Even the broken one had value to him. Yet twice within the last week, they had been taken from him.

While Hamman Drew tucked his weapons carefully into place, the elf came back to him and picked up the blanket. Quickly, unshouldering his backpack, the elf folded the blanket. As Drew placed his weapons, he admired the elf's field readiness. He loved how neatly the blanket fit in the backpack and made little bulge. As the elf put the pack on, he also noticed how the pack hugged tightly to his back. He recognized how such a perfectly fitting backpack reduces the hassles of moving through brush.

"Okay, what's your name. I'm Hamman Drew."

"Brighton Scarlet," the elf replied. Then he looked at the hand that Hamman Drew had extended. "Ah yes, one of your odd customs." Then Scarlet extended his hand and shook Hamman Drew's hand awkwardly.

"I spoke on your behalf, last night," the elf began. "I told Captain Phillibus that you had probably saved my life during the fighting. Since I spoke to save your life, your life now becomes my responsibility until you are out of our valley."

Looking at this elf, Hamman Drew realized that he was younger than most he had ever met. Yet he wore his short sword like a seasoned veteran of many battles. He was also a little ashamed of the fact that he didn't recognize this elf from the fight. He didn't say a word. He just let the elf speak.

"Once I get you across that stream, I can return to my ranks," he explained.

Looking below, Hamman Drew could see a stream that flowed away from the base of the waterfall. He was relieved to have this help because he had no idea how to remove himself from this ledge. Feeling as though he had regained his composure, Hamman Drew turned to his new Elvan friend and said, "Then lead on."

Scarlet had shown Hamman Drew how he had to squat and shimmy along the face of one rock while ducking under the rushing water. Hamman knew to stand up was certain death. The powerful cascade would certainly knock him right off this rock ledge. Staying low as he could, he followed Brighton Scarlet under the wave of water and to the other side.

Once they had cleared that wall of water, a downward trail had become more apparent. The two weaved in and out of the waterfalls, commonly having to jump from one ledge to another. Though this elf clearly knew where he was and where the right rocks were for them to use, it in no way reduced the risk. Every time Hamman Drew paused, he found himself needing to lean away from the edge.

After a couple of hours descending the bluffs through the rushing water, they came to the riverbank. There a large tree had fallen into the stream and made itself into a bridge. The bridge went most of the way across the river. From where they stood, it would have been a short swim had the tree not fallen.

As Scarlet made his way to the fallen tree, he paused to look back at Hamman Drew. "We will part ways once we reach the other side." Hamman Drew seemed fine with the idea. He was getting hungry and guessed he didn't have much left in his pack to eat. One mouth was half as many to feed.

He had stayed on the forest path, just as Scarlet had suggested. This part of Namron Rae was foreign to Hamman Drew. The woods here were not at all like the Elvanwood. These trees were much smaller in size and grew much closer together. There were times that the trail was barely a trail at all. Fortunately for Hamman Drew, he had traveled enough to follow a trail and to track, if he needed to.

It had been about an hour since leaving Scarlet by the river. He wasn't sure where this path was taking him. He was just happy to know that it was away from the fighting. He knew he was going to have to flee this part of the continent, now that he could be identified as a traitor of the Zel Camber army. He was fine with that. All he really wanted to do was to make enough silver to get a boat ride home.

A pang of hunger made Hamman Drew consider how long it had been since he had eaten. Having been unconscious, he wasn't really sure. He knew his stomach had a better idea, and it was telling him it was time. Realizing that he had been on the move all morning, he took a moment to sit and grab a bite from his pack.

The jerky was a little tougher than he thought it should be. He knew this was some of the backup stock he liked to keep in the dark recesses of his pack. The stuff he only used when he had to. He had grown accustomed to eating around a campfire. He was thinking about some of the fresh warm meals he had recently enjoyed as he took another tug from the stick of venison. As he pulled a bite free, his head jerked, and it reminded him of its pain.

Then his ear caught the sound of crunching underbrush; he stopped chewing and listened carefully. This sound wasn't like that of a grazing deer or some restless bird. This was the sound made by a pack of beasts moving through the underbrush. Hamman Drew quickly took cover behind a tree and crouched low into the underbrush. As he listened, he could tell there was an unusually large group of beasts coming through the woods.

Just as he realized this was a small army advancing, he saw their advance scouts coming down the trail. Two men darted nervously from one cover of underbrush to another. Both had daggers pulled, and they moved quickly to make sure this trail was safe. Each examined their own side of the path. Looking high and low, they searched for any signs of ambush.

Hamman Drew was considering his best move when he heard overhead the faint whisper of an arrow in flight. Checking to see if the scouts were shooting at him, he saw one scout suddenly grab his chest and fall backward. At that moment, he knew he was in the wrong place…again.

The other scout turned to look at his fallen comrade. He began to take cover by lunging for a large rhododendron. Just as he scrambled behind the shrub, an arrow flew into the bush. The thud he heard left him sure this man had been hit too. Then the scout fell from behind the bush with the arrow buried in the center of his chest. There was no alarm sounded.

Hamman Drew whipped around to see where the arrows had come from. When he didn't see anyone, he listened carefully. The movement in the brush had stopped. This wasn't good. If fighting were to break out, he would be right between the two forces. If the group marching forth found him, they might assume he had shot the arrows. He knew he was supposed to keep moving, but he couldn't continue down this forest path.

With the river still on his left, Hamman Drew had very few options. He knew staying on the trail would only leave him exposed. Hamman Drew crouched down and crawled into the underbrush, moving slowly toward the sounds beyond the tree line. He did not have to go too far off his path before he found a legion of riders flying the black Flag of the Crow. Quickly he realized this small legion of Zel Camber's army must be planning an attack at the flank of the Elvan kingdom.

He had no choice; Hamman Drew retreated back into the cover of brush. He began retracing his steps toward the riverbank where he had left Scarlet. He knew he could move faster through these woods than those men on horseback. So as soon as he was certain to be beyond any scouts, he began to run.

He ran for several minutes and felt he was putting some distance between himself and the horsemen. Darting in and out of trees and under branches, Hamman Drew knew this was a situation he could easily survive. He was very comfortable in the woods. If nothing else, he could just slip away into the underbrush and disappear.

As he came to a clearing, he moved to the edge of the path to avoid the direct sunlight. As he got to the other end of the clearing, he was surprised by Scarlet stepping out from behind a large tree. "What do you think you're doing?" Scarlet asked. "I thought my directions were very clear."

Looking over his shoulder to ensure the riders were not directly behind them, he waived for Scarlet to step into the cover with him. Pausing to catch his breath, Hamman Drew explained that there was a mounted force of Zel Cambers men coming down this trail toward his kingdom. He was coming back to warn the elves.

The urgency he used to explain this to Scarlet was lost on the elf. Looking at Scarlet, it suddenly dawned on him that it had been Scarlet who had killed the scouts. Putting it together Hamman Drew asked, "Have you been following me?"

"It is my job to make sure that you leave our land." It's also my job to make sure that these trails are closed," Scarlet said.

"Well, I can't go back that way," Hamman Drew noted as he pointed with his thumb over his shoulder.

"I certainly cannot take you with me," Scarlet reminded him. Then thinking, Scarlet said, "You better just come with me. I will need to blindfold you."

"I'm more than willing to let you blindfold me, but don't hit me in the head. My head is still pounding from the last time."

The forces of Zel Camber were dealt a serious blow that evening. The ambush the elves were able to create was brutal and efficient. Scarlet's warning was timely. For that night, the elves could rest.

18

Jarius's eyes shot open as he woke to the reality that he was lying facedown in a bed.

Instinctually, he forced himself to roll onto his back. As his torso tightened, pain shot across his shoulder blades. Then nausea hit, reminding him of events from the night before. As he collapsed onto his sore shoulders, he heard Amanda say, "Just lay still."

Before he could fully relax, he noticed Amanda and a strange man standing at the foot of his bed. His instinct was to get up, but this time the pain stopped him. "I said, be still. You are safe here." Trying his best to analyze his situation, Jarius thought there was nothing unusual about the man. He had the medium build of a middle-aged human. The man looked somewhat like Amanda. He was fair haired as well. His clothing looked ordinary for the people of this town. Still, seeing them there, Jarius tried to shift into a position that might allow him to get out of bed quickly, if he had to. The pain from his shoulder would not allow him the full movement to sit up. Amanda held up her hand to encourage Jarius to lay still. His pain convinced him to do as she said. Jarius reclined back onto the pillow so that he could face this person who was with Amanda.

The man wasted no time. "What is your name, and where are you from?" Amanda's dad asked in a serious tone. Amanda looked at her dad a little surprised by the terse tone he used. This was not his usual kindness she had known her whole life.

Jarius, startled by the direct nature of his question, responded honestly, "I am Sir Jarius Rafael, a Knight of the Elvan Army of Namron Rae. I come to your village from the holy city of Hollywondra."

Amanda was shocked as her dad began speaking in a language he had taught her as a child. She had always believed it was their special language she thought they had created because nobody else spoke it. She was surprised to find her father speaking this language to this stranger. In Elvan, Amanda's father asked, "Who commissioned your journey?"

To Amanda's surprise, Jarius not only answered her father, he answered in the same silly language her father had taught her. Jarius now gingerly sat up in the bed and began to explain the same strange story he had already told Amanda and Titus. He described the great war aimed at the Elvan nation. He explained how he had been sent here on an important mission. Then last night, Jarius and Titus encountered an assassin who had been sent by the evil Zel Camber. "Zel Camber sending that assassin required great magic to engage the Tree Gate. It also means Zel Camber must be concerned for the purpose of my mission," shared Jarius. He stopped short when he considered telling this man about his quest for the Ray of Light.

Jarius's pause seemed almost expected and appreciated by Amanda's father. With a short smile, he turned and took a small step toward the door of the bedroom. Running his right hand through his hair in contemplation, he stopped and turned back to speak further. "You never told me why you are here." He stared at Jarius carefully.

Jarius considered everything he had experienced since coming to this small town. Amanda appeared to be an elf in another land. Her dad knew his native tongue and did not flinch at his explanations. He examined Amanda's father very carefully. He knew that if this man was a path to the Ray of Light, he would have to confide in him. He surveyed the room to locate his weapons. He saw his daggers resting on a dresser two strides away.

Seeing Jarius looking for his weapons, the father took a small step away from the dresser. This small step seemed to almost provide Jarius with enough space and time to make it to the dresser and arm himself. This was a code of battlefield honor for an unarmed man. If this man was truly afraid of him, he would have stepped between him and his weapons.

Looking back at the man, Amanda's father raised both his hands as if he were defenseless. Then he said to Jarius, "You are not my prisoner. You may take your weapons and leave, if you chose. You have come to my home and town, and I am simply inquiring about the objectives of your mission."

In the Elvan kingdom, it is considered rude to visit another home without the direct invitation of the elder of that home. What her father stated was the fact that Jarius was not truly invited into his home. Realizing this implication, Jarius painfully began to pull his legs from under the blankets.

Amanda stepped forward and said, "What do you think you're doing?" Turning to her father, she pleaded, "What's going on here? And how does he know how to speak our language?"

Just then her dad seemed to get an idea that could break this stalemate. Raising his hand to quiet Amanda, her father stepped around the edge of the bed, between Jarius and the dresser that held his dagger. "You call yourself Sir Jarius Rafael? That might suggest you are a knight of the Elvan Kingdom. Tell me about your being knighted."

Understanding that this could be a way for her father to finally have faith that Jarius was good, and the father was the right contact in this new world, Jarius began to recount the events of his knighting ceremony. As Jarius began describing the details of this ceremony, Amanda kept looking back and forth at the two of them. Thinking that this might reveal some important detail, she carefully examined their tones and words. As Jarius began describing the holy sword used to knight him, Amanda's heard he father whisper, "Perdition."

At first, wondering how could he know the name of this holy sword, Jarius realized this man's knowledge of Elvan Knighthood was real. That brought a small smile to his face as he answered, "Yes."

Looking very carefully at the man, Jarius asked, "Who are you?' You are not of this land. There is no way you could know of the name of Perdition, unless…"

Jarius paused to consider the possibility that he could meet another Elvan Knight in this foreign land, when he was interrupted by the man's reply. "Sir Bartlebee Allendale," Amanda's father announced proudly, placing his right hand over his heart in an Elvan salute.

Jarius grimaced at his reflex to return the salute. Deep in his subconscious mind, he knew this man. He could see this man wearing Elvan armor and being knighted under the blade of Perdition. In some way, Perdition kept the memory of all the Elvan Knights it had knighted and placed all those ancient memories deep into his subconscious mind. This revelation gave Jarius a huge surge of faith and confidence in his progress.

As the two Elvan knights exchanged a smile, Amanda's words were barely audible in the background of their emotional revelry. His little girl was emerging as she pleaded, "Daddy! Daddy!" She did not understand what was going on, but his knowledge of this stranger and the sharing of their childhood language was shaking the core of her very existence.

Turning to see the panic in the eyes of Amanda, Sir Allendale quickly told Jarius he was safe and that he needed to rest. Allendale needed time to explain things to Amanda. Allendale put his arm around Amanda's shoulder and escorted the bewildered girl from the room. Peace and safety welled over Jarius as slumber wrapped him in warmth.

*****

For the next few days, Jarius rested in the home of Sir Allendale. Once he felt strong enough, they all met in the parlor of the home and began talking about their missions. "How can I be certain that you were not sent here to steal the Ray of Light?" Allendale asked Jarius.

"How can I be certain you were not placed here to foil my efforts?" Jarius replied with guile.

Realizing that they shared knowledge of Perdition, Allendale began to recount the story of his coming to this land. He told Jarius about how he was assigned this mission of the greatest urgency and security: to hide the Ray of Light in this distant land. He was told to stay in this land and to blend into the culture so as to not be easily be detected. In time, a messenger would come to bring them home. Then he asked Jarius, "What do you know of the Ray of Light?"

Jarius paused and then realized he really didn't know much detail. Feeling as though he needed to make a reply, Jarius explained that he understood he would recognize it when he came upon it. This caused Allendale to throw his head back and laugh.

"That sounds so much like Barnabus," Sir Allendale replied. "I can't trust you enough to reveal my secrets. You can't trust me enough to reveal yours. It's perfect! We must all return to Hollywondra."

"All of us," Jarius repeated as he looked slowly toward Amanda.

Smiling, Allendale said, "Well, you did come looking for the Ray of Light, didn't you?"

Perplexed, Jarius slowly nodded his head as he looked at Allendale for the answers. Allendale smiled broadly, "Then we had better be taking the Ray with us."

19

Prowling had become an art form for Titus. It had allowed him to move in and out of a lot of difficult situations in his life. He wasn't sure if this was a blessing or a curse. He knew it would be frowned upon, if anyone ever caught him snooping.

A few days after the knife fight, Titus found Amanda and her father in the field gathering up the body of the assassin. When he asked if he could help, his presence surprised them both. Amanda's father told him that he would be wise to just rest his shoulder and let himself heal. Besides, he should not have anything to do with this death, if he could avoid it. Walking away, Titus couldn't imagine how he could not have anything to do with this body. Surely evidence would show his presence. How could they have dismissed him and his involvement? He figured it must have been his surprising them that resulted in them discounting him like that.

This only made Titus wonder even more about what was going on. From a distance, he watched Amanda and her dad wrap the body in a blanket and draped it over the back of a horse. Then the two rode off toward the woods. Titus knew he could not keep up with them. He also knew he didn't have to. He knew they were getting rid of the body. He just couldn't understand why. This attacker was clearly a criminal. Why would they risk their standing in the community to hide the body of a murderer?

This only fed his curiosity. Titus began watching Amanda's house very carefully. One night Titus had been outside the parlor window eavesdropping. Through the single paned glass, Titus was able to track the majority of the conversation. While there were some things that did not make total sense, he was able to piece together several facts. The most important of which was that they were planning to leave Rile. He knew that wherever Amanda went, he wanted to be at her side. He also had a sense that they would not be inviting him, so he had to make himself ready to move in a moment's notice.

Over the course of the next couple of days, Titus had changed his sleeping patterns. He intentionally avoided school, knowing he could always catch back up if he needed to. Instead, he altered his sleeping hours so that he could keep an eye on Amanda's house. He noticed she hadn't been going to school either. When he had tried to talk to her, she seemed distant and distracted. This only made him more curious.

One night, almost a week after the knife fight, Titus had gone to his favorite window to listen to their plans. This time what he heard was more movement than talk. When he heard an odd metallic sound, it enticed him to peek in the window. He saw Amanda's dad holding a drawn sword. Extending his arm toward Jarius and Amanda, her father displayed this weapon with a certain ease of confidence and pride. The two examined it carefully. At one point, the dad took the sword by its blade to show them the hilt. The two examined it carefully. Jarius craned his head as if he were reading something then pointed at something for Amanda to examine more carefully.

Amanda nodded and then left the room. Jarius and her father spoke too softly for Titus to understand. It sounded like her dad was giving Jarius instructions on how to behave. Then he extended his left hand and took Jarius's right. With the sword in his right hand, her father extended it in front of them. Jarius, as if taking a cue from Sir Allendale, pulled a dagger from his hip and extended it in a similar fashion. Almost as if they were practicing for some ceremony, they seemed to practice moving their weapons in sync.

Amanda came back into the room. She was carrying something rolled up under her arm. She had changed clothes. She was now wearing a thin white lacey gown. The gown was so thin that it pressed against the contours of her body as she walked. Coming toward the two guys, she addressed her father.

HOLLYWONDRA

With his sword, Sir Allendale pointed at a spot on the floor in front of the fireplace. Then he turned to a large silver cross that stood on the mantle. Bowing his head in a movement of reverence, Allendale then shifted the cross to the center of the mantle, adjusting it so that the cross squarely faced the room. Turning, Allendale instructed Amanda to alter the location of the rug she had just laid on the living room floor.

This rug that she had just brought into the room was something Titus had never seen in all his visits to her home. It was a thin silky bright green fabric. As Amanda unfurled it, the rug gently fell into place. Amanda had only to pull it into the exact place Sir Allendale directed.

From less than ten feet away, Titus was mesmerized watching this rite unfold. Sir Allendale instructed Amanda to kneel on both knees facing the cross on the mantle. To Amanda's left stood the man she had only known to be her father, and to her right stood Sir Jarius Rafael. Sir Allendale extended his hands to the other two. Reaching up from the floor, Amanda took her dad's hand and the left hand of Jarius, thus forming a circle. Then Allendale instructed them to bow their heads in prayer.

It was only natural for Titus to bow his head as well. He had been brought up in the church and attended weekly services at Sir Allendale's church. When he said, "Bow your head," it was only natural for him to follow Allendale's direction. Titus could not clearly hear the prayer, he just knew that in his heart, he truly desired that all of these people would be safe in whatever it was they were planning. When he heard Allendale's tone change from reverent to normal, he lifted his eyes and continued to spy on them.

As the two men released Amanda's hands, they both drew their weapons. Titus began to rise in a defensive concern for the safety of Amanda. Then he realized that something else was happening. The two men lifted their weapon to their faces. Upright they pointed, as each man kissed their blade. Slowly, each man moved their blade from their kiss to the shoulders of Amanda. Jarius's magical dagger came to rest on Amanda's right shoulder at the same moment that Allendale's short sword blade gently came to rest on her left.

113

The two men began to chant words that were inaudible to Titus. All he could tell was that they were chanting the same words repeatedly. After what appeared to be a couple of times saying the same series of words, both weapons began to glow light blue. The two men, with their eyes closed, continued their chanting. Amanda kneeling with her head down remained motionless.

Suddenly, the light blue glow intensified. The glow raised to a brightness that caused Titus to lift his arm to block the glow from his night sensitive eyes. Then the glow exploded into a bright flash of blue light. Somehow, this explosion of light permeated the walls of the house and knocked Titus backward into the shrubbery. Realizing that he had been knocked back into the bushes, Titus carefully pulled himself out so that he could remain unnoticed.

Slowly pulling himself back to the window, Titus snuck a peak to see what had happened. At first, all he noticed was the three of them hugging in the center of the room. Then he noticed Amanda.

Amanda had always been radiant in his eyes. But now she appeared to almost actually glow. As Titus starred, he realized, it wasn't just the dress; it was her. Her face was also glowing with a supernatural radiance. Titus had always seen Amanda as a beautiful young woman that one day he hoped to marry. Her beauty was now awesome. Even the two men in the room could not take their eyes off her.

As Titus considered that she was well out of his league, he realized that he was feeling different. As he held out his arms and looked down their length, all his hair was standing on end. He had goose bumps, but it was from a rush of warmth and not from the chill of the night. He felt different. It wasn't painful. It was…different. This caused him pause. Titus concealed himself against the side of the house, afraid he might be glowing too. Then he slowly stood to examine himself more carefully. He couldn't see any distinguishable difference. He felt fine. Actually, he felt better than fine. The soreness that had been pestering him all week from the dagger wound was gone. Reaching inside his shirt, he noticed that there wasn't any pain at all, where the bandage was. Pulling back the bandage, Titus could feel that the wound was completely healed and only a small scar remained. His wound had been scabbed over and sore.

Titus was even more surprised when Amanda's voice asked him, "Did you watch the entire ritual?"

Looking up, Titus saw Amanda standing in the dark. Her luminescence jumped off her like a bright moon bounced off frosty grass on a winter evening. Behind Amanda stood Jarius and Allendale.

Uncertain what to say, he simply spoke the truth. "I think so."

The two men shot each other a glance and then looked back at Titus. Then Allendale gave a quick survey of the yard and calmly suggested, "You'd better come inside, Titus."

20

The antechamber was a circular room with a single entrance. Like many of the structures in Hollywondra, this room had been carved from the inside a gigantic oak tree. This was the largest such chamber and oldest oak in the city. The walls, ceiling, and floor were smooth and polished from centuries of use. The hundreds of rings that would normally be counted to age a tree had been carefully polished away. The wall carvings were older than any of the elves who had assembled in this room. The artist's work transcended centuries of Elvan rule. His name had been lost over the centuries, but his work could still be found in the most sacred Elvan quarters. The warm comfortable atmosphere of the room was a contradiction. Just a few leagues away, Zel Camber's army closed on Hollywondra.

The craftmanship was exquisite. The seam of the door was virtually invisible. The easiest way to find the exit was to look between the two guards who stood watch. The door was made from the original tree and had been incorporated into the intricate carvings and rings that decorated the walls.

The two guards looked straight ahead at the five men standing at the table in the middle of the room. While the four Elvin leaders met, Chronus kept note. Chronus was the keeper of Namronian history. Mystically, he could be found attending any event or conversation that might dictate the outcome of historical events. He came and went unannounced and uninvited. Over the centuries, his presence had come to be expected at all significant historical conversations or events. He was too tall to be considered an elf and too old to be human. He almost never spoke a word. When he did, it was usually to remind folks that he cannot alter the path of the future.

Chronus would never make predictions. He claimed to have no powers beyond this realm.

"It was a calculated risk," stated Barnabus Malactus defensively. "We know we can't keep the humans at bay much longer. There are just too many of them. Our only real hope is that Sir Raphael returns with the Ray of Light." Across the table from Malactus stood King Elfanwisel. While they did not always agree on how the king chose to run his kingdom, they both agreed that time was running out.

King Elfanwisel was an ancient frail elf with bright green youthful eyes that glowed more life than his body seemed to hold. The royal robes and thin gold gilded crown made his presence regal. His frail appearance made one wonder how his body could manage the weight of such ornate robes. He moved slowly and paused before speaking. He was considered wise and very capable of managing his kingdom. The urgency of the situation did not seem to fit into how slowly the king spoke.

Sir Kluvarner stood to the right of his king. Considered by many to be the greatest living Elvin warrior, Kluvarner had been compelled to a new role of leadership. The Elvin army had suffered so many losses, one such casualty resulted in Kluvarner's promotion in rank. Often assertive, Kluvarner held his tongue as the priest and king discussed the progress of defending their forest. While he was honored to be in their presence, he knew the success of the army now rested on him and Sir Bracanthorpe. This was Kluvarner's first strategic meeting with the king.

Bracanthorpe stood to Kluvarner's left. Bracanthorpe was in command of all the Elvin forces that patrolled Hollywondra and kept their perimeter secure. In these days, his men had been stretched so thin, they were seldom afforded rest. Zel Camber's forces on the fields of Shayna had kept his men busy. "We've had some unusual fortune," shared Bracanthorpe. "We had a human defect from the enemy army and run into our ranks. He was quick to share details of a sneak attack Zel Camber tried from the north. We were able to ambush and route those forces. It had to have been a significant setback for Zel Camber."

Kluvarner had been listening patiently, but finally had to insert, "It was only a setback for Zel Camber. The humans and their Klofgar are slowly burning their way to Hollywondra. We've been able to slay any man who so much as picked up a torch, but the Klofgar don't die so easily." Kluvarner turned to Malactus and said, "I don't know what this Ray of Light can do for us. I am here to tell you that we need to begin considering a plan to evacuate Hollywondra."

Kluvarner had said what the others refused to consider. Being rational, Kluvarner spoke with the interest of keeping the Elvan race alive. He did not have the political acumen to consider his audience or how he might best phrase his concern. He just put it out there for the others in the room. Sir Bracanthorpe shot Kluvarner an angry eye. Kluvarner knew the look. Bracanthorpe was not the first person to suggest Kluvarner might not be good at reading a room.

Before he could reprimand his new second of command, the king interrupted, "Our history and prophecies have always held true. I see no reason to abandon our faith, our prophesies, or our home in this holy sanctuary." The notion of leaving this sacred wood was preposterous to the king. Appalled at the idea, the king turned from Kluvarner to look at Malactus. Then turning back toward Kluvarner, the king slowly asked the warrior three questions. "How do we move Hollywondra? Do we move from here to create a new Hollywondra? Do you believe the Elvin people want to surrender Hollywondra?"

Realizing how irrational his suggestion to retreat sounded, Sir Kluvarner tried to correct what he had stated. Speaking with sincerity and humility, Kluvarner explained, "Please forgive me, your Highness. I only suggested a retreat to secure the safety of our women and young. Maybe through their escape, we could preserve our race."

The king gently smiled and replied. "Kluvarner, you have given so much of yourself to our kingdom. You have endured countless wounds in securing the safety and well-being of our nation. Your service and your commitment are beyond question. Your success and honor have come from your faith in your sword instead of our God. There are greater forces at work in this world. I would encourage you to visit the temple to rekindle the faith you knew as a child. The

HOLLYWONDRA

same faith that gave you power and glory in battle will show us how to overcome this assault on our kingdom."

A bit ashamed, Kluvarner deeply bowed his head to show respect for the king's suggestion. He dwelled on the fact that he felt he was only thinking practically. Then taking the king's suggestion, Kluvarner tried to recall his innocent years. Soon he found his thoughts returning to defensive strategies to better defend this forested city. He knew Zel Camber's forces were great in number. He was just being realistic. The elves could not keep them at bay forever.

Sir Bracanthorpe began to offer suggestions for how his men could use the Scurriers to create a trap. Kluvarner stopped his planning to carefully listen to his general's thoughts. The general's idea was both clever and deadly. Yet in the back of Kluvarner's mind, he knew that the trap was only a stop gap for an army that outnumbered the elves twenty to one.

*****

The fact that Hamman Drew was allowed to move freely about the camp gave him a sense of freedom. In truth, he knew every elf kept a watchful eye on him. As he sharpened his scimitar, he casually looked around at what he figured was the Elvan camp. This camp was different than the human camps he was accustomed to. Instead of everyone being centrally located, the elves seemed to intentionally spread as far apart as they could and still see at least another. As he looked around, he continued to notice more and more elves that were in different trees and in different locations throughout the area.

The elves kept no campfire. Their camp kept moving. Every four hours, they would move from one area of the forest to another. They always kept a trailing party to erase any evidence of their previous camp. Hamman Drew was learning Elvan tactical behavior and the types of things they tried to conceal. He knew an unskilled eye would never notice that the area had been an Elvin camp.

After a couple of days, Hamman Drew realized the party was moving in a strategic pattern. They were clearly working with a network of other patrols to keep certain trails into Hollywondra watched from different positions at different times. After about a week into his stay with the elves, an alarm was shouted in his encampment. As quickly as the alarm was shouted, the elves responded.

From the ground to the tree tops, they all broke their rest and began running as fast as they could to the north. Drew ran as fast as he could to keep up with the fleet elves. The elves were not just fast, they could move quickly through the brush that covered the forest floor. Drew was only able to keep up by following the brush that still moved from the passing of elves. He wasn't really positive he was running in the right direction. He just knew he could not afford to be separated from the squad he had been camping with. It would be too easy to be mistaken for a human enemy, if he was not at the right place at the right time. Hollywondra was no place for humans.

The smell of burning wood was quickly followed by traces of smoke. What had started out as light wisps of smoke soon grew to a haze that began to blur the trails through the underbrush. Hamman Drew had to slow down but kept moving in the general direction the elves had been running. He knew their ways well enough to know that they would not have wasted time by circling around; they were moving in a beeline for the assault on their forest.

Soon he heard the clash of metal on metal, so he knew he wasn't far from the fighting. The smoke was getting thick, and it was beginning to affect his ability to breathe. Hamman Drew slowed to a walk. Then he heard something crashing through the branches above him. He paused to spot his attacker. As he looked overhead, he saw a large burning limb falling through the tree branches, lightly igniting leaves on its way to the forest floor. The torch landed about twenty feet in front of Drew and began to ignite a large bush at the base of an oak. Hamman Drew knew he had to address this right away, or the tree would certainly be in flames.

Quickly, he ran to the burning bush and pulled the large torch out. The bush had been ignited from the middle, so he figured pulling the torch out would be the best way to slow the fire. With the torch safely away from the bush, Hamman Drew began smothering the flame with dirt and debris. Looking back at the bush, he could see that it was still on fire, but the flames were slowly dying out.

HOLLYWONDRA

Hearing the crash of brush again, Hamman Drew looked up just in time to see a Klofgar swing a large piece of wood at his head. Drew ducked under the swing, but the wood glanced off his shoulders. That alone was enough to knock him to the ground onto the smoldering torch he had just put out. Drew knew the Klofgar were not agile, so he quickly rolled from where he landed on the ground. Sure enough, the wooden branch the Klofgar was using as a club crashed down right where he had been.

Springing to his feet, Hamman Drew turned and looked up into face the Klofgar. Hamman Drew instinctively drew his scimitar and immediately missed having his other scimitar. So he pulled a knife to provide himself a second weapon. Drew began to circle the Klofgar. The Klofgar was not nearly as tactful. Lifting his club, the Klofgar lunged at Hamman Drew. Drew easily slid to the side and sliced at the stomach of the beast. Then jumping past the Klofgar, he made a downward strike at the backside of the Klofgar. Both blows hit the beast, but the sheer size of the monster made his attack seem almost pointless.

The Klofgar, seeming unphased by the attack, spun around. As he turned, he swung his club in a long strong arch. Drew danced back to avoid the blow then quickly moved in to attack the creature at point blank. The Klofgar was very muscular and stood a little over ten feet tall. Its hairy leathered torso was barely covered by crude clothing. The strike he made to the side of the Klofgar bled, but it appeared to be little more than a bad scratch.

As Drew advanced, he waved his scimitar in a flashing figure eight. He knew this approach intimidated and caused as much damage as possible. He had hoped that this assault might put the Klofgar on his heals and off balance. What Hamman Drew did not expect was the Klofgar's total disregard for personal safety. Instead, the beast dropped his wooden club and began to swing his bare fists at Drew. His first swing was met by the blade of a scimitar. The blade struck the Klofgar's hand and sheared off his little finger. The Klofgar's other fist struck Hamman Drew in his shoulder. The blow lifted him off the ground and sent him flying.

Pain shot through the entire left side of Hamman Drew's upper body. He knew he needed to roll, or the Klofgar would be upon him. As he rolled to one side, he saw that the Klofgar had picked up his club and was moving in to finish him off. Hamman Drew's shoulder was seriously damaged. The pain was so intense, he could not imagine lifting a scimitar with his left arm.

Drew determined to put a tree between him and his attacker, hoping to dodge or out run the Klofgar. Getting off the ground was not as easy as he thought it would be. He had to make a second roll. As he turned over, he saw the Klofgar closing on him with the club held high. Lying on his back, he watched the beast strike down at him. He quickly rolled out of the way to his left. Forgetting that he had been injured, the pain alone almost knocked him out. He knew he could not outlast the Klofgar at this game.

Scrambling to his feet, Hamman Drew realized that he had lost his scimitar. He was using his right hand to support a useless left arm. Hunched over, because that somehow made the pain lessen, he watched the Klofgar raise his club and step toward him. The beast had what could be called a smile on his face as he closed in. Drew bounced from side to side, hoping to make himself a tougher target. Each movement shot pain into his shoulder. He watched the musculature of the beast to sense when he was going to strike. His read was good, and he was able to leap out of the way as the club struck the ground with a heavy thud. The Klofgar quickly lifted the club and then decided to try a new tactic. Stepping forward, the Klofgar swung the club like a bat. Trying to duck under the blow, Hamman Drew was knocked to the ground as the club glanced off his back.

Quickly he rolled just as the club hit the ground where he had laid. Only this time, he rolled right into the trunk of a great oak. His motion was stopped. He could only roll to his left. His painful left shoulder. He considered how much pain would be involved if he allowed the Klofgar to just kill him with the next blow.

Looking up he saw the beast draw his club high overhead and take aim. Hamman Drew knew he had to muster the strength to roll onto his left shoulder. He just hadn't mustered that courage just yet. He was still considering the options of a quick and painless death.

HOLLYWONDRA

While watching the Klofgar to time his move, Drew saw an arrow suddenly sink into the left eye of the beast.

Screaming in pain, the Klofgar dropped his club and reached for its wounded eye. Just then his second eye was hit, and a third arrow struck him in the brow just above the right eye. Crying out in agony and blinded by the attack, the Klofgar began to scream a deep guttural roar. Blood trickled down his face from the wounds to the eyes, but the beast still stood and thrashed about, trying to gently extract the arrows from its eyes.

Seizing this moment of opportunity, Hamman Drew made his way over to where he thought he had dropped his scimitar. Digging around through the leaves of the loamy forest floor, he was finally able to find his trusty sword. Picking it up with his right hand, he carefully moved up on the Klofgar from behind. Hamman Drew lifted the scimitar high and drove the blade as deeply into the back of the beast as he could with his one good arm. Just striking the beast shot a horrible pain through his left side and made him weak at the knees. What he didn't expect was for the Klofgar to spin around and swing at him. His instinct allowed him to dodge the blow. That movement shot more pain through his left shoulder and reminded him that he did not have the strength for combat any more. He needed to kill this thing and kill it quick.

Moving quietly so the beast could not detect his location, Hamman Drew pulled out his last dagger. Realizing the futility of attacking this beast with a knife, Hamman Drew knew he had to try something else.

The Klofgar had broken one arrow when trying to remove it from an eye. He was now fumbling with the other one. Hamman Drew saw the beast was standing in front of the same tree he had used as a club. He wished he had the strength to shove him. He knew he would stumble over the log and then be on the ground. Hamman Drew just could not hit him hard enough. The pain in his shoulder would not allow him.

Then, with a little smile, he carefully advanced on the back side of the Klofgar. Once he had quietly moved directly behind the beast, Hamman Drew carefully shoved his knife into the right buttocks of the Klofgar. The bite of his blade made the creature lunge. Stepping forward, the beast tripped over his own weapon. Stumbling forward, the Klofgar lost his footing and fell to the ground.

This gave Hamman Drew the chance he needed to make a fatal blow.

The smoke from the fires created a haze that made seeing difficult. Though it was midday, the smoke combined with the underbrush made it almost impossible to see more than ten feet. With his scimitar in his one good hand, Hamman Drew slowly moved toward the fighting. He knew he couldn't be much help. He also knew he could not be separated from his Elvan allies. He approached the combat but was careful to not rush in.

Hamman Drew was startled when three elves suddenly jumped through the underbrush. Smoke swirled around them as they approached. They approached without any regard for his presence or threat. Hamman Drew was relieved to see one of them wore a bright green ribbon tied around his thigh. That elf addressed him first. "Let's get you some help for that arm," he said as a matter of fact. Surprised by the elf's quick assessment, Hamman Drew watched as they walked past him and continued into the woods behind him. Assuming his weapons were no longer needed in the battle, Drew turned and followed them deeper into the woods of Hollywondra.

*****

Laying on a loamy pile of turf, Hamman Drew looked up at two elves standing over him. One was an older elf that did not look able to be much help in combat. The other was clearly battle ready and tested. The old elf reached down and examined his damaged shoulder. The pain was horrible, but Hamman Drew tried to look as though he could handle the pain. It was so intense, he was growing nauseous.

"This shoulder is a seriously damaged. Why should we waste our magic on a human?" the elder elf asked the fighter.

"We need every hand we can get for combat. This human has chosen to fight with us. He's not the smartest warrior we have, but

HOLLYWONDRA

he's willing to die trying. Please place your hands up on him," the fighter pleaded. "I must return to the fight." Without another word, the fighter turned and ran into the underbrush.

The old elf stood over Hamman Drew considering the idea of using his power on a human. It just seemed wrong to him. He knew these were desperate times. Finally determining, if this guy was of any value to the Elvan cause, then who was he to keep his blade out of combat. The old elf leaned over the top of Hamman Drew. Using both his hands, he grabbed his shoulder and began to pray. The pain was too much. Hamman struggled a little, but the old guy had a tight grip on him. The pain was too much. Hamman passed out as the old elf continued to pray.

*****

Upon waking, Hamman Drew chose to lay still. Slightly stirring on the ground, he could tell the pain was gone. He slowly wiggled his left fingers and found that he had complete use of his left arm. It was a miracle. He wasn't sure what magic the elves had used on him, but his left arm felt whole. He had his whole range of motion.

As he rested, he heard stories of how Zel Camber's men had catapulted large fireballs into the woods to create a distraction. While the blazes were underway, hundreds of Zel Camber's men and Klofgar rushed into the woods north of the blaze. The catapults changed the direction of their fire and shot blazing balls of fire into the woods ahead of their attack party. As the elves rushed to the second fire, they encountered Zel Camber's men.

The Klofgar were carrying large unlit torches. They stuck them into the blazes to ignite them. Then they flung them deeper in the forest. By the time the elves had reached the insurgent force, the fire had quickly spread to five times the size. A Klofgar could throw one of their fiery torches a great distance. This attack was more than a distraction; it was a direct assault on the hallowed woods.

21

Taking Titus by the chin, Sir Allendale looked carefully into his eyes. "Yeah, that's what I thought. Come here, Jarius. Look at his eyes and tell me what you see." Jarius did as he was told. All of this attention was starting to make Titus worried that he might be sick or something.

Leaning close to his face, Jarius searched his eyes for some kind of sign. Jarius wasn't sure what it was that Allendale wanted him to see. Whatever it was must be small, because these looked like the eyes of his friend. Jarius continued to search carefully. Then he noticed something rather strange. Deep in the green cornea of his eyes, there was a faint glow. As Jarius focused, the glow seemed to almost grow brighter. It was so bright, Jarius did not understand how he could not have seen it before. Jarius pulled his gaze away and looked at Allendale. Then he turned back to look into Titus's eyes again. This time he was able to quickly see the greenish glow in his eyes.

Turning back to Allendale, Jarius asked, "What is that?" Titus was now starting to freak out. Something was in his eyes. He began to consider the possibilities of various bacteria or maybe radiation from the bright flash. Standing up, he rubbed his eyes. Walking over to the mirror that hung above the fireplace, he searched his eyes while listening to what Allendale explained to Jarius.

"The Rite of Purification changes a person. It would appear Titus was close enough to the aura that he, too, has been changed. Look into my eyes, or Amanda's," Allendale offered. Looking into Allendale's blue eyes, Jarius could now see the same glow that he had just seen in Titus's eyes. Jarius then joined Titus at the mirror to look into his own eyes. Allendale told him, "It doesn't work that way. You can only see the power of this blessing by looking directly into the eyes of the person. For some reason, a mirror corrupts that."

Amanda seemed unaffected by the whole conversation. She spoke with a stern authority and insight to the situation. "Titus, you cannot tell anyone what you've witnessed here. It's not that anything bad happened. It's just that the townsfolk would not understand. That, combined with the death of that assassin, might make you look more suspicious than you should be."

"Well, what about you and your dad?" Titus quickly fired back. "You don't think that body will be found? They'll follow the horse tracks back to where the fight took place? It's only a matter of time before we're all discovered."

Amanda shot a quick glance at her dad and then Jarius. No words were said, but Titus quickly picked up on the fact that other plans had been made and he was not a part of them. He also knew that the evidence of the murder was clear and easy to understand. They had to be planning to leave Rile.

"Wait just a minute!" Titus quickly jumped in. "You guys are not taking off and leaving me here to defend myself in your absence. That's just wrong! I know I am innocent, but I'd have a tough time proving it without you." Then Titus looked down and whispered, "Without you." It was as if he realized he might never see Amanda again.

Jarius approached Titus. "You can't come with us, Titus. It's far too dangerous...and...we're not ever coming back."

"With us leaving town so suddenly, it will be easy for you to place the blame on us," suggested Sir Allendale. "You can even be the eyewitness. That could explain any of your DNA or footprints they might find."

This struck Titus right in the heart. The idea of Amanda leaving Rile never to return was just not acceptable to him. Titus refused to accept this option. He knew Jarius was a strange guy who claimed to come from a strange land. Scientifically, Titus knew there were wonders of the world that could not be easily explained by modern science. All the possibilities were more than he could wrap his mind around. Titus knew one day he'd leave Rile. He also knew he did not want to stay in Rile without Amanda. The thought of her leaving was too much to bear.

"I'm going with you!" Titus declared.

"That's not a good idea," Allendale quickly answered.

"I must tell you, Titus, the place to which we journey is a violent land. It is a land in which people would kill you, just because they do not know you," Jarius offered.

Thoughts of the war-torn Middle East or violent jungles of Africa came to Titus's mind. The thought of fighting had always been frightening to him. He was a kind spirit who had always been able to use his wits to avoid conflict. Would this place be a place where his mind may not serve him well? He could not imagine that his intelligence could not be a resource for the group. He'd always realized that Rile held no future for him. Titus firmly stated, "I'm going! Wherever it is that we travel, it must be to a land where I cannot be known or tracked in connection to this murder. So, it is in my best interest to join you and offer my knowledge as a tool for our survival."

The other three looked at each other. Amanda and Allendale knew Titus well enough to know he had to have weighed the options. He had always been a rational intelligent person. They knew that to abandon Titus in Rile was to surely set him up for legal troubles.

Amanda nodded at Sir Allendale.

Allendale went to Titus and told him, "Sit down. I need to explain some things. You need to keep an open mind, because this is not going to not make a lot of sense to you."

*****

While on his knees, Jarius bowed to pray. After a short pause, Jarius looked up at Titus, as if to examine him for the first time. In an all-knowing way, Jarius reported, "I see you are not yet committed. We will have to work on that." Getting up, Jarius came nose to nose with Titus and said, "Because of this specific situation, I am forced to trust you with some very important information. You can never tell anyone the reason for our mission or who Amanda is. You would put my entire kingdom at risk. Sharing this with anyone would be a direct betrayal and absolutely unforgivable."

Jarius's posture and tone was so serious that it sent a chill down his spine. Titus knew what Jarius was capable of doing. This was not some schoolyard pinkie promise. This was life or death. He knew if he were to betray Jarius that he would probably not survive. There was something about Jarius that made Titus trust him. Then there was this other side of the young elf that Titus knew was dire and urgent.

Looking around the room, Jarius directed Sir Allendale, "Get the key." Titus wondered what key he was talking about. Titus watched Allendale walk through the front door and out into his front yard. Allendale's shadow moved gracefully along the faint dusk horizon. He walked over to the picket fence and began counting the fence pickets. After counting more than a dozen pickets, Allendale stopped and grabbed hold of a picket. With one strong tug, he pulled it from the fence line. Then he returned to the house.

Entering the room, Jarius smiled. "How very clever. Hide something so precious right in plain sight." Taking the picket from Sir Allendale, Jarius examined the Tree Key. At the top of the picket, two iron nails stuck through back side of the picket. The white paint was thick. He scratched it with his fingernail then looked carefully at the scratch that he had made. Titus looked at Amanda, as if she might tell him what was going on. She shrugged her shoulders. Amanda appeared every bit as curious as he was.

Jarius smiled. Careful to avoid the nails, he took hold of the picket at each end. Bending the stick, the shaft broke. Jarius examined the short piece with nails and then looked at the jagged end of the long piece. He threw the short piece to the floor and said, "We have no time to waste." Shooting one more glance at Titus, Jarius said, "There will be no coming back."

Titus nodded, acknowledging he understood and was ready to go. Titus knew he had no idea what he was getting himself into. He was simply ready to leave Rile. His father had tried his best to raise the two boys, but Titus was miserable. This was really his only choice. His dad and brother had done just fine after his mom left. He figured they would do just fine after he leaves too. Besides, Webster was always his father's favorite.

As they began to run through the tall grass, Jarius whispered back without looking, "Keep up, you two!" Amanda and Titus took a fleeting glimpse at the only home they had known. The homes of Rile began lighting up as families came in from their fields for their evening meals. Neither of them knew exactly where they were headed. They just knew there was a good chance they may never see Rile again. Sir Allendale lagged behind them and had since slipped all the way out of sight. They could see he was trying to hide their trail. It had just gotten so dark, they could no longer see him bobbing up and down in the tall grass.

"What's he doing?" Titus asked Amanda. As they followed Jarius, he leaped from one foot to the other as he moved through the tall grass. Not using the entire sole of his foot, Jarius lightly bounced from one step to another. He was so adept at this strange movement that he commonly had to slow down or stop to wait for the others.

Amanda said, "I don't know, but I think I'll try it. He moves pretty quick like that." Amanda then tried the same hopping lope that Jarius had been using. She was pleasantly surprised to find that she quickly grasped the technique. It did require more balance than running, but once she found a rhythm, she found herself able to almost keep pace with Jarius. This did not help Titus much. Seeing Amanda beginning to slip away into the darkness, he tried it too.

This loping was very awkward for Titus. Struggling to keep up, he landed wrong on a root cluster. Realizing he could easily roll his ankle, he allowed himself to fall to the ground. Jumping back up, Titus could barely see Amanda's silhouette loping away. Giving up on this new skipping technique, Titus took off running after them. Gradually they made their way through the grass field toward the forest.

Their backpacks were already a bit of a burden. Once Jarius explained that they would have a lengthy hike from the Key Tree to Hollywondra, they packed their backpacks with food. They also stuck a couple of other items in their backpacks they thought they might be useful in this foreign land. Right now, Titus was wishing he hadn't packed it as full as he did.

As they made their way to the edge of the tall grass, Jarius stopped to speak to the two of them. He told them to stay hidden in the grass until he can be sure there have not been any new trackers. Titus and Amanda enjoyed the rest while Jarius carefully examined the path and area surrounding his camp. When he came back, they entered the woods together. Once they reached the camp, Jarius said he needed to do a little more searching. He checked for tracks in concentric circles. Starting from the center of this camp, he circled the area to see if there was any evidence he had been followed by anyone else. By the time he was satisfied that nobody else had come into his camp, Sir Allendale had caught up to them. With a sense of accomplishment, he reported, "I'm a little out of practice, but you can be sure no human is going to be able to track us here."

For the first time, Titus realized that his pastor and the teenaged object of his affection were not human. He concluded they were the same race as Jarius. Titus was unclear what the differences were. He knew about the earlobes, but outside of that, he was puzzled. This also made Titus wonder how much he might stand out, if he did not have the same earlobes.

From his camp, Jarius led the party to the same burl-based pine tree that brought him to their land. Jarius began explaining the situation to everyone. He described what they had to do to effectively transport everyone through this Tree Gate. He was emphatic that they understand that they will very likely be attacked immediately as they arrive. Jarius reminded them that the goal of his entire mission was to bring Amanda back to Namron and to get her safely to Hollywondra. Jarius could not be specific about how she was the Ray of Light. He knew that, somehow, she played a role in what the Elvan kingdom needed. Once he delivered her to the priest in Hollywondra, the safety of the elves would somehow be secured.

Titus had always considered Amanda to be special. As he looked at the others in the party, he saw Sir Allendale looking at her with awe. It was not the awe of a parent enamored with their child. It was an awe of wonder. It was as if Allendale was just seeing Amanda for the first time.

Jarius went into great detail on how they should pass through the Tree Key. He explained the blinding light and how that can put you at a disadvantage. The detail included the order they would pass and the ways that they should arrive ready. He only wanted to ensure everyone came out the other side and didn't stumble over each other. Amanda and Titus looked at each other. Jarius's words reinforced his warning for how deadly this new world would be.

Before Jarius engaged the key, Titus wanted to get some facts straight. The notion of jumping through time and space to a place where he was almost certain to be under attack had him frightened. He had a good mind, but his fighting skills did not even exist. "What should I do?" Titus asked.

As if they were realizing for the first time, everyone recognized that Titus was not physically equipped to be any form of asset in this quest. Amanda walked to him. Quietly, she reached out and touched Titus on the chest and said, "Titus, you have always been so good to me. I know you would do anything for me. I can see the love in your eyes. Know that I too love you. It may not be in the same way you feel for me, but there is no mistaking that I truly do love you. I do not want harm to come to you. I don't think I could live with myself if I were responsible for you being hurt on my behalf. Please…don't come. Stay here. Answer questions for us. You are so brilliant. You could spin a yarn the whole town would believe. But please, don't follow us. I am afraid you will be hurt or killed."

Looking deeply into Amanda's eyes, Titus could see her sincerity. He also knew that she was right. She did not love him the way he loved her. He could not let her go knowing that she could be in harm's way. If he were not present to stop anything from happening, his life would lose meaning. Letting her walk away now made his life meaningless. She was all he looked forward to in each day. The ignorance of most of the ranchers only gave him distain for this small town. Sure, he loved his dad and his brother, but he wasn't so sure they would miss him if he was gone. In his mind, there was no choice. He knew he had to go with her. He also had to find his role in serving this party.

Titus mustered as much nerve as he had ever displayed and spoke to the entire party. "I know I do not present a physical threat to anyone or much of anything. What I do have is the ability to learn things quickly and apply that knowledge. I believe I can quickly learn how things work in this new world and be of service to this team." Turning to Amanda, Titus told her directly, "I can't let you walk away. I could never let anything happen to you. Worse, would be living the rest of my years wondering whatever became of you. I'd rather spend the next hour of my life protecting you than to spend the next fifty years dreaming of what could have been. I am coming with you. Even if this means the end of my life, I am ready to sacrifice myself just to be at your side."

Titus was shocked when Amanda leaned forward and kissed his cheek. As quickly as she had done that, she turned to Jarius and coolly stated, "We should go."

Jarius explained how anyone guarding the other side of this teleport will have very little warning that they are coming through. "By the time I come through, they will be jumping to alert. That's why I should be followed by Sir Allendale. Amanda should follow Allendale, and then Titus should be last. Whoever's guarding the door will probably not expect to see four of us coming through.

"Which do you prefer, Sir Allendale?" Jarius offered his bow while looking at the short sword Allendale wore on his hip.

"If you truly don't mind," Allendale said as he took the bow and arrows. He slung the quiver over his left shoulder. Then taking an arrow, he lightly nocked it in his bow and held it in place with his right hand.

Jarius pulled the Tree Key from his pack and began examining the burled base of the pine tree. Then Amanda suddenly broke out of the line. Jarius stopped and watched her as she jumped over to a bush. There she found a long wooden shaft. Rapping it against the trunk of a tree with a *crack*, she smiled. "It's not much, but it'll do in a pinch."

"You cannot break rank!" Jarius stated sternly. "Once this key is engaged, there will be no coming back. We have to be in physical contact with one another. Sir Allendale, certainly you know this?" Jarius asked.

Sir Allendale simply nodded. The nod was as much agreeing with him as it was suggesting he was ready. Everyone in the line held tight, so there could be no gap in their chain of connection.

Jarius found the niche where the Tree Key fit. Looking back at his team one last time, he nodded. As they all nodded back at him, he clicked the Tree Key into place. The familiar green luminescent glow began to grow from the key and up his arm. Titus watched from the back of the line. Amazed at what he saw, the green glow suddenly became a blindingly bright green flash.

22

A bony black finger made another deep scratch into the soft piece of leather. Then the finger tapped slowly back over the scratches to count a total. The fingernails made it easy to be exact. They grew to a thick sharp point, more like a claw than a fingernail. The Kobold captain then turned to address Sythene. Looking up at the human magician, the Kobold captain said with suspicion, "I count exactly one hundred. How strange that you caught exactly one hundred elves."

Leaning into the face of the Kobold captain, Sythene whispered, "I see that you understand, captain. That is why you are a natural leader." With his thick praise and a smile, he added, "You know there is more where these came from."

The Kobold captain's sneer revealed filthy jagged teeth, more suited for tearing flesh than mustering a smile. The captain's eyes trailed over to the captured elves. Then he paused to wipe drool from corner of his mouth with the sleeve of his tattered tunic. Giving Sythene one last look, he turned and ran up a rocky slope to where a group of Kobold elite awaited his report. There he handed the piece of leather to what appeared to be the leader of this Kobold clan. They began to chatter in a language that Sythene could barely understand. Kobold language was crude and simple. Their mouths were not made for clear speech.

After some pointing in the direction of the Elvan prisoners and choppy discussion, the captain turned from the Kobold king and made his way down the hill to confront Sythene. "You say you have the Elvan nation cornered and your victory is imminent. How many elves are we talking about?" The Kobold captain seemed excited about the possibility of so many elves at his disposal.

Sythene paused and smiled. "The rest of them. It is the last of them. That's right, you can tell your king that his reign can be one of Kobold legend. He will be known in Kobold history as the king who rid Namron Rae of the Elvan race." This suggestion brought what one could only imagine was a smile to the face of the Kobold captain.

Pausing for a moment to consider the magnitude of this allegiance, the Kobold captain replied, "Very well then. You tell Zel Camber we have an agreement. That is so long as we get all the elves, young, old, dead or alive. We want them all. No more holding back a few for your own personal desires." The captain spoke as if he were striking a carefully crafted deal.

"What level of support can we expect for so many elves?" Sythene asked.

"King Bantwable promises to send ten legions now and another twelve legions, once we are sure things are what you say they are. If you betray us, your entire human empire will be crushed by the Kobold hordes of King Bantwable."

Pausing, Sythene had to hold back his smile at the captain's empty threat. The Kobold horde would be a nice addition to Zel Camber's army, just for the sheer numbers they would bring to the ranks. They were no threat to Zel Camber's army. Zel Camber's Army was too large and mighty. Sythene found the threat amusing but still agreed that they had a deal. "You may tell King Bantwable to send his legions to the Crescent Crags. There they will find our army under the command of a man named Nictovius. He will tell your military how best to join the ranks." Sythene threw out a few exaggerated unsolicited compliments about Kobold wisdom and strength to seal the deal.

With the negotiations completed, Sythene stepped to a flat piece of ground. Turning to a sergeant of Zel Cambers army, he explained, "This regiment is now in your command. I am sure Zel Camber would like you back to the Crags yesterday. Do not dawdle." The newly assigned leader, rigid with pride, nodded sharply.

HOLLYWONDRA

As the sergeant turned and began barking orders at the men, Sythene took his staff and began drawing in the dirt. He first drew two circles around the place he was standing, one circle inside the other. Using the butt of his staff, he quickly scrawled magical runes inside the two rings he had just made. After completing his runes, Sythene took one last look at his surroundings, pulled his staff to his side, and began an incantation.

The Kobold guard ignored the magician and began surrounding the ranks of Elvan captives. Many of the elves were wounded and tattered, yet the caution the Kobold took in closing in on them showed a high degree of respect for their ancient foe. A ring of no less than five hundred Kobold encircled the unarmed Elvan captives.

The elves were bound by twine at their wrists. A thin iron wire was woven into the twine and ran from one captive to the other. The Elvan aversion to iron had made them move carefully. Now with this small army of Kobold closing on them with their short spears, they knew their chances for being released were gone. Elvan flesh was a Kobold delicacy.

The elves began to struggle. As their movement caused the iron to slap and burn others, those who were burned jumped and caused more chaos. Some of the elves knew their only chance was to break free and fight for their life. A couple of those who had been wrestling with their bindings were able to break loose in time to meet the closing ranks of Kobold spears. A few elves were able to fight back. But they were entirely overwhelmed by the sheer number of Kobold.

Sythene could not care less. His last view of the conflict was blocked out as he began to focus on his spell. As he began quietly murmuring, the rings he'd drawn into the dirt began to glow a faint purple. Suddenly, the deep purple glow turned into a bright flash, and he was gone. A little cloud of dust settled where once stood the mage.

The bright purple flash and the priest's sudden disappearance startled those Kobold who were not attending to the elves. The Kobold captain who had been negotiating with Sythene ran up the hill, as if to join his king. There he turned to watch the last of the elves fall under the swarm of Kobold spears.

The human guards, who had escorted the Elvan captives, tried to remain calm. The chaos of the riotous Kobold and screaming elves was unnerving. Some of the men had to simply turn away from the slaughter; others busied themselves by preparing themselves for their march back to the Crescent Crags.

*****

Not a moment was being wasted. The women and children of Hollywondra had been making arrows for days. The Elvan archers were using arrows faster than they could be made. Each day the elves would launch attacks on Zel Camber's army. They knew they were inflicting damage, but the sheer size of the Zel Camber's army was so large that they felt ineffective. When the elves were not launching their own assaults, they were defending their sacred forest from the assaults launched by the army. The humans had no regard for the treasure this ancient forest was to Namron Rae. Their efforts to stop the fires were every bit as exhausting as the combat.

"We do that every night!" complained Hamman Drew. "I'm sure we kill fifty to a hundred of them every night. They have thousands! At this rate, we better hope they plan to stay camped there a long time." Hamman Drew's words seared into the minds of the elves planning their next attack. They knew their efforts were futile. They did not need a human to remind them of it. His words left an awkward silence around the table. Hamman Drew knew he had angered them, and now they were waiting for him to offer a better scenario. He had none.

The only reason the elves had been successful in holding off the humans as long as they had was because of their ability to move so deftly through the night. They were able to sneak into the camp and cause enough mischief that delayed the strategies that humans had been designing. That also provided them with information about plans the humans were making for future assaults. The problem was their reconnaissance had brought back troubling news.

If what they had heard was true, this human army was about to double in size. The information suggested that Zel Camber had recruited another twenty thousand men, and they were expected within the next two weeks. There was also a rumor that Zel Camber had enlisted the support of the Kobold nation. If that was the true, that alliance could bring another fifty thousand beasts into the valley.

"We need some help!" Hamman Drew suggested. "I don't know if this is Elvin pride or your inability to count, but if we don't get some allies to support us, we are all going to be a memory in some bard's song."

"Who do you suggest we enlist?" Barrick snapped. "It doesn't appear much of Namron Rae cares that we parish. Maybe if we all assemble and cry help, someone might come save us," he stated in sarcastic frustration. Turning his gaze away from Hamman Drew, he looked back at the map they had on the table.

"I know not all humans share this same passion to destroy us. If we could find a nation that was willing to rise up and support us, then we might be able to offset their numbers," suggested one of the elves.

"Enough!" shouted Sir Bracanthorpe. "We know our hope rests solely in the coming of the Light. That is our legend. That is our future. We cannot be distracted by false hopes offered by humans." Barrick shot a glance at Hamman Drew that was very cold. Hamman Drew knew that he was treading on thin ice. He was the only human in a city being attacked by humans. He was bright enough to know when to shut up.

The conversation returned to a strategy in which they used the Scurriers to move quickly around the perimeter for the human camp, launching random attacks. The attacks were designed to come from the back side of the human camp. They hoped to raise fears that the Elvan army had allies that might have them surrounded. This plan had several problems. The use of the Scurriers was only a hope that they might raise fear in the ranks of the army. In doing this, they would risk spreading their ranks too thin. If they failed, then their forces could be severely damaged.

Most recently, Zel Camber's camp had set some net traps on their perimeter. Those traps had snared several of the Scurriers. The result was the loss of nine Scurriers and their armed escorts. This plan just seemed too risky for the reward they hoped to generate.

"What about their water sources?" Hamman Drew offered. This caused Sir Bracanthorpe to pause. Looking at Hamman Drew, he waited for his explanation. "Well, I was just thinking. They have to be drinking water from the streams that pour into the valley. Maybe there is some way that we could…alter the water quality?" he suggested carefully. The elves were attuned to nature. The notion of poisoning anything was heinous. Hamman Drew knew better than to suggest that…explicitly.

"What are you suggesting?" Sir Bracanthorpe sternly demanded. "Are you suggesting we poison the human and poison our land?"

Hamman Drew could tell that this idea appalled Bracanthorpe and maybe the sense of elves in general. He changed his thinking slightly and offered, "Not the streams, but maybe where they store their water in their camp? You can't be entirely against poisoning them, you poisoned the Klofgar."

"Klofgar are an abomination," Bracanthorpe stated firmly. "They are the creation of an evil wizard. They are not fruit of Namron Rae. They have no right to live. We have a responsibility to kill them in any way we can."

"The same goes for the Kobold," Barrack added. "They are not creatures of nature. What kind of a beast eats its own?" he stated with absolute disgust.

Grasping the Elvan thinking for the first time, Hamman Drew came up with a new idea. "Well then, what if we dammed the creeks that ran into the valley? They have to be getting water from somewhere?" They have a lot of mouths to feed and drink. This caused the group to pause and consider.

"If we did it far enough upstream, we could work out of harm's way," suggested Barrack. "There are three major streams that flow into valley. If we set up guard posts to ambush anyone who comes to scout out the problems, we could even reduce their numbers further."

The conversation took a turn as they made plans to alter the camps water sources to their strategies. Sir Bracanthorpe gave Hamman Drew an appreciative nod as their brainstorming began to evolve into a plan. Drew felt that maybe his contributions might be seen as authentic, and he need not worry that they might take his life at any time.

23

Jarius considered the lay of the land at the base of the Key Tree. Recalling that the tree rested on a slight slope, he tucked his head and rolled into this forest he knew so well. Rolling down the slight incline, Jarius quickly jumped to his feet and drew his sword. The magical flash that came from this teleportation temporarily blinded him. It was night in Namron Rae, and as his eyes began to adjust, the Tree Gate exploded with the familiar magical green light. Tumbling out of the tree came Sir Allendale. Much like Jarius, Allendale rolled as he came through the Tree Gate.

Jarius stepped aside to make room for Sir Allendale as he rolled away from the tree. Allendale came to a quick stop on one knee next to where Jarius stood ready. Just as Jarius saw Allendale balance himself, an arrow flew between them and into the dark. There was no way he could have seen the arrow. His eyes were still adjusting. From shear instinct, Sir Allendale quickly drew back the arrow he had readied in his bow.

Then came another flash of light from the trunk of the tree. Amanda appeared standing at the base of the Tree Gate. She used one hand to steady herself as she arrived on the uneven terrain. Steadying herself with staff in her right hand, she paused to survey this new location, totally unaware her party was already under attack. As her eyes adjusted, she realized how this area of the woods was not fully embraced by the dark of night. This area had been partially illuminated by a perimeter of torches. The torches been placed in a wide perimeter that surrounded the Tree Gate. Many of the torches were placed high in the trees so that they could cast the greatest possible light on the area around the Tree Gate. Their placement up in the trees resulted in the torches not being well maintained. Most of them were only partially ablaze.

Amanda was in awe at the size of the tree from which she appeared. Then it occurred to her that this area was illuminated by torches for a reason. Standing in this light is probably a bad idea. Amanda deftly stepped to her left and into the shade of the Tree Gate, just as Titus came through the gate.

Had Amanda pulled her staff a little quicker to hide behind the tree, Titus might have been killed. As he came through the Tree Gate, a chorus of bow strings thrummed. Arrows began to fly from all directions around the Tree Gate. Unsuspectingly, Titus stepped out from the green magical flash of the Tree Gate to immediately trip over the butt of Amanda's staff. Her staff caused Titus to trip and fall forward. Just as Titus fell forward, three arrows buried themselves into the bark of the mystical tree, right where Titus had entered this hostile new world.

The evasive moves taken by Jarius and Sir Allendale had mixed results. Jarius was lucky. His movement placed him at the dark edge of an archer's range of sight. The arrow intended for him hit a thick limb, glanced off the branch, and fell into the leaves of the forest floor at his feet. Sir Allendale was not so lucky. He was hit squarely in his left thigh by an arrow.

For the first time in several years, Allendale found himself experiencing the agonizing fire of an iron-tipped arrowhead buried deep into his thigh. His first instinct was to drop his bow and grab the shaft of the arrow. Instead, the wound ignited his fighting instinct and reflexes. He knew if he did not make a quick move, he'd have two or three more arrows in him. Allendale quickly hit the ground and crawled for the cover of a nearby tree.

The torchlight cast wildly unnatural shadows in the forest. The flickering light made it hard for Jarius and Sir Allendale to see into the darkness. They anticipated an ambush; they just did not know what it would be like. They thought returning in the dark of night might provide them some advantage. While the six torches illuminated most of the area, the light did not reveal the location of their attackers. Strangely, in the first salvo of arrows, two of the

HOLLYWONDRA

six torches had been knocked down and landed in the underbrush. Those torches hit the ground with enough force that the flames were busted into embers. The torchlight was reduced considerably after these two hit the forest floor.

Both torches fell from the side of the circle that Amanda had stepped toward. The sudden loss of light on her side of the tree supplied her even better cover. She took one careful step around the back of the Tree Gate trunk to conceal herself from the light and battle. There she hunkered down between the tree trunk and some brush. She peeked around the side of the tree; the brush provided her enough cover to survey the attack.

It all happened so fast. Even though they expected some kind of ambush, this method of attack and the speed of the assault still surprised them. Titus was unaware of any of it. He had stepped from the Tree Gate and immediately tripped face first into the loamy floor of the forest. He heard the sound of arrows hitting a tree. He just didn't know the sound he heard was arrows sticking in the wood where he had just been standing.

Concerned the others might laugh at his clumsiness, Titus tried to recover quickly. Scrambling around in the loose leaves, he jumped up and began to brush himself off. Looking for the others to ensure they were not making fun of him, Titus saw a torch hit the forest floor. When one flame burst into an explosion of sparks and embers, Titus could clearly see the silhouette of an archer standing between him and the dying light. The archer quickly notched an arrow and spun to aim at Titus. Startled to think someone would shoot an arrow at him, his instinct still made him quickly drop to the ground.

The illumination of that archer gave Sir Allendale a perfect target. He quickly buried his arrow into the chest of the archer shooting at Titus. Unfortunately, the arrow did not strike him before he shot his last. Sir Allendale's arrow struck the archer in the right upper chest and buried itself deep with a loud thump. Allendale wasn't sure if he had seen things correctly, because he thought he had seen another arrow strike the archer at the same time. But that arrow looked to have lodged in the left side of the archer. That made no sense, but he did not spend a moment dwelling on it.

Jarius knew his sword was no good from a distance, so he quickly got down and slipped into the shadows. He knew where the arrows had come from. Looking in that direction, Jarius was able to make out some movement in the shadows. He could not be sure who or what he was looking at. He just knew they were not members of his party. Jarius quickly looked around to see if everyone had come through the gate safely. Sir Allendale was exchanging arrows in combat. Titus had dropped to the ground take cover. But where was Amanda?

Out of the shuffle of leaves and loam came a sudden cry of alarm. It was human voices crying out for help and reinforcements. The cry was quickly cut short with what Jarius could only imagine as a well-placed shot by Sir Allendale. As quickly as the alarm began, it ended.

Now that he was beyond the perimeter of light, Jarius moved into position to the attack. He began weaving his way through the shrubbery, toward the shadows of the archers. Arrows rattled through low hanging branches in an attempt to find his heart. They were shots of desperation, because they were fired into such deep brush. Jarius could tell the archers struggled to see him by how badly they were missing him.

Sir Allendale went immediately into a rolling attack maneuver taught to the youngest of elves. It teaches them to roll on the shoulder they will pull their arrow with. This allows them to keep their bow arm straight and steady. Coming out of the roll, the warrior need only string the arrow, because the bow is ready. Favoring the side that had already been hit, Allendale tucked and rolled. Coming out of his first roll, he was able to find a target and hit it solidly. Sir Allendale's pride almost killed him. Rather than tucking immediately into another roll, he hesitated to admire his shot. This time an arrow hit him in his left shoulder, the same shoulder he used to steady his bow. The arrow struck hard. The arrowhead drove to the shoulder's bone.

Surveying her surroundings, Amanda knew they were being attacked. She just wasn't sure how she would be any help with her stick. As she pondered what she could do, she caught sight of three

HOLLYWONDRA

humans carrying long swords sneaking up on the fight from her heavily shadowed side of the tree. She wasn't sure if they had seen her. She didn't think they could, since they were looking directly into the fire and the fight. She was still concealed in the shadows.

They carried their swords low as they approached the conflict. They were not ready for her attack. As they got within five feet of Amanda, she jumped at the nearest one and shoved the butt of her staff into his stomach. His ribs made a loud crack. The man dropped his sword and fell straight to the ground on his knees. The other two did not have a chance to react before Amanda pulled back her staff and swung it in a large overhead arch. Her shaft came down sharply on the back of another man's head. He stiffened and then fell limp into the darkness of the underbrush. The third man was not so easy. He had turned to find his attacker. With his sword drawn, he carefully closed on Amanda.

Titus had crawled to the base of a large bush. From there he could see Allendale was horribly wounded. Arrows seemed to be flying from all directions. Titus couldn't be sure any of them were meant for him. Strangely, more torches had fallen from trees. It was as if the trees were spitting them out. Soon, all the torches had fallen. The only remaining light came from the smoldering embers dying on the moist forest floor. As he looked around, he could not find Jarius or Amanda. All he could hear was the sounds of fighting and the screams that accompanied only the most severe wounds. Unsure of how he could help, Titus held tight to the base of the shrub and watched carefully.

The light had died down considerably. All Titus could really see was shadows jostling in the glow. Some had swords and others had bows. Titus could only make out Allendale. Allendale was trying to fend off attackers. He watched as Allendale struggled to steady his bow to shoot. Then Titus noticed two armed men approach the other side of his bush. After pausing, they started closing in on Allendale from his blind side. Titus knew Allendale would not see them coming. They used the shadow of a large tree to hide their approach. Titus knew he could not stand by and watch Sir Allendale butchered. He also knew he had no way to help him. While trying to figure out what he could do, his time had simply run out. Titus shouted a warning at the top of his lungs. "Allendale! Behind you!"

The two men lunged out from behind the tree before Allendale could fully spin around. The first sword strike Allendale was able to partially block with his bow. Unfortunately, the blow ran down the bow shaft and severely slashed the back of Allendale's left hand, causing him to drop his bow. With his shoulder already almost useless, Allendale looked up into the eyes of his attackers. As the man who hit him drew back to deliver a fatal blow, an arrow struck him in the center of his neck at his Adam's apple. He quickly dropped his sword and fell to his knees, grabbing at the arrow shaft. The man who was right behind him heartlessly shoved him out of the way so he could attack. Allendale grabbed his bow and held it up. The frame of the bow was his only defense. Stepping forward, the man's blow came down on Allendale's bow, snapping it in half. Fortunately, the blow was not strong enough to break the bow and reach Allendale.

With no way to protect himself, Allendale could only hope to dodge his next attack. The man quickly pulled his sword overhead and closed in on the couching Allendale. Trying to anticipate the man's next move, Allendale was surprised when the man stiffened and fell toward him. Unsure if this was just an unorthodox attack, Allendale rolled away from the falling man. His attacker landed face-down next to him. Three arrows were grouped in his back as if they had come from a single bow. Puzzled by the arrows in the back of his attacker, Sir Allendale would not hesitate again. He quickly picked up the man's long sword and began to launch another attack at an enemy who just came into view.

Jarius had made short work of the first two human swordsmen he encountered. It was almost as if they did not know who or what they were up against. His next opponent was much more skilled. Jarius and this man fought in the glimmer of a few small flames that had sprouted up from nearby embers. This man was a serious challenge for Jarius.

By yelling his warning to Allendale, Titus had revealed himself. Now two swordsmen were closing on him. Titus quickly looked around, hoping to find a way to protect himself or hide. All he knew was that he wished he could not be seen. It wasn't as if he didn't want to be here. His words to Amanda were his truth. He just wished he couldn't be seen. He knew couldn't do anything to help. Terrified by the warriors striding toward him, Titus simply froze. Standing absolutely still, Titus looked directly into the fierce resolve of his enemy. Titus saw the swordsmen looking directly at him and then suddenly past him. It was as if they saw someone behind him. Titus could not take his eyes off his attackers as they approached. Then the swordsmen stopped and began quickly looking around, as if they couldn't find him.

"He was right here! You saw him, right?" one of the fighters said to the other. "You heard him shout the alarm?" he began to question.

The other fighter offered the only explanation he could manage. "Who knows what sorcery we are up against? He's clearly not here now." That fighter turned and started to move toward the fray.

Titus could feel the hair on the back of his neck standing straight up. His fingers tingled. The fact that they could not see him while they were less than ten feet away was something he was willing to accept. He didn't understand it, but it resulted in one of the fighters walking away. As Titus stood still, he slowly looked down at his right arm. He could see the faint outline of his own arm. As he wondered how he was able to do this, the outline on the arm began to disappear and Titus began to reappear. Startled to see himself becoming more visible, Titus tried to concentrate on just not "being there." His arm disappeared again.

The second warrior wasn't so easily convinced that nobody was there. He began to randomly swing his sword back and forth as he got closer to where Titus stood. Eventually, Titus would have to move out of his way or be hit. Titus was afraid that if he moved, he might reappear and then this man would kill him. Titus also knew the guy was going to kill him if he didn't move.

Titus tried to mimic the same emotion he used when he wished he was not visible. He knew when he began to let that slip away, he began to reappear. He also had a sensation that made the hair on the back of his neck stand up. Realizing he would be killed helped Titus focus on his need to be invisible. Slowly stepping to one side and out of the arched path of the man's wild swings, Titus was able to slowly step out of the way.

Soon the man found himself in the bush Titus had been using for cover. Realizing he was wildly swinging at nothing, the man paused, then turned around to search for his next attack. In that moment, his options were stolen from him by three arrows that diving squarely into his chest. Looking down at the arrows, Titus saw confusion in the eyes of this dying man.

Titus quickly realized the arrows that struck the man all came at an angle that suggested they were not fired from ground level. Not risking a move, he stood still to search the branches above.

For most people using a stick to wage war on a steel blade might seem a disadvantage. Amanda was so comfortable with her weapon that she found herself able to keep her swordsman at bay. He tried talking her into surrender, but she knew better. She felt a very strong sense of evil from this man. The sinister dark kind of evil most people don't understand. You only know it has to exist for so many evil things to be wrong in the world. Somehow, this man had more than his fair share of wrongdoing.

Amanda explained to him calmly, "I believe I may need to kill you."

The soft tone coming from the face of a young girl so skilled with a staff made her attacker wonder what he was doing. Her words only caused him to increase the speed of his assault. Amanda was able to easily deflect his blows and countered his attack by rapping him on the back of his neck as he parried past.

Turning and pausing beyond the reach of her staff, he surveyed the situation as best he could. She was very skilled to have blocked all his blows. The sounds of fighting were lessening, but there wasn't any celebratory yelling. He knew what this meant. If his gang had been successful, they would be here rooting him on. It dawned on him that he could possibly be the last remaining member of his attack party. He refused to let that cloud his mind. He made a couple of light lunges Amanda was able to easily deflect.

He figured his only chance was in his experience as a fighter. So suddenly he yelled, "Get her!" and pointed at her with his sword.

HOLLYWONDRA

Amanda fell for the ploy and gave a quick glance over her shoulder. That was all the time the man needed to make his move. As her eyes left him, he turned and ran as fast as he could. Jumping over brush and ducking under bows, he rushed into the darkness of the forest.

Realizing her foolishness, Amanda dropped her head in temporary shame. She made no effort to follow the man into the darkness. She only wanted to make sure everyone else as safe. She came around the trunk of the Tree Gate to see the forest floor was ablaze. She could see people trying to stomp out the fire, but there was no fighting.

"Amanda! Over here!" Jarius yelled. She was able to make out a couple of people in the distance. One seemed to be kneeling down next to the other. As she arrived, she found Jarius examining the wounds of Sir Allendale. Amanda could see Allendale had two arrows in him and his hand was bleeding badly. She still could only look at him for a moment, as her eyes kept being drawn to two unknown elves stomping out the fires.

"They are friends," Jarius whispered with a smile. That very statement suddenly made sense of everything.

Quickly looking around, she asked, "Where's Titus?"

"I don't know. The last time I saw him, he fell as he exited the gate. Then I saw him crawl under a bush," Jarius explained as he pointed behind her.

"Would you make sure he's okay? I will tend to my father," she asked.

Allendale corrected her with a serious tone and a strained smile. "That's Sir Allendale to you." Allendale looked up at the young lady he had raised as his own. Lying in pain on the ground, Allendale took in a deep breath. It had been years since Allendale had smelled the crystal clean air of Namron Rae. These woods felt remarkably familiar to him. Even though he was laying wounded on the ground, he felt a sense of accomplishment. After years of posing as a peaceful minister, he had returned his charge to Namron Rae.

Jarius went to look for Titus.

Even though silence had come to the forest and the fight appeared to be over, Titus wasn't confident he was safe. He could not make out all the shadowy figures. There were clearly more than his three companions. He was certain he had seen Amanda walking toward some flames. She seemed safe, so Titus turned to move in her direction. Then he saw a figure carrying a sword coming toward him. He froze and concentrated on not being visible as Jarius walked past him. The glow of the fire was the only light. Jarius's face was covered in shadows. Titus was able to tell it was Jarius he had walked past him.

After passing Titus, Jarius suddenly stopped. Titus didn't know what it was about Jarius, he was his friend, but he knew this friend was a trained killer. If he didn't let him know who and where he was, what Titus thought a joke might be his last. Wishing Jarius could see him, Titus appeared saying, "It's me, Jarius. Don't strike."

Jarius spun quickly with his sword ready. He was easily able to stop himself, but he was a little bewildered. "How did you do that?' he asked.

Titus shrugged and said, "I dunno. I just wished I wasn't in the middle of this fight, and then suddenly I vanished."

Dropping his sword, Jarius looked at Titus with a new respect. "Well, we'll will have to talk about this."

24

Hamman Drew reflected on how he had become a part of this patrol of elves skirting the Zel Camber army. The trek was not an easy one. Just the small change in elevation resulted in the group marching through about six inches of snow. They made their way up the rugged slopes in a single file line to avoid detection from the army sentries. The woven baskets of quivers carried by the men made their climb even more challenging. This crew of twenty elves had some large tasks ahead of them. Hamman Drew knew the plan but could not comprehend how this small troop was going to accomplish all that work. As he looked at the crew he walked with, he knew a few of these elves from battle. It made him wonder if this mission wasn't just an effort to just get him out of the way. He wondered how large of a burden he may have become.

While Hamman Drew had been working with these elves for the past few weeks, he still struggled to read their emotions. He knew he was being tolerated. He just wasn't sure why or for how long. Drew knew he was trapped. Working with the elves was his only option. He felt as though the elves knew it and were only biding their time with him.

The group moved quietly through the late afternoon light. The easiest terrain was behind them. They knew they were going to have to climb some very steep slopes in the dead of night, if they were going to move undetected. In daylight, they could possibly be seen. Their only hope was to do this in the dark of night.

By midnight, they had reached the end of what had appeared to be a rugged deer trail. The trail opened into a clearing that exposed them to the muted moonlight. Stepping carefully out into the open, the line continued forward for another hundred yards before their trail ended abruptly at the ledge of a cliff. There was not enough moonlight to show a safe way around or down the cliff face. As Hamman Drew eased up to the edge, his stomach sank a when all he could see below was darkness.

As the rest of the party arrived at this location, the two perimeter scouts caught up and joined the group. One of the scouts turned to look around the area. After making his way through the group, he began to backtrack and wander around the area, as if he were looking for something he had lost. Following the ledge, he walked off into the darkness.

Even in this moonlight, Hamman Drew felt very exposed as he stood out on this promontory point. It didn't help that he stood almost a foot taller than anyone else in this party. To reduce his exposure, Hamman Drew took a knee and wondered if these elves even knew where they were. He had hardly rested when the party began to move off in the direction the scout had gone. Without making a sound, they all moved off in unison.

Hamman Drew followed them down a gentle slope for about thirty yards where they found the scout tying a rope to the base of a small lone pine. Walking to the ledge, the scout took the rest of the rope to toss over the side. He walked along the edge looking for a target. After taking a few steps to his right, the elf stopped then threw the rope as far into the darkest as his strength would allow. Tugging on the rope, the scout explained they could descend one person at a time. The rope would get them to another ledge below. Everyone would wait there until all had been able to safely descend.

Then turning to Hamman Drew, the scout said, "You must go last. We cannot be certain how well this tree will sustain your weight. If you went first…well, you seem intelligent enough to understand how that could set us back." The elf spoke without emotion. It was a simple matter of fact. If someone died descending, then they'd have to try something else. Sending the largest person down first might entirely damage their chances of using this route.

The elves seemed to negotiate the descent into darkness without any trouble. Finally, Hamman Drew found himself alone on the dark

HOLLYWONDRA

mountaintop. The rope had gone limp from the last elf descending. The rope jumped, as a signal that the last climber had safely arrived, and it was finally his turn.

The little pine tree had been a great companion in this task. It stood fairly strong through the various climbers. Not that the task didn't take a toll. The tree now listed slightly toward the cliff. Hamman Drew considered his options. He could grab hold of this risky looking rope and descend down to this troop, or he could take this opportunity to make a run for it. If he just took off down the slope, he could cover a lot of ground before they came looking for him. Then he wondered, if they would even bother looking.

Finally determining that he really had nowhere else to go and that he ran the risk of encountering Zel Camber troops, he picked up the rope and carefully tested the tree. As he leaned back with the rope, it looked like the little pine should hold on to let him descend. Moving to the edge of the cliff, Hamman Drew tried to move slowly over the side. He tried his best to not jar the tree with his sudden weight. As he slipped off the edge, the rope pulled tight with his weight. A smile only Hamman Drew could feel came over him. He realized he had been holding his breath. Dangling an unknown height off the ground, Hamman slowly descended one hand over the other.

Repelling straight down the face of the cliff, Hamman Drew began to worry about how much rope he had left. He could faintly see the cliff above him as a shadowy edge against the starry sky. When he looked down, all he could see was the blackness. He was growing worried that he might run out of rope, when a couple of hands gently grabbed his ankles to let him know he was nearing the landing. The shadow from the face of this cliff made things even harder to see.

As his eyes adjusted, he wondered why one of the elves came over to the rope and gave it the tug to signal safe arrival. He was sure he was the last to climb down. Sure enough, two Elvan archers were the last to descend. One of them he recognized as Brighton Scarlet. Suddenly, Hamman Drew did not feel very trusted.

From this landing, the trail was easy to find. It was rocky and slow, but after about a mile of descent, they entered a forest line.

They did not have to travel far into the forest, before the gentle roar of a waterfall could be heard. The group marched directly toward the sound. The descent was enough that they no longer walked in snow. Emerging from the tree line, they found themselves on mist-covered rocks below a small waterfall.

What little moonlight they had glimmered off the large pond that had formed at the base of these small waterfalls. As they walked away from the falls, they found that the pond had a partially built beaver dam that had caused the pond to form. The dam had been ransacked. The damage to the dam had created a stream of water that was significant. This was their first task: to somehow plug this gap and close off this water source. Looking at the size of this breech and the stands of timber, Hamman Drew began to wonder how they were going to pull this off. He knew the elves were not going to be chopping down trees, yet that gap would take a family of beavers a generation to plug.

One of the elves started whispering orders. The others began to gather large and small branches from the forest floor. Hamman Drew began wondering how they planned to place this debris in the gap. The elves pulled the branches and sticks to the water's edge. After dropping off what they had found, they went back for more.

Hamman wasn't entirely sure what the plan was, he just wanted to help speed things up. He had just dragged one of the largest of logs to the edge of the water when he noticed three of the elves were not helping. Instead, they stood at the water's edge looking out into the pond. This somewhat angered Hamman Drew. He knew they could be doing more if everyone helped. Just before he interrupted them, he noticed that they all appeared to be praying or chanting something at the pond.

Respecting their need to pray, Hamman Drew stopped himself and went back to gathering wood. When he returned to the bank with more branches, he noticed the calm surface of the pond was disturbed by small ripples. The ripples were moving toward them. The elves seemed to be calling beavers to their shore. He couldn't believe his eyes, so he paused and watched as the beavers took the wood from the shore.

HOLLYWONDRA

Pulling the chunks of wood into the water, they dragged the wood to the dam. Some of the elves gently placed some of the larger pieces of wood in the water to make the beavers work a little easier. A small group of elves took fresh branches out onto the dam and wove them into small snags for the beavers. Hamman Drew was amazed to see how the elves worked so closely with the beavers. At his best guess, he figured there must have been almost a dozen beavers working with the elves to block this stream.

Soon, the elves started taking some of the larger broken pieces of tree fall and sticking them into the water at the dam's gap. As Hamman Drew watched, an elf came up and picked up the end of the large log he had dragged to the shore, waiting for Hamman Drew to grab the other end. Grabbing the log, they made their way carefully out onto the dam. They discussed how best to drop the log so that it did not destroy the work that was being done nor hurt the beavers at work. Finally, they set the log into place. This log crossed the entire span of the remaining hole. It would serve as a major support for their final branches.

The work went well into the morning. Everyone worked non-stop to rebuild the beaver's dam. At midmorning, Hamman Drew had stepped off dam to throw some sticks into the pond. For the first time, he noticed how much they had actually accomplished. They had successfully slowed the flow of water by over 90 percent. There was now only a trickle where there once was a creek that fed the Valley of Shayna.

Feeling a sense of satisfaction, the group rested. The beavers did not seem satisfied with their work and continued to pull wood that had been gathered for them. The party discussed their next stop and how that job would be different than this one. They had to grab what rest they could so they could travel under the veil of nightfall. They also knew the other jobs were going to be a greater challenge, as they were going to have to leave a few archers behind to guard this dam. They knew with certainty that a patrol would come to open the dam again. They had to be ready to ambush Zel Camber's men. By the time they got to the last stream, they would be significantly shorthanded.

25

Biander's Bluff was an ancient fortress built on the face of a large stone mesa. The fortress was considered virtually impenetrable. The single largest entrance to this mountain fortress was from the top. The top of the mesa slowly sloped upward toward an entrance that was just yards before the cliff's face. Where most gates present a weak point on the perimeter of a fortress, this gate was different. To reach this gate, you had to first scale a three-hundred-foot rock face to reach the top of the mesa. The mesa's top served as an unwalled courtyard for stables, farming, fighter training, and a place for holding large ceremonies.

The halls of Biander's Bluff were dank and cold. The stone floor and walls gave the inhabitants security and a chill. Even when the summer heat was at its greatest, the halls of Biander's Bluff were still insulated and cool. The main halls were large enough to allow two mounted riders to easily ride side by side. The ceiling in these hallways were high enough that any rider could sit erect in his saddle. A large spiral staircase ran down the face of the fortress. The stairs were spaced wide enough that horses could navigate the climb or descent. The windows at the top of the spiral staircase were large and open-aired. They all framed the same picturesque southern landscape. The light coming through the windows easily lit the stairway. This ancient craftsmanship was not without wear. Hundreds of years of boots and horse hooves had worn down the stone.

The bottleneck was where the fortress met the valley floor. At the valley floor entrance, the hallways narrowed, and only one rider at a time could exit. This also meant only one rider at a time could enter. With such a small entry, it made assaults almost impossible. An

HOLLYWONDRA

entire army could die at the base of this fortress trying to get in while they were picked off by arrows or flaming oil from above.

The door to the valley floor was a double thick steel plated door inset in the bedrock. It had no hinge. A large counterweight was used to lift the door open. The rock face above the door was devoid of any significant window for the first hundred feet. The only windows were narrow archer portals from where archers could pick off anyone attacking the fortress. It's no wonder why history had never recorded a successful military assault on Biander's Bluff.

Sythene, the Arch-Mage of the Boar, stood before Zel Camber in his royal chamber atop Binder's Bluff. "They should arrive by the full moon."

Zel Camber sat on his padded throne of gold and black silk. The silk of his cloak matched that of his throne. It looked like the two were cut from the same bolt of fabric. Zel Camber was looking out a distant window as he considered the magician's report. Then turning toward the mage, he pulled back the hood of his cloak so he could look into Sythene's eyes. In a low slow voice. Zel Camber replied, "Good. We cannot afford any delays. My sources tell me the plight of the elves is beginning to fall on some sympathetic ears. We need to finish this before someone thinks saving those tree monkeys is a good idea."

Feeling as though his report satisfied his liege, Sythene bowed deeply and asked, "If I may be excused?"

Waiting until Zel Camber nodded his approval, Sythene slowly backed away. He backed himself all the way to the chamber entrance and backed out into the hallway. There he found himself standing between two of Zel Camber's royal guards. They didn't impress him. Sythene had more urgent tasks to attend. Making his way down the wide hallway, Sythene stepped quickly into the staircase to descended three floors.

After leaving the stairwell, Sythene immediately encountered a sextet of palace guards walking their patrol. The guards knew Sythene, so it was not in their best interest to question him. At the western end of the corridor, Sythene stopped in front of a large oak planked door. The oaks planks were held together with a steel frame and girded with thick strips of steel. If you looked carefully at the steel frame, you could see the entire door had magical runes etched into the door frame and lock. As Sythene approached his door, he cast a spell, and the magical runes that had encircled the door disappeared. He pulled a leather thong from under his tunic. At the end of the strap was a large iron key. Sythene gently inserted the key and unlocked the door. After closing the heavy oak door, Sythene used the key to lock the door and then tucked it safely back inside his tunic. He cast another spell on the inside of the door to further secure his room. He did not want to be disturbed by anyone.

Always untrusting, Sythene slowly looked around his room to see if anything was out of place. His room was simple. The few items he had in his room were covered in a thick coat of dust. Even his floor showed the only paths he regularly walked. His quarters did not have any windows. Each wall had a candelabrum. These provided enough light to satisfy his needs.

Once he felt everything was as he had left it, he walked to the stone wall opposite his door. Even though he was sure he was alone, he still glanced around his room one more time before casting a spell. The stone that had formed this impenetrable wall suddenly fell into a pile of small pebbles. Then Sythene stepped through the pile of rock to the other side. With a single word, the pebbles quickly regrouped into the rock wall they had always been.

Now Sythene felt safe. Here was his true sanctuary. He felt Zel Camber had no eyes or knowledge of this location. While the other room had a bed, this was where he felt safe to sleep and where he kept his most prized possessions. It was a large room with stone walls. Two candelabrums illuminated the space, though they sat on each end of a work bench. His work bench was a long wooden table pushed up against the western wall of this smaller chamber.

Sythene plucked a long dry sliver of wood from a small stack at the end of the table. He lit the sliver by placing it into the flame of a candle. Taking the fire, he lit two smaller candles that sat directly in front of his only stool at the table. Blowing it out, he tossed the smoldering twig on the table.

HOLLYWONDRA

Then he picked up a pipe. It looked like something he may have made himself. The stem of the pipe looked to have been made from a thin black bone. At the end of the stem, the bone went through the skull of a small creature. The head was about the size of a bat. The mouth of the creature was open, and some of the fangs were still intact. Sythene pulled a purple felt bag from across the table, extracted some herb, and loaded his pipe. Picking up the still smoldering sliver, he ignited it again and lit his pipe.

Three large tomes were stacked at the across the table from where he sat. He pulled the middle one out and drew it forward. Opening the large book, he was able to turn to almost the exact page he desired. Turning the final page, Sythene leaned over the book and gently caressed the page as he read it. There in the ancient Elvan script, Sythene read about the Mansuranthra's Rod of Might. A picture had been drawn from an eyewitness account. The art provided detail right down to gold leaf and where the various gems were mounted. The picture itself was a piece of art.

For days, Sythene had been trying to make sense of this one passage that stated this magical rod empowered the user to "deliver nature." What did that mean? Flora and fauna? Insects? Weather? Earth? To what extent did this rod give you power over nature? The boundaries of his imagination made time quickly pass. Sythene envisioned himself holding the rod in one hand and commanding the universe to do his bidding.

He knew the Rod of Mansuranthra held some kind of powers of persuasion over man and beast. Mansuranthra was a renowned Elvan cleric. Centuries ago, his power created natural domains for the elves that no man dared to enter. With the rod in his hands, Sythene knew he could rule all Namron Rae. Blowing a large billow of smoke, he allowed himself to ponder different ways he would kill Zel Camber with this newly acquired might.

As quickly as he had allowed himself to dream, he drew his attention back to his work. The following pages contained the story of an evil elf who had witnessed this very rod while visiting Hollywondra. The visitor spoke about how the rod had been temporarily displayed for a large religious celebration, only to be returned to some secret place of security inside a holy Elvan temple.

For the past two years, Sythene had let Zel Camber believe that he was afraid of him. Zel Camber was using Sythene and his powers to advance his cause on the elves. What Zel Camber did not know was that this was all a part of Sythene's plan to reach Hollywondra and have the Mansuranthra's Rod of Might for himself. He was confident Zel Camber did not even know of the rod or its powers. Sythene would play his part in Zel Camber's mission to destroy the elves. Zel Camber's goals cleared the way for Sythene to achieve his.

The next page in the book revealed a crude map of Hollywondra. Much like any treasure map, it only showed the most important landmarks. Hollywondra was so remote and inaccessible for anyone other than elves, there was never a way to verify the accuracy of this map. Sythene had to have poured over these pages a hundred times. He grew excited as he began to think how soon he might be able to walk the streets of Hollywondra. Sythene knew that Zel Camber's forces would soon crush the elves and give him the power to walk right into the Elvan Temple of Hollywondra. This map would help him identify the building he needed to enter to find this mighty Elvan artifact.

Taking a quill and a small piece of parchment, Sythene drafted a note. "Use this whistle to call this servant. When you give the servant the whistle back, he will return it to me. That will be my sign that you have finally defeated the elves, and I will come join your ranks. You will be rewarded beyond your greatest dreams for this service. Do not try to procure this magic without me. Tell no one of our agreement, or I will incinerate you with a slow burning holy fire." Taking what looked like a short wooden tube, Sythene twisted the piece of parchment until it fit snuggly inside the whistle. Checking it to make sure that it was snug, Sythene then made a shrill whistle.

From the dark end of his room, five large black bats flittered suddenly into his candlelight. Four of them moved quickly around the room and settled back into the dark end of the cavern. The fifth one flew directly a crude T-shaped perch at the end of table. The bat struggled to grasp the bar. When the bat had finally stopped flapping his wings, Sythene poked the whistle with its note at the claws of the

HOLLYWONDRA

bat. The bat grasped a hold of the whistle with one claw. Then while the bat fluttered its wings to sustain its balance, Sythene cast a spell over the large black bat.

When he was done, he was a little surprised to see the bat still hanging from its perch. Pausing to consider he might have said his incantation incorrectly, Sythene took a puff from his pipe, stood up, and shooed at the bat. The bat took off and flew away into the darkness of his room. Sythene knew the bat would fly through the cracks of the mountainside and into the night. The bat would follow his commands and take his note to his servant.

26

Taking a moment to reunite with his Elvan clansmen was a short-lived celebration. "It's good to see you, brother. Which way is their camp?" Jarius asked. One of them pointed to the southwest. Jarius recognized their camp to be directly between them and the King's Highway. The King's Highway would be the quickest way west to Hollywondra. It was also the most obvious route.

Realizing the elf had chosen to not respond verbally, Jarius whispered, "How many more are there?"

The same elf carefully flashed an open palm at Jarius five times.

Jarius took stock of his party. He saw Allendale's arrows had been removed and Amanda was praying over him. Titus and Amanda both came through the fight without a wound. Even with two seasoned Elvan archers, the odds of them defeating twenty-five armed men were pretty slim. He considered the advantage they might have if they were to surprise them. Even then, the risk was too high that they could lose Amanda in battle. He couldn't take the risk. Jarius suggested, "Well, at least we should have enough time to slip away before they post their next guard?"

Standing up from Allendale, Amanda added, "Uh, one of the guys I was fighting got away."

At the realization reinforcements could be returning any moment, the elves waved for them to follow them. Seeing Allendale struggle to his feet, Jarius checked, "Can you travel?" Allendale nodded his approval. Just that quickly, one elf took off to the east, the other elf fell back to hide their trail. Jarius stepped in behind the lead elf, followed by Amanda, Titus, and the Sir Allendale.

For the next few hours, they loped through the forest under-brush. The six of them pushed a hard pace through the night. Titus found himself struggling to keep pace. Just when he thought he would have to ask the group to rest, the group slowed to a walk. Then the lead scout held up a hand for the group to stop. While the rest of the group stood still, the elf slowly walked out into the open and up to the bank of a small creek. Kneeling down, the scout sipped creek water from the cup of his hand. Realizing it must be safe, Jarius joined the lead scout at the water's edge. Taking a drink of his own, he encouraged the others to get a drink. "It could be hours before we find another water source as cold and fresh."

The others went to the water's edge and began drinking. While they drank, the other scout stood watch. Jarius went and asked the scouts their names. "I am Palcombine, he is Ellerson." The elves both had long straight blonde hair. At first glance, their physical appearance could lead one to think they were related. Palcombine wore his hair back and in a braid. Ellerson let his hang loose. Nodding at Ellerson, Palcombine explained, "We serve under the command of Phillibus."

"I think it's safe for us to start moving to the north," Palcombine offered. "We should cross the creek and then lightly pepper our trail with some spice. They have dogs. I'm sure by now they are on the move. To the north, there are some shallows we could cross at. We can be sure they will be watching for us at Bierland's Ferry. Not too far from here, there's a little hamlet. There's a farmer there who owns some dogs. That could cause them a little more distraction."

Jarius simply nodded his approval and turned to walk back to where Amanda was talking with Titus. Amanda did not seem tired when compared to Titus. He was just getting his breath. As Jarius approached, he overheard Titus whispering to Amanda, "You know how many times I wished I could have disappeared while in school. My brother made me just miserable. Well, this time I was wishing I could disappear, and I did!"

Jarius watched Titus as he approached. Titus extended his right arm and seemed to glare at it. Nothing happened. Jarius asked, "What exactly did you do to conceal yourself during that fight?"

Titus thought about it, "Well...I was afraid for my life. I was wishing I was somewhere else." Then realizing it for the first time, he added, "Oh, and I closed my eyes."

"Closed your eyes?" Amanda asked.

"Yeah. I shut my eyes and squeezed them tight as I wished I'd just disappear. When I opened my eyes, I could tell they could not see me. I looked at my arms and could see them, but they appeared kind of blurry. Then I moved slowly to the side and out of their way," Titus added.

"Well?" Jarius asked. Amanda and Titus turned to look at Jarius wondering what he wanted. "Well, let's see if you can do it again. Who knows, this might be the one thing to help keep you alive in Namron Rae."

Titus was a bit discouraged that this new trick might be his only salvation. Then he reminded himself that he really didn't understand the dangers of this new land. So he held his arms out in front of himself and examined them with a glare as if his gaze would make him disappear. "Try closing your eyes," Amanda suggested. Titus closed his eyes and seemed to squeeze them tight.

The morning dew had made their toes numb. The moon had gone, and the glow of the early morning sun made the high branches black against the first light. The party was taking time to see if Titus could control what he had done. With his eyes closed, Titus concentrated. Suddenly, he began to blur in and out of sight. Then he opened his eyes.

"What are you doing?" Jarius asked. "When you tried it with your eyes closed, you started to disappear."

"I didn't disappear?" Titus asked with a surprised tone. "My arms looked like they had vanished."

"It looked like you were flickering in and out of visibility," Amanda added.

Titus closed his eyes again and began to concentrate. Quickly he began to blur again. This time he let himself flicker for several moments. Then Jarius got an idea.

Jarius moved slowly behind Titus while he continued to focus. Taking the hilt of the short sword, Jarius quickly pulled the sword from its sheath. Intentionally, Jarius pulled the blade against the sheath to maximize the sound of his weapon being drawn.

At that very moment, Titus disappeared.

"What do you think you're doing?" Titus's squealed as his voice seemed to come out of thin air.

Jarius smiled. Slowly inserting his sword back into his sheath, he explained, "I thought you could use some motivation."

After reappearing, Titus paused and then disappeared again. "I think I get it," Titus claimed. "It's a state of mind," he explained. Then Titus gave a wry smile he had meant only for himself. Titus wondered what other thoughts might have power in this realm.

Instinctively, the entire party stopped as Jarius raised his hand. Making their way through the forest in the morning light had just become a little more complicated. Standing behind Jarius, the party could see the forest give way to rolling plains of farmland. The party looked back over their shoulders toward the distant sound of hunting hounds. The idea of leaving the cover of the forest and rushing out into open daylight frightened them.

*****

Larimore's face was cold. It should be. It was the only part of his body that had not been covered by the thick pile of blankets that covered the bed. He knew with certainty his leather moccasins were going to be every bit as cold. He also knew the cow wasn't going to milk itself. Pausing just long enough to listen to his wife make a hardy snore and to soak in the warm comfort of his morning bed, Larimore pulled back his blankets and sat up on the side of his bed. His movement made his wife shuffle under her blankets. He knew he had chores to do before she rose.

Bending over to stoke the morning coals wasn't getting any easier for Larimore. Most of his days were behind him. Now it was a simple life he made for Maggie and himself. After Larimore bent over the coals and blew on them to ignite the kindling, he found himself having to stand upright to catch his breath. He chuckled at himself for being winded after such a simple chore. As the kindling caught fire and he began to lay wood upon the small flames, he found himself struggling to get a full breath again. As he stepped back from the hearth, he knew his wife would be pleased with the warmth the morning fire would bring the front room of their cottage.

Taking a moment to enjoy in the early morning fire, Larimore looked at the shield and sword that rested on the mantel of their fireplace. The shield was military. The coat of arms had two crossed longswords overlaying an oak tree. A long sword laid on the mantel in front of the shield. The rectangular shield stood tall over Larimore's fireplace as a daily reminder of the sacrifice his son had given the kingdom. For his death in battle, Larimore and Maggie had been given his shield and sword. Many mornings Larimore would stare at this artifact of his son's life and service, trying to make sense of his death. Larimore knew his only remaining purpose in life was to care for Maggie.

Enjoying the fresh flames of the fire, Larimore added a couple larger pieces of wood and turned to warm his backside. Grabbing his cloak from the back of a crude chair, Larimore flung the cloak over his shoulders and tied it at his neck. Sitting in the chair, he pulled on some filthy old stockings and then his moccasins.

Walking across the room toward the front door, Larimore paused. Much like many other mornings, he paused to wonder what this day might bring. Exhaling, he lifted the latch that secured the door from the inside. Stepping out onto a wooden deck he had built to keep from tracking mud into the house, he paused again, as if he were building momentum to start his day.

Larimore walked around the side of his cottage to where a manger provided his cow shelter from the elements. There he found her slowly chewing straw. The cow looked at Larimore and knew what was to come. She had grown accustomed to their morning ritual.

Larimore's cottage sat at the edge of the forest. The King's Highway ran past the front of his land, though it was still a couple hundred yards away. The gently rolling hills provided comfort and peace. It was seldom that Larimore saw any riders. It was even rarer to have guests. Not more than a rock's throw, a gentle creek flowed from the woods past the back of his cabin.

HOLLYWONDRA

Pulling up a three-legged stool and grabbing an old wooden pale, Larimore sat down to milk his cow. His old sheep dog came up to greet him and took his morning taste of the cow. The dog sat watching Larimore do his chores, as if inspecting his work. The dog really didn't have much else to do. When the sheep needed to be walked to a summer pasture, he'd get some exercise, but this cool lazy fall day was a good reason to sneak into the house and lay by the fire.

"What is it, Albert?" Larimore asked his dog as he stopped his milking. Albert had left his spot next to Larimore and trotted to the edge of the creek. There he stood, looking off into the distance. Raising his snout to the distance wood, Albert howled, as if he were speaking to a distant friend.

Albert sat facing the tree line. Larimore watched him for a moment and decided it must have been a muskrat in the creek that had drawn his attention. Larimore began to massage the cow's udder when he heard the distant bay of a hound. Albert returned the call. Larimore was unsure what that meant. It sounded like it was coming from the forest. The forest was deep and went for hundreds of leagues. Surely this had to be a lost dog Albert was calling to.

Even at that, Larimore could not sit by and find himself unprepared. Albert howled again. This time his howling brought Maggie from the door. Coming off the stoop and around the corner, Maggie called out to Larimore, "What is it?"

His first instinct was to just assure Maggie. Then he decided he'd best be safe. Untying the cow, he told Maggie to walk the cow into the house. "I'll get Albert. Close and secure the shutters." Larimore handed Maggie the rope to the cow, and she began to slowly walk the cow toward the door. Larimore turned to get Albert. As he came to the side of his dog, Albert stood and barked, the same sharp type of bark he made when one of the sheep strayed from the flock.

Looking up, Albert saw a small group of people running from the forest. It looked like a half dozen or so were racing from the cover of the tree line and toward his house. "Come on, Albert, now!" he commanded. Quickly Larimore and Albert raced into the house. They were slowed a little by Maggie and the indifferent cow. Neither of them understood the urgency.

167

Scooting past Maggie and the cow, Larimore went directly to the fireplace. There he pulled down the long sword. Maggie had never seen him pick up the sword but to dust it off. Maggie had known Larimore most of her life. She knew he was a farmer, not a fighter. She could tell by the look on his face, he was prepared to use the sword, if he had to. Dropping the rope to the cow, Maggie grabbed Larimore as he ran past her. Maggie began to shake frantically. She pleaded, "What are you doing, you silly old man? I can't lose you."

All Larimore had time to do was shoo Albert into the house while Maggie pleaded for him to "Lock the door and stay."

Stepping inside with his dog, Larimore assured Maggie, "Of course, I'm locking the door. There's at least six of them out there." Larimore quickly slammed the door shut and then secured it with a cross member of wood. "Hopefully, they are just rushing past and only need a head of lamb," he suggested, hoping to calm his wife.

"Hello inside!" came a yell from a strange voice. "Can you offer us shelter?" Suddenly, three sharp raps were made on the door. "We are in urgent need of shelter." This time the voice was that of a woman.

Larimore and Maggie looked at each other wondering what a woman would be doing this far from town. Larimore went to the door with his sword in hand. Then as if he was trying to hold the door shut, he slowly reached toward the door with both hands and dropped his sword. His hands caught his fall, as he dropped to one knee at the door. Maggie didn't understand what was happening. Grabbing his chest, Larimore looked over his shoulder to his wife. Then he smiled, grimaced, and slumped to the floor.

Maggie let out a blood-curdling scream that startled the troupe of travelers. Pausing from knocking at the door, they listened for someone to come. Instead, they heard the wailing of a lost soul. The sorrow in her cry was profound. The entire party stood on the other side of the door and wondered what horror could have occurred to create such trauma.

The crying suddenly stopped. Then the group heard a shuffling on the other side of the door. Then it sounded like the door was being opened. A sense of security rushed over the group as a weath-

HOLLYWONDRA

ered old human woman pulled open the door. Slovenly dressed, this woman's face had clean little lines of skin where the tears had recently washed away the grime of farm work. Still crying, she clumsily swung a long sword back and forth as she rushed outside screaming.

"I'm not dying without taking one of you with me!" she sobbed. Launching her attack at Allendale was fortunate. He had the skills to quickly block her blows and disarm her. Having lived so many years in the presence of humans, he knew the sound of anguish. Unarmed, she fell to her knees and began wailing. She showed no regard for the farm dress she wore. She didn't care what they might do to her. She simply bent over and sobbed without restraint.

Titus felt horrible for this lady he had never met. He didn't understand anything that just happened. He just knew she was crying uncontrollably.

Almost everyone was distracted by her sorrow, except Ellerson. He always seemed to be strictly business. He came walking out the front door of the cabin and yelled back at the group, "I think I have found the source of her sorrow."

The group turned to walk into the house. Maggie had a sudden burst of speed that defied her age and weight. Rushing past the party, she shot past the party and to the side of Larimore. Larimore laid on the wood planked floor of their cottage. Maggie had taken his right hand and wrapped it inside her hands. She pulled his hand to her breast and began to plead to Larimore to not leave her. Falling on him, she began sobbing again.

The party stood by not knowing what to do for the woman or her man. Then Amanda knelt at his head and peeled back his eye lids. "He's still alive," she pronounced. "If you want him to live, you'll have to trust me," Amanda told Maggie. Maggie wasn't so quick to trust this stranger who just invaded her home. Amanda reminded Maggie, "If we had wanted to bring you harm, we would have done so by now, don't you think? Let me see if I can keep him alive for you."

Maggie realized what this girl had said was true. It was out of desperation that Maggie slowly extended her arms and handed Larimore's hand to Amanda. Sitting with both her hands on her knees, Maggie placed all her faith in this young stranger. Amanda took his arm and laid it by his side. Pulling a blanket off a nearby couch, she placed it under his moccasins. Then Amanda straddled his stomach and began administering chest compressions.

After less than a minute, Larimore began to cough. Then the color began to return to his face. Amanda asked for another blanket. Maggie quickly brought two more from the bedroom. Looking down at her man, Maggie still cried, but now they were tears of happiness.

Amanda explained to Maggie, "His heart is failing. If I don't do some work on him right now, he may not see tomorrow morning's light."

Maggie knew she had no options. Larimore was everything to her. She asked, "How can I help?"

"Let's get him in the bed," Amanda directed the men. Larimore did not have the strength to stand. It took the four men to move and lift him onto the bed. This was one chore Titus knew he was not meant for.

"Give me some privacy," Amanda directed. Initially, Maggie did not want to leave Larimore's side. Then she realized that she needed to do whatever this girl asked, if she was going to see her husband survive. Maggie quickly found she could not leave the door. She stood outside the door touching it with both hands, as it were an extension of her husband. There she began to cry again. She knew she could not care for this farm or sheep by herself. Certainly, she could not do that and care for her husband too. What was she going do?

Maybe it was the tears that created that strange glow. Maybe the tears were blurring her vision. Maggie wasn't sure. The glow was bright enough to make her wipe her eyes to refocus. She peeled her gaze through the planks that formed the bedroom door. All she could make out was that this young girl was on the bed next to her husband. His shirt was open, and she had her hands on the center of his chest.

This time she saw it with her own eyes. As Amanda murmured a prayer, a bright blue light flashed from under her hands and onto the chest of Larimore. Maggie didn't even know what to think or say. Her first instinct was to cry sorcerer. Then again, she was surrounded by this group. She slowly looked around the room at the rest of the party and found that they were more curious about what was outside than what Amanda was doing in the other room. So Maggie took another look into the room; this time she was even more shocked.

Larimore was awake and was holding the hand of the girl. He was speaking softly to her. It looked like he was thanking her. Maggie couldn't wait. She began pounding on the door. "Let me in! I want to see him. He's *my* husband." She paused long enough to try looking through the planks again. This time she saw the girl walking toward the door. Maggie stepped away just in time. As Amanda pushed the door open, Maggie didn't hesitate to rush past her and to the side of Larimore.

"You old ram. You scared me to death. You know you aren't allowed to die before me. I thought I'd made that clear." Larimore was happy to be chastised. His smile only brought more affection from Maggie. Her tears of joy rolled from her chin onto his face and pillow.

27

Hamman Drew managed the hillside to the best of his ability. The light snow had made the footing treacherous. Drew tried making each step land on a tuft of grass. The grass was far more stable than the snow slickened mud that had built up on the soles of his boots. The cold wind blowing directly into his face seemed to make travel even slower. While paying such careful attention to his footing, he failed to notice the line of elves had come to a halt. Hamman Drew bumped into the elf he had been following and slipped to one knee. Before he completely fell, the elf in front of him caught him by the shoulder of his tunic. The elf who had caught him placed his other hand to his mouth to signal silence. Then removing his hand from his mouth, he pointed toward the tree line. Hamman Drew's eyes had to adjust from the bright white of the snow to the dark shadows of the woods. The breeze rustled the foliage enough to make the Kobold movement hard to see. The Elvan patrol drew their bows and began backing slowly up the hillside. Following the moves of his counterparts, Hamman Drew pulled his scimitar and carefully backed his way up the slope. Never taking his eyes off the Kobold army, Drew began examining his surroundings.

The elves had been hiking a deer trail that slowly descended the hillside. The elves could have hiked level ground, but they also know that increases their chances of encountering others. Plus, by taking the higher ground, it can offer them an instant tactical advantage. That standard practice saved them this time.

Hamman Drew could not tell how many Kobold had already passed. All he could see was that their ranks disappeared deep into the woods. They could be walking a hundred abreast for all he knew.

The line of Kobold extended beyond their view to the east and west. Then Hamman Drew realized why the elves were slowly backing away. Wolves!

Skirting along the edge of the Kobold ranks loped several Great Gray Wolves. The Great Gray Wolf was almost as tall at their back as the average Kobold stood in height. Having been a scout, Hamman quickly realized that they were currently upwind of the wolves. He also knew that as the wolves run ahead of the Kobold, it would not be long before the Elvan party was going to be a fresh scent in their wind.

The elves tried to use their location to their advantage. They knew they were probably going to be attacked, so they needed to find good cover on high ground if they were going to have any luck fending off these attackers. After slowly backing away, they quickly picked up their pace. They moved up the hillside trying to reach a rocky shelf. While this group could do serious damage to several Kobold, it was hard to tell just how badly they were outnumbered.

Making their way to a boulder lined landing, they watched what appeared to be the last of the Kobold army pass. They knew the direction of the wind, and it was only a matter of time before the wolves caught their scent. They quietly discussed how many they believed had passed. After a short discussion, they determined it had to have been at least a thousand Kobold and fifty Great Gray Wolves.

When this patrol set out, they had about twenty-five elves. Each time they set an ambush, they left a few more men behind. Their patrol was now down to nineteen elves and one human ranger wondering what he was doing in the middle of their war.

The hillside was covered with grass that had browned from the bitter cold and lack of sunlight. There were trees, but you could not call this hillside wooded. The trees were too far apart to move without being seen. They all knew the Kobold were marching toward the northern end of Hollywondra. They knew these trails, and that was the only logical point of attack. plus, the elves had recently stopped another group from attacking that northern point of the forest. These Kobold must be their backup plan.

As they discussed their positions behind the rocks, the first howl came. It was unmistakable. Then suddenly a second wolf joined the first. Quickly it turned into a chorus of howls. They figured the wolves would take the route with the least slope. That meant they would have to come around the bend in front of them and charge up the landing. It was possible the wolves could come running over the top of the hill, but that just did not seem likely. The elves knew this position was going to give them several shots before the wolves could reach them. The howls grew nearer.

As the elves took cover behind the line of large boulders, they quickly assessed how many arrows they had. The elves held the higher ground. Their entire defense was based on the belief that the wolves and Kobold would take the same trail they had taken. The landing in front of their boulders stretched three hundred yards to the bend. They were about to find out just how outnumbered they really were. Hamman Drew was given a bow by an elf he did not know. All he had to do was nod that he knew how to use it and that was good enough for this elf to hand him a bow and quiver with about twenty arrows.

As Hamman Drew began to take the quiver from the elf, the elf pulled back on the quiver. Hamman was momentarily startled by this act. Then when he looked at the elf, the elf told him, "Make every arrow count." Hamman Drew knew the importance of that message. What the elf really meant was that they did not have enough arrows and he better be ready for the hand-to-hand combat that will come.

Hamman wanted the highest ground he could manage. He knew the higher he was, the more trouble they were going to have reaching him. He also knew he would be able to shoot over the top of the others. When it came to hand-to-hand combat, it might also give him some advantage. Hamman Drew was mostly concerned about the wolves. He knew he could outrun Kobold. The wolves could run faster than him and for days at a time. They all understood their only chance for survival was to kill all the wolves.

Hamman found a small boulder that served as a perch behind a larger one. By standing up on top of the smaller boulder, he was able to shoot down onto the charging army. What concerned him was how tough it was getting up on the small boulder. As he made his way around the larger boulder, each stride he took, his footing slipped halfway back down the hillside. This did not slow him down. He knew it would be the same problem for anyone coming after him. The slope leading up the line of boulders would be slick for the Kobold too.

One elf was sent up the hillside to get a visual on how many wolves and Kobold were coming. He was also sent there to assure them that the Kobold were not coming straight over the top of the hill. They could hear the howls of the wolves getting nearer. They just wanted to know how bad this was going to be. The other elf could not be heard. The howling was too loud, so he simply turned around and headed back for cover.

Just before the elf was able to rejoin the party, the first of the Great Grey Wolves came charging around the bend. There were at least twenty of the large wolves rushing toward them. The elves knew the wolves would have outdistanced themselves from the Kobold warriors. They needed to dispatch these as quickly as possible.

The entire party had an arrow ready for their charge. When the arrows flew, wolves began to fall. In the first salvo, they killed five. Quick to the quiver, the second salvo dropped another seven. Hannan Drew felt good about his efforts. He was certain one of his arrows single-handedly killed one wolf. They only had time left for one more salvo before the wolves would be upon them. The third salvo killed all but three of the wolves.

Then the wolves were upon them. The elves with short swords drawn did their best to hack at the beasts and kill them before permanent damage was done to anyone of the party. The elves all converged on the wolves and killed them as quickly as they could. Nobody was killed, but two elves had been badly bitten.

After all that effort, they looked up to see a wave of Kobold rushing around the bend. The Kobold were able to see the last of the wolves killed, so there was no mystery as to where the elves were hiding. There was a moment when Hamman Drew thought, *Hmm, only a hundred Kobold. We could do this."*

As the Kobold cleared the corner and rushed forward, Hamman Drew could see one that had stayed back. He carried some type of crude horn. He was well beyond arrow shot. As the first flight of arrows came from the elves, at least fifteen Kobold died. They were slower than the wolves, so the elves would get at least three more arrows off before they had to fight any of these creatures. The next three salvos had a similar result. They had already cut the number of Kobold in half. That was when they heard the distant Kobold blow an alarm. That sound of that horn was quickly met by the distant sound of wolves howling.

Hamman Drew had used half his arrows by the time the last of those Kobold had fallen. The elves had done a good job of fending off this first wave of Kobold. They were able to kill the entire group without losing a single man. That did not mean they had not suffered injuries. Anytime an enemy used steel weapons, the elves suffered. Now more were on the way, and they were not done killing the wolves.

As the new wave of Kobold came running around the bend, Hamman Drew realized that this brigade of Kobold did not have any wolves. The howls were getting nearer, but they were not mixed in with this part of the Kobold army. Hamman Drew began to pull draw back an arrow, when an elf came up behind him and said, "You and I need to go."

Releasing the tension on his bow, Hamman Drew listened more carefully. "We must go now. We must let the Elvan nation know. We cannot allow ourselves to be a part of this battle."

Hamman Drew did not realize retreating was an option. Looking back at the wave of Kobold, he immediately realized this was not a wave of Kobold; this looked like the entire army. The wave just kept coming around the bend. There must have been three hundred of them around the corner before the first of the wolves made the corner.

Realizing the arrows would better serve those elves that were staying behind, Hamman Drew pulled his arrows from his quiver and placed them in the quiver of another elf. Then he and the other elf descended their perch in the boulders. Getting back down onto

HOLLYWONDRA

the ground, the two took off running directly away from the location of the fellow elves. They hoped the boulders would give their retreat cover and they might not be seen.

As a ranger, there had been plenty of times Hamman Drew had run from a violent situation. That's how you live to fight another day. Looking over his shoulder, he felt this time it just didn't feel right. He knew he was abandoning a group that was horribly outnumbered. Then he realized, there was no guarantee that he was actually going to get away. As he looked back around at his Elvan friend, he found that the elf had not wasted any time, and Hamman Drew had ground to make up. The elf was running as fast as he could away from the fight.

Hamman Drew picked up his pace and tried as hard as he could to catch the elf. Even when he heard the howling of wolves, he still seemed unable to close the distance the elf had created between them. *Wolves*, he thought. Hamman was beginning to regret leaving his arrows.

As they ran away, Hamman Drew was trying to imagine the fight. Dozens of Kobold would fall under the arrows of the Elvan archers. Even the remaining wolves would be primary targets. But Hamman Drew knew the sheer number of Kobold he had seen was greater than the force of those elves. They would be overtaken. He refused to let them die in vain. The thought of their sacrifice made him focus on running faster to take the warning to the elves of Hollywondra.

28

Titus wasn't sure which was worse, the cold pouring rain or the carnage he could not get out of his mind. They had been on the move for a couple of hours, but all he could think about was the ambush they had set for the men who had been tracking them. Titus was still shaken at how quickly and savagely everything happened. When their trackers cleared the forest line, their dogs immediately bolted for Larimore's farmhouse. The elves laid low and let their trackers get good and clear of the woods before they attacked. These men had no chance. The elves rose from their hiding spots and shot their arrows with precision. The sound of the flights thudding into the torso of the trackers was quickly followed by screams of pain. Those who screamed were less fortunate. They were not immediately killed. The tracking party was dead or dying before they even knew they were under attack. Once their trackers were down, Palcombine and Ellerson moved quickly to finish off the wounded. The dogs stood just as little chance. All the bodies were dragged off the road and into the underbrush. The team quickly worked to cover as much of the trail as they could.

Maggie begged them to stay for a hot meal. As good as a warm meal sounded, they all realized killing this group of trackers gave them time to put some distance between them and anyone else who might take up their scent. The King's Highway was the primary road that through this region. If they chose to turn east, they could find themselves in Planceon by nightfall. They needed to travel west for the Eastern Jor River. The further they got down the road, the more their scent might blend in with the smells of other travelers.

HOLLYWONDRA

The blood and cries from the dying men was all Titus could think about as they moved along the King's Highway. Their pace was anything but casual. After hours at this pace, Titus found himself struggling to keep up. Titus scoffed at the notion that this was a highway. The muddy dirt road they followed was just wide enough to accommodate a single car. It was very uneven. In several places, the water puddled. The size of the raindrops exploded in the puddles. Everyone in the party was soaked, but nobody complained. There was no escaping the downpour, so there really was no reason to complain. One blessing the heavy rain did provide was very little traffic. The few travelers they did see were not actually on the road. They had pulled off and made camp under nearby trees waiting out the rain. The campfires made it easy to tell when they were approaching the camps of other travelers.

The King's Highway ran just north of the Rocco Forest. The Tree Gate was inside the Rocco Forest. It was much further west than their current position. By rushing off to the north, the party had distanced themselves from the Tree Gate and the shortest route to Hollywondra. They still needed to backtrack and head southwest to get on route to Hollywondra. The road wove miles through slow rolling hills. About midday, they found the highway descending the hills and stretching out into a grassy plain. This was the first time they really felt exposed. They could see the highway heading into another wooded area in the distance. That didn't change the fact that they all felt exposed as they walked out onto the plains of west Planceon.

They were already tired, but now they had to pick up the pace. They could not afford to be found out here in the open. Ellerson began to break into a light jog. The others quickly followed suit. Sir Allendale looked over his shoulder to check on Titus. Titus, too proud to admit he was already taxed, nodded his head as if he were fine. The group moved quickly across the plains and into the woods.

Trees lined both sides of this section of the King's Highway. Everyone enjoyed the cover of the trees. The rain had not slowed at all, but tree bows caught a fair amount of the rain. It made it seem like it wasn't raining as hard. Titus was relieved to reach the trees, because the group had decided to start walking again. About an hour after entering the trees, Ellerson raised his hand in warning. The group froze for a moment. Then following the wave of his hand, they all scurried into the underbrush on the north side of the road.

Pausing in the confines of the deep brush, they could only hear each other breathing. Amanda took note of how the other elves covered their mouths with their tunics. Looking at Titus, she noticed how his breath was creating a cloud of steam in the cold. Tapping him with her staff, she silently blew a little cloud at him. Then she covered her mouth and pointed at the rest of the party. Titus understood and buried his mouth into his wet sleeve.

Slowly a distant thrum began to rise. At first it seemed like a low rolling thunder. Then as they carefully listened, it sounded more like the thrum of horses. Sure enough, a patrol of armed riders emerged on the highway. The leather armored militia rode two abreast and a score deep. The troops sat tall in their saddles despite the pouring rain and the mud flying from the hooves of their horses. The last two riders each carried a white flag emblazoned with an oak tree on shield with two swords crossing the oak tree's trunk.

In these days, many men of the countryside had been pulled away from their families and forced to serve in the army of Zel Camber. There were still some kingdoms that were intact and proud. This militia was a hopeful site to Amanda and Titus. All they had seen in this new world was chaos. This patrol of armed knights gave them a sense of order in this new world.

After the riders disappeared over the hill, Amanda began to step from the cover of brush when Sir Allendale raised his arm in front of her to stop her. Then Ellerson waved his hand to suggest they step back and down from sight. Seeing Ellerson squat low into the brush and cover his breath, the others followed his lead. The sound of the first patrol had hidden the sound of the second. No sooner than Amanda had settled back into her hiding spot, a second Planceon patrol came trotting around the corner. It was another forty armored riders. This was not the time for this pack of travelers to show themselves. They could not afford to be detained.

Once the second patrol passed, they stayed in the brush until Ellerson waved them out. Sir Allendale suggested they take a break,

HOLLYWONDRA

since they had not stopped all day. Palcombine reminded Allendale that they couldn't rest long if they wanted to make it to Bierland's Ferry by nightfall. Allendale suggested they give these youth just a little time to get their wind back.

After about ten minutes, they set out again. The group followed the northern tree line of the highway the rest of the day. All day the rain was unrelenting. Just when it seemed like it might be slowing down, it would start to pour again. Titus wasn't sure why they had stopped. That little rest had only provided him false hope that he might actually get off his feet.

As the cloudy gray day started to get darker, Ellerson raised his hand to halt the party. Everyone paused to listen for what Ellerson must have heard. Then he waved for everyone to follow him slowly. They all eased up over a little rise. There in the distance they could see the forest's edge opened up and distant land permitted the great Eastern Jor River to flow through.

Walking back up the road and using the rise in the road to conceal their presence, the party moved south across the highway. They slipped inside the tree line and slowly approached this place where the King's Highway was abruptly stopped by the muddy brown torrent of the Eastern Jor. The King's Highway ran directly to the ferry landing. Bierland's Ferry was obviously the only way to cross.

From their cover in the tree line, they could see the ferryman was midstream pulling six riders to the other side of the river. The muddy brown river was deep and the current strong. Swimming this span of water was not an option. As it were, the ferry sagged downstream from the strong current. The team of mules on the other side struggled to make ground. The circle they walked was a muddy mess. Even though they were being whipped by a young boy shouting at them, the mules could only move slowly.

By the dock on the other side of the river were two small wooden plank buildings. Smoke rose from the chimney of the one that looked like a house. The other looked more like barn. In the fading daylight, they could not be sure. Both buildings looked like good shelter. As the ferry arrived on the far shore, the riders walked their horses onto a shallow bank and broke into a light cantor. The

181

last of the riders stopped, handed something to the ferryman, and then raced off to catch up with the others.

The ferryman turned to look carefully at the other side of the river. Since the party was hiding in the tree line, the ferryman began tying his ferry up for the night.

Tired of being in the pouring rain, Titus whispered, "What are we waiting for?"

"Rushing is a reckless human quality," Palcombine said as he shook his head at Titus. "We can wait for the morning light. We need to plan how best to cross this river. We need to make certain we are not all caught out on the water at the same time. What if our enemies await us on the other side of the river? It is in our best interest to move away from the highway and set up a camp a little way into the woods. We can cross tomorrow, once we have made our plans."

Titus had never thought about the possibility of someone waiting on the other side of the river to ambush them. The comments only reminded him how little he really knew about their situation and this new land. From where they stood, it was obvious this area had previously been used for camp sites. Titus considered, even this close to the road was not going to be safe. What was going to be safe? He really didn't know. Thinking about the men he saw slaughtered this morning, he shuddered at the idea of anyone wanting to harm him or any of his friends in a similar way. This was a cruel and ruthless land. He knew the wisest thing he could do was listen and learn from those sent to protect him.

The group turned from the highway and made their way a few hundred yards deeper into woods. Along their path were plenty of old campfires showing they were not the only ones who preferred solitude while waiting the night for the ferry. They walked past four or five more campsites, before settling into an area they felt was far enough away from the road.

It was as if the clouds had taken their cue from the sun, the rain ceased just as night came. The group settled into a small clearing that was fairly flat and free of brush. The gentle slope that did exist was kind enough to allow much of the day's rain to run off. The thick forest blocked most of the night sky. The group allowed themselves the luxury of a small campfire to dry and warm themselves.

While Jarius stood at the edge of the campfire light, Amanda approached him. "I don't get it. I feel a true sense of belonging and urgency to be in Namron Rae. I just don't know what good I can possibly be to your cause."

Jarius turned to answer her. Before he could speak, the man she had only known as her dad stepped from the shadows to explain. "Honey, there are great powers at work in Namron Rae. I, too, do not understand them all. I know that my mission was to ensure your safety at all costs. In some way, it is your destiny to bring great power to our cause." Waiting to hear more of Sir Allendale's knowledge, she was disappointed when he just turned away and returned to the fire. Jarius gave a gentle nod and followed.

The group dug into their backpacks for rations. When members of the group pulled sandwiches and chips from their backpacks, they had the attention of Ellerson and Palcombine. The elves mostly wanted to inspect the plastic bottles of water. The screw-on bottle cap was pure genius. They examined the plastic bottles and discussed the various uses they would have for such technology.

After eating some food, they let the fire dim, and everyone tried to find a comfortable place to rest. The ground was wet. The driest spots seemed to be under trees. Still, there was not a lot of difference between a wet bed of needles versus the wet grass when your clothes were still wet. Ellerson had climbed a nearby tree to stand watch for the night. The rest of the party tried their best to get comfortable enough to get some rest.

It wasn't long after they had decided to try to get comfortable that Ellerson whistled an alarm. Quickly, everyone jumped to their feet. From having seen the brutality of the morning, Titus frightened quickly and seized his emotions to become invisible. With their weapons drawn, the party looked around for a sign of attack. Slowly they formed a circle with their backs to one another. Several moments passed. Amanda was just beginning to think it may have been a false alarm when a small robed figure stepped from the tree line.

Jarius was not certain if this was an intrusion or if the person was looking for them. The small robed figure did not appear to be armed. It looked like he was…eating something. As their eyes adjusted, they could see he was eating nuts. Slowly strolling into their camp, he cracked a shell with his hands, tossed the nut in his mouth, and dropped the shells on the forest floor. Jarius decided to make this person aware of their presence and yelled, "Halt! You are surrounded. You have strayed into a private camp." Generally, such a warning would startle a single traveler. Jarius was surprised to see how calmly this person managed this situation.

The warning made the man stop in his tracks. Then the man took a moment to crack and eat what must have been his last nut. Dusting his hands of the shell residue, he slowly raised his hands to indicate no aggression. The hooded traveler calmly spoke, "Weary friends, I mean you no alarm. I too await the morning ferry. We simply share the wisdom of avoiding the highway as we camp. My name is Ezen Kroach. I am on my way to Haverford."

"What? By yourself?" asked Jarius. Then he shot a glance in the direction he knew Ellerson had gone to stand watch. Jarius figured if there were more intruders, Ellerson would alert them. No further sounds came from Ellerson's direction. Jarius was surprised to see them speaking to this loan traveler.

"Yes, I know it seems a bit reckless. I have found over the years that there is not always safety in numbers." While speaking to the group, he showed them the palms of his hands then slowly raised them to the hood of his cloak. Pulling back his hood, he revealed that he, too, was an elf. Not an elf that anyone of them recognized, but an elf nonetheless.

The fact that he was an elf did not make the party relax. Knowing he was an elf prompted Sir Allendale to ask, "Where are you from? You certainly are not from Planceon, nor were you born in the mountains of Haverford." Sir Allendale knew that Planceon and Haverford were both human communities. Certainly, others were welcome to visit, but it was mostly humans who lived in those cities. It seemed unlikely that this elf came from either place. Ezen Kroach

HOLLYWONDRA

was of an age that he would have been recognized, if he had lived amongst the elves of Hollywondra.

"You are clearly an honorable Knight of Hollywondra," he calmly replied to Allendale in a very matter-of-fact way. "I was borne in an Elvan community in the far eastern foothills of Axel Major. It is at least two moons east by horse and the better part of day on the back of a dragon."

After pausing to consider what he had just heard, Sir Allendale raised his left hand and directed the visitor, "Just a moment. You speak so casually of dragon flight. Do you wish us to believe that you have flown on the back of a dragon?" His question was not to verify that he had flown on the back of a dragon as much as it was to challenge the truth or sanity of this stranger.

The visitor did not even honor Sir Allendale by looking directly at him; instead, he just shrugged his shoulders and explained, "Well, not lately. I mean, I wouldn't be walking the King's Highway if I had such noble company." Quickly raising his hand and flashing a smile at Sir Allendale, he said, "No insult intended. You are clearly a noble lot."

Putting his sword back into his sheath, Sir Allendale told the rest of the party, "This elf is no threat to us. He is clearly mad. Walking this countryside alone and speaking of riding on the backs of dragons. We are not fools! Nor or are we tolerant! Be on your way." Sir Allendale waved his hand at the elf to dismiss him.

Seemingly undisturbed by the suggestion that he was insane, Ezen Kroach turned to walk away. "I just figured this young band of six could use a little hand with that ambush that awaits you on the other side of the river." Then pausing as if to recall something, he shared, "My first wife loved to remind me that I wasn't always right." He continued murmuring something to himself about a mistake she had made in picking poisonous flowers, as he strolled into the dark of the woods.

This elf had to have known that a sentry had spotted him, but only four of them stood visible. How did he know there was a sixth person, unless he had scouted them out? What was it that he knew about an ambush? "Halt!" yelled Allendale. "You cannot throw the suggestion of an ambush at us and then walk away. What ambush are you talking about? Why do you think this ambush is set for us?"

Titus looked at his hands and legs to makes sure that he had not suddenly reappeared while listening to this traveler. He was very sure he had not. So he took extra care to stand still and monitor his breathing so he would be quiet as possible and sustain his invisibility.

Kroach stopped, turned, and returned to the light glow of the campfire. As he approached the group, he waved with his left hand and asked, "May I sit for a moment. I have been traveling all day, and it would be nice to get off my feet for a bit."

"If you have been traveling all day, why aren't you soaked like the rest of us?" asked Allendale. For the first time, the group realized this guy's cloak was dry. Allendale was right. How could this be? It had poured all day.

Kroach flippantly replied, "Because I dodged the rain." He took a few steps from where he entered their camp, then turned his attention to a snag where a tree had blown over. The trunk of the tree was twisted and still partially attached to the stump. Jagged shards of wood rose as high as eight feet above of the stump. Walking toward the snag, Kroach suddenly slapped his gloved hands together. Kroach then, after a brief pause, opened them just as quickly. Suddenly, the tree broke loose and rolled a few feet away from the stump. The thrashing of the branches in the brush did not distract the party from the fact that this guy just willed the tree to move. Looking at the rugged stump, Kroach then turned his hands flat and clapped them together. The shards of wood rising out of the stump exploded from an unseen impact. As the debris settled, Kroach moved to the stump, dusted it off, and took a seat. Then he turned to speak to the group as if nothing had happened.

The party looked at this small elf in awe. He was clearly a mage of power. What was his interest in them? And…did he really dodge the rain?

Seeing the group somewhat speechless, Kroach waved his arms in a welcoming way. "Oh, sit down. Surely you have seen magic before." As the group began to step closer, Kroach turned in the direction of Titus and called to him. "You too, young mage, just relax and come join us."

Titus checked again to make sure he was still invisible. He could not see any indication that he had lost control of his invisibility. Cleary, this elf could see him, so his efforts were not worth continuing. Titus dropped his invisibility and came to join the rest of the party that had now moved closer to Kroach.

As Titus arrived, Kroach took a quick interest in him. "If you'd like, I can give you a couple of tips on how to manage that spell."

"What spell?" thought Titus. This was an inert talent that Titus felt he had acquired in this new land. This guy thinks it's magic?

Sitting comfortably on his stump, Kroach began to explain that he is somewhat of a businessman. During his travels, he commonly has an opportunity to hear the conversations of other travelers. He had heard that a group of armed men were searching the King's Highway for a group of elves. Kroach spoke somewhat proudly of the fact that he found them first. It sounded as if it might have been like a game to him.

Then he turned and addressed Titus again. "But you, young mage? I heard nothing about a human mage being in their ranks."

Then he explained, "If they don't find you tonight, then you can be sure they will set an ambush on the other side of the ferry. They know you have to cross the Jor to get to Hollywondra. There is a cavern a little more than a mile west of the ferry. If you use that cavern, you would find that it is very extensive. A traveler could take that cavern for several leagues to the southwest, thus circumventing their ambush."

"That sounds like a great solution, Mr. Kroach, but I have traveled into a couple of caverns in my days. I know that they can be very dangerous travel as well. You also need to know where you are going, as caverns commonly have multiple directions one could go. We could go into this cave and be in there for months," explained Allendale.

Considering his point, Kroach nodded. "Indeed. I suppose I could escort you through the passage?" suggested Kroach. "I wasn't really thinking of traveling toward the southwest, but I don't know why not."

Allendale quickly replied, "I thought you were headed for Haverford. This would take you leagues out of your way."

Nodding his head to Allendale's comment, Kroach replied, "True. True. But I must say, I am curious to see how all this turns out." Kroach then looked at the members of the party as if he had more knowledge about them then he should have.

"We do not have the luxury of wandering aimlessly," stated Allendale. "We must make haste."

Kroach turned a quick glance back to Allendale. "The land of Hollywondra is a very dangerous place right now. But then, as I look more carefully at you, I can see that you know that." Tossing his thumb in the direction of Titus, he said, "I can't begin to understand what good this one will do you in your travels to Hollywondra. He seems undisciplined and ill fit for such a formidable conflict." He looked at Titus. "I can't begin to imagine where you found such a boy."

When Ezen Kroach was able to quickly identify their direction as Hollywondra, Allendale felt he had created unsafe exposure to the party. He racked his mind to recall if he had inadvertently mentioned the Elvan homeland as their destination. Allendale decided to cut this encounter short before more information became exposed. Even if this guy were to travel with them, there was no assurance that he would not be more trouble than good. "Mr. Kroach, your stories and company have been most entertaining. I am afraid I will have to ask you to move on. We all have road to cover tomorrow, and I feel our journeys should be in two different directions."

Taking the cue from Allendale, Kroach stood up and gave a graceful bow. "Very well." Pulling his hood over his head, he turned south and walked deeper into the woods and away from the highway.

After he had gone, Ellerson came from out of his hiding and joined the group. They talked about their visitor and the likelihood that his story had any truth. They agreed to double their watch for the night to make sure he did not return to their camp. Ellerson explained that he would track the guy for a distance to make sure that he didn't double back on them.

Titus made his way to the stump that Kroach had so casually turned into a chair for his use. He examined the surface that been flattened by his power. Titus could not imagine such telekinetic power.

29

His tent was guarded and larger than the rest. It was proper accommodations for the captain of such a large army. A large center pole held the tent up high. Just above eye level, two brass arms stuck out from the sides of the pole. The unlit lanterns that hung there had already cooled from earlier use. Between the pole and the door sat a small table with three chairs. At the back of the tent lay Nictovius on his cot.

The shadows of men walking by danced across the walls of his tent. Slipping in and out of sleep, he wondered if maybe he had not gotten enough practice today to earn him a good night's rest. When he would open his eyes, he could make out the shadowy figures of the two guards that stood watch outside his tent door. Their silhouettes were keenly cut against the tent wall by the large campfire that burned just beyond them. The fire was as much for seeing as it was for the warmth. One time he woke wondering if his personal safety was what was keeping him awake. As he considered it and realized he was perfectly safe, he just kept closing his eyes to see if he could find rest.

After hours of restlessness, Nictovius cracked opened his eyes, just like he had done at least a half dozen times that night. Only this time there were three silhouettes, not two. His first thought was that it must be a changing of the guard. Then he realized there was only one other figure. As best he could, he tried to focus his slightly opened eyes to better understand what he was seeing. As his focus adjusted, he realized this third figure was in his tent.

Nictovius was a battle-tested veteran of several military campaigns. It was not unusual for him to rest with what seemed like one eye open. His combat instinct took over. He tried his best to not alter his breathing and focused as best he could on the figure standing still on the other side of his tent. When he became certain that there was a person in his tent, he quickly sat up and reached for where his long sword laid beside his cot. Quickly sitting up, he was surprised to find he could not bend over to grab his sword. He tried to lunge a second and a third time. It was as if he had suddenly gained a hundred pounds of weight around his belly. He could not bend over. Looking over at the silhouette, Nictovius strained to lean over, but he could not reach his sword.

The silhouette moved slowly toward him. As it passed the center pole of his tent, he was able to more clearly see the invader. It appeared to be a heavily armored human carrying a long sword. That was where everything normal seemed to end. This fighter wore no belt or sheath for his sword. Strangely, his armor made none of the normal clamor associated with wearing clothing of iron. No, this person was able to move quietly past his guards and walk into the center of his tent without making a noise.

In the same moment Nictovius began to shout an alarm, the man raised his right hand and pointed his palm at Nictovius. His voice was immediately stuck in his throat. He could breathe just fine. He could not utter a sound. Standing directly in front of Nictovius, the man lightly planted the tip of his sword into the soil and rested both his hands on the hilt. Nictovius did not recognize this man nor the ornate armor he wore. It bore no insignia of allegiance to any army or realm. The armor was highly polished and unblemished.

Unwilling to sit idle and unarmed, Nictovius tried to lurch forward to tackle his intruder. Again, he found that his weight was so great that he could not lift himself from where he sat at the edge of his cot. The most he could manage to do was rock himself slightly forward. At no point was he any threat to his intruder.

Then his visitor began to speak. "Nictovius, son of Albikur of Answad, hear me. You have stained the land with enough blood. You have dragged man and beast unwillingly to this valley and into this assault. You have compelled innocent lives to die in your zeal to kill the Elvan kind. Your army has been a parasite to the land. You burn down trees and kill wildlife without purpose. The carnage you have made will take generations to repair. No more of this destruction will be tolerated."

Initially, Nictovius wondered how this figure could know the name of his father. That thought quickly faded as his anger rose. He was angered more by the insolence than the intrusion. Nobody speaks to Nictovius in this tone. Nictovius didn't know how this person had found their way into his tent, let alone kept him from moving or speaking. Nictovius struggled even more to move, speak, and grab at his sword. It seemed the more he struggled, the less he was able to actually move. The person standing in front of him allowed him to exhaust himself without saying anything to him. Once Nictovius stopped writhing, the person continued to speak.

"You will disband this army and permit them to return to their homes and boroughs. You will turn your back on this Elvan nation never to speak ill of them again. You will see that your camp is removed from the valley and every effort is made to make it appear as if you were never here. This is the will of God."

After pausing for a moment, the figure raised his hand, pointed his index finger at Nictovius, and then gently rubbed the tip of the finger to the tip of his thumb. Nictovius could feel his throat loosen and recognized he might be able to speak. The first word that came from his mouth was "Guards!" Strangely, it came out as a whisper and the guards could not hear his cry for help. "Guards!" he whispered again. Then realizing he could not call the guards, he tried to grab his sword again, but found he was still unexplainably paralyzed. Pausing to stare up at his invader, he whispered, "You are nothing but a bad dream. I don't know why I should have such a nightmare, but that is all you are. You are clearly not real. My guards would have killed you in your tracks, if you were truly trying to invade my chambers." Then he tried to struggle free again.

Then the figure spoke. "Understand, Nictovius, son of Albikur of Answad, if you do not heed this warning, then you will stand witness to the annihilation of your army. Those who are allowed to live will run in every direction of the compass. Many will die before they stand. Some will disappear as if they were nothing but sand. But rest assured, they will all be gone.

"And you, son of Albikur of Answad, if you do not heed this warning, you will perish before the next winter's snow. Your death will mean nothing to anyone, because you have done nothing of good. Your name will disappear like a breeze that blows past someone who stands in the field. They cannot see it or know where that wind truly goes. Nor do they care or think about it, but for a moment. Those who try to recall your name will struggle to put together the syllables. Yet they will never be successful in actually recalling your name. Your name will hold no meaning, and any recollections of you will trickle by like the water of a river. They will be woven into the other thoughts of the day and lost among them. Even your liege will quickly replace you and forget anything that you ever accomplished for him. Your life will have been for nothing. Heed my warning. Turn away now. Your fate is at hand."

Just that quickly, Nictovius could feel the constraints that held him in place loosened. From instinct, he lunged forward to tackle the man, only to find that lunging forward resulted in him quickly sitting up in his bed. Reaching over the side of his bed, he snapped up the sword that had rested next to his cot. Pulling it from its sheath, he quickly looked around his tent. He could no longer see the figure that was just speaking to him. Slowly rising from his cot, Nictovius circled his tent's pole searching for the man. He was just relieved to be mobile again. Moving to the flap that serves as a door to his tent, he lightly pulled it back to check on his guards. There they stood, alert and at the ready.

Stepping back inside, Nictovius thought the whole thing had to have been a nightmare. It seemed so real. It was as if it had actually happened. Wiping the sweat from his brow, he returned to his cot to rest. He still couldn't sleep. All he could do was think about the intruder. He was certain it had to have been a nightmare. Nictovius thought about what was said to him, and he knew he had already become famous in the service of his liege. Nobody could take that away from him. Nobody knew Nictovius's upbringing, let alone the name of his father. Who could come to him with such detail? He was absolutely convinced it was just a nightmare.

*****

Nictovius stood over the thin leather hide he had stretched across the top of the table in his tent. Alec, Silas Pei, and Tallarand stood looking down upon the map that detailed the battle lines. The tree line was a lot different than when they first arrived. Many efforts to burn the tree line back and use the wood for their siege engines scarred the face of this once majestic valley.

They were making their plans for their final assault. Any day now, they expected a reinforcement of several hundred Kobold to joint their ranks. Nictovius did not care much for Kobold nor did he think they offered much for combat strength. Adding the Kobold to his army added an entirely different dimension. The Kobold and elves were ancient enemies, mostly because Kobold consider elves a delicacy. The idea of a thousand Kobold rushing through their forest would make the elves fearful for the safety of their loved ones. They know they travel in huge hordes. Where there were ten Kobold, there are surely a few hundred more.

The map showed the location of each of his lieutenants' camps, the siege engines they had built and the camp of the Klofgar. It showed each regiment under their command. Nictovius used small stones to mark the location of the siege engines and how he wanted them utilized for this assault. Nictovius was deeply engrossed in explaining the strategy and timing of the assault. As he looked at Silas Pei to explain how the Kobold would be joining into his ranks from the north, he noticed Silas Pei was not looking at the map. When Nictovius paused, Silas Pei quickly turned his attention back to what Nictovius was saying. It was too late. Nictovius had already seen that Silas Pei was distracted.

Lifting his arms from the table and stepping back to squarely address Silas Pei, Nictovius asked, "What? Have you got a better plan?"

HOLLYWONDRA

Silas Pei realized that his captain had just directly challenged his loyalty. "No, no, sir," he quickly said and then added a bow.

"Am I boring you?" suggested Nictovius.

Silas Pei raised his head to look Nictovius in the face. "No, sir, please continue."

Nictovius was not accustomed to being ignored or disrespected by his men. He carefully considered the words of Silas Pei before looking back at the map. Nictovius knew his men feared him. That's the way he liked it. They should fear him, because he was not afraid to kill any of them to forward his plans. What he couldn't tell was if the fear he saw in Silas Pei's eyes was the same fear he always saw each time he raised his voice. Silas Pei just seemed a little different this time.

Slowly turning his attention back to the map, Nictovius ran through the details one last time. In closing, he reminded the men, "As soon as those Kobold arrive, we should be ready to launch this final offensive." After providing his men the chance to answer any questions, he excused them.

As the three exited the tent, all three turned to the right and walked away in the same direction. Once they knew they were a safe distance from the tent, Tallarand asked Silas Pei, "What? Are you insane?"

Silas Pei shot Tallarand a sideways sneer and did not offer him a response.

Tallarand continued, "You better get your head on straight. This would not end well for you. What were you thinking about? Were you just going to ask Nictovius to withdraw because you had a bad dream? That would probably be the last stupid thing you ever said."

Silas Pei stopped walking to turn and look Tallarand in the eyes. "You don't find it a little weird that we all had the same dream last night? You don't think that accounts for something? Maybe he had the same dream. I don't know." Silas Pei began silently questioning his role in this campaign.

"Now stop it, you two!" Alec inserted. "You know damn good and well you are going to follow whatever orders that man gives you. You know he is ruthless, and he will have you and every living relative of yours killed if you fail him. So knock it off, and let's get to work." Alec turned and walked off.

Silas Pei turned to Tallarand and said, "Something's just not right about this. We have fought with Nictovius for years. That was the strangest experience I have ever had… It just seemed so real."

Tallarand reminded Silas Pei, "You know Alec speaks the truth. This campaign is coming to an end. Failing Nictovius now would be a mistake worse than death. He would assail you with an unbridled fury. Just steady yourself and return to your work. Soon we'll all be laughing about his over a large tankard."

Seeming to calm down and agree with Tallarand, Silas Pei said, "Yeah, you're probably right. I best be getting back to camp. I've got to figure out a way to keep the Kobold and Klofgar apart." Then he turned and headed north toward his camp.

Tallarand watched Silas Pei walk away. He couldn't explain how the three of them could have possibly had the same exact dream. It bothered him too. What bothered him more was if Silas Pei would follow through with his part of the attack strategy. Tallarand considered going back to Nictovius and telling him. Then he realized, he would be personally responsible for the death of Silas Pei. It wasn't that Silas Pei was a close friend. The greater concern was that they would have to promote someone to take charge of his platoons. Promoting someone to that level of leadership just prior to a massive battle was just not wise. Tallarand determined it was just best to let it be, turned to ready his troops.

30

Everyone was glad the rain had stopped. The skies were cloudy, the wind could give you a chill, and every now and again, the sun would throw a few warm rays of sun on weary travelers. Not enough to make them dry, just enough to give them hope. After careful consideration, the group decided they needed to split up to make the river crossing. They feared if someone was looking for a group of six, then they should break the group down to smaller less obvious sizes. They decided to split up and cross in two groups. Planceon and Titus were going to cross first then lay low until the rest of the group crossed. The others would follow on the next ferry. Planceon cut a piece of forked wood to use like a crutch. He was trying to disguise himself and make it appear Titus was escorting him in his travel. The bad weather made wearing their hoods a logical way to hide their Elvan heritage.

The group had quietly moved through the brush and up the highway a few hundred yards. From there, they could sneak out onto the highway without being seen by the ferryman. It was there that Planceon and Titus left their forest cover and hurried out onto the highway. As soon as they were on the road, Planceon placed the crutch under his arm and assumed his role. Titus took the arm Planceon was not using for his crutch and awkwardly draped it over his shoulder. As they cleared the rise and the ferryman could see then, the ferry started across the river to meet them. Down in the confines of the forest, the rest of the party followed alongside the two as they made their way to the ferry. They watched carefully as Planceon and Titus hobbled the final yards of the King's Highway to the ferry's landing.

As Planceon and Titus began to pull away from the shore, the others discussed how they could join the ferry as a group of three and then one person acting as a lone traveler. It was possible that even a group of three might be scrutinized from someone watching ferry traffic. While they were discussing who the odd person out should be, they noticed a donkey-drawn cart coming down the highway toward the ferry landing. Quickly Allendale ran out to talk to the farmer. Unable to hear what they discussed, the group felt better when they saw the man nod agreement.

Allendale returned to the group and asked Ellerson for some coin to give the farmer. "I need a couple pieces of copper. He has agreed to let me ride on the bench of the cart with him as he crosses on the ferry. If you three join us on the same ferry, then we can all cross at the same time. Turning away from the other three, Allendale ran back out to join the farmer on the bench of his cart. Jarius, Ellerson, and Amanda ran back up the highway to where Titus and Planceon had entered the road. They crossed over the highway to the north side and then ran down the tree line. They figured if they appeared to be coming out of the north side of the tree line, it might make it look like they were not associated with of the others and they were just rushing to catch the next ferry.

Allendale thought catching a ride with this stranger was a solid plan. That was until he realized that he had left Amanda's side. He was confident Jarius and Ellerson would protect her at all costs. He just knew these were wicked times and anything could happen. As he got up onto the seat next to the man, he simply nodded and handed him a coin. He knew the other three would be watching carefully from the brush. The farmer's donkey slowly pulled his load of hay to the ferry landing and waited for the ferry to return. The driver never offered conversation to Allendale.

Running down the northern tree line, Jarius, Ellerson, and Amanda watched the cart stop at the landing. When they looked across the river to find where Planceon and Titus waited, they were shocked. They were nowhere to be seen. They had been so busy hatching their plans, they had lost track of the other two. Now they

HOLLYWONDRA

nervously searched the other side for any sign of the other two, but the ferry was arriving.

The ferryman got the cart and donkey centered on the ferry. Just has he turned to see if there was anyone else who might want a ride, Jarius, Amanda, and Ellerson shot out of the brush and ran toward the landing, waving their arms for him to wait. As they got to the ferry, they tried to act casual, but they all kept searching the other shore some sign of the others.

The ride across was stressful. The current was fierce, and the muddied ropes left everyone worried if they would hold this craft in this current. When the ferry had crossed the strongest current and began to slowly move up stream toward the landing, the four party members couldn't help but try to read if one of them might have spotted the others. Once they reached the other side, Planceon paid the ferryman, and the three of them quickly left the ferry. With a quick step, they made their way to the highway and quickly out of sight. Allandale knew his role was to stay on the cart and to ride a little way down the road. They knew it was necessary, so the ferryman didn't consider him as being with the other three.

Everyone knew any ferryman at any river crossing was a wealth of information. The ferryman knew all the locals. They also knew the details he'd overheard between fares. Without a doubt, any ferryman would more easily recall a party of six strangers. Allendale had to keep up the illusion so the ferryman would never make the connection.

Allendale took the cart about a half mile down the highway. He figured by that time, the ferry should be heading back across. The trees from the riverbank and woods also made a nice cover for Allandale to get off the cart. Allendale gave the man another coin, and the farmer hastened his cart down the road. After the farmer was out of sight, Jarius, Ellerson, and Amanda came out from the woods to meet Allendale.

After Ellerson offered, "I can't imagine they would be walking down the center of the highway. My guess is we will pick up their tracks somewhere near the river." The party left the road and moved back into the cover of the riverbank. Under the safety of cover, they spread out to see if they could pick up their trail.

It didn't take long before Ellerson stopped. Shaking the branch of a nearby shrub, he signaled the others. As they joined him, he pointed, "It's clearly their path." The group of four all nodded knowingly. This struck Allendale. He knew the other two were experienced trackers. He had learned some tracking while in his service. It wasn't like Amanda to fake knowledge, so he just asked her. "What are the signs you see that reveals their trail to you?"

Amanda only paused a moment to consider. Then she explained how one path was very easy to spot. There were several more natural disruptions that she could almost see as Titus fumbling through that undergrowth. Then she pointed out a couple of footprints and a small broken branch.

"Honey, I'm glad you can see that. Frankly, if you couldn't find that trail, I'd be a little worried," Allendale said with a smile.

His humor and comment were accurate. Amanda knew she had to be at her best. Looking at Allendale, she felt his love for her but also his mentoring eye assessing what she could and could not do. Smiling at this man she had only known and loved as her own father, she turned his attention back the trails. "Well, the other one would have been really tough to pick up by itself. But you see how many of the leaves are pointing parallel with the riverbank? That is not a nature a natural occurrence." Then pointing off to the side, she said, "See how those are in total disarray?" Then pointing back to the trail, she explained how "a higher ratio of the leaves on their trail are parallel to the riverbank." That suggested to her that someone was moving in that direction. Then pausing to look at her father, she smiled. "Titus's trail might have helped me to notice that."

Allendale smiled proudly. Amanda was always a bright girl, but her knowledge of the subtle ways of nature impressed him. Allendale examined the path left by Planceon and realized that finding that path would challenge a moderately good tracker. He looked back at Amanda to see a girl who was still looking at him for his approval. He smiled warmly and nodded.

The group relaxed a little bit when they realized Planceon and Titus must just be scouting things out ahead of them. Since they had no desire to travel openly on the King's Highway, the group chose to follow the path their friends had made. Even though the rain had stopped, the ground was still very soft from yesterday's heavy rain. It didn't take them long before they caught up to the others.

The woods on the western side of the river were not as overgrown as were on the eastern shore. There was far less underbrush, and the travel was much easier. They continued to follow the riverside for a few hours. When the shoreline started to turn north, they realized that another stream was coming into the river. Staying well within the cover of the forest, they scouted the best way to cross the stream. The mouth of this stream was too deep and wide to cross. They could see the King's Highway crossed the stream at a wooden bridge. Even at the bridge, the water was deep and moving too fast to ford. There was a good reason that bridge had been built.

Unfortunately, the bridge had no brush cover on either side. It was probably a hundred yards from the last tree to the first plank of the bridge. The trees on the other side of the bridge were equally as far from the bridge. They studied the distant tree line for any evidence of travelers. They could not see anyone. The creek was about twenty yards wide. The stream was full and fast after collecting the recent rain. Both sides of the creek had some tall shrubs that offered some cover, but that wasn't going to help them get across. No matter what, they were going to be exposed crossing the bridge.

Ellerson said he had an idea and asked the others to wait. Following the shoreline, he made his way to the base of the bridge. Ellerson examined the structure carefully. Securing his bow on his back, Ellerson climbed up the side of the bridge. Since the bridge construction was simple cross members on poles, there would not be very many handholds. The group became nervous as Ellerson's plan unfolded. All they could do was watch as Ellerson carefully swing out onto the edge of the planking. Suspended by only his fingertips, Ellerson worked one hand after the other to slowly make his way across the bridge. As he reached the other side, he dropped down onto the grassy shore and took cover in the high weeds on the other bank. From his cover on the other side of the creek, Ellerson pulled out his bow and nocked an arrow.

Palcombine turned to the others and explained that he was going to do the same thing Ellerson had just done. They decided that Allendale would make his way to the base of the bridge to provide them cover from that side as the other three crossed. Once Palcombine crossed and Allendale took his place, Jarius, Titus, and Amanda slipped out onto the highway and started down the road toward the bridge. Trying their best to appear casual, the three walked side by side. They were not taking their time, but they were careful to not appear in a hurry. As the three of them reached the middle of the bridge, they saw Ellerson and Palcombine scurry up the slope to the roadside. Just as they reached the end of the bridge, riders came out of the woods toward them.

The idea to play it cool went away quickly as one of the riders shouted, "There they are!" then dug in his heels. The others followed suit. Uncertain how many riders there really were, the three took off running to join the two Elvan archers. Hearing the three of them running made Allendale jump out from his cover and begin running across the bridge to join them. The elves opened fire and dropped four riders before they had closed half the distance to the bridge. The riders were not in uniform, carrying a flag, or riding in formation. They appeared to be aggressive and rushing toward them with their long swords and bows drawn.

Hopelessly, outnumbered, it looked like about thirty riders came charging out of the woods. Only two more riders fell to their arrows before the riders and horses suddenly collided with some invisible barrier. It was as if they had suddenly hit a wall. The first riders and horses were crushed against this wall by those who were riding behind them. Their arrows seemed to hit the same wall and fall to the ground. More than half the riders and their horses ran into the invisible obstruction. Their speed caused them to pile up and crush one another. Some riders had been knocked from their steeds, and the rest reined in behind the massive pile.

Rising from the creek bed on the north side of the bridge appeared the Elvan mage they had met the night before. He scampered up onto the highway and then ran past the group into the weeded shoreline to their south. He did not stop to explain. Looking over his shoulder, he said, "That wall won't hold them long. You might want to follow me." The riders were already moving along the wall trying to find a way around it.

With no reasonable options, the group quickly followed Ezen Kroach into the high shrubs that lined the shore of the creek and river. "You may want to hurry. After all, they do have horses." After rushing through the tall grass, the soft saturated ground turned to river rocks. This will make it harder for them to follow us on horseback. "Come on," Kroach urged. Behind them, they could hear the riders reorganizing and shouting commands.

The rocks turned to larger ones as they got closer to an approaching hillside. This made the running very awkward, as many of the rocks would roll out from under their feet as they moved across them. They followed the hillside to the river's edge. There was still some vegetation among the large rocks. Sometimes the occasional tree helped to provide cover for their escape. Their path was narrowing as the river and hillside converged. Suddenly Kroach slowed down and began to look at the large rocks and boulders that rested just up the hillside. Ellerson and Palcombine moved to the rear of the party and drew their bows. It looked like they had run out of room, and they were going to have to stand their ground at this place.

Ellerson shot Allendale a look of concern. They knew trying to a swim for it would be extremely dangerous. There they stood watching Ezen Kroach surveying this hillside and mumbling something to himself. They could hear the hooves of the horses clacking their way through the large rocks. They knew the riders were getting closer. They were about to panic as Kroach declared, "Oh, here it is." Then he waved for the others to follow him. The party crawled their way up the short rocky slope to a large group of boulders. At the base of the boulders was considerable overgrowth of young aspen. Kroach showed them how to pull it apart and stride through. On the other side of the saplings was a short path that led to the opening to a small cave. With a sense of pride, Kroach turned and reminded the party, "See, I told you there was a cave over here."

31

Quellen had just begun his service as an acolyte in the Elvan Temple. He was much younger than most acolytes awarded this rare honor. Unfortunately, one of the realities of war was that it pulled all able-bodied men from their homes and jobs to protect their kingdom. Quellen had only been serving as a confidential aide for about six moons. Yet some of the conversations he was privy to were those of legend. In this sacred antechamber, it was common for Barnabus Malactus to speak with Knights of the Royal Order, other priests, or even King Elfanwisel. Quellen had taken a sacred oath of secrecy. Certainly, he never intended to divulge things he had heard in this room. He knew he was truly honored to just be present. Quellen was never a part of the conversation. His role was to do whatever Barnabus wanted. So mostly he stood to the side and served when called upon.

This day seemed no different than others. Barnabus Malactus was conferring with a scroungy looking human and Bellard, an archer Quellen had known in his youth. Bellard had dedicated himself to military service and was an honorable fighter, recognized for his skill and wit. Why he would bring this human into this holy chamber was truly beyond anything Quellen could imagine. Standing by the door, he could not entirely hear what the three of them were discussing. Whatever Bellard was saying quickly captured the attention of Barnabus. Moments after Bellard and the human came into the room, Barnabus pulled a map from a pile of parchments he kept laying open on a table against the wall.

Bellard pointed to a place on the map and said something about "the High Creek Pass." Quellen had never traveled beyond the security of Hollywondra. There really was no reason to go anywhere else. Hollywondra was a beautiful place, and the woods provided all anyone needed for nourishment. He had begun training in clerical healing, so he was not much of a resource for the fighting. So when Bellard mentioned the High Creek Pass Trail, the story intrigued Quellen. He tried to imagine what this trail must look like and where it might be in a land beyond the great sacred woods. He took parts of the name Creek High Pass Trail and began imagining what the terrain must look like, when suddenly he was startled by Barnabus yelling his name.

"Quellen! Would you please pay attention? I told you. I need you to go to the king's court. Tell the king's couriers that you are coming on my behalf, and it is of the utmost importance that I speak at once with the king. Do you understand me?"

Now Malactus had Quellen's undivided attention. His nodding grew uncomfortable after the fifth or sixth bow. Of course, he understood. He was just embarrassed that he had been caught allowing his mind to wander. He took a moment to look at the two men who stood with the priest at his table. This delay only resulted in Barnabus yelling, "Well? What are you waiting for? Make haste!"

Quellen shot out of the room and onto the high bows of the ancient oak. He used every short cut he knew to quickly make his way to the forest floor. Running was socially undignified inside the city, but after a moment of reservation, he took off in full flight. He needed to get to the king as fast as he could. Everyone knew the priest was of the highest standing. But for the priest to say he must have an audience with the king seemed almost inappropriate.

Showing no concern for the carpet of alyssum, Quellen flew through Hollywondra as if he were being chased. The city of Hollywondra was much larger than most people realized. With the homes and shops carved into the trunks of the gigantic oaks, it could be mistaken for just an ancient oak grove. That is if you failed to notice the absence of the debris that normally litters the floor of the forest. Inside Hollywondra, not so much as an oak leaf littered the hallowed ground. Quellen was able to move quickly to the other side of the city. Even at his top speed, it still took him ten minutes to reach the king's court.

At the north end of Hollywondra, the creek turned east as the ground rose to a mound. At the top of the mound was the king's estate. Four enormous oak trees grew close enough together to intertwine their branches and create one gigantic canopy. The Royal Green of Hollywondra was a large grassy patch of turf that lay on the southern face of this large knoll and extended out into the city. The Royal Green was the large open space where many of the public ceremonies were held and large crowds could assemble. At the top of the Green, one of the four trees stood forward, with two tree trunks on either side, and the fourth tree grew directly behind the frontmost. The pattern in which they grew was so symmetrical that you could not see the fourth tree trunk if you stood in front of the first one. This tree formation covered the majority of the knoll. The King's Knoll was at the northeast end of Hollywondra and at the very edge of the Raven Rift. There was no back door entrance to the king's residence.

Two armored Elvan guards stood at the entrance to the first tree. They stood tall and each held a polished mithril javelin. The Green was such a large gentle slope that nobody could approach without being seen from over a two hundred feet away. If someone were to rush these men, they would clearly be able to get off the first shot and even retreat into the royal quarters, before anyone was within fifty feet of them.

As Quellen approached the grassy green slope, he noticed the two guards cross their spears at the front of the entry. Quellen then slowed to a walk, stopped, and raised one hand, as if to wave. From a distance, he announced, "I am Quellen, the personal acolyte of the High Priest Barnabus Malactus." Quellen was a little disappointed that he had to announce himself. He knew that many of the high priest's acolytes had become very famous and highly honored citizens of Hollywondra. He realized he was new to the position, and he still had to earn the respect that came with the position.

"I come with urgent business at the request of the high priest. He requests the king's company at the Temple as soon as the king can come. He has urgent news to share with his lordship."

HOLLYWONDRA

At this, the guards pulled their javelins back to their sides. Then they turned to face each other. As one of the two guards stepped inside the wooden door, the other guard took a post directly in front of the door to wait. Quellen thought the formal guard seemed a bit defensive, but then remembered they were at war, and this was the residence of their king. The enemy army was still days away. As he stood and waited, he suddenly became saddened at the realization that they were indeed under attack and their forest was besieged. Just as he was done processing the grave nature of their reality, the guard retuned and announced to Quellen, "The King shall be there soon. Tell the high priest to make ready."

At that, Quellen turned and ran as fast as he could back to the temple.

*****

"There were more than we could count," reported Bellard. "It looks as though they are sweeping in from the northwest. I think they will try to come over High Creek Pass."

"Yes, of course," interrupted King Elfanwisel. "We understand that is really the only way they could come undetected. The real questions are how quickly did you get here and how fast were they moving?"

Then the high priest interrupted the king with a gentle clearing of his throat. Turning his attention to the high priest, the king paused as if he was just now reminded. Then looking back at Bellard and the human who escorted him, he said, "Well...we must know how quickly they will arrive and of course the names of the men in your patrol. We must honor each of them and their families."

Bellard began to speak, when the king quickly raised his hand and said, "But first, we must know more of these details of his new army." Then the tactical questions began. Hamman Drew knew the elf was the only one they would listen to, so he tried to remain interested. As he stood nearby, his mind wondered to how badly his thighs throbbed. Then after he considered his level of fatigue, he couldn't decide if he'd take rest over something to eat. Then his mind began to wonder back to the last time he had eaten anything.

As Bellard recounted the events, the king seemed particularly interested in the type of wolf that ran with this band of Kobold and the number of them they actually saw. It seemed he was calculating the possible size of the army by the number of wolves deployed. He didn't reveal his thoughts. He simply gave the high priest a glance and then asked more questions of the Elvan scout.

After what seemed like hours, the two of them were finally dismissed. The high priest ordered Quellen to provide food and quarters for Hamman Drew. Quellen escorted Hamman Drew from their meeting. Walking beside the tall human ranger made Quellen uncomfortable. Besides the fact that the human stunk of mud and sweat, Quellen knew he had to be a warrior of great stature to have been invited into this temple. Quellen escorted Hamman Drew to an acolyte's quarters. It was a simple room with a bed and a chair. A little daylight came into the room through a hole that was high on the wall. Not a lot of light, just enough to let you know if it was day or night. Drew went straight for the bed and began taking off his moccasins. It was then that Quellen realized he didn't have any reason to fear this man. He simply wanted rest and nourishment.

Quellen brought Hamman Drew a large bowl of berries and nuts and a carafe of water. Pausing as he exited, Quellen suggested to Hamman Drew, "You should not leave this room unescorted. The temple is a holy place, and you could easily wander into sacred areas of the temple. That would be unforgiveable. It's just safer for you to stay here and wait for me to serve or direct you." Hamman Drew nodded his understanding and stood up to pull back the wool blanket on the bed.

As he turned to walk away, Quellen felt empowered by the way this human listened to his suggestion and moved to the cot so quickly. For the second time that day, Quellen's stomach sank. As he left Drew's room, he found that four armed guards had been posted outside the door. Again, he was reminded just how few of humans the elves could actually trust. Many humans had banded together to

HOLLYWONDRA

form this army to extinguish the elves from existence. This man, for some reason, was different.

*****

The next morning Quellen brought Hamman Drew a basin of water and some raw oats. Quellen did not want to engage the human because he did not want to anger him. The guy did carry a sword and was savage enough to use it. Why take the chance of inciting him? So after dropping off the food and wash basin, Quellen intentionally avoided eye contact and scurried quickly for the door. He was not fast enough. "Pardon me," Hamman Drew asked. "Is there any chance I might have an audience with the Elvan hero who brought me here yesterday?"

Quellen's first thought was that this human either didn't know what the word *hero* meant or he was exaggerating kindness. Turning to him, Quellen decided to keep it simple and proper. "I will inquire." Then bowing, he backed out of the room. As he exited Drew's room, Quellen realized that he found comfort in the presence of the guards that stood outside his door.

*****

"Listen! This was not my war, but I've decided to make it mine. I cannot fight it from some comfy room in a distant temple. If you guys are launching any assaults, please count me in. In combat is where I can help the most. I don't care which assault you want me in, just get me out of this bed and into the fight." Bellard listened to Hamman Drew's plea. He did look unusually restless for a man who had just been chased out of the wilderness and into the safe confines of this temple.

"All I can do is tell the captain about your willingness to fight. I am a soldier like you. I carry no rank or authority. I will let them know you are willing to fight." Then Bellard paused and said, "No. I will remind them how you fought bravely with us and how I had to pull you away from the fight."

"Thanks," Hamman Drew offered with a solemn respect. "I am confident you will do your best. I will honor whatever decision is made by your superiors."

Nodding in agreement, Bellard left Hamman Drew in his room. Looking around at his meager lodging, Hamman took a seat at the edge of the bed. As he had done a hundred times after a fight, he pulled out his out his scimitar and examined its edge. Sharpening the one scimitar always reminded him of his broken blade. Then pulling out his stone and spit on it. In long careful strokes, he pulled his blade across the coarse surface of his whetstone.

32

As the party rushed into the cave, they found the large rocks turned to boulders, and the boulders soon turned into walls. The walls closed quickly to form an obvious path. The clear path made it easy for them to quickly rush down the trail, until the darkness overtook them. At the very edge of daylight, Palcombine slowed everyone to a stop. Pulling an unlit torch from his backpack, he said, "I wasn't sure if we might need this." The need was obvious, his humor didn't get a response from anyone in the party. As Palcombine began to pull his flint from a pouch on his waist, Ezen Kroach stepped forward.

"I can help," he offered. Slowly waving his left hand over his right, he mumbled a short incantation. Suddenly, a small flame appeared above the palm of his right hand. The flame was not burning him. It seemed to dance just above the surface of his skin. Stepping toward Palcombine, Kroach gently tossed the flame onto the pitch saturated end of the torch. The torch immediately ignited, and the party got their first real glance of their new surroundings. To their left was a dirty stone-faced wall that was impenetrable. To their right, stalagmites rose up from the floor. It looked as though they could weave in and out of the field of stone pillars, but following the wall to their left seemed the most logical and expeditious. The group wasted no time and tried to distance themselves from the cave opening. If they were being pursued, their followers would have to light torches was well. They wanted their torch to be out of sight by the time the others entered the cave.

Recognizing that Kroach had again used his magic to support the group, Titus decided to share a little of his own fire-making "magic." Titus slowed down so he could get into his backpack.

Slinging his backpack from his shoulder, Titus quickly found what he was looking for. Putting it in his pocket, he slung his backpack back onto his shoulder and quickened his pace. The search of his backpack resulted in Kroach getting slightly ahead of him. Easing into stride beside Kroach, Titus said, "I have a little fire-making magic of my own." Amused at the notion, Kroach gave the boy his undivided attention. Pulling the lighter from is pocket, Titus flicked the lighter. A spark jumped, and the flame quickly appeared. Kroch slowed his pace and leaned in to examine what his young friend held in his hand. He was both amazed and curious about this instrument that created fire. Titus showed Kroach how the lighter worked. Once Kroach understood it was a tool, he remarked how he knew "some tinkers who would enjoy replicating this machinery."

The mage's interest in Titus's raw talents endeared the boy to him. They talked quietly as the party wove their way deeper into the cavern. The cool dank surroundings made everyone wonder just how far they were going to walk into this place. At least it was shelter from the rain and a place to hide from their pursuers.

Allendale had taken the torch from Palcombine and chosen to light the way. Palcombine and Ellerson complained about not needing the torchlight. They could see better without the illumination. Allendale had to periodically remind them that not everyone in their party had Elvan vision and everyone needs to be able to see their way. Palcombine moved well out in front of the torchlight to scout the way. Ellerson fell back behind the group to see if their pursuers had followed them into the cavern. Titus and Kroach walked behind Amanda and Jarius, while Allendale led the smaller group.

After traveling downward into the cavern for several hours, they still had not heard any sounds of pursuit. Kroach became a bit cavalier about the path, suggesting that "you can't really get lost in here, because we'll eventually come out the other side." The rest of the party didn't share his lighthearted enthusiasm. Their silence suggested they were a bit restless and unsure what they might have gotten themselves into. When they first entered the cave, the ceiling was only head high to a human. Now the torchlight could no longer illuminate the stalactites that hung overhead. If anything,

HOLLYWONDRA

what had been a tunnel in the side of a hill had turned into a huge, cavernous chamber. Their path continued to weave down through moist stone structures. They moved carefully through the cool damp moldy smelling darkness. The only thing that seemed to break the unending darkness were the distant echoes of water dripping into a nearby pool. The torch Allendale carried continued to light the wall and their dusty path.

For several hours, their path had followed the wall to their left. At one point, the stalagmites forced their path away from the wall. They moved carefully out into the rock formations. Then the stalagmites were becoming more sparse and an obvious path emerged. Black emptiness still hemmed them in. It was as if their torchlight was being pushed back by an insurmountable darkness. The path had become uneven and crude. Small little trickling streams of water made parts of the floor puddle and slick. The slippery path made everyone slow down and exercise more caution.

Titus asked Kroach, "How do we even know where we're going?"

"Our friend Palcombine is scouting things out for us. He won't lead us wrong. Just watch your step."

The group was a little started when Palcombine came out of the dark to direct them to their left. After a short walk, they reached a wall of large stalagmites. Palcombine showed them where to step between a couple of stalagmites, as if they were pillars at an entry. Walking past the pillars, Titus looked up the side of one pillar. The stone rose up into the darkness of the cavern. After entering this pillared pathway, the floor had become drier and more level. They wove through the rock formations on a path of least resistance. After having followed this path for just a few hundred yards, Allendale raised his hand to halt the party. He'd noticed Palcombine had stopped scouting and was waiting for the party to catch up.

The path ahead was split by an enormous stalagmite. The side of this enormous stone formation could easily be mistaken for a cavern wall. The path to the left looked like it might move toward the wall of the chamber. The path to the right seemed to wander off into a maze of stalagmites. Ezen Kroach made his way to the front and quickly explained, "We go left. Do not go that way," pointing to the trail to the right. Realizing he had been a bit unclear, he explained, "That trail would take us deeper into the mountains. No man nor elf were meant to travel that path." Almost shuttering, Ezen Kroach didn't wait for the torchlight and started off down the trail to the left. Over his shoulder, he suggested, "Besides, we're not far from a great place to set camp."

As the new line formed, Palcombine quickly scooted past Kroach to take the lead and to continue to scout. Kroach seemed to not care. Then Allendale strode past Kroach to move the torchlight back to the front of the group. As if Kroach had slowed down, Jarius nudged Amanda to pass him and move in behind her dad. After they had passed the mage, Jarius came into an even stride to Amanda's right. This was the first time Titus realized his party was organized in a specific marching order. Titus quickly moved in alongside Ezen and asked, "So have you ever taken that other path?"

Initially, Kroach did not even look in Titus's direction. He just began explaining that he had taken the other path before. "It is much longer, turns to the north, and is inhabited by unfriendly sorts."

"What kind of unfriendly sorts?" Titus naturally asked.

"Nothing for you to be concerned with, laddie. Just know that this way is a lot easier."

Just as Kroach had suggested, about a half hour from the stalagmite junction, the stalagmites dissipated. The path turned to the left, and it seemed they may have found a new wall. This time the wall was to their right. The ceiling of the cavern dropped down and could be seen at the very edge of their torchlight. At one point, the rock forming this corridor's wall had a vein of fragile rock that had crumbled, and small boulders had rolled out onto the floor of the path. It was there that the party decided to rest.

Using the different-sized boulders as places to rest their aching feet, the party sat quietly eating rations from their packs. This was a lot more exercise than Titus was prepared for. He could never understand the emphasis the school put on physical education classes. He just saw them as "fluff" or an "easy A" for the athletes. Now he was getting a strong sense for the value of that physical conditioning. All this walking and running was taking a toll on his feet. He knew they

HOLLYWONDRA

were blistered, but he was afraid to see just how badly. The dripping of water into a pool sounded so close that Titus picked up the torch and moved slowly in the direction of the sound. He thought he might be able to take off his sneakers and soak his feet in the cool water for a just moment. Tired from their travel, they all watched Titus move slowly away from where they sat. Titus quickly found the edge of the water. Excited by his discovery, he shouted back to the group, "Hey, it looks like there might be some fresh water over here."

Turning back to the water, Titus squatted down to examine it more carefully. Cupping his left hand, he reached into the pool. The clear cold water and fire light made it hard to judge the depth of the pool. His hand was able to scoop up a handful of water, but it also stirred the sediment at the bottom of the pool. Smelling the water, Titus could not find any reason to not try drinking it. The swirling sediment revealed an odd-shaped shadow just under the water a few feet from the edge of the pool. Momentarily frozen by his curiosity, he quickly spit out what remained of the water as he recognized human skeletal remains lying in the shallow pool and lightly covered with silt.

Choking from the surprise, Titus began to stand when a dark blue frog with bright orange spots jumped onto the back of his hand. He didn't even have time to shout for help. The frog quickly snapped the back of his hand with his sharp tongue and caused a small cut to open on the back of his hand. Startled by the sudden attack, Titus shook the frog from his hand. Immediately he became dizzy, fell to his right, dropped the torch, and narrowly missed falling onto its flame. Titus made no noise. There he laid wide awake, but unable to move or speak. Breathing was becoming more difficult. All he could hear was the echoes of his party yelling his name and drawing nearer. He wanted to tell them what had happened, but he couldn't speak.

The aurora of the torchlight had fully illuminated Titus as he walked from the group to the edge of the water. From their seats, the group saw Titus kneel down to check the water. When they saw him slip to the ground and drop the torch they rushed to his side. As they came to his side, they saw a small dark blue frog jump from the water and jump again toward the rest of the group. Ezen was the

215

first to notice that several more of the frogs were now coming out of the water.

The dark color of the frogs made them hard to see in the torchlight. Those they could see they were able to quickly kill. Even a wooden staff was a formidable weapon to the flesh of a small frog. The challenge was that they could not see them very well. One had struck and paralyzed Palcombine as well. In a very short time, the group felt certain they had staved off the poisonous frogs. Then they dragged Titus and Palcombine away from the water's edge and back toward the cavern's wall. By this time, Titus wasn't breathing and his face was turning blue.

Amanda came to the side of her friend. Kneeling down on the rocky floor, she placed both her hands on Titus's chest and prayed. In very little time, Titus's chest began to heave deeply, and the color began to return to his face. Amanda asked Titus if he was feeling better, but all Titus could do was point to his mouth. After Amanda examined him further, she suggested that it would probably wear off slowly. Then smiling at her friend, she suggested the group could possibly benefit from not hearing him for a while anyway. The look Titus gave her assured her that he was on the mend. She returned his look with her warm smile. Her smile made him forget that he was in a foreign land, and she'd just saved his life. For just a moment, her smile took him back to a warm summer's day sitting on hay bales.

Ellerson arrived just in time to see Amanda place her hands on the still body of Palcombine. Her prayers seemed to have an even stronger effect on Palcombine. He was able to stand and begin speaking almost immediately. Titus wanted to ask the others if he was the only one wondering about these skills of hers. So Amanda can lean over Palcombine and with a few words of prayer transform a dying man into a vital warrior? He couldn't even begin to comprehend the science of that healing. All he knew is that he'd love to talk to someone the about it.

The party took turns standing watch while everyone rested. After everyone had a chance to get some rest, they continued to head what they felt was west through the cavern. They had not been traveling an hour before Palcombine raised his hand for them to halt.

HOLLYWONDRA

Everyone froze in their tracks. It only took a moment before they could also hear what first found the ears of Palcombine. It was a disorganized thrumming sound. As they stood still to listen more carefully, they realized it was the sound of armored men marching.

Quickly the group huddled and Ezen suggested, "We should backtrack to that intersection of the trails at the stalagmites. We could go up the other path a short ways and let them pass by. I'm sure they are just passing through."

"What if they decide to take the path we're hiding on?" asked Jarius.

"Well, we could still outrun them. But I think if they knew how to find this cavern, they also know not take the other path." Ezen seemed confident anyone traveling this trail would not turn north at that intersection. They knew they still had the advantage of not being discovered yet. So they extinguished their torch and held each other's hands as they moved quickly through the darkness. Titus was very uncomfortable moving at the speed they moved. He could not see his own hand if he were able to hold it in front of his face.

Titus was holding Amanda's hand as they moved through the dark. He welcomed her warm soft touch. Even though the cavern was pitch black and he blindly rushed forward, he found himself wishing he could see her face, as he felt her guiding him through the dark. Then Titus remembered the gravity of their situation.

Amanda was slowed by having to pull Titus along behind her. She was surprised to find how well her eyes adjusted to the darkness. It wasn't perfectly clear, but she could pick out gray shapes that made her better at keeping her balance as they moved through the dark. She could very clearly see the figures of her father, Jarius, and Palcombine rushing along the path in front of her.

This method seemed to work for them as they made their way back to the intersection of the trails. As they arrived at the intersection, they stopped and immediately noticed the glow of torchlight coming from the path to the east. The path to the east rose slowly, so the torchlight flickered between the columns of giant stalagmites. They couldn't hear who was coming from the east, but they suspected their attackers had followed them into the cavern.

Huddled in a tight group at the intersection, Ezen Kroach calmly suggested, "Well, it looks like we best head north. It's best if we do not use torchlight. There are creatures that call this trail their home, so the less attention we draw to ourselves, the better."

"Why don't we wait them out and see if they simply pass each other?" Titus suggested. "Then we could let them light the way and take our time following them at a distance."

Allendale explained, "If we wait nearby to what choices they make, we forfeit any advantage we have in being ahead of them."

"I could do it," Titus offered. "I could stay far enough out of sight and up the trail to see what they do. I could remain invisible to them, and they wouldn't know I was even there."

Allendale turned to Ezen Kroach and asked, "What's to stop these guys from just turning up this northern path? If both armies are from Zel Camber and they meet, why wouldn't they just turn north to seek us out?

Kroach paused, then sheepishly explained, "Well…nothing, I suppose. Then again, if they had the knowledge to enter this cavern from the west end, they may also know about the Kayuni. The Kayuni are subterranean folk who rarely, if ever, go to the surface. They subsist on the creatures they hunt here in this cavern. They are vicious and cannibalistic, so they don't have friends or allies."

"Well, it seems we are hemmed in on all sides," Ellerson said, stating the obvious.

"Maybe, we try the lad's idea," suggested Kroach. "If the two armies pass, then we can follow one of them out. If they unite and march in one direction, we can either follow them or go the other way. If they fight each other, we could take the path they leave for us. If they meet and turn to the north, well then, we just do our best to stay ahead of them."

The group discussed it for a few moments and realized they could no longer see the torchlight from the east. They knew that group would soon be coming out of the stalagmites and arriving at this intersection. Running short on time, they agree to move up the northern trail and listen. Titus got them to agree to let him hang

HOLLYWONDRA

back down the trail, but far enough away from the intersection that he would not be seen if he were to become visible.

The pack of elves moved quickly and quietly away from where they left Titus. Titus focused his mind to make himself invisible. Then he slowly made his way south toward the intersection. He was about one hundred feet away from the intersection when he saw torchlight emerge from the path through the stalagmites on the western trail. He could see there were at least a dozen armed men and four torches. As they reached the intersection, they stopped. He could easily overhear two of the men talking about which path to take.

One of the men near the front stopped to tell another, "He was perfectly clear that we keep moving to the east." Not even pausing to consider the path to the north, the group of men began to move east. The last of the troops had not even passed the intersection when shouts arose. The echoing shouts in the cavern made it hard for Titus to understand what was going on. All he could here was some name calling and confusion. When the shouting quieted, he noticed that the last man had turned around and was now beginning to slowly make his way back toward the intersection. Then more torches began appearing. Soon, there had to have been more than thirty armored men standing at the intersection.

Titus could hear the accusations and blame as one human leader accused the other, "How could you have let them past you!"

"What do you mean let them past us? We combed the cavern for hours searching every crack and crevice for any sign of them. They did not slip past us. I think you better take another look at how your men searched your path," suggested the other lieutenant.

"We had twice the men," he scoffed. "There is no way a group of four or more slipped past us.

Then the two paused and considered the path to the north. "You don't think they went north, do you?"

The other man chuckled, "Well, dumber things have happened."

The two leaders realized the same thing at the same time. The man leading the western group turned to the larger group and said, "You men, wait here. We are going to take a brief look at this." Then the two leaders took a torch and began moving slowly up the northern path toward Titus.

Realizing the men were coming his direction, Titus began to slowly move back up the path toward his party. As he started to move, his shoulder jarred loose some small rocks that had been sticking out of the cavern wall. Quickly he leaned into the rock to hold it into place. He knew if he moved, the rocks would fall and make his presence known. He couldn't tell how much rock he was holding in place with his back. He could only tell that it was gravel and not just one big rock.

Standing as still as he could, Titus found himself starting to hold his breath as the two men drew near. They both carried a torch. Not five feet from him, they stopped. "Okay, here's the deal. I know neither of us want to go north on this trail. We both know we had better check it out, or we risk not finding them, and that could be worse than taking this northern trail."

"Hey, I've got an idea," the other man offered. "I have a man in my ranks who is my sister's husband. He's a drunkard, and I know he's been terrible to her. He is constantly asking for promotion, though he has never done a thing to deserve it." The man began to smile. "Maybe we offer him an opportunity at glory? We send him and a handful of our biggest hungriest dolts to check out this path. We can always report back that we sent a regiment up that trail while we doubled back to make sure neither of us lost let them slip past us."

The other man smiled and nodded. "Yeah, that's a great idea. I've got a couple of guys that come right to mind."

The two men turned and began making their way back to their troops. Titus continued to stand still until the men made their way back to the group at the fork. Then being as careful as he could, he slowly squatted to the ground to let the rocks fall gently to the ground. The little sound they made was hidden in the orders being given by the lieutenants. As soon as he was sure he had not been heard, he slowly made his way back to his party.

"They're sending a small detail of men up this trail. The rest of them are going to backtrack the other two directions looking to see if they had overlooked us. Every route's taken," Titus shared.

HOLLYWONDRA

"Let's move," Palcombine suggested. "They will be able to move a little faster with torchlight, then we will be able to without torches."

The group quickly clasped hands and began moving up the trail. For the next hour, they were able to keep a steady pace and never really heard their pursuers. As they reached a place where a large stalagmite pushed the trail away from the wall, Ezen Kroach told the party to stop. The path narrowed sharply between two gigantic stalagmites.

"Hold your step, and cover your eyes," he directed. Then Kroach made a small flame erupt in the palm of his hand. The bluish flame was clearly not a natural flame, but it did create enough light to show the party that a few thin fibers ran from one side of the trail to the other. Under careful examination, they could see that the fibers appeared to be a single thread that had been woven back and forth over this passage. Tiny rings had been set in the stone to thread the fiber through. At the bottom was a small brass bell.

Individually, each member of the party slowly wove through the trap while Ezen held the bell still. After taking considerable time to safely pass through, the group was startled to see how much their pursuers had closed on them. On the path beyond the trap, the stalagmites were still very large, but there was space between most of them. This made finding the path very confusing and far less clear. The group chose to move to the far western side of the path and take cover. They knew they couldn't afford to be out in the open if the Kayuni came. They also wanted to see what they were up against and what happened if the men set off the trap. They moved as far west of the path as they could and still have a view of the torch coming down the path toward the trap.

*****

As the men bumbled into the fine filament, you could barely here the jingle of the bell over the clanking of their armor. Just like that, the men were past the trap. Now the group was frozen as the military men slowly made their way toward them. The men had to slow down a bit, since the path was not clearly defined. The group of eight fighters walked right past them to the north.

Amanda and her group collected their breath and tried to stay as low in the glow of the torchlight as they could. They realized they had just given away any advantage they thought they may have had. They were now surrounded on all three sides. As the men moved further north, they were suddenly attacked. Not more than forty feet away, several small humanoid creatures jumped down from the tops of stalagmites and onto the patrol of eight. The men were quickly covered in a countess swarm of lean little humanoid creatures. These small creatures were naked, except for the small filthy loin cloth they wore. They all appeared to be slashing the solders with short little daggers. They slashed and stabbed with a ferocity that almost seemed random. Even the men who were carrying swords in their hands had no time to defend themselves. The entire group was overtaken and killed in a matter of moments.

The Kayuni hunger was just as viscous as their attack. Many could not wait to eat. Without hesitation, they began cutting into the flesh of the men and sliced off chunks to devour. Some took time to even eat a second portion. Amanda and her friends watched the gore in horror. Fortunately, the torches carried by the militia had fallen to the ground. Much of what could be seen was just the chaos. They had to make sure they were not seen and attacked as well. They remained frozen waiting for the creatures to leave. After a while, the Kayuni dragged the bodies from the area.

Now everyone had a clear understanding why Ezen said nobody who knew this path would choose this path. As the Kayuni left the area, the group backtracked to the intersection of the two main trails. The other soldiers were gone. Still, nobody dared to say a word, until they had made their way around the corner and all the way back to the frog's pool. Once they paused, Ezen Kroach broke the silence. "Kayuni are not friendly to outsiders."

Titus could only shake his head and whisper, "Kayuni," to himself.

The group knew the question they had to answer, so Ezen Kroach offered the answer before the debate began. "You know we have to take that northern path." All heads quickly turned and looked

HOLLYWONDRA

at him for his reasoning. Then Kroach continued, "Those troops, that so willingly sent those men to their death, are going to be waiting at both ends of this tunnel. Few know where the northern exit is since that path is not traveled by people who live to tell about it."

"So why is that a good idea for us?" asked Amanda. "What makes you think we will have any better luck then those guys?"

"Well, I have indeed taken the northern path before. There are some strategies we will need to employ, but I am confident that most of us can make it through safely," he answered.

"Most of us?" she challenged.

"Well, of course," he answered in a quick cavalier tone. "All three of these paths carry risk. You don't think those men are looking for you just to get your opinion on the next lunar eclipse, do you?" Waving his arm at the rest of the party, he continued, "Don't you think these men are willing to lay down their lives to protect you? Eastern and western routes carry the certainty of attack. At least there is a chance that we can skirt past the Kayuni. They are warm-blooded creatures. We will be able to spot them in the dark. They will also be able to spot us, so we need to be very sneaky."

Ezen mumbled, "And they might be busy right now."

Suggesting the required level of stealth would have to rise to the level of "very sneaky" made Ellerson shook his head in doubt.

"I have to agree with the mage," offered Palcombine. "As far as those men are concerned, they have us trapped in here. They do not consider the other route an option, so they will not let so much as an ant out of here without a siege. Well, wizard, what kind of strategy do you suggest?"

"Their timing was almost perfect," Kroach thought as he considered the attack they had just witnessed. "There's a good chance the Kayuni may not have reset the trap at the stalagmite gate. That band of eight men probably created a feast like the Kayuni hadn't seen in a generation. I say we move now. If we're lucky, they may be distracted with dinner." Looking at Palcombine, Kroach urged, "I think we should move as soon as possible."

*****

223

Titus had become a little envious that Amanda and the rest of the group could see so well in the dark. That was until the time came for them to slip past the Kayuni camp. The slurping and growling sounds made him wonder if he wanted to see what these beasts were doing. The others later told how the bodies of the dead were not as bright as those of the Kayuni. But the flesh was still warm enough that they could tell it was being ripped from the bone and devoured as quickly as it was pulled off.

Once they had skirted past the Kayuni encampment, they followed the cavern wall until it funneled them toward a place where two large stalagmites formed a gate north of the Kayuni camp. Recognizing this type of rock formation, the group had no trouble finding and disarming another alarm trap. What they didn't expect to find was a pit fall trap that had been dug into the path about a hundred yards past the gate.

The floor of the path quickly descended into a bed of stakes. The stakes appeared to be broken tips and shafts of spears buried in the dirt and sticking upright. On the other side of the pit was a wall of dirt that rose back up to their path. The party had to meander through the shafts and hoist each other up the other side. While making their way through the bed of stakes, Titus stepped on something that made the ground very uneven. It wasn't a stake or anything so sharp, so he bent over and picked up the gnarly shaped stick he'd stepped on.

The stick was thin and a little bulbous on each end. Initially he thought it must have been one of the knobs that he felt through his boot. The strange thing was that there was something on the stick. Quickly he realized it wasn't a stick, it was a bone! It was a finger bone. Loosely dangling from the bone was a ring. He quickly pulled the ring off and quickly threw the bone back to the ground in disgust. Immediately, he began wiping his hand on the leg of his pants.

With a little teamwork, they were able to get everyone pulled up out of the pit and back up on the path. Finally, they were able to put some distance between them and the Kayuni.

33

Hamman Drew's suspicions were correct; the elves needed every capable man to support the defense of Hollywondra. What he could not have guessed was that he was going to be sent right back from where he'd come. While he stood waiting for his orders, Drew watched how this mysterious city came together to prepare this regiment. The town square had become a staging area. The elves pulled together a regiment of about a hundred archers and a handful of fletchers. The townsfolk were quickly organizing the Elven archers for their next foray.

Kids, just large enough to wrap their arms around the quivers, carried arrows to the Green. Ladies prepared patties of dried smashed berries they packed between thin yellow leaves. They took these paddies and then packed several of them at a time into packs. The packs of arrows and food were being loaded onto the back of two of the three Scurriers standing in the Green. The men were organizing into units, and the entire operation was coming together very quickly.

Through the field of chaos emerged Bellard carrying a mithril scimitar. Approaching Hamman Drew, Bellard extended it out to him hilt first. "I remember you whining about needing to use two of these at a time. You insisted you were better when you had two. It would only collect dust in the armory. Here, put it to good use."

Hamman Drew could not be sure if Bellard was ribbing him or not. He was just appreciative of the gesture. Reaching out, he took the scimitar by the hilt and said, "Thank you." Then turning slightly away from Bellard, Drew slowly drew the scimitar from its covering. Then he looked down the length of the sword and balanced it mid-shaft to see how its weight was distributed. Taking the scimitar by the hilt, Hamman Drew began slicing thin air. Looking back to Bellard, he registered his approval with a nod and said, "This is outstanding craftsmanship. I will put it to good use defending your people."

Nodding back at Hamman Drew, Bellard turned away and made his way back to the men who were making ready.

Hamman Drew took off the belt that held his two sheathes. Even though the one scimitar had been broken, Hamman Drew still carried the broken blade in its scabbard. Now he pulled that scabbard and broken blade off his belt. Then he put the new Elvan sword in its place. After putting his belt on, he adjusted his scabbards to ensure they were exactly where he needs then for fluid access. Then he practiced pulling his two swords and making slashing attacks with them. It wasn't his old sword, but it was every bit as good. For the first time in days, Hamman Drew felt fully prepared for war.

*****

The elves seemed to lope along at only one speed, and that was almost an open run for Hamman Drew. He had forgotten how quickly they moved through the brush and woods. This small force was charged with intercepting the Kobold army and decimating as many as they could. Their primary objective was to not let the Kobold join the enemy forces already assembled in the Valley of Shayna. The elves knew they had to make good time. The time it had taken Bellard and Hamman Drew to bring their warning to Hollywondra suggested the Kobold army could arrive any day.

Their regiment consisted of ten small bands of ten. Half of them peeled off and headed more westerly, in case the Kobold were making a forced march to the valley. The other half headed in the direction they felt they felt they should find the Kobold. Each half of the force had their own Scurrier of supplies. A third Scurrier was ridden by a scout. The scout rushed out in front to see if he could locate the Kobold army and offer intelligence about how the elves could best ambush the Kobold. The elves hoped to intercept the Kobold before they passed the lake that formed Shayna's Tears. They could use the lakeshore as a natural boundary to pin them in, if they could just get there in time.

After pushing hard all day, Hamman's group stopped at a western edge of the forest. As night began to fall, they could look out onto the grassy plane and see no visible sign of the Kobold army. Staying inside the tree line, the group began to slowly move westward while they sent a scout out into the planes to search for signs that the army had already passed. Before they could get any answer from their scout, an alarm was sounded. Hamman Drew had not even begun to recover before he had to take off with the elves to the west.

About a five-minute run from where they first arrived at the forest's edge and just inside the tree line, they found the body of the Scurrier that had been carrying the scout. There was no visible harm done to the Scurrier, yet it was surely dead. There was no sign of the Elvan scout. The idea that the body was not there sent shivers through the morale of the squad. As they assessed the area, they could tell that the body of the Elvan scout had been picked up by a group of Kobold and carried off to the west. The trail was warm.

Without hesitation, the elves took off in pursuit. Several elves grabbed the extra arrows from the back of the Scurrier. Several more went right up into the trees. The rest had taken off in pursuit. Hamman Drew followed the group on the ground. In the dusky lighted sky, Hamman Drew was still amazed at how quickly the elves could move through the trees while he ran across the ground.

It did not take long before he could hear the fighting. The elves on the ground slowed down so they could choose where to enter the fray. This gave the elves overhead time to move out ahead of them.

Hamman Drew could tell his group was coming into the battle on the left flank of the Kobold army. Since the Kobold army was partially in the trees, it was impossible to tell just how large the army was. He could tell that the two sides had been engaged for only a few minutes. It appeared that most of the wolves had been killed and the Kobold were backing away from the Elvan arrow fire. About fifty Kobold were engaged with Elvan forces that were on the ground. The fighting was right below the Elvan archers shooting from the trees. Those fifty Kobold were left behind by their retreating army.

The elves held an advantage from the woods. If the army was permitted to retreat out onto the plains, then the Kobold would have the advantage. This strategy was not lost on the elves. Instead of outwardly diving into the fray, Hamman Drew's squad stopped and redirected themselves toward the tree line so they could cut off Kobold trying to make it into grasslands.

This strategy changed right after the archers released their first flight of arrows into the Kobold. Shortly after Hamman Drew saw the first rain of arrows drill into the Kobold ranks, a bright blue-white flash of light shot up from the Kobold ranks and into the trees above. The flash erupted into a type of chain lightning. Suddenly, it began raining the smoldering bodies of Elvan archers.

Hamman Drew had seen his share of Kobold and knew them to be crude and uncivilized. He had never heard of any Kobold commanding magic. He didn't really have time to wonder what they were truly up against. A wave of Kobold fighters rushed in his direction to finish off the elves who had fallen from the trees.

Hamman Drew was in his element. He sliced and stabbed his way through countless Kobold. As soon as one fell from the edge of his scimitar, his other scimitar was cutting into another. The Elven fighters were also doing well. The group of Kobold that had rushed Hamman Drew's party were all now dead or dying.

Drew looked around to see that his party was holding their own at the edge of the Kobold army. In that moment when Hamman Drew could have snuck away into the night, he didn't hesitate. He quickly rushed into the fray, joining the elves in hand-to-hand combat with the sea of Kobold militia. Hamman Drew was killing them two at a time and in a deadly rhythm that made him wonder why they would even approach a killing machine like him. The Kobold army had taken a serious blow. Many had turned and begun to retreat from the fight.

The tree cover made it hard to tell how many Kobold were left. The success they had in killing the Kobold in the woods left Hamman Drew looking at the army in the grass. Then he thought he had noticed a Large Gray Wolf among the sea of Kobold. As his eyes adjusted, he realized it was a large Kobold wearing a gray wolf cloak and carrying a staff. He watched as the cloaked Kobold pointed his staff up into the trees. Suddenly, another bolt of lightning shot from the staff. This explosion blasted another half dozen Elvan archers from their perches. This shaman was surrounded by scores of Kobold. There wasn't an elf within a hundred feet of the magic user. The shaman continued to slowly retreat with the rest of the Kobold force, as they backed out of the woods toward the plains.

The surviving Kobold had retreated from the forest and back onto the open grassy plains. Fighting had subsided as the elves rushed to outflank the Kobold to the west. They had to stop them from joining the Zel Camber's army. By sheer luck, Hamman Drew caught up to Bellard, who had stopped to help a wounded elf. "Did you see the shaman?" Drew asked him between his labored breaths. Bellard looked confused by the question and the fact that this human had stopped to talk with him during battle. "The shaman!" Drew stated again, pointing in the direction of the Kobold shaman.

"What is this nonsense?" Bellard asked. "I gave you the scimitar in hopes that you might put it to use."

This insulted Hamman Drew. Had they been resting at a tavern's table, he would understand Bellard's tone. But they were in the field of battle. For a moment, he thought he might have to reassess his relationship with Bellard. Then he realized the comment could mean anything. He decided to let Bellard tend to the injured warrior and rushed off to join the fighting in the west.

His band of elves were now fending off their second wave of Kobold. Rather than stop and join the fighting, Hamman Drew ran alongside the edge of slowly retreating army of Kobold in an attempt to get ahead of it. It didn't take him long to find that half the Kobold army had already retreated onto the plains. If what he'd found on the plains was half of the Kobold army, then the elves had dealt them a serious blow.

A flash of lightning shot out from the ranks of the Kobold to remind Hamman Drew that a shaman was still in their ranks. The shaman was about fifty feet and twenty-five Kobold warriors to his left. They were still slowly retreating but looking straight ahead at the tree line. Hamman Drew approached from their right flank.

The elves could have killed Hamman Drew any time they wanted. They saw something in him they believed to be pure to their cause. This was a different faith than Drew had ever known. He had always been a mercenary, willing to do another man's bidding, as long as there were enough coins in the purse. The trust they had extended him was something he had never had. He didn't really understand it. He just knew it was driving him to make one very irrational decision.

Feeling this strong sense of allegiance to the Elvan cause, Hamman Drew rushed directly into the Kobold ranks. Most of these warriors were still watching the battle in front of them as Hamman Drew attacked. The Kobold were not expecting a one-man assault. Hamman Drew spared them the awesome blood-curdling battle cry. The only thing flashy about his attack was how quickly his scimitars slashed through the Kobold. His surprise attack into the Kobold ranks resulted in him making about half the distance to the shaman before the Kobold guard even turned to respond. When they saw the enemy in their ranks, they came at him from all directions. Hamman Drew was slashing and spinning as fast as he could. He wasn't making the headway he had hoped to make. He did take note that he did slash a couple of Kobold who were already falling forward from arrows in their chests.

What Hamman Drew could not see was that his attack had slowed their retreat to focus on his insurgence. This also provided the other elves time to regroup. This time they launched a ground offensive directly in Hamman Drew's direction. Hamman didn't know this. He was swinging, slicing, and stabbing as fast as he could move his arms. At the same time, he had some narrow misses from arrows that were flying directly into his fray. The clamor of swords, the screams of the dying, blood flying from savage wounds left no time for anything but slashing and reacting as fast as he could. It was absolute bedlam.

Wounds to Hamman Drew's arms and legs began to burn. He knew the Kobold were not going down without a fight. He also knew he could not afford to pause to check the severity of his wounds. He could only go as fast as he could and kill as many as possible. And… hope.

Hamman wasn't sure who was more surprised, him finally reaching the Kobold magician or the shaman finding a human fighting among the ranks of ancient elves. It didn't matter. They were both skilled and experienced. Drew struck first, because the shaman was just another Kobold, until Hamman realized whom he was fighting. Hamman's new mithril scimitar stuck the shaman's staff and cleaved the bottom third of it off. Angered by the damage, the shaman reached out his hand, as if to touch Hamman Drew. Instead, a blast of cold energy overtook Hamman Drew.

The blast of cold did not freeze him in place, but it did chill him to the bone and force him to take a step back. His pause allowed a couple Kobold clean slashes at Hamman Drew's midsection. Flitching away from the swipes of the sword may have saved his life, but the gashes still cut through his leather tunic and across his abdomen. Drew returned the attack and quickly killed the two Kobold that had wounded him so deeply. By now a group of elves had joined Hamman Drew in this assault to the right flank of Kobold horde. Their swords were a welcome addition to Hamman Drew's solo assault. The Kobold dropped quickly, and the Kobold army were forced to shift their focus to respond to this sudden assault.

Hamman Drew wasn't entirely sure what to do. He knew if that shaman did that to him again, it would probably kill him. So using his new mithril blade to keep the Kobold at bay, Drew raised his familiar old scimitar overhead and flung it with all his might. His blade found its mark and buried itself into the chest of the Kobold mage. Hamman Drew had successfully thrown his blade at an enemy before. He was never more satisfied with the result.

Unwilling to part with his trusty old blade, Hamman Drew continued to lead the Elvan surge into the Kobold with just his mithril blade. The fighting was fierce, but the Elvan forces pushed the Kobold into a full retreat. Maybe it was the death of their shaman, but the Kobold turned and ran eastward into the grassy plain by Shayna's Tears. There the Kobold regrouped. They were not half the army they had been when they had left their ancestral home. The elves watched from the woods and knew there had to still be over five hundred Kobold. They also knew that if they went out onto the field, they were giving away their strategic advantage. So they watched them from the tree line to see if the little beasts dared to step back into their sovereign woods.

The elves had sustained tremendous losses and had been outnumbered ten to one. Even with their losses, the elves were excited for having chased the Kobold out of their trees. More importantly, they had been able to stop the Kobold from joining Zel Camber's army in the valley. They knew the small stretch of forest that separated the two plains was all the elves needed. They didn't need to have their entire force in those woods. They just needed the Kobold believing that they were.

The elves quickly took stake of the injured and the supplies they still had. Elvan clerics moved between the wounded and provided healing and first aid. One approached Hamman Drew. Surprised to find a heavily bleeding human in their rank made the cleric pause. As the two stood looking at each other, Hamman wanted to ask him for help but stood frozen and in shock from his heavy loss of blood. Suddenly, the disappearance of the adrenaline that had powered his assault him made him weaken. Hamman Drew fell to his knees. From his knees, he slowly fell on his face at the feet of the cleric.

As Hamman Drew laid bleeding, all he could hear was the elves discussing how they would set up watches on both sides of the woods so they would not be surprised. Anytime the Kobold would come within fifty yards of the tree line, the elves could unleash a rain of arrows to leave them thinking they might be outnumbered. It wasn't a perfect solution, but these Elvan fighters were needed with the main force that had been repelling the other major assaults. This facade would have to buy them time.

34

Traveling through the dark made it difficult to tell how long they had been underground. With no sun to reference the start or the end of a day, they could only guess how much time had actually passed. When the party came through a tight channel that required them to travel single file, it opened into a flat open room. Some larger rocks made fine looking places to sit and rest. Since they finally stopped to rest, Allendale approached Kroach. "Okay, old man, how much more of this cavern do we have ahead of us?"

Kroach was visibly tired from the march. The party had been careful, but they were trying to put some distance between them and the Kayuni. Besides a few rats, the group had not really seen much of anything or anyone for several hours. They were also unable to find any more water. This path they were on seemed to slowly slope upward. It was dusty and very dry. The cavern walls had closed in, and at a few places, they had to march single file.

Looking at Allendale, the mage could see the protective posture that caused him to speak so tersely. "Well…" Ezen Kroach began, as if measuring the path from his recollection. "It's been a few years since I've felt so rushed that I've chosen to take this particular route."

Rubbing his chin, as if to figure the actual distance, Allendale interrupted his thought. "Years? How many years?" Allendale realized they knew little about this man and he was an older elf. There was no telling how long ago it had been.

Turning his attention to the ground Kroach pondered, "Well… I'd have to say…oh, maybe a hundred fifty years."

Allendale understood the aging of elves. A hundred fifty years is a long time, but not too long for Kroach to have some clear idea about what they were doing. "Okay, then. How much further do we have to go before we can turn our path back toward Hollywondra?"

"Hmmmm? I'm pretty sure we won't have to spend two more camps in this hole," Kroach suggested.

Disgusted at the thought of traveling so many days in the wrong direction, Allendale just turned from the elf and walked over to Titus and Amanda. Titus was making quick work of a sandwich. "Titus, you may want to ration your food as much as you can," Allendale suggested.

Slowing how fast he chewed, Titus had never considered the idea that he might run out of food. There was no point in trying to put any of this sandwich back in the bag. Titus had devoured all but the last bite. Allendale's suggestion did guide Titus to not take another sandwich out of his pack. He knew he could easily eat another, but resisted the urge.

After a hard day's march, sleep came surprisingly easy. Most of the party just propped themselves up against the wall of the cavern and slumped over into a deep slumber. Leaving behind the challenge and stress of this journey made their sleep and dreams even more welcome.

Until Palcombine woke everyone with a shout of alarm.

As a torch was lifted, the flicking light and drowsiness made it hard to see what Palcombine was doing. All they could see was Palcombine backing up into the camp firing arrows from his bow as quickly as he could. None of what they saw made any sense. They would hear the twang of his bowstring and then a *clack* sound shortly after the arrow left his bow. Allendale and Jarius pulled their swords as Ellerson pulled his bow and moved in alongside Palcombine. Ellerson had barely got off a shot before the enormous mandibles of a gigantic ant reached out for them.

The gigantic black ant was taller than anyone in their party. Palcombine and Ellerson's arrows bounced off the ant's face. Allendale struck the jaw of the enormous ant. His blade bounced off the ant as if it were made of stone. Jarius dove under the ant so he could attack its underbelly. He didn't find anything softer than the others had found.

HOLLYWONDRA

The ant's reflexes were quicker than they thought. It suddenly seized Ellerson by his left arm. As quickly as the mandibles snapped down on his arm, Ellerson let out a scream that echoed down the corridors. The ant then lifted its front two legs and began to fling Ellerson around by his arm. Ellerson had dropped his bow and had pulled out his dagger in hopes of prying himself free of the ant's jaws. The swaying motion of the ant flinging him from side to side made it impossible for Ellerson to do much with his knife.

Palcombine continued to shoot arrows that glanced off the face of the ant, while the ant seemed like it was trying to rip Ellerson's arm off his shoulder. Since the ant had stood up, Jarius and Allendale attacked the stomach area as Jarius had tried earlier. Suddenly a blue flash of light illuminated the entire cavern. For just a moment, everyone could see the terrain of the entire cavern.

The light emanated from the hand of Ezen Kroach. During the struggle, Kroach had made his way to the ant and had grabbed one of its middle legs. There he applied this blue light that forced the ant to freeze. For just a few moments, the ant stood still. Ellerson still screamed in pain as he dug at the maw of the beast with his knife. That moment was all Palcombine needed to finally hit this beast in the eye. Quickly he sank an arrow in each of the ant's eyes. Strangely, the ant did not respond to the damage to its eyes. Ellerson continued to scream in pain. Blood was dripping from the limp arm that hung in the mandibles of the giant ant.

Feeling a moment of satisfaction, Palcombine paused to see what happened next. Between his cries, they could hear the blades of Jarius and Allendale striking against the thick exoskeleton of the ant. The rapid nature of their attacks left others wondering if they had found a soft spot yet. Oddly, the ant continued to stand still.

"Here! Right here!" yelled the mage, pointing at the leg of the ant. Kroach was pointing to a joint in the ant's leg. "Quickly, sever its leg!"

Amanda and Titus could only look on in amazement. Amanda was deeply disturbed. She had always had a passion and kindness for animals. This creature was unreal. This ant looked like it wanted to eat Ellerson. Titus simply couldn't make up his mind if he should disappear or just watch. A type of panic had set over the both of them, and it was the two of them that first noticed the smell.

"Hurry, you haven't much time," Kroach yelled as Jarius and Allendale began to attack the ant at its middle two legs. Rushing from out of the dark, Jarius swung his sword with a fury. The edge of his blade landed right in the gap that someone might call a knee on the ant. His blade cut cleanly through, severing off the bottom of its leg. Jarius's momentum saved him from the ant falling on him. As the strength of Kroach's spell ebbed, the ant fell onto the stub that remained of its left middle leg. The ant still held Ellerson high overhead. As the ant slipped, Ellerson's cries were noticeably getting weaker. Then the ant seemed to come back to life.

The ant initially toppled but quickly regained balance as it came back down on its front legs. Just as it came into balance, Allendale hacked off his front right leg. The ant showed no emotion. It just continued to thrash Ellerson around. As the ant tried to regain its balance, Jarius took out its other front leg. This caused he beast to fall forward and use its face to manage its balance. Unfortunately, the ant buried its face into the chest of Ellerson.

Then ant smashed Ellerson's body to regain its balance. The loss of both its front legs seemed to anger the ant. Now it decided to use Ellerson as a weapon. Still clamped tightly onto Ellerson's arm, the ant swung the elf back and forth at the others. This was when they noticed Ellerson had dropped his knife and was no longer screaming. Ellerson's limp body struck Allendale at the legs. The impact knocked Allendale to the ground and snapped Ellerson's arm off at his shoulder.

Ellerson's body slid across the floor of the cavern and came to rest at the feet of Amanda and Titus. Ellerson stared blankly up at them. They knew Ellerson could not see them. The blood that had been gushing from his arm wound had slowed to a trickle. He laid lifeless at their feet.

Kroach snuck around behind the ant to grab it by one of its by two legs. The bright blue light of his magic signaled another blast of energy that temporarily froze the ant. "Quickly!" Kroach shouted.

HOLLYWONDRA

"This is a huge creature, and it takes a lot of energy for me to cast this spell. I'm not sure I can do it again."

Allendale and Jarius quickly tried to cut the last three legs off the ant. "Enough of that. Cut off his head!" shouted Kroach. With so many legs gone, they could now reach the neck of the ant. Allendale and Jarius took turns hacking at the neck of the beast until they were able to sever the head from the body of the ant.

The head fell to the floor of the cavern. It might have rolled further, but of the arrows buried in the eye of the beast caused it to stop. As the body of the ant began to squirm and writhe, a smelly substance dribbled out of the ant's wounds.

After finding his arm on the floor, Palcombine rushed it over to where the rest of the party stood around Ellerson. As he arrived, he saw Amanda leaning over his body. This gave Palcombine hope. He knew she possessed healing powers. He had seen it with his own eyes. As he offered the arm to Amanda, as if she would simply attach it, he saw the tears in her eyes. Looking up at Palcombine, she cried, "I've tried. He's lost too much blood. There's nothing I could do." Turning back to look at Ellerson's body, Amanda buried her head into his chest and wept aloud. Her sorrow brought Titus to tears. He had never heard such anguish from Amanda.

*****

It had taken the group several hours to gather enough rocks to create a satisfactory resting place for the body of Ellerson. They had intentionally made his resting place off the path, fearing what might become of his body. They piled the heaviest rocks they could find on top of his grave. The pile of rocks was substantial. They tried using as many large stones as they could find. They wanted this stone pile to mark his body but also protect it from the creatures of this huge underground world.

While they stood beside of the large mound, Titus and Amanda were surprised to hear Palcombine begin to sing a salutatory dirge. "*You rose up on the field of battle,*" he sang, as he stepped forward and bent down to one knee. Then Palcombine was joined by Jarius. "*You rose up to stand and fight by me.*" Then Allendale took a knee and joined. "*You rose up to honor our Elvan fathers.*" The three continued singing as the other three stood by somberly. "*You rose up to fall beside me.*"

Your name will echo thru the ages
Your name will guide fighters how to be
Your name is honored throughout our kingdom
Your accomplishments are greater than any tree

Time has come we must part our ways
Time has come for family to cry and morn
Time has come that we should sing your glory
It's time for the Lord to take you home.

They trudged along, wondering how much further it could be. The slope of the trail had narrowed, but they were periodically getting wafts of fresh air. They had been breathing stale dank cavern air for days. The gusts of fresh air were welcome and refreshing to their senses. As the party came around one of the last twists on the path, their eyes were suddenly assaulted by a ray of defused sunlight. Muted as it might be, they could tell the light was trying to find its way to them. The glow illuminated the remaining path.

After just a few more corners, they saw the opening they had been seeking for the last several days. The trail was steep now, but that was not going to deter this group from getting out this cave. As they drew nearer the opening, they could see the daylight of an overcast sky. As gray as the sky might be, the light had no trouble piercing through the tree boughs outside the entrance. As they reached the mouth of the cave, they found the cave opened onto a small landing. Over the edge of the landing, a rocky slope swept down the mountainside and through tall firs. To their left, a small trail seemed etched into the face of the hillside. It was their only choice.

35

The Kobold scout slowly moved away from the cover of the rocks and trees and out into the grassland of the Valley of Shayna. Staying as low as he could, he was hoping to avoid detection. So far, the Elvan archers had killed anyone that got near their tree line. He had been wise enough to backtrack all the way up onto the hillside before trying to skirt south around the trees. This left him with less cover but kept him out of arrow range. He still needed to move undetected, or his progress might cause the elves to rush from the woods to attack him.

Moving slowly gave him time to consider his next move. All he really knew was that his regiment was joining an army led by a human named Nictovius. His hope was to find this guy and alert him to the fact that the Kobold army was just beyond the trees at the north end of the valley. He was smart enough to know he had better not go running into the camp. He felt a sense of relief to have successfully skirted the Elvan army. It would simply be stupid to rush into Nictovius's camp and be killed as an intruder.

After crawling on his stomach for several hundred yards, he was able to put the Elvan Woods behind him. He determined it was now safe to get up and walk. As he made his way across the valley floor, he took in the awesome size of the army he approached. The campfires that dotted the horizon were more than he could count. The sheer size of this force frightened him.

Feeling a degree of success and pride, he allowed his mind to wander. He began to wonder if there were any other Kobold legions in this army and if they would have to share the bodies of the elves with them. The idea that they might have to share began to anger him, and his pace began to grow. Just as this notion was beginning to seize his emotions, the silhouette of a large human figure brought him to a quick halt.

Standing perfectly still, he slowly began to dip down to hide himself in the grass and dark horizon of the trees behind him. Squatting down in the tall grass, he craned his neck to survey his surroundings. He could see a human guard approximately a hundred feet directly in front of him. As he looked around, he could see there were several more guards. It looked like there was a human guard about every hundred feet on the perimeter of this camp. Then he noticed a second perimeter of guards inside this outermost line of defense. The Kobold stayed low to consider how best to manage this without getting himself killed.

After several minutes of considering, the Kobold finally weighed his hunger against the fact that he wasn't bright enough to come up with any unique approach. Slowly standing, the Kobold raised his hands over his head, as if he were trying to surrender. Then he slowly began to approach the guard. The Kobold was sure this would either work or get him killed. He had been marching for days, and for him, it was worth the chance they might feed him. He figured he would just get close enough to say Nictovius's name and maybe they would listen to him.

As he got near enough that he could almost be certain the guard could hear him speak, he realized he'd just forgotten the name of Nictovius. He was frozen by the fact that his ignorance might just cause him to be killed. Standing with his hands over his head only fifty feet from one of the sentry guards, he could not recall the name of their leader. His fear seized his breath and his rational mind. He began to tremble and sweat. Still standing with his hands over his head, he began looking around as if he might find the answer. Shaking with fear, he accidently let out a little squeak.

That was all it took for another sentry to yell, "Halt! There on the perimeter!" The other guards all pulled their swords and began to look around themselves for intruders. At first, the guard he had been approaching looked right over him. When his eyes swept past the second time, he saw the Kobold. Raising his sword, the guard yelled,

"Here!" and began to rush the surrendering Kobold scout. The other guards, seeing the direction he ran, began moving toward them both.

The Kobold scout tried his best to stand his ground. He had considered how this might go down. In his mind, his best approach would be to simply surrender. He could only hope they took prisoners. As the guard approached, the Kobold waved his hands over his head hoping this might help the guy see he was no threat. As the large burly human got within striking distance, he could see the man slightly lower his sword. That glimmer of hope with his hands over his head that he would be taken prisoner was all it took for his intellectual gridlock to bust loose. Excited that he actually remembered the name, the Kobold startled the fighter by yelling, "Nictovius!" Yeah, that was it. "Nictovius," he repeated in confidence.

Just as he finished announcing the name of the man he sought, another of the guards arrived. "Did he say what I thought I heard him say?"

"Yeah, I think so," confirmed the first guard.

"Well, I don't know why we should be too surprised this freak is coming to join our ranks. We already have a half dozen different strange beasts I never even knew existed. What's one more? At least he can pronounce the general's name."

The guard, whom the Kobold had been approaching, was not so sure. If anything, he was a little shaken by how close the guy got to him in the dark. He wasn't ready to trust the little creature.

As the Kobold said the name Nictovius a third time, the other suggested, "We'd better take this guy into the camp and make some sense of him."

By this time, more of the perimeter watch had arrived. Four of the sentries escorted the Kobold into camp. The Kobold walked with a purpose. He had a job to do, and he could be rewarded handsomely for what he had accomplished. He knew enough common tongue that he could make out much of what the men were saying. They did mention someone other than Nictovius, and that began to concern the Kobold. He felt he needed to speak to Nictovius. Where were they taking him? Who is Silas Pei?

Reaching the first of the camps, the Kobold was shocked to find Klofgar lounging about the camp in groups of five and six. He could not take his eyes off the giants as they marched him deeper into the camp. The Kobold could smell the burning flesh of beasts as they wound their way through the tents. He knew that cooking beasts was a choice in this culture. He preferred his food uncooked. But right now, he thought he could eat something if it were still on fire.

Finally, the escort brought him around between two large wagons and into the light of a large campfire. There humans sat around on large chunks of wood that had been pulled into a ring around the flames. In the center of the flames was a large pot hanging from a tripod. It was steaming hot and smelled like something he would be willing to eat.

As the men came into the fire light, one of them called, "Captain, you'll want to see this. Look what we found out in the grass."

Then the one guard who had let the Kobold get too close suggested, "I told them we should have killed him where he stood."

Peering over the rim of his tin cup, Silas Pei moved his eyes from the Kobold to look at the guard. "Yeah, that would have probably been the dumbest thing you would have done today. I'm glad someone stopped you."

Silas Pei turned his attention to the Kobold. Before Silas Pei could set down his cup, the Kobold played his best card and said, "Nictovius."

The name made Silas Pei straighten up in his boots. "Wha'd you say?"

"Nictovius," the Kobold repeated.

*****

Staring into the campfire all Gormund could think about was how much he hated this assignment. He was sure Sythene had sent him into this battle hoping he might die. Gormund pondered the fact that he had been learning so much so fast, he had never considered that he might become a threat to Sythene, but maybe it was possible. Maybe that was why he had sent him into this battle.

HOLLYWONDRA

Gormund knew he learned magic quickly. Maybe it was his own foolish thirst for knowledge and power that drove him to this place in his life. Maybe his desire was so obvious that Sythene knew he could use him to do his bidding. Wythargle's Tome was a treasure trove of Elvan mystical knowledge. If Gormund could access this tome, he could advance his skills considerably. He and Sythene both knew that. What Gormund didn't understand was that he was expected to go into battle to get this book.

The idea of entering Hollywondra made this mission more compelling. Few humans could ever say they had visited this center of Elvan civilization. This Elvan city of mystery could contain any number of unknown wonders. While his thought excited him, the overbearing stench of war turned his stomach. The smell of rotting flesh might be something campaign tested warriors might know. For Gormund, it was a stench he could rarely escape. The smoke of the campfire helped. But, feeling his stomach turn, he had to get up to see if he could find a fresh breeze.

Walking only a few feet from the fire, he turned and sniffed for any sense of fresh air. Suddenly, Gormund found himself ducking under the ariel assault of a large bat. The bat initially startled him. But when it circled back and came at him again, he began to consider spells he could use. As he prepared to cast a spell on the bat, he noticed the bat drop something. The bat then flew off into the dark of night.

Searching through the trampled grass, Gormund quickly found Sythene's whistle and note. After reading the note, his charge was now clear. He was a watchman. He did not even have to enter the forest. He just needed to hang back and let Sythene know when he could safely arrive.

At first, Gormund was relieved to know that he was not expected to follow this army into battle. Then he began to wonder, what could be so important that Sythene wants to be present to retrieve it for himself. The more he thought about his assignment, the more he thought how capable he was to simply gather and transport something of value. What does he not trust me to transport?

Gormund was not a fool. He knew very well that Sythene was not going to just hand over the Tome of Wythargle. No. Gormund knew he had to help Sythene see that allowing him to study from that tome was in Sythene's best interest. This was a wicked balance. Among the magic users, there was a ranking of power. If Sythene became threatened by Gormund's ability, then he might just stop him now before he grew too strong.

The next spell Gormund needed to cast was one of wits. He had to make himself appear to be the greatest ally Sythene could hope to attract in this time of war. That was, of course, until Gormund could kill him.

36

The group marched through the early morning with hardly a spoken word. The uneven path could barely be considered a trail. At times, the single file line had to slow down to pass more challenging rock outcroppings one person at a time. Most of the path was loose gravel that had come to rest on a more level shoulder of the mountainside. How anyone had ever found this path was a mystery. The brisk cool breeze and gentle slopes made the descent down the eastern face of the Kellene Mountains steady but uneventful. When the party finally paused for a break, Palcombine climbed atop a tree snag and looked off to the north. Allendale walked up to the base of the tree trunk to see what he might see.

"We're going to have to follow this hillside a while longer. We should make the tree line by afternoon. We may need to cover and camp in the seclusion of the forest. I'm not exactly sure where we will finally be able to turn west. After these woods, the valley floor opens up, and there will be very little cover for us. The valley extends to the north about as far as I can see," shared Palcombine.

Turning away from the Elvan scout, Allendale turned to Ezen Kroach. "Okay, wizard. I do appreciate you getting us out of that cavern alive, but we are far afield. We need to redirect our march. We need to get to Hollywondra as soon as possible. This path seems to be taking us in the opposite direction."

Kroach had taken advantage of their respite to stoke himself a pipe load. As he exhaled a thick gentle cloud of smoke, his gazed turned to Allendale. "Indeed. You are correct. I'd guess this little trek added almost a week to your journey," he said with hardly a care.

Frustrated with Kroach's cavalier attitude, Allendale emphasized the urgency to get to Hollywondra. Kroach calmly took another puff from his pipe and asked, "Are you rushing to your fate, or is your fate going to wait for you? I have found that my fate always seems to be waiting for me." As quickly as he finished saying this to Allendale, Kroach began pondering the thought and forgot the fact that he was engaged in a conversation with Allendale.

Allendale paused to consider Ezen's question, then like the smoke that was gathering around his head, he wiped away the thought and reengaged Kroach. "Wizard! When can we turn west through these mountains?" Then Allendale paused to consider the location of the sun and asked, "We should turn west before heading south, shouldn't we?"

Tapping the ash from his pipe on the heal of his leather boot, Kroach looked down the valley and paused to think. Then looking up at Allendale, he said, "Yes! I believe you are correct, Sir Allendale. We need to journey west through these mountains before heading south." Then running his fingers through his beard to consider their location, he shared, "I recall a mountain stream down this way." Now he had everyone's attention. "It comes out of the hills from the west. If we follow that creek up into the hills, we will surely find a pass that drops us right back down into the civilized world," he said with a gentle chuckle. "If I were to guess, I'd say it would take us two full days to reach the valley floor west of the Kellene."

"Kellene?" Amanda asked.

"Yeah. These mountains and this valley are known as the Kellene. I understand this region was named for an ancient queen with the uncanny talent for propagating and rearing children. The legend was that she cared deeply for all the children of her kingdom. The way these mountain walls hug this valley reminded royalty of her care for the youth, so they named this region after her." Pausing to consider her fame, Kroach slowly shook his head and shared, "I don't get it. What use could anyone have for a brood of little ones?" He seemed to ask with sincerity.

HOLLYWONDRA

Palcombine did not honor the conversation with any more of his precious time. He jumped down from the snag and began walking down the mountain trail, expecting that everyone else would follow.

As they recognized Palcombine's movement, everyone got up and fell back into line. As they continued their descent, Kroach stepped up alongside Titus. Then whispering to him, he suggested, "You really should show me what you found back there in the cavern."

Titus, trying to feign confusion about the statement, quickly realized Kroach had to somehow know he had found a ring. "How did you know?"

Kroach shared, "When powerful magic is imbued upon an object, it can emanate a mystical glow. Most humans can't see it. For that matter, there are plenty of elves who can't see it either. You're bright enough, I may be able to teach you how to see magic. Right now, I'd just like to take a look at what you found. Just because it's magical doesn't mean it's good magic. If it was that good, would that guy have died wearing it?"

The logic made sense and kind of scared Titus. So he pulled the ring out of his pocket and handed it to Kroach. Kroach examined the ring closely. The finely crafted silver band looked very old. Besides the grime of sitting in that pit, the years of wear had done little to destroy the beautiful details that had been so carefully etched around the circumference of the ring. After a couple of steps, Kroach stopped in his tracks. He stopped so suddenly that Allendale almost ran into him. "Easy, old man," Allendale offered as he skirted past the two of them. The rest of the party kept walking as Titus watched Kroach examine the ring.

"Oh?" was all Kroach was able to offer. Titus began getting anxious curious to hear what the mage might say.

"Oh, what?" prodded Titus.

Fully forgetting his whereabouts, Kroach pulled his concentration away from the ring and back to his young friend. "Well, this is very nice. You will definitely want to clean it up." Then Kroach handed it back to Titus and took off to follow Allendale.

"Wait! What? That's all you can tell me? You seemed to be surprised by what you saw," Titus asked.

Kroach just kept walking. "When we have a bit more time, I can give it a more thorough examination. What I can tell you is that you do have a magical ring there. You can choose to wear it and hope it brings you good fortune or keep it in your pocket so nobody sees something of such high value."

Walking alongside Kroach, Titus tried to imagine what he should do. This world was unlike anything he had ever imagined. What did Kroach mean that someone might see its value and try to take it? What does he mean that it glows? It looked like a normal old silver ring. Titus tried to look more carefully at the ring, but it just looked like a dirty silver ring to him. Considering Kroach's words, Titus slipped the ring into his front pocket of his Levi's.

*****

Kroach's recollection had served him well. After descending for a couple more hours, the path dropped below the tree line and began to open up. The late afternoon was pleasant without the constant wind. The rocky path had turned to a thin grass. Soon the group found themselves walking through light forest underbrush. Ahead, the trees began to dissipate and turn to a green grassy field. From the west, a small creek trickled out of a willowed thicket and pooled into a small lake.

Still several feet away from the edge of the tree line, Palcombine raised his arm to stop the group. Quickly they took cover behind nearby trees and looked toward the lake to see what had alarmed Palcombine. In the distance, they saw an old woman standing in a rowboat pulling in a fishing net. She wore a dirty white tunic and a rust-colored dress. The boat teetered as she leaned over the side to pull the net into her boat. After pulling the net into the boat, she lifted each fish to her face to examine it. After looking each fish in the eye, she said something to it and then paused, as if waiting for it to answer her. Then she flung each one as far as she could away from her boat and back into the lake. When she was done throwing her entire catch back into the lake, she didn't waste a moment to cast her net again. This time she threw it off the other side of her boat. The group watched in curiosity, as she pulled in her net, examined her catch, then began to methodically throw each creature back into the lake.

"She's killing fish!" Amanda stated in disgust. As the others considered what Amanda had said, they noticed that many of the fish she had thrown away were floating dead on the still surface of the lake.

"Wait here," Palcombine directed the group. Then he stepped through the tree line and headed across the grassy shoreline toward the lake. Palcombine was about halfway across the grassy field when the woman in the boat noticed him. As soon as she saw him, she stood up straight and pointed a finger at him. Palcombine stopped in his tracks as the woman began to yell and thrust her finger in his direction. The group was too far away to hear much of what she was saying. Palcombine waved one hand, as if to be peaceful in his approach. This only seemed to enrage her. Growing more angry, she bent over in her boat and quickly lifted a bow and arrow. When she pointed it in Palcombine's direction, Palcombine immediately stopped and raised both hands. As he began to slowly back away, the woman nodded her approval. Trying to be emphatic, the woman shook her bow and arrow at Palcombine, as if that increased the power of her threat. Palcombine retreated to the group as the woman watched him carefully walk into the trees.

Walking behind one of the larger trees, Palcombine smiled for what must have been the first time in days. "I think she's mad. That bow and arrow is not a threat. I walked away because I did not want to have to save her when she fell into the water. She is crazed."

Allendale asked, "Crazed fishing woman?"

"Yeah, I don't know what to tell you. She wouldn't even let me get close to the shore. She seemed to be protecting the lake from intruders. I think we should just skirt down the tree line a little and avoid her. She does not seem rational."

Amanda was perplexed and a bit upset. "Why's she killing the fish?"

Palcombine slowly shook his head. "I couldn't tell you. She didn't seem very interested in having a conversation. She seemed more interested in chasing me away."

Amanda could not permit this to continue. "Oh, she'll have a conversation alright!" Amanda stated indignantly. Before Jarius could step in front of her, Amanda marched out from the cover of the trees. The woman in the boat did not see Amanda right away. She was busy casting her net off the back of her boat.

"*Hey*!" Amanda yelled at the woman. "You need to knock it off."

The woman looked up, saw Amanda approaching, and quickly spun around to pick up her bow and arrow from the floor of the boat. As the woman picked up her bow and arrow, the rest of the group rushed from the trees after Amanda.

Notching an arrow and aiming at Amanda, the woman yelled, "Stay back. I don't want to kill you, but I will. Don't come another step closer!" Now the woman was shaking the bow and arrow. "I'll shoot you. I swear. I've warned you, so I can't be held responsible." After only a moment's warning, the lady let her arrow fly. Her boat was not fifty yards from shore. Her arrow only made it a little more than halfway to land. The flight was pathetic and horribly inaccurate. Dejected by her shot, the lady threw down her bow and slumped down onto the boat's bench and began crying.

Now Amanda felt bad for the woman and yelled, "Are you alright?'

She just kept crying. Uncontrollably, the woman sobbed. Sometimes she began coughing when she could not catch her breath to cry more. Her anguish was very real. It froze Amanda on the shore. The lady was a portrait of despair. An older human woman in an old filthy dress caked with fish guts and lake water. Amanda yelled again, "Is there anything we can do to help." She just swatted her arm at Amanda in anger.

As the party joined Amanda at the edge of the lake, they began to fill their water skins. This caught the lady's attention. This made her crying stop, and she began yelling aggressively at the group to get away from the water. When he saw that the group was not leaving, she began paddling toward them.

HOLLYWONDRA

Aware that she was slowly approaching, the group was mystified by her aggressive tone. There were six of them and only her. What did she think she was going to do?

As she drew nearer, she could see what they were doing. She stopped rowing and informed them, "Oh, that's fine. Take water. Take all the water you want. Just leave the fish for me." She seemed to calm down but carefully watched the group fill their water skins. Each time they looked up, they could see the old woman watching them.

After filling all their water skins, the group turned west and started to head up stream. This caught the woman's attention, but she did not comment. She seemed interested but not enough to stop her from returning to her fishing regimen.

*****

The group quickly found a trail that meandered through the willows and along the creek. Their path gradually climbed as they pushed their way through the willows. As they reached the edge of their cover, they could see the trees gave way to a grassy slope. A few hundred yards up the slope was a small village. The creek flowed right through the center of the hamlet. To their right was the shore of the lake and a long pier. The number of boats tied to the pier seemed to almost outnumber the homes in the village. A half dozen people sat on the end of the pier with fishing lines in the water. In the distance, smoke climbed from the chimney of a lodge that towered over the homes that surrounded it.

Palcombine had been quiet since the death of Ellerson. It seemed he had been putting all his effort into pushing them forward and trying to keep them safe. It was as if that focus might keep his mind off the loss of his friend. Recognizing that Palcombine had taken this role upon himself, Allendale offered, "What do you think, Palcombine? Should we see if we can find us a room for the night? These kids are not accustomed to a forced march, and we've been pushing them pretty hard."

Palcombine considered Allendale's suggestion then pulled a small leather bag from the belt on his hip and tossed it to Allendale. "That should be enough to get us a night and some food."

Allendale bounced the weight of the bag in his hand. "Yeah. Keep an eye on these guys. I'll see what I can do."

Palcombine asked everyone to step back into the cover of the willows as Allendale made his way up to the village. The town consisted of less than fifty buildings. Even the smallest of the homes were made of a study stone plank construction. Palcombine suggested the group pull back and off the path, in case someone just happened upon them. As everyone backed deeper into the trees, Palcombine watched Allendale disappear into the town.

While huddled under the cover of countless willow branches, everyone stood hoping that Allendale would be safe and successful in finding them a warm comfortable place to rest. Titus, Jarius, and Amanda took the opportunity the find a tree to sit up against. As they enjoyed the solace of the cool breeze, Amanda suddenly asked, "What is that?"

Everyone turned and looked at her. "There it is again," she stated.

Listening carefully, "I don't hear anything," Jarius said as he slowly pulled his short sword from his scabbard.

Amanda turned toward the water and started to make her way toward the shore of the lake. Palcombine pulled his bow and quickly stepped in front of Titus and Ezen. Jarius quickly made his way to her side and scanned the surroundings for any clue.

As Amanda came to the shoreline, she suddenly turned to her right and said, "See." Jarius still could not hear what she was talking about. Amanda walked a short distance down the shoreline and found a fish splashing in the shallow water. Then she noticed it was hanging from a fishing line that came out from under nearby willow's branches. While Amanda grabbed the line and pulled the fish toward her, Titus followed the line toward the tree. Flopping at the end of the line was a fat silver fish, unlike anything she had ever seen before. The bright silver fish had very small scales that made the fish almost look like polished chrome. The body was short in length but very fat.

HOLLYWONDRA

Its body looked like it had swallowed a ball. The body was far too large for the fins and tail, but not for its mouth. The mouth on this creature looked big enough to swallow itself.

Amanda lifted the fish by its lower jaw and worked to loosen the bone hook. The fat fish writhed and gasped, making the task more difficult. Fortunately, Amanda had plenty of experience catching fish, but this odd-shaped thing struggled aggressively. Happy that she got the hook out, Amanda didn't waste any time dropping the fish back into the water. At first, the fish rolled onto its side and gasped rapidly. Then as its breathing stabilized, the fish righted itself. Then staying at the surface of the water, the fish began to swim backward. Still in only a foot of water, Amanda could clearly see the fish struggling to get its mouth above the surface of the water. Then as if it was trying to grab a breath of air, the fish shuttered and convulsed. Suddenly, it spit a large black ball into the air. The ball flew about ten feet and then splashed back down into the lake. This made the fish seem suddenly more lively, and it quickly swam away.

As everyone returned to the shore, they noticed a fishing pole had been snuggly stuck between three large rocks. Just beyond the pole laid a dead man with an arrow in his eye.

*****

As everyone quietly ate their rabbit stew, they knew everyone in the lodge was watching them. "They must not get many visitors," Jarius suggested softly under his breath. The others just looked in his direction and worked at finishing their meal.

Then Allendale shared, "The innkeeper wasn't even going to give us a room. I had to explain that we had been traveling several days without proper rest. He only agreed after I assured him that we would be gone at sunrise."

What remained of the daylight was just enough to allow the group to confidently assess the comforts of the room Allendale had bought for the night. The room was not very large, but it did have two beds. Everyone agreed that Amanda and Titus should take the beds while the rest of them made themselves comfortable on the floor.

Allendale stated that he would take the first watch. He promptly began taking off his belt and tried his best to make himself comfortable against the door. Palcombine tried to make himself comfortable under the window. Seeing everyone settle into place, Jarius suggested he would take the second watch. That was about all Palcombine needed to hear before crossing his arms and closing his eyes.

Amanda was surprised how comfortable the straw mat was for a mattress. She remembered falling asleep almost instantly. It was hard pulling herself out of that deep slumber as Jarius gently rocked her shoulder to wake her. Disoriented by the absence of sunlight and her location, it took Amanda a moment to become aware that there was some citizen unrest in the streets of this little town. As she sat up in the bed, she realized she was the last one to wake. Even Titus had already swept the sleep from his eyes and stood by the door.

"You've got to keep your hoodie up," reminded Jarius. "The length of your hair and the fairness of your face will not conceal your femininity much longer. You may need to cut your hair."

Unprepared for such scrutiny, Amanda ran her hand through her hair. She realized it was getting longer than she normally wore it. Jarius's words reminded her of her need for diligence.

"We've got to get moving," Palcombine stated.

"It seems the town is upset about some lost trophy or something," Ezen Kroach added.

"We don't have time to get caught up in their drama," added Allendale.

Amanda was quickly on her feet, and the group made their way down the stairs. They found the lodge hall was empty, but the front doors were open. Outside the lodge, a group of people were gathering. They could hear bit and pieces of the public outcry. It was clear, the town considered them as suspects for the theft of some prized fishing trophy.

Rather than defend their character, Palcombine insisted they exit out the back and make quick for the distant woods. As they exited the lodge, they walked quickly through the streets until they got in plain view of the distant tree line. Then Palcombine broke into a run that Titus dreaded. It would take everything he had just to keep up.

As they reached the tree line, Titus had hoped that Palcombine might slow down a bit. His wish would not be realized for several hundred yards into the trees. Palcombine had chosen to follow a trail that ran right along the creek. It kept the branches out of their face and allowed them the cover the greatest distance. After reaching a large boulder at the edge of the creek, he stopped to check on everyone. As the group arrived, they realized that Titus was not the slowest. "Where's the wizard?" asked Allendale.

Everyone looked around, as if he might be standing in the brush, and they had overlooked his diminutive stature.

"We cannot wait for him," Palcombine stated. "We have to move."

Everyone knew Palcombine was right. It just seemed so odd to leave behind someone who had fought at their side. "We need you to take the lead," Palcombine directed Allendale. Then he suggested that Jarius to stay close to Titus and Amanda. "I'm doubling back to make sure that we are safely away from any threat. Until we can be sure we are not being followed, we will need to break off this path. I will be back as soon as I can be sure we are not being followed."

Everyone knew their role. Titus was pleased to know that Palcombine would not be setting the pace for a while. Allendale didn't wait for a signal. He turned and began heading up the path. Titus had only turned to look at Allendale's movement. When he turned back to see what else Palcombine might suggest, he was already gone.

37

The lush green valley below ran a great distance to south until it hit distant forested hills. This perch on the western slope of the Kellene Range gave them a clear view of the miles of travel they had ahead. They could see they had almost a day's travel to reach the valley floor. A large marsh sat at the base of the hills and reached about halfway across the valley floor. It was in their direct line of travel. They would either have to gently navigate through that muck or go several hours out of their way to skirt the fens. Taking the western route around the marsh would be longer and force the party to travel the open grasslands of the valley floor.

Jarius came to stand next to Amanda and Titus. Then pointing off to the southern horizon, he said, "A few days beyond those hills is our homeland, Hollywondra."

Then turning toward Allendale, Jarius suggested, "If we take the rest of the day to descend this hillside, we could spend most of the night skirting that swamp."

Allendale replied, "Yeah, but then we're exposed in the middle of the valley and tired from pushing through the night. I don't know. I think we'd be smarter to camp at the edge of the swamp and then push thought it in the light of day. We'd be fresh, we'd save the extra steps on our legs, and there probably wouldn't be any search parties in there."

While making these plans, Jarius noticed movement from the trail behind them. In reflex, he reached for his short sword. This caused Allendale to turn to see the threat. Then they saw Palcombine coming into view. He lifted his hand to hail his arrival. As Palcombine approached, the others gathered to hear his report.

HOLLYWONDRA

"I found no sign of the wizard. Evidently, this little town had been on edge for a few days. They make their living from the fish they pull from Lake Kellene. When the moon moves in front of the sun and turns day into night, a strange fish comes to poison the other fish in their lake. They call this thing the Sepien. When this happens, the townspeople know they have until the next full moon to catch this creature or it will secrete poison into the lake and kill all their fish. It can be devasting for their community.

"I understand that while we were making our way through the caverns, the moon's shadow covered this town during daylight. That put the whole town to the task of trying to catch this creature. This is such an urgent need that the entire community compensates the person who catches this creature with a reward. Every household gives the person two pieces of silver or a favor bartered of the same value. So anyone who catches this thing is instantly a wealthy hero. The town is then safe until the next time day turns to night."

"No wonder they were uncomfortable with us being there. They all wanted to be the one to catch this thing," Titus suggested.

"All the fish don't die at once," Palcombine added. "Dead fish begin to surface on the lake. By the next full moon, they are all dead. The outcry we heard this morning was because dead fish began surfacing."

Titus turned to look at Amanda. He was going to say what they were all thinking, but he could see in her eyes that she was thinking it too. Amanda was very caring and kind. When it came to animals, her love and compassion seems even deeper. Amanda turned, hung her head, and walked away from the group.

This saddened Titus deeply, so he turned to follow her. Allendale quickly lifted his hand to get Titus's attention, then he gently shook his head no. He knew her better than anyone. So Titus paused and only looked at her as she softly sobbed.

The somber feeling that overtook the group made Allendale wish he could lighten spirits. Then he realized, "So, Palcombine... that is an awful lot of detail. Tell us more about how you came to learn so much information."

Immediately, Palcombine shot Allendale a sharp suspicious glance only to find a light smile on Allendale face. Allendale had his suspicions, but he needed Palcombine to be honest about them.

"Well, I backtracked to the edge of town. Staying in the shadows, I was able to hear the people screaming about their discovery of dying fish on the lake. I also heard the townspeople forming a search party to come after us," Palcombine shared.

"Are they still pursuing us?" Allendale asked. He'd come to know Palcombine well enough to know that he would not have taken the time to share this story, if they were in pursuit.

Palcombine continued to explain. "The search party only went a few hundred yards into the woods, until they realized they were not fighters and they needed to catch as many fish as they could before they all died. So they turned around."

"Hmm? That still seems like an awful lot of detail for guy who was trying to stay ahead of a small search party."

As if forfeiting his efforts to conceal some details, Palcombine sheepishly admitted that he did hear most of this detail from a bard in their street.

Allendale's playful tone caught Amanda's attention. Gathering control over her sadness, she turned and was slowly returning to the group. Wiping away the last of her tears, she began to smile. She knew Allendale as her father. She knew from his tone that he was up to something.

"Oh! A bard!" noted Allendale. "Please share. Don't spare us a single detail."

Bards were musical historians whose songs were ways people were able to sustain the exact facts and details of significant events. Since the integrity of the information was attached to music, the song helped sustain the message accuracy over time. Sharing details from the song of a bard carried a cultural responsibility. You did not simply share the chosen details you heard in a bard's song. If you wanted to share any part of what you heard, you had a social obligation to actually sing the song so nobody could misinterpret or misunderstand the details or order of events. This practice also ensured historic details of such stories would stand the test of time.

HOLLYWONDRA

When Allendale asked, "What exactly did this bard sing?" Palcombine knew he was being compelled to sing. He looked at Allendale, cleared his throat, and raised his tenor voice to sing.

> "When the sky's go dark, and quiets the lark, the Sepien comes for prey.
> All must amass and forward cast, so we might save the day.
> The lucky is lauded and openly applauded for saving our little town.
> For the Sepien must die or all will cry and even our will children frown."

It wasn't much, but Palcombine having to sing this short lilt still made him smile for a moment. This was the first smile any of them had seen even a glimmer of warmth in Palcombine since the death of Ellerson.

"I'm not sure I understood that last line," goaded Jarius.

Palcombine lightly shoved Jarius as he walked past him to take a look down the valley.

The marsh was larger than it looked from above. A light morning fog tried to lift itself from the puddled landscape. When the breeze picked up, the wind just made the fog swirl in place. The smell of the stagnant water and rotting fauna was to be expected. That was not it. There was some other putrid odor woven into the smell of this place that nobody seemed to recognize.

"This place just looks so dead," Amanda said.

"Yeah, I'm not liking this very much," Titus added.

Jarius explained, "We really need to shoot straight through this thing. We lost days going through those caverns. We really can't delay. It might take us another day or two to hike around this swamp. We will just need to be alert and stay together." Then in an effort to lighten the task, he added, "Maybe the fog will lift with the afternoon sun."

As the group looked up, the sun had been muted enough that you could look directly at the bright pink circle in the sky. Allendale knew Jarius was right. Palcombine didn't wait for the discussion to continue any longer. Pulling his bow, he knocked an arrow and began to move his way into the fetid fen. The rest of the party fell into place, just as they had marched through the caverns. On this day, Allendale took up the rear.

The ground was very uneven, and the turf varied from solid and dry to spongelike. The ground was covered with grayish green thick bladed grass. The thick blades sometimes created slippery slopes on the uneven ground. Through the morning, everyone, including Palcombine, had lost footing and slipped into the muddy mire. Everyone in the party was wet and cold.

By what they could only imagine was about midday, the group stopped to rest on a large tuft of turf that was drier than most. They had spent their morning meandering from one soggy patch to another while trying their best to travel due south. They could not be certain, but they had faith that Palcombine would lead them through this place.

This swamp was a dead still landscape. The water was still. There were virtually no trees. The fog had not lifted. The day was gray as far as their eyes could see. Everyone quickly ate some of the smoked fish they had bought in Lake Kellene. Even Palcombine took jerky from his pack and pulled off a few bites while standing watch. Whispers were the only conversation. Folks preened at their boots by kicking off some of the muddy buildup.

As if removing some of the mud might make their feet get warm sooner, everyone had hoped that this rest might reenergize them. What they found was that it just made them colder. So after grabbing a quick bite, they pushed on into the mist.

Shortly after leaving their lunch, Palcombine raised his hand to signal a silent stop.

Everyone stopped to look in the direction he pointed. It seemed he was looking at something in the water off to everyone's left. Drawing back his bow, he fired a shot into the water.

HOLLYWONDRA

Immediately, a large reptilian creature began splashing around in pain. It looked as though Palcombine had hit the creature right between the eyes. In most cases, that might be a perfect shot; in this case, it just seriously injured the creature.

The party watched as this reptilian creature thrashed and splashed about. They were just waiting for it to die. When suddenly six filthy humanoid creatures jumped out of the water and onto a tuft of sod next to the dying beast. They wore crude crafted fur pelts that covered their upper torso to their waist. Working as a team, they pulled out crude little knives and jumped onto the dying creature. Even as they began stabbing the creature, they pulled it away from the group, as if they were claiming it as theirs.

As they disappeared around the corner of a large tuft of grass, everyone looked at one another, reminded they that were in strange, hostile lands. This just reminded them that they had to be alert at all times.

The death of the reptile and the discovery of the other swamp beings kept everyone on their toes. By late afternoon, the fog had begun to lift, and a thin tree line could be seen in the distance. It wasn't a forest, but it was at least a place where they could conceal themselves and maybe dry out.

The trees were a welcome friend to everyone. Allendale explained that this was where they would have hoped to arrive after skirting the swamp. His comment helped everyone understand how much time they saved by getting wet. Allendale continued, "We can follow this tree line all the way down the valley. We can cross the King's Highway at night. Once we are on the other side of the highway, we are home free." Those hills bordered on the Elvan kingdom and were very familiar to Palcombine, Jarius, and Allendale.

38

Nictovius sat high and proud in his saddle. For the first time since entering this valley, things began to go his way. There had been far too many setbacks for his liking. The loss of water to his camp and the Elvan ambushes had been challenging. The ignorant Klofgar and the nonsense they brought to his organization had him doubting the decision to enlist their might. Now as he looked out onto his invading army and could see the Klofgar easily cranking the trebuchet wheels, on this day, things were finally falling into place.

The army of Zel Camber was launching a full assault into the woods of Hollywondra. For the first time in this siege, Elvan arrow fire was not enough to slow their charge. The men and beasts rushed into the woods with a bloodlust and hope that this day might finally be the day they eradicate the elves and dance in the streets of Hollywondra. Nictovius realized he could add the strength of the Kobold forces after launching this assault. He knew the elves' tendency would be to fall back. That created a window of opportunity for him to connect with the Kobold forces and give them directions on how to join the assault.

As his horse nickered, Nictovius patted her neck and promised, "Alright. You'll get your chance. Let's go see what we can do." Urging his horse forward, they began to descend the hillside perch and make their way to the fighting.

Hamman Drew leaned against a giant oak sharpening a scimitar as the Elvan patrol under the command of Phillibus gathered or their next campaign. As Bellard approached, he acknowledged, "I'm glad I got you that second sword. It looks like you know how to use it."

HOLLYWONDRA

Bellard's attempt at humor continued to catch Drew a little off guard. There had not been a true moment of levity the entire time he had been in Hollywondra. Certainly, the tasks ahead could lead them both to death. Hamman Drew paused long enough to smile at Bellard. Before he could return his attention to his ritualistic preparation, he was startled by the blast of a nearby horn sounding an alarm. Hamman Drew had heard these horns in the woods, but never had he heard one in the city. The bow was quickly off Bellard's shoulder, and an arrow was nocked before Hamman Drew could comprehend the invading foe was upon them.

Suddenly, everyone in the city was rushing in panic. Women gathered children as quickly as they could. Everyone seemed to be rushing from one place to another. Drew quickly joined Bellard. As they reached Phillibus, they overheard an Elvan fighter report, "They are coming from all three sides! Bracanthorpe has fallen. Bracanthorpe's entire legion is lost. Kluvarner is still up there, but he sent a message to let the king and Malactus know, they cannot hold them back. We need to evacuate the royal family."

Phillibus turned to Bellard, saying, "You need to let Malactus and the king know. Take these two with you," signaling that Bellard should take Drew and the scout who had just arrived. Just that quickly, the three of them sprinted off for the temple.

The horse Gormund had won at dice was worth everything to him in this moment. Nictovius's army was in a full charge, and the elves could not stop them. Gormund rode tight to the neck of his horse. He had no desire to fight with anyone. He had only one thing in mind. He rode strategically to keep safe but fast enough to stay right behind the first wave of marauders. He was on a mission. He was excited about the possibility of what this day might bring him.

He didn't even realize he had ridden into the city of Hollywondra until he recognized that this area of the forest was gardened, the underbrush was clean, and a carpet of alyssum covered the ground. The fighting seemed chaotic as it no longer seemed to move in a wave, but it was now all around him. He decided that being mounted might be too dangerous, so he quickly got off his horse. Wanting to make sure he could use the horse to escape the fighting, he looked for a good place to tie it up. All the trees were larger than his reins. Realizing his efforts were taking too much time, he walked his horse to the backside of a large tree and tied him to the branch of a large rhododendron.

Gormund realized he could be shot by an archer at any moment, so he cast a spell of invisibility on himself. Once he could see that it had taken hold, he began to sneak his way through the shadows in search of an Elvan temple of worship. He wasn't waiting for the fighting to get over. Technically, the battle raged, so he did not have to send a message to Sythene. He was now on a mission to find whatever it was that Sythene wanted.

As Gormund snuck around the shadows of the trees, he found this search more challenging than he thought it would be. All the structures were in the trees themselves. Gormund had never seen such large trees. Some had stairs carved into the bark that led to a second layer of the city. Gormund looked above and saw there were even more elves up in the trees. As he looked more carefully, he realized that the city went upward several levels. He could not tell if the city climbed higher or if these were just elves trying to stay out of the fight. He could see the elves freely moving from one tree to another as they made their way around the city. Pausing, he realized that finding any one place in this town was going to be extremely tough. Whatever he was looking for could be fifty feet up some other distant tree.

*****

Bellard, Drew, and the scout stopped short of the King's Green to request an immediate audience. Bellard's tone and the sound of the alarm helped the guard recognize the urgency and allow them to pass. After winding their way to the King's Chamber, they found Barnaby Malactus already in audience with the king. As they approached, they could hear Malactus saying, "You have no choice! You must go now, or our entire race will be erased from the annuls of Namron, if you do not flee."

"I will not be known as the king who ran away," argued Elfanwisel.

Before Malactus could continue to persuade the king, Bellard barked, "Their army has entered the city."

Malactus and King Elfanwisel spun to see who had interrupted them then looked quickly at each other. Malactus reminded him of his duty, "You have no choice in this matter. You have a responsibility to your kingdom. If you do not move for the stairs right now, you may not have a chance later."

The king looked away for a moment to consider, then back up at Malactus. "I know you are right. It's just...this is not how my reign was supposed to end."

"Your reign will not be remembered for how we were attacked, as much as it will be for how we respond. This is not over just yet, your highness," Malactus reminded him. "I must urge you to go now. I must return to the temple before I can follow. I will not be far behind."

The king turned and quickly disappeared behind a tapestry. Malactus waved at the guards in the room to follow him. They left their posts and quickly followed after their king.

"You three. Let's go. We must hurry," Malactus commanded.

*****

Gormund was carefully prowling Hollywondra, when through the chaos, he noticed a group of armed men escorting one regally appointed older elf. This was just the type of clue he was hoping to find. Picking up his pace, Gormund caught up to the group and filed in right behind them. As they made their way to the base of an extremely large oak, Gormund was pleased to see the regal elf casting an incantation. Suddenly, magical runes appeared in the bark of the old oak. Then the seams of a door appeared where no door would have ever been detected.

Gormund knew he had to be quick and agile to follow and not get caught by them quickly closing the door. With one quick hop, he was in, just as one of the guards reached to close it. The group stood in the hallway and began discussing some plans. Gormund realized this was his chance to get some distance from these fighters and start searching for the tome. Gormund was thrilled with his progress. He was pretty sure he was on the right track, and he had not had to confront anyone yet. He knew Sythene had knowledge and desire for whatever Hollywondra had to offer. Gormund hoped that he might be able to find it and maybe procure a few valuable things for himself in the process. This might also show Sythene his ability and worthiness.

Surveying the corridor, Gormund was impressed by the beauty of the hallways and structure of this temple. The floors, walls, and ceilings were polished oak. He had never seen anything like this. The hallway wasn't very wide, but he knew he was still standing in a hallway inside a huge tree. He didn't want to take any chances, so he pulled out his dagger, held it ready. Gormund began to slowly make his way through the temple.

He was surprised to find how unattended the temple was. It was as if the temple had already been abandoned. After leaving the men who let him in, he had not seen a soul. His hope for finding anything of value seem dashed. Certainly, the elves would have grabbed something of great value before evacuating. Still, he moved in and out of rooms carefully searching each one for wealth.

Feeling a bit disappointed, Gormund rested against a wall to reconsider what he might have overlooked. There certainly were several precious items of gold and silver adorning the rooms. He just couldn't seem to find anything more meaningful than a few gold sconces and candelabrum.

As he paused to give one room a second more careful look, the wall next to him burst open. Falling to the floor in front of him was an elf and a human. They wrestled for control of a short sword that the human was trying to use on the acolyte. Looking inside, Gormund realized this was a room he had not seen yet. Ignoring the two engaged in a fight for their lives, he stepped around them and into the secret chamber.

The room was not large. It was more of a short hallway than a room. The room was illuminated by golden sconces. One was on the wall by the door he entered. There was an identical golden sconce at the other end of the room. The door at the other end of the room had been left open. The hallway beyond seemed poorly lit compared to this room. On the wall to his left were two bookcases that had been crafted into the wall. They held several large dusty tomes. Standing between the two shelves of books was an ornate pedestal. The ornate pedestal rose up from the same oak wood that made the floor and walls of this chamber. Atop the pedestal's post was a rectangular display case. The display case appeared to have been carved from the same piece of wood as the post on which it sat. The whole thing was a part of the tree. The insides of the rectangular box were padded with a thick red silk cloth. Resting on the red cloth was an elegant bright silver rod. This rod was easily the most beautiful thing Gormund had ever seen. The entire shaft of the rod was etched with intricately crafted vines of ivy. A colorful array of emeralds was embedded in a straight line from the top and bottom. Though they were perfectly aligned, the emeralds did not connect in the middle. Countless smaller emeralds were embedded in each of the leaves of ivy. The artifact was mesmerizing. Gormund had been excited by the knowledge in this library of tomes, until his eyes fell on the beauty of this silver rod.

His short trance was shattered when a burly human burst into the room. Having dispatched the acolyte, the human wiped the blood from the blade of his sword as he stepped back into the short hallway room. Forgetting that he was invisible, Gormund's instinct was to step back from the intruder. Looking around to make sure the room was empty, the man almost turned away. Then his eyes caught sight of the exquisite silver rod. He paused and looked around. Then sheathing his sword, the man stepped over and grabbed it for himself. Before he could fully turn to the door, the man stiffened then fell to his knees and then onto his face. The rod bounced out of his hand and spun out onto the floor. Slowly it rolled toward Gormund's feet. Gormund took a small step back and allowed the rod to come to a rest on its own.

Gormund stepped around the rod and then began searching through the tomes in search of the Wythargle's Tome. As soon as he picked up the tome, his spell of invisibility ended. He was so excited when he found the tome that he almost forgot his desire to steal the beautiful silver rod as well. Considering the death of the man at his feet, Gormund then pulled the silky red scarf from the display case. Using the scarf, Gormund picked up the rod and carefully wrapped the scarf around the silver rod. Realizing he needed to cover his tracks, he used the candles from the candelabrum to set the room on fire. He knew the room held a wealth of clerical knowledge, but he didn't care about that. He had what he wanted…and a little something extra for his efforts.

Gormund moved quickly to escape this strange tree structure. Wythargle's Tome was large and challenging to carry with a rod wrapped in silk. Gormund imagined he could not afford to accidently touch this rod, so he tried to be careful carrying both. Moving carefully, Gormund found an exit from the temple. As he exited the temple, he found the fighting was all around him, and it had only intensified. He was no longer invisible as he started the journey back to his horse.

*****

Smoke poured from the room, but it didn't slow Barnabus Malactus. He went rushing into the flames, yelling for others to help. Using elemental incantations, the Elvan high priest was able to single-handedly stop the spread of the flames and expel the smoke from the room. Immediately, Barnabus realized that the Mansuranthra's Rod had been stolen. The damage to the tomes was considerable. It made it hard for the high priest to recognize if any of the tomes had been stolen.

Quellen rushed into the room. Bellard and Hamman Drew were just a few steps behind. They arrived in time to hear Malactus explaining the theft. "He was probably with this lout," Malactus suggested as he lightly kicked the shoulder of the dead fighter on the floor. "My guess is that he had enough brains to wrap the rod in the bright red cloth it rested on. If not, we'll find him lying in the street with the rod nearby. Whatever you do, under no circumstances

HOLLYWONDRA

should you try to touch the rod." Then as he realized the gravity of the theft, he added, "Under no circumstances can we allow that rod to leave Hollywondra."

As if they were waiting for more direction, the three of them stood silent, before Malactus emphatically yelled, "Well?" and then waved his arms at them as if to shoo them away.

Realizing the urgency to find this rod, the three men rushed from the room. As they ran for the door, Drew tried to clarify, "What are we looking for? A bright red cloth?"

Quellen quickly responded, "We are looking for Mansuranthra's Rod of Might. It is the most holy and powerful of all Elvan artifacts."

While that helped Hamman Drew recognize the urgency, he was still pretty unclear as to what he would be looking for.

As the three rushed out into the streets of Hollywondra, the chaos of the fight made their mission even more challenging. As they looked around, Hamman Drew saw a human soldier strike down an elderly elf who appeared to be standing between the fighter and a child. As the elder fell to the ground, the child began to scream. The soldier started to lift his sword on the child, as Drew bolted in their direction. Hamman Drew, yelling as loudly as he could, caused the man to pause. That was all the time Drew needed to close on the man. As the fighter turned to look in Drew's direction, he was assailed by a flash of scimitar blades. The fighter was quickly on the defense.

It did not take Hamman Drew much time to kill the soldier. After killing the soldier, he turned to check on the little Elvan girl and the elder elf. He found Quellen tending to the injured old man. "Go!" Quellen directed Drew. "I've got this. Go find the rod."

As Drew stood up to survey the chaos, he noticed a horse and rider. The rider was clumsily caring something very large as he tried to hold his reins. It seems this rider was not interested in fighting. It looked like he was trying to escape. The challenge of caring for his cargo made him unsteady in the saddle. Drew watched for only a moment before he realized the rider was carrying a large book. As Hamman Drew saw this rider trying to balance himself, he noticed a bright red fabric flagging in the wind from under the rider's arm.

Acting on instinct, Drew took off running after the rider. In very little time, the rider began distancing himself from Drew. From his left, Drew was surprised to see Bellard running after the rider too. He was hopeful because it seemed Bellard had a better angle to intercept the rider. Unfortunately, the rider saw him coming and turned his horse away from Bellard. Having found his balance in the saddle, the rider was now spurring his horse up to full speed.

Just as Bellard slowed his pursuit, Drew ran up to Bellard. "Where do you guys keep those tree spider things?"

A bit perplexed by his question, then Bellard processed his thinking and said, "Oh! This way."

39

Gormund didn't care that he was riding north and away from the Zel Camber's camp. He was just excited to be out of the combat and in possession of some very valuable items. Every time he allowed his mind to wander to the wealth he possessed, he found himself suddenly struggling to control his horse and the balance of carrying these items. He knew he was being chased, so he knew he had to ride as fast as he could. He also knew it made no sense to ride so fast that he dropped his treasure—or worse, accidently touch that magical rod.

He considered arching his path back toward the camp of Nictovius's army. While he knew he had two very important items, he also knew he could not make Sythene an enemy by simply trying to run off with this ancient spell book. He knew if he started to turn back toward the camp too soon, he risked the chance to riding back into the battle's fray. He used this logic to keep his northern course a little longer. He knew there wasn't anyone back at camp waiting for him. He might as well be safe in circling back.

*****

The last two days of travel had been different than any of their previous days. Palcombine, Jarius, and Allendale had each found signs of things that troubled them on their path to Hollywondra. Much of it made no sense to Titus and Amanda. The one thing they did understand was that they needed to move faster, yet somehow more cautiously. The elves had found evidence that Kobold and giant wolves had been traveling this same trail. They could tell it had been several days since these enemies had passed this way. That only made the elves feel more urgency.

The group had chosen to follow the very path that had been taken by the Kobold army. The path was at least a few days old. Palcombine took the point to ensure the group didn't run into any lagging Kobold scouts. The others tried their best to keep up.

Just after noon of their second day of travel, the group was surprised to find Palcombine suddenly returning to them. As he arrived, the rest could see that something was wrong. Palcombine stepped up to the group and began to speak rapidly in Elvan. Amanda knew some Elvan, but she could not keep up with what she heard him saying. Titus had no idea what was going on. He knew something wasn't right when he saw Allendale drop his head and Jarius instinctively touched the hilt of his short sword.

Amanda turned to Titus. "This is bad. It sounds like Palcombine found evidence of a slaughter of his countrymen."

Titus could not imagine the horror. The few conflicts he had witnessed turned his stomach. He only listened as Amanda tried to translate snippets of information for him. "It sounds like we may be taking a new route. It sounds like it might be a little bit dangerous, but it will get us there much faster than this path we're on. I think we might have to climb some waterfalls." As she said that, Amanda realized what she was saying and said, "Wait! Let me check on that."

Allendale turned to Amanda and said, "You heard him right. We are going to take a trail that literally scales through some waterfalls. It's a little bit slippery. Then pointing at the other two elves, he explained, "We've all gone that way before. It's always easier coming down that climbing up, but it will cut several hours off our travel."

"There's more," Allendale said solemnly. "Palcombine said that just up the path, he could smell smoke. He's afraid that the army might be using fire to burn the elves out of their homes."

The idea that anyone would destroy ancient wildlife really upset Amanda. Immediately, she found herself anxious and ready to move. "Then let's go!" she barked. "Why are we still standing here?"

*****

HOLLYWONDRA

Palcombine had spent many nights away from his home tracking and hunting in the wild. He knew the exhaustion that came from forced marches or running for hours on end. It was a life he had chosen for himself many years ago. With it, he also knew the risks that he was choosing to adopt. The sunrise was still over an hour away, but he had already grown restless. He was anxious to get to Hollywondra. He knew that they could join the battle this same day, if he could just get his group up and moving.

As Palcombine shifted his weight, he was pleasantly surprised to see that the muted noise was enough to wake Jarius. It was not intended, but it did remind him that Jarius was an experienced soldier. His ability to be awaken by such a subtle shift was encouraging to Palcombine. As Jarius made his way to his feet, he moved over to speak quietly with Palcombine.

"I think the push and the waterfalls really knocked them out," Jarius suggested. "I know we are close. I think we should let them rest as much as we can afford. We will need them to be as fresh and capable as possible. There is no telling who or what we will be encountering."

Looking down at the ground, Palcombine nodded his head in agreement. This made it clear to Jarius that his friend was willing to wait, though he'd probably prefer to set out on his own at this point in their journey.

Allendale woke just before daybreak and immediately surveyed their camp. He quickly realized that the two Elvan fighters were waiting patiently for the others to get their rest. "I'll wake them. I know we need to go." As Allendale went to wake the others, Palcombine pulled his quiver off his shoulder to take stock of the arrows had left.

*****

Titus understood why they didn't have a campfire. That didn't change the fact that his cold legs were still sore and his joints stiff. Through the misty morning fog, they pushed their way through dewy forest underbrush. If this was a trail, it didn't look like it had been used in a long time. Their trail ran along the edge of a steep hillside and followed the river that ran below them. As they climbed, they found that they were able to quickly rise above the blanket of morning fog that tightly held to the river's water. The warm morning sun felt wonderful after spending a night without campfire. As they climbed higher, they could see the river's route determined by the thick gray ribbon of fog weaving off into the distance.

After about an hour, their path started back down toward the river. The group walked back into the thick blanket of fog. The trail opened up, and the slope disappeared. Soon, they found themselves walking along the riverbank again. The fog here was so thick that Palcombine could only scout a few dozen yards ahead of the rest, or he risked losing them.

Shortly after the trail pulled away from the stream and began heading into the woods, they heard Palcombine shout a warning. He usually used more subtle whistles and cues. For him to shout out a warning meant that the danger was immediate. Everyone pulled their weapons, except Titus. He was initially flustered, then he remembered he might be able to disappear. He had been working on this with Ezen, so he quickly found himself able to focus and disappear.

Through the fog came a single rider. The sound of his horse was lost in the roar of the river. The rider shot right past Palcombine and unknowingly right into the rest of party. The speed of the rider was such that none of the fighters seemed able raise a weapon, before he was past. It was all they could do to step aside and not be trampled by the careless horseman. The only one able to raise a hand was Titus. As the rider came past him, Titus could see that the man had no concern for the safety of his friends on the trail. Out of anger, Titus reached up to strike at the man. As he reached up toward the rider, he inadvertently grabbed a red silk cloth that flapped from under the arm of the rider.

Pulling on the cloth caused the rider to lose his balance. While he tried to keep hold of the cloth, the rider spun in his saddle. It seemed the cloth was a part of his clothing. In an instant, the rider was faced with releasing the cloth or being pulled down from his horse. Before the rider could recover his balance, Titus's grip on the cloth pulled it right out from under the rider's arm. Immediately, the

HOLLYWONDRA

rider lost hold of objects he was carrying. The stuff he carried was tossed up into the air as the rider tried to grasp what he had just lost and manage his balance in the saddle.

The rest of the party watched in wonder. The fog was thick. They couldn't tell what caused the rider to lose his balance and his cargo. Being only a few steps away, they stepped toward the rider who was now reining in his horse. As the group looked more carefully, they saw Titus holding a red fabric. Some random objects had fallen to the ground near his feet. As the rider turned and began walking his horse back, everyone raised their weapons.

"Whoa, now," the rider said as he recognized their readiness. He held up his hands as he slowly walked his horse back to their location. "My apologies. You came out of the fog so suddenly. I didn't see you until I was upon you," he suggested. As he reached Titus, he said, "I just need to grab my stuff, and I will be on my way. Again, my apologies. I hope nobody was injured by my recklessness."

Hearing the man offer so many apologies, everyone began to consider that this encounter was indeed accidental and without malice. Sheathing their swords, they approached common ground. "What do you know of the war with the elves?" asked Jarius.

While dismounting, Gormund chose not to look Jarius in the eye as he answered, "I heard the fighting and was riding as far around it as I could." Not allowing their questions to slow him, he easily found the tomb and finished his thought. "As you can tell, I am no mercenary. I am simply running an errand for my master. It seems to have put me in greater peril than we realized." Then he began looking around for the rod. Titus offered him his red fabric. Gormund gladly took it but started to become panicked that he didn't immediately see where the rod had fallen.

Seeing the man kicking around the grass, Titus asked, "What else are you looking for?"

Gormund was carefully beginning to calculate what he might have to do, if this situation turned violent. He knew he could quickly immobilize three or four of them, but he knew the further apart they got, the less likely he would be able to capture that many in a single spell. Those he did not capture would be his immediate threat. So as

275

he looked for the rod, he tried to keep them grouped together as best he could. Each moment he looked for the rod, he knew he pressed his luck.

There were no human communities in the valley. Realizing this, Jarius asked, "Where is it you are riding from?"

This was the type of question Gormund feared. He didn't have enough detail to fabricate a detailed lie. This made him quickly weigh whether to cast a spell or just leave the rod behind.

Before he could answer, Amanda said, "This is what you must have been looking for."

Gormund's head spun in a panic, knowing that she would be instantly killed if she touched that rod. Then he would immediately be in the fight of his life. "Wait!" he yelled. With the tomb tightly wrapped in his right arm, he raised his left arm as if to make her halt.

He was too late. The young man he thought Amanda to be had lifted Mansuranthra's Rod up from a large tuft of grass and held it out for him to take.

Gormund moved toward her as quickly as he could. "Noooo!" he cried, reaching his left arm toward Amanda. He was only a few steps away, but he was too late to stop Amanda from picking up the artifact.

As she extended her arm to return the rod to the rider, Amanda paused to stare in awe at the magnificence of the rod. Spinning it in her hand, she marveled at the beautiful etchings and jewels embedded into the art. She quickly realized why the man would stop to recover such a precious thing. It had to be extremely valuable. Before she could stand up straight, a warm surge of power shot through her body. This surge of power made Amanda suddenly stand erect and stiff. As that surge of power grew, it climaxed in a brilliant flash before her eyes. The flash of light blinded Amanda for just a moment. Then instinctively, her grip on the rod tightened. She was a little confused by her own behavior. What she knew was that holding this rod felt very good to her. It fit in her hand as if it had been made for her. Looking down at the rod, Amanda slowly rotated her wrist to examine all the details she could take in.

HOLLYWONDRA

As Gormund neared Amanda, the rest of the party saw her holding this heavily bejeweled rod in her right hand. Then by rolling her wrist, Amanda spun the rod in a figure eight. At first, she seemed to roll the rod to examine it. Then she began rolling it faster. The speed that she was able to spin this rod seemed to increase beyond anyone's natural ability to spin such a thing with their hand. The details of the spinning rod began to blur as Amanda made it spin faster and faster. The amazing speed made the rod look like it was simply flashing at the end of her arm. Then she spun it faster. The bright silver rod spun so quickly that it blurred into what seemed to be a silver ball.

Gormund did not understand what was going. He knew she should have collapsed by now. Extending the red velvet tapestry with his left hand, he asked if she would "kindly wrap it up" for him.

Amanda did not respond. She seemed mesmerized by the silver ball at the end of her hand and gave no indication that she even heard him. She gave no sign of slowing down the spin of the rod. Her mind was somewhere else. She continued spinning the rod. It moved at such an unnatural speed that the glistening ball began to glow and make a low hum.

Gormund did not understand what he was witnessing. He knew that she should be dead by now. He began slowly backing away from Amanda. He'd seen enough magic to know power greater than his own. "I...uh...don't know what's going on, but..." He didn't even know what to say. Gormund began slowly backing his way to his horse as the others watched Amanda in wonder.

As Gormund reached his steed, he quickly mounted it and tried to make the horse turn to ride away. As he kicked his horse and pulled the reins, it jumped a little but did not turn. His horse seemed to be mesmerized by the ball of light coming from Amanda. He kicked it again and again, but it would not move. Suddenly he found Amanda standing in front of him. Her hood had been pulled back. Her blonde hair and face glowed with a magical aura. She had stopped spinning the rod.

Standing next to the horse, Amanda lightly patted its face with her left hand while she held the rod out toward Gormund. "This was not your rod to take, now, was it?" Amanda asked.

The rest of the party were startled to find that Amanda had moved in one moment from where she had found the rod to now stand in front of this rider's horse. She seemed to have moved faster than the blink of an eye. So they turned to see her addressing the rider.

"I...I...uh don't want any trouble. I found that rod and...I mean it is beautiful, wouldn't you have picked it up," Gormund suggested.

"Where?" Amanda asked sternly. "Where did you 'find' this rod?" Her tone was intense, and Gormund knew this was going to turn bad. Realizing the rest of the group was still behind her, Gormund determined to cast a quick spell on Amanda. Not something that would kill her, but something that would stun her enough that he should be able to get away. He knew the incantation was short and the hand gesture very concise. As he began to speak his incantation, Amanda was no longer standing in front of him. Just that fast, he had no target. Amanda had moved from in front of his horse to right up beside him.

Amanda was not sure why she was able to move so quickly. But when she made her mind to move quickly, it was as if time slowed down and she could still move at her normal speed. She recognized this rider to be a mage of some type. She noticed him start some intricate gestures with his fingers. The gestures reminded her of the same gestures Ezen Kroach made before unleashing his magic. She figured that he was about to cast some spell at her. So she moved.

"You need to dismount. This horse will not be taking you anywhere. He refuses to let you ride any longer."

Gormund was bewildered by her movement and her words. Knowing that she was now directly beside his steed, Gormund yanked his reins away from the girl and gave the horse two huge kick to the ribs. The horse lunged forward at first. Then it stepped back and began bucking wildly. Amanda took a step back, but the rest of the party spread out as the horse's kicking was unpredictable. Gormund had no chance of staying on the horse or holding onto the tomb. Quickly, he found himself on his back with the tome on the ground at his side. The horse jumped away from where Gormund laid in the moist grass and walked up to Amanda. Amanda gently petted the horse's face and spoke softly to it.

Gormund just wanted to live. He knew he needed to keep the tome and get away as quickly as he could, so he grabbed the tome and quickly dove toward the taller grass. As he rolled into the taller grass and fog, he cast a spell of invisibility on himself and tried to remain still. As the party began moving in his direction, he tried to move quietly to skirt them.

Amanda stepped forward and said to them, "He cannot hide from me." Amanda began spinning the rod again. As the spin accelerated to the point that the blur became a bright glowing ball, a bright flash of light burst out of the ball. The flash of light was bright in the midday sun, and it burst out in every direction. Then she slowly stopped spinning the rod.

Gormund was scared. There was definitely something supernatural about this girl, and he needed to quickly get as far away from her as he could. He was frightened at the thought of her being able to harness the magic of this rod at him. Feeling he might have backed far enough away, he began trying to skirt their perimeter to some nearby trees to his left.

No sooner than she had stopped spinning the rod, Sir Allendale was startled by a large timber rattlesnake that just slithered past him. Stepping quickly aside, he began to lift his sword to kill the snake. "No, leave them alone," directed Amanda. Then two more slithered past Titus. The three of them crawled in the same direction. The rest of the party grew more concerned when they heard the low guttural growl of a mountain lion coming from the brush not fifty feet away.

Before the snakes were able to reach the tall grass, Gormund came running out from the high grass swatting at a swarm of bugs that surrounding him. His sudden appearance caused all three snakes to coil for a strike. His movement made his spell of invisibility dispel. As he jumped forward, the party could see he was swatting at a swarm of bees and wasps that surrounded him. The snakes looked like they were ready to strike, if he came any closer. Behind him, a large mountain lion appeared from the undergrowth. Again, Amanda assured the group that everything was okay. The mountain lion stopped after it emerged from cover. It seemed to stand and just watch everyone carefully. Gormund no longer carried the tome. He needed both hands to keep the pests from eating him alive. Hopping out into the open, he cried for mercy. "Okay! Okay! Make them stop. Make them stop!" he cried.

Amanda stepped closer to the man and said, "I will only ask them to stop this one time. Do you understand me?"

"Yes! Yes! You will have my full cooperation. Just make them stop!" he yelled as he continued to swat at the flies, mosquitos, and wasps that were all over him.

Suddenly, the swarm spun away from him and dissipated. Gormund continued swatting though the bugs as they flew off him. This face and hands were swollen and severely bitten. As he realized the swarm was gone, he raised both hands in surrender.

"Go fetch that book you were carrying. I want to take a closer look at it." As Gormund turned to fetch the book, he saw the mountain lion and froze. "It's okay. As long as you do as you are told, he will not bother you. Though, I would not make any sudden movements." Amanda turned to chuckle with her friends. They all stood speechless, staring in amazement at the powers she displayed. Amanda, not really understanding this power or her purpose for receiving such power, smiled and shirked her shoulders to show them that she doesn't fully understand either.

Gormund slowly picked up the tome and slowly walked over to Amanda. As Amanda took the book, she could tell it was very old. She really had no idea what she was looking at, so she turned to her friends and offered them the chance to examine the book. As the group looked down at the ancient tome, they were all a little surprised to find the first observation came from Titus.

"See that mark right there? That little squiggly mark looks just like one I had seen before." Everyone in the group stopped their inspection of the book and turned to look at Titus. Where could he have seen magical markings in this limited time in this world? Realizing that he had just exposed a bit more information than the rest of the group knew, he explained how he had found a ring, how Ezen had told him it was magical. Then pulling the ring out from his pocket, he showed Amanda where one marking inside the ring looked just like one of the markings on the tome. "I don't know what that means. Heck, I don't know what this ring does. I just think these two marks look the same."

Amanda began nodding her head in agreement. Jarius noted that one of them looked like a marking from his dagger. Then Allendale, Jarius, and Palcombine each identified different Elvan markings on the leather cover.

Just as they flipped the tome to examine the backside, they heard the thrashing of tree bows overhead. Gormund was almost too busy caring for his wounds to care. Out of the branches landed a Scurrier. From the back of the Scurrier, two riders jumped and rolled. When they came up from their roll, one elf had an arrow nocked and ready to fire, and the other had pulled two scimitars and stood ready to fight.

Standing just a few feet away the mountain lion, Gormund could no longer imagine his fate. His only hope was that these two factions would break out in a fight that provided him enough time to slip away. Those hopes were dashed when Bellard recognized Palcombine. "Corporal Palcombine!" he announced. Quickly Bellard returned his arrow to his quiver and his bow to his shoulder.

"What is the meaning of this?" Palcombine asked, pointing at the Scurrier. He knew the Scurriers were a rare military commodity. "What brings you so far afield?"

Bellard turned to look at Gormund. Gormund stood quietly, wondering if this could be the day he dies.

Barnabus Malactus felt the depressing dread of failure. Amidst the chaos of this invasion, he had lost the holiest of all Elvan artifacts. His dread was not for his personal safety. It was for his failure to protect the Rod of Mansuranthra. Somehow, it had been stolen right from under his nose. He had no idea where it could have gone or who could have taken it. Worse was the fact that Zel Camber's army was clearly stronger than the remaining Elvan forces. The elves would not surrender and continued to fight from the upper reaches of the trees. The fact was that they did not have enough men to push this force out of their ancient city. Malactus knew the temple's fire had been extinguished and all the exterior doors were sealed shut. Yet he roamed the hallways of the temple frantically searching behind every tapestry and fixture, hoping that somehow it had been left behind.

The high priest wasn't ready to surrender the temple to the godless louts outside. The more he searched his halls, the more certain he became that the rod had been stolen. Hanging his head in shame, he realized he could no longer do any good from inside the temple. After hours of searching, Barnabus Malactus paused to accept this reality. Pausing to pray, the priest prayed for comfort and guidance, comfort he had always had in his faith. He'd hoped that God might actually show him how the prophecy would unfold. His prayer did not provide him the comfort he had sought. He determined he needed to seek out the king and the remnants of the Elvan nations that were able to escape into the Raven Rift. Standing by the door, he waited to make sure he could no longer hear fighting or noise. Once it sounded safe, Barnabus Malactus cracked the door to check.

HOLLYWONDRA

As soon as he opened the door, he was startled to find the face of Sir Jarius Raphael staring right back at him. Startled to see someone face-to-face, the priest quickly shut the door in reflex. Pausing for a moment, he realized that it was Sir Jarius Raphael he'd seen outside. Sir Raphael was the one man tasked to retrieve the Light. Barnabus Malactus quickly opened the door to let Jarius into the temple. He was surprised to find Jarius had a young girl with him. This young girl carried the rod. This caused the priest pause. He wasn't sure what was unfolding in this critical moment in Elvan history. Jarius raised his hand to assure the priest. "It's okay. I think she may be the Light."

Shocked by this sudden development, Barnabus Malactus hurried them into the temple and secured the door. Backing slowly into the hallway, the priest was agog at this young lady who could safely carry the rod in her bare hand. As Amanda began to speak, she paused as she saw the figure of Chronus come around the temple corridor to join them. Coming from the hallway to their left, he approached quietly and with a measured step. Stopping short of their company, he stood to listen to Jarius's report to Malactus.

The high priest had seen many significant events over the past several hundred years, each time Chronus would suddenly appear and record the significance of those events for his ancient annuls that nobody had ever seen. The return of the Rod of Mansuranthra was a huge event in their history. If this girl is the Light of Elvan legend, then this could be the single greatest moment in Elvan history. The significance of this moment affected the high priest's poise. Unsure how to process the conversation, Barnabus asked Amanda, "What do you need?"

Not skipping a beat, Amanda said, "Take me to the Sanctuary."

Barnabus didn't pause. He turned and led her to the holy sanctuary of the Elvan Temple. Leading her into the room, the rest stood to watch what amazing thing she might do next. To their surprise, she knelt down and prayed. Setting the rod on the floor in front of her, Amanda raised her face and arms in praise to her God. She thanked her Lord for her safe arrival to Hollywondra and for his grace in preserving the Elvan race. She praised his kindness and compassion for everyone compelled to war. Then she asked for strength and wisdom—strength, because the use of this magical rod took a physical toll on her each time she made it spin in her hand, and wisdom, so that she would know how best to use this divine tool to better the world in the way God would want it.

The three watched her to see what she might do next. The silence seemed to go on forever. Jarius was the most anxious. He wanted to be outside killing the marauders who had entered his holy city. He knew Amanda was his primary charge and that waiting for her is what he needed to do.

Finally, Amanda stood up calmy and began spinning the Rod of Mansuranthra.

*****

From the back of his horse, Silas Pei could evaluate the progress his forces were making. The resistance they had experienced before was entirely gone. Not that they didn't suffer loses. It was simply not the level of resistance they had encountered before. Silas adjusted himself in his saddle to sit a little higher. He had been pretty uncertain about this invasion. The dream he'd shared with the others seemed very real. But on this day, everything had changed. The Elvan resistance had failed, and victory was certain.

As Silas navigated between two large rhododendrons, he recognized one of his division leaders running back in his direction. The man was swatting at something that was around his head. As he came nearer, Silas Pei realized that several of the men from that division had emerged running in a retreat. They were all swatting at bugs that swarmed around them. Some of the men fell to the ground to cover their faces. Others dropped their weapons so both hands could be used to swat at the pests. As Silas Pei began to comprehend what he was seeing, he noticed that the woods beyond the men were turning dark with a swarm of insects. As far as he could see to his right and left, the swarm only grew. Silas Pei knew his horse could only carry so much, so he turned and determined to outrun the swarm himself. As he turned to see the progress of the swarm, he lost sight of his men who had been overtaken by the dark mass of insects.

HOLLYWONDRA

As he urged his horse to move faster, Silas rode past a troop of about fifty Kobold. They were in the fight of their life with what looked like a menagerie of wild cats. It looked like a couple dozen bobcats and mountain lions had joined forces to attack this group of Kobold. Even thought they had weapons, the Kobold were falling fast. Silas Pei knew he could not help their cause, so he kept riding for the valley floor.

When Silas Pei finally made it to the open grasses of Shayna's Valley, he was surprised to see the Klofgar had left their positions at the trebuchets. They were running around swatting at birds that continued to dive and harass them. Not just a few birds. This flock of birds had targeted the large beasts. Their harassment had sent several of the Klofgar to run. When the Klofgar ran away from the woods of Hollywondra, they found the birds would stop attacking and go to attack those who stayed behind.

Silas arrived just in time to see the last of the Klofgar abandon their post and run for the hills. Silas realized he should have heeded the warning of his dream. Reining in his horse, Silas began to assess his surroundings. The birds did not seem interested in him. The swarm of insects must still be behind him. There was nobody in the camp.

Looking around, he realized he might be the only living human in the valley. The moment gave Silas the time he needed to reconsider his role in this army. He knew the risks of abandoning the army. If Zel Camber ever came to know, he would be hunted down and killed. Then Silas realized, he'd better get going before someone else comes out onto the valley floor and sees him riding away. Assessing his belongings, he knew there was no reason for him to return to his tent. So Silas asked his horse to give it everything it had and to rush to the nearest forest line of northern hills.

*****

Nictovius had entered Hollywondra from the southernmost edge. He'd taken this route in hopes of skirting the fight and maybe cutting off any sneaky elves who might try to escape his frontal assault. His route had taken him deep into the forest. Since he was not leading any of the fighters, his arrival was not attracting any attention. It seemed the elves had surrendered their perimeter guards for fighting the core of his forces. He was able to ride to a place where the forest floor became very uneven. It even seemed to slope somewhat to the east.

The sound of battle was remarkably familiar to him. He could hear the screams of battle, but the sound of those screams included cries of pain. Nictovius noticed bugs had begun to swarm around him. He stopped his horse and swatted at them. As he paused, he noticed that the swarm was thicker ahead of him. This was very strange. It in the distance, the swarm was so thick, it was almost a wall of swarming pests. Then he noticed that the wall was moving. It was moving toward the valley to his left. After sitting for a few minutes, he noticed the bugs that pestered him had left to join the wall that continued moving further into the woods.

He walked his horse forward to see many of his men lying dead on the forest floor. Some had been killed by arrows. All of them were unrecognizable from the countless stings and bites on their skin. Nictovius paused to consider the damage this might have done to his army. He could not see a single living person in the forest around him. He kicked his horse to move forward. As he went deeper into the woods, Nictovius could still hear the clamor of hand-to-hand combat. This excited him. For a moment, he feared all hope was lost. He moved his horse in the direction of the fight.

*****

The fighting was furious. Jarius, Hamman Drew, Allendale, Bellard, and Palcombine formed a small circle on the street outside the temple. They were fighting intruders as fast as they came into town. They did not have time to leave the group before another arrived. They did have some support from the archers overhead, but the number of marauders seemed endless.

They knew that Amanda was doing something to help. They just did not know what it was and when it would happen. They had

HOLLYWONDRA

to stop as many of these invaders as they could. Titus remained hidden against the nearby wall of the Temple Tree. The gore was every bit as bad as any horror movie had had ever seen. But he knew the difference. These men were people he had come to love and adore. He felt so powerless as they fought for their lives.

Watching them fight, Titus realized they fought in a very intentional and strategic manner. This new friend used two swords. He was quick to kill his target, but he did not leave the side of the elves. It was as if they were waiting for something. Their little circle only moved to provide them more targets to attack. But they never left the side of the other four fighters.

Suddenly, it seemed all their prey were gone. It appeared that they had killed all the intruders who were nearby. Just as they paused to look around, they noticed another wave of intruders to the west. Turning to the west, they moved as a group to address their attackers. All Titus could do was watch. He knew if he became visible, they would be having to protect him while fighting off these attackers. He realized his best role was to remain invisible and not worry anyone.

Titus watched as his friends dispatched that group of attackers. Titus recognized that there were no more Zel Camber forces coming from the north or the south. This allowed Titus time to watch as things unfolded from the west. Looking up into the trees, Titus could see several elves moving from branch to branch heading west. The sudden focus of Elvan forces seemed like a good sign, until Titus saw the wave of Kobold rushing into the city. There were dozens of them that had not yet engaged with Elvan forces. It was as if they had skirted the lines and found a way into Hollywondra.

There was Elvan shouting from the trees, as the archers began to backtrack to the Kobold insurgence. The savagery Titus had seen so far was worse than he could have imagined. That savagery amplified as the Kobold appeared as interested in eating the dead elves, as they were in killing them. The sheer number of Kobold made it hard for him to remain out of the way. As they rushed by, they ran all over the city streets. There numbers were almost as if the fighting had just started.

He could no longer see his friends. There was a swarm of Kobold where he knew them to be. Occasionally he could catch a glimpse of one of their swords arching down on an opponent. His frustration was greater now than ever. Most of the Kobold rush had run past him. One of the last ones to run past him slowed down, when it realized the rest were running ahead. He stopped not five feet from Titus and paused. Looking around, the Kobold moved over to the dead body of an Elvan archer who had fallen from above. Grabbing the dead elf's arm, the Kobold shoved the elf's hand into his mouth. The Kobold bit and tugged on the dead arm, trying to tear fingers off this hand. After finally securing a bite, the Kobold looked around to make sure he was still safe. Then digging into its mouth, the Kobold pulled out a bone and began nibbling at the flesh that was still attached. After doing that to the second finger he had eaten, he turned his attention back to the dead elf.

Titus could not take any more. He moved quietly to where he saw a short sword laying on the ground. He knew he would become visible as soon as he picked it up. So he timed his attack. He waited for the Kobold to turn his attention for another bite. When he did, Titus quickly picked up the short sword, took two quick steps toward the Kobold, and shoved the sword through the Kobold's back. Titus had never been a fighter. But this felt right. After all, this was not a person. This thing is an evil beast that needed to die.

Titus did not have any illusions of grandeur. He knew he was still best serving this group by being out of the way and invisible. Not even bothering to pull the sword out, Titus backed over to the tree and refocused himself to become invisible. If he continued to carry that sword, he could be seen. Titus's heart was racing. The only thing he had ever killed before was a chicken. This was entirely different. He knew this thing would have killed him, if it had seen him coming.

As he stood to process his kill, he noticed that the Kobold were being defeated. Suddenly, momentum of the fight had changed, and they were being chased back from where they had come. Four of the five fighters had now broken their circle to pursue the retreating Kobold. Titus could see the elves above him giving chase as well.

HOLLYWONDRA

Jarius had made his way back to the Temple Tree and began quietly calling for Titus.

"I'm over here," Titus cued, causing himself to reappear. Jarius approached to explain that it looks like they might have staved off this wave.

Titus was sweating from the one blow he had landed. He was considering telling Jarius about the Kobold he killed, when he noticed an armored rider walking his horse into the camp.

This was no Kobold. This rider was the most formidable person Titus had ever seen in his life. His horse was even armored for battle. The rider's helm made it hard to see his face, but he confidently walked his horse through the alyssum into the center of Hollywondra. Jarius was so concerned for Titus's well-being, he did not see Nictovius arrive. "Jarius" was all Titus had to say.

Jarius turned to see the approaching rider. All his friends had given chase to the Kobold. Yet without hesitation, Jarius pulled his short sword and began to stride out to meet him in battle.

As Jarius approached, he offered, "This war is over. These attacks on our sacred forest have failed. Spare yourself from certain death. Turn your horse around, and ride back to your home."

Nictovius looked at the fighter walking toward him and replied, "This war is over when I say it's over!" Seeing that this elf was not deterred, Nictovius dismounted and drew his longsword.

Titus watched with fear. He had seen Jarius fight courageously, but he had never seen a warrior the size of this man and dressed in such heavy metal armor. The way the rider dismounted showed Titus that the fighter was clearly comfortable with the weight of this armor. His longsword was at least a foot longer than the short sword Jarius carried. Titus wished Jarius at least had some type of metal armor. The fighter stood a foot and a half taller than Jarius. Jarius looked seriously outmatched. Titus looked around, but he could not see any one to help Jarius as he squared off with this large human fighter.

Nictovius could not believe the brazen stupidity of this elf to square off with him. He took two strides then skipped into a two-handed crushing blow on Jarius. Jarius jumped to the side, avoiding the powerful blow. Nictovius spun around before Jarius could launch any type of counterattack. Realizing that his prey was quick and agile, Nictovius slowed his approach.

Realizing this man was in full armor, Jarius drew his magical dagger and threw it with all his might. Jarius was thrilled that the dagger found a crease in the armor and stuck Nictovius in the front of his left shoulder. Surprised by the pain, Nictovius grabbed the dagger and pulled it out. As he tossed it behind him, Jarius attacked. He hoped that this might catch the man off guard. Jarius took a large swipe at the knee of Nictovius. Nictovius quickly planted the tip of his sword in the dirt and was easily able to block the blow. Jarius rushed past him and spun around to see if there was a counterattack.

Nictovius did not seem in a hurry to kill the elf. "You got any more of those children's toys?" he teased Jarius. Then holding his sword at the ready, Nictovius closed on Jarius.

Jarius stood his ground, as Nictovius slashed and parried. Jarius was able to deflect both attempts. He even countered, but his short sword only found the stout metal edge of Nictovius's long sword. That block led Nictovius to arch another overhead swing down on top of Jarius. As Jarius stepped aside, Nictovius let the momentum of his swing push his sword into a level slash at the midsection of Jarius Raphael. The strength and speed of this attack surprised Jarius. The tip of his steel sword cleanly cut through the thigh of his leather pants and into the flesh of his thigh.

Jarius's leaping backward from the burn of steel did not deter Nictovius. It only encouraged him. Now he came hard and fast at Jarius. Nictovius launched a heavy overhead blow at the head of Jarius. The elf was just able to get his sword up in time. This time his sword met the edge of Nictovius's long sword and snapped in half. Nictovius then slashed at his midsection. Jarius was just able to use the broken short sword to deflect that assault. But Jarius knew he could not fight this way. He turned quickly to grab another short sword from a nearby body. As he turned, Nictovius swung and slashed the back of Jarius as he stepped away.

Titus was absolutely beside himself. He couldn't do anything to help his friend. It also appeared Jarius was going to be killed right before his eyes. He had to do something. Totally unarmed, Titus decided to try to distract the fighter and yelled, "Hey! He's over here!" hoping to suggest that he was calling reinforcements. That did make Nictovius pause and look back in Titus's direction. That was all the time Jarius needed to pick up the short sword.

Not seeing any threats, Nictovius returned his attention to Jarius. As the two of them fought, Jarius was unable to land any more significant blows to this man in armor. Nictovius had more fortune. He had hit Jarius two more times. Now Jarius bled from his left arm and shoulder.

Titus could see Jarius weakening and knew he would be killed. So he quietly moved up behind Nictovius to give him a huge shove in the back. Titus knew what it was like to fight with someone much larger than himself. He channeled all the hatred he had for his brother and how his brother had treated him into this one push. Titus was not going to be cheated. He knew he had to hit this guy with everything he had. He also knew he couldn't let the guy know his was coming, or he'd surely be killed. As he approached, Titus got within ten feet of Nictovius as Nictovius moved toward Jarius. In the last few steps, Titus sprinted to the back of Nictovius to hit him with everything he had in his weight and strength. Just as Titus came crashing into the back of Nictovius, Titus became visible to Jarius.

The impact threw Nictovius off balance. Jarius took the opportunity to lunge a blow for the face of Nictovius. The seasoned fighter saw the attack and tried to duck down below the blow. The blow did not land directly on Nictovius, but it did slice his face as it passed by his head.

Regaining his balance, Nictovius turned to see what had hit him. He found Titus quickly backing away. This allowed him to return his attention to Jarius. Reaching up to his face, Nictovius felt the slick warm blood that trickled toward his scarred cheek. The thought made him laugh. That cheek had been ruined years ago.

Titus began yelling for help. He was out of ideas. He started picking up stones and any object he could find to toss at the back of Nictovius. Nictovius did not let those things distract him. He closed on the wounded elf. Jarius knew he was weakening, and he could not hold this man off for much longer. Fleeing the fight was never an option. There was no greater honor he could imagine than to die in defense of his homeland.

One particularly large rock struck the back of Nictovius's helmet. Now that one hurt a little. This caused him to pause and address the kid who was yelling behind him. Stepping back from Jarius, Nictovius turned and said, "I will take care of you when I am done with him. This is your chance to run." Without any more to say, Nictovius turned around to find Jarius launching an aggressive frontal assault. The elf lunged forward to stab the man at the base of his breastplate. Then using his momentum, he rolled past to slash twice at Nictovius's backside. The jab seemed to find its way into a seem of the armor, enough that when Jarius rolled past, he was slightly off balance. None of the slashes struck Nictovius's back. He didn't hit anything but armor.

Nictovius slashed but missed Jarius, as he had rolled too far away. Then Nictovius lunged his own attack. Jarius was still slightly off balance from his rolling away. Nictovius's sword came down on the short sword with a loud clang. The weight of his overhead blow knocked Jarius's sword to the ground. Nictovius pushed a follow through and stabbed Jarius solidly in his right shoulder. The blow made Jarius step back from where his sword had fallen. Nictovius was a skilled fighter and knew how to sustain his balance to keep his sword actively hurting his opponent. As Jarius backed away, Nictovius lunged forward. Jarius could not take the pain of the long sword's blade in his shoulder. The searing pain from his wound, his poor balance, and the forward push of Nictovius cause Jarius to fall to the ground.

"*No!*" shouted Titus, as he watched Nictovius standing over Jarius. The warrior pushed down harder on his longsword. Titus saw the tip of the blade poke through Jarius's back as he screamed and writhed on the ground.

Laughing at the fact that he had this elf pinned to the ground, Nictovius taunted him, "Now, what were you saying about this war being over."

"That's right! This war is over!" came the shout from behind Nictovius. The tone in this threat seemed far more confident than

HOLLYWONDRA

that cowardly boy who shoved him and threw rocks at his back. Nictovius quickly spun to see Hamman Drew striding toward him. "You should have left while you had the chance," Hamman Drew stated as he pulled his scimitars without breaking stride. Sir Allendale was right behind Hamman Drew and moved to the right as the two closed on Nictovius.

Nictovius quickly stepped on the chest of Jarius and pulled his sword out of his shoulder. Then Nictovius thrust it back at Jarius's chest to finish him off. Just as Nictovius pulled the sword, Jarius tried to roll away. Nictovius was too quick. He quickly sunk the sword back into Jarius's abdomen then quickly pulled it out to address his new foes.

Nictovius heard the screams that commonly were associated with battle. He was able to block them out as he considered the two men he was about to fight. As Nictovius squared with Hamman Drew, he asked, "Aren't you the tracker who killed one of my men?" Feeling sure this man fit that description, he said, "Yeah, I think you really need to die today."

Lunging into battle, Hamman Drew offered, "I don't think it will be today." Hamman Drew slashed wildly at the warrior. Nictovius was able to block one blow, but two others struck his armor. Allendale closed in, and Nictovius spun to keep the both of them on one side of him. Allendale lunged, and Nictovius easily blocked. But that gave Hamman Drew an opening, and he slashed past Nictovius. One blow struck him in the shoulder, where the blood from Jarius's dagger showed a gap in the armor. The other slash struck Nictovius on the back of his waist under his breastplate. Again, Nictovius spun to keep them both in front of him.

Nictovius considered Allendale almost a decoy compared to the damage this two-handed fighter could cause. Nictovius bent over to pick up the short sword that Jarius no longer held. Fighting two handed, he felt he might be able to keep Allendale at bay while killing the tracker.

Allendale made an intentionally futile strike at Nictovius. Nictovius was able to easily block it. He was able to also anticipate Hamman Drew coming right afterward and countered his attacks as well. As they circled, Nictovius noticed that boy and a girl trying to help the elf he'd just run through. The futility of their efforts made him smile. All he could think about was that that was one less opponent for him.

Allendale watched carefully how this guy was managing his attacks. Allendale tried to jab Nictovius like he had the last two times. Each time Allendale tried to parry, Nictovius blocked his parry but did not launch a strong counterattack. Allendale could tell he was mostly concerned for the threat posed by Hamman Drew.

So Allendale took a different approach this time. He made what looked like the same type of parry he had done in the past. Again, Nictovius easily blocked the parry and prepared to defend the serious assault he expected from Hamman Drew. To his surprise, Allendale allowed his sword to be batted away. By not keeping much tension on his sword, Nictovius as able to push his sword well out of the way. That did not keep his sword between Allendale and himself. Allendale used the momentum of his sword's arch to roll past the arc of Nictovius's blade and into the fighter with a lunging blow for his knee. Allendale's blow came down hard on top of Nictovius's knee. Nictovius was busy deflecting blows from Hamman Drew when the pain caused him to drop to one knee. Hamman Drew did not hesitate. He came back at Nictovius with a wave of slashing blows. This caused Nictovius to focus everything on him, while Allendale was able to thrust his sword under the chest plate of his armor. Suddenly Nictovius stiffened. Hamman Drew did not stop. He continued to slash even after Nictovius had fallen.

41

A deep complete warmth filled Jarius. As he laid there, he could only think of all the men who had the great honor of Elvan Knighthood bestowed upon them. As his thoughts cleared, he opened his eyes to see. He thought he recognized this room…he was in the Elvan Temple. Quickly his hand went to his stomach, where he remembered the burn of Nictovius's sword. He felt a raised scar where his fatal wound had been. He sat up and began to look more carefully at the wound. He quickly pulled back the tunic to look at his shoulder. All of his wounds were healed.

An acolyte who had been watching him brought him a drink of water. "Here. You are supposed to drink this." While Jarius raised the cup, the acolyte left the room. Within a few moments, Amanda, Titus, and Allendale came into the chamber.

"It's about time," teased Titus, very glad to see his friend looking well.

"How are you feeling?" asked Amanda.

Not really sure how he came to be safe and comfortable inside the temple, Jarius simply said, "Well." Puzzled, he repeated, "I am very well."

"That's great news!" offered Allendale. "When you think you're up for it, we'll want you on your feet. We need to talk. The army that came to our valley and burned our forest has been dispersed. That arm of the beast is gone. The problem is the beast itself."

About the Author

For almost forty years, Joe La Fountaine served Oregon schools as a teacher and school administrator. After decades of service, he has retired to a new home in Southern Oregon with his wife, Kelli. *Hollywondra* is the second book he has published. It is also the first in his Namron Rae series. His first book, *Colastic Moon Temple*, was published in 2003.

Printed in the USA
CPSIA information can be obtained
at www.ICGtesting.com
LVHW040529150624
783212LV00001B/102